DREAD HOUSE

A NOVEL

A.C. HESSENAUER

DREAD HOUSE PUBLISHING

Dedication

To my family, for all your support and help making this book a reality;
to my husband, Jan-Michael for reading and re-reading and listening to
me talk endlessly and obsessively, at all hours. Thank you for helping me
with the added details. To my Mom and Dad; my first and biggest fans;
who helped me believe I could do anything I put my mind to. To my sister
Sophie, for all your editing help, your knowledge of grammar and punc-
tuation (I still don't know the rules), as well as your ideas and suggestions.
To my brother Brad, who shares my love of all things horror; thank you
for proof-reading and your feedback on the ending. To my brother Matt,
thank you for encouraging me and helping me with the cover art! To my
Nanna, Margaret, who taught me from a young age a love of reading and
helped me to see the magic in the world. I couldn't have done this without
all of you. And to the little girl who dreamed of being a writer, for as long
as she could remember, this one is for you.

"And all the woe, that moved him so
That he gave that bitter cry,
And the wild regrets, and the bloody sweats
None knew so well as I:
For he who lives more lives than one
More deaths than one must die."
-Oscar Wilde,
The Ballad of Reading Gaol

CONTENTS

MONDAY

My hands gripped the steering wheel tightly, knuckles white. My stomach twisted in apprehension. I squinted ahead, trying to see any break in the trees. My only companions were the hum of my car and a faint ding whenever a rock hit the undercarriage. Otherwise, the forest surrounding Hideaway House seemed dead silent and perfectly still. I wondered if there was anything living in here. I rolled my window up. Having it open was making me feel oddly vulnerable. I sighed loudly.

The first mistake I made was the dress. To be fair, my options were limited. I certainly couldn't roll up in my bridesmaid dress to arrive at the house, even if it was my nicest dress. But perhaps something in between the skin-hugging mermaid gown that I could barely afford and the black cotton dress I was wearing tonight would have been a better choice.

I take that back. My first mistake was saying yes in the first place. I had been feeling nervous as hell all day and if I'm being honest, all week. It was one of those situations that left current-me wishing past-me had just said no. I had been caught up in the excitement and had readily agreed without a thought to stay a whole week out in the country with Emily's entire wedding party at her fiancé's family estate. She had actually used the word "estate." Apparently, they called it "The Hideaway House." Emily was one of my best friends, so I doubt I honestly would have tried to get

1

out of it. But here I was, driving alone in the middle of nowhere, through the forest at night, left to fantasize about the excuses I might have invented had I been smart enough to anticipate this at the time. I could have gotten out of a few days, at least. Maybe arrive on Thursday or Friday, in time for the rehearsal dinner. Instead, I would be stuck out here for an entire week, trapped with a horde of strangers, who would surely be drunk at least fifty percent of the time and hung over the rest.

Emily had been planning this week for months, and I knew how much she looked forward to it. I had been at first as well, at least in the moments when I was feeling more social. But as the date drew nearer on my calendar, a feeling of reluctance, and then eventually dread, had started to set in.

It wasn't just that I didn't know anyone; that fact alone was bad enough. But I had met Emily randomly, and I wasn't part of her world. The crowd she usually hung out with was way out of my league. As was Emily herself, really. What would I even talk about with these people? Nothing I said or did would make me fit in, and neither would my wardrobe. The bridesmaid dress had been an extravagance I truly couldn't afford at the moment, and I had scrambled to come up with acceptable outfits for the rest of the week. I had even sent Emily a picture of one of them while I was packing, just to make sure she would approve. I threw my phone in the open suitcase on the bed afterward in disgust. Since when did I care what other people thought of me? Or obsess over my outfits?

I took a deep breath as my hands gripped harder on the steering wheel. Google Maps said there were only seven minutes left. I would be there before I knew it. I turned left down a narrow dirt road into the woods about fifteen or twenty minutes ago. I never liked driving down dirt roads and always drove well below the speed limit. The road was so narrow I wasn't sure two cars could fit side by side going either direction. My eyes were starting to sting. I had been so hyper-focused on trying to see any vehicles coming on the road ahead that I had forgotten to blink. It was just getting on towards dusk now, and while that had made the forest feel a little spooky, I figured at least most cars would automatically have their headlights come on by now. That would hopefully give me a few seconds warning to avoid a head-on collision. *Where in the heck was this place?* I was starting to worry I had made a wrong turn somewhere. Emily had said it was out in the boondocks. Now I understood why it was called the Hideaway House.

While more than a little ominous, the woods were also oddly peaceful. The quality of the light flickering through the leaves gave the forest an ethereal, almost surreal atmosphere. My overactive imagination pictured a myriad of creatures roaming through the undergrowth. If I wandered off the path, who knows what I might find?

Suddenly, I shot out into the open, exiting the forest without warning. The road changed to gravel. I passed through an open black gate with an ornate wrought iron scroll arching over the road that read "Haverford."

My jaw dropped open as the house came into view. It was more like a manor, rising from the middle of a vast field with a circular drive out front. There was an empty fountain in the middle of the drive. Off to the right was a narrower gravel drive that must lead to the garage or some sort of parking situation. No cars were parked out front, and I could not be the first to arrive. I wasn't sure where to park, but I opted to enter the roundabout and pull up to the side of the front door.

Old-fashioned streetlamps lined either side of the stairs leading to the front door, giving off a warm, comforting glow. It was truly getting dark now, and I breathed a sigh of relief. Grateful to have made it safely, I sat in the car for a moment and grabbed my phone to check for any new messages. Nothing new had popped up, and I noted with dismay that the signal strength looked pretty poor. A week stuck with pretentious strangers, and now no internet?

I debated grabbing my bags and heading inside with everything at once, but I thought better of it and sent Emily a quick text message letting her know I had just arrived. I waited a minute or so but got no response. Climbing out of the car, I stopped for a moment, staring up at the house, rising into the night sky before me. I felt strange, almost like I had been here before...stood in this exact spot. I shook my head to clear it. It must look similar to another house I'd seen; obviously, I'd never been here before.

I felt nervous walking up to the front door. Should I try knocking? It seemed unlikely anyone would hear me in a house this size. They must have a doorbell or something. I scanned either side of the intimidating double doors and couldn't find anything resembling a doorbell. There was a large metal door knocker in the shape of what appeared to be a deer skull with antlers. Sort of odd, I thought as I gripped the one on the right and gave three short, gentle but firm taps. A minute or so went by with no response. I could hear nothing stirring on the other side of the door. I checked my phone, and still no response from Emily.

Sighing, I gingerly grabbed the door knocker and knocked three more times, much harder this time. I looked around me as I waited. The cool night air held a slight chill now, scented with the first hints of fall. I breathed deeply for a moment; one of my favorite smells. I scanned the shadows on the forest edge in the distance behind me as though someone could be watching me lingering on the doorstep. The black fence, which appeared to run around the property, at least on this side, stood between me and the woods. Somehow, that didn't feel very comforting at the moment.

I couldn't just stand out here all night. Reluctantly, I tried the door handle, and it turned easily in my grasp. Sighing again, deeply this time, I turned the handle and pushed the heavy wooden door open a few inches.

I peered inside and, scanning the entryway, didn't see anyone in my line of sight. I swung the door farther and ducked in, head swiveling right and left. I took in a massive sweeping staircase straight ahead, with a landing at the top that branched to the right and left. A large chandelier hung over my head. The entrance was dimly lit with warm, golden light, with the hallways off to either side drenched in darkness. A set of double doors stood shut on either side of me. Great. No one seemed to be around, and I had no idea where to go. I stood there, debating what to do next and feeling frozen in place with indecision. Then I heard a faint laugh—voices, off to the left down the darkened hall. I started to make my way towards them, hoping Emily would be in there.

I saw several paintings hanging on either side of the hall. I would have to stop and check them out later. I certainly was not an artist of any type, but I loved looking at paintings and learning about the artists. This house felt like a museum. The carpet underneath my feet was plush and deep, my feet sinking slightly with each step. I hoped I wasn't tracking in mud. I knew Josh's family was wealthy, but clearly, Emily had been downplaying just how rich they were. I could not believe they owned this place. This wasn't even where Josh's parents lived year-round. I was pretty sure he had grown up here, but now it was more like a vacation house.

The voices grew louder as I drew nearer, although I still couldn't make out anything they said. I passed several closed doors and additional hallways branching off the main hall on either side. Finally, I turned a corner and saw light up ahead through a door that stood ajar at the end of the hall. I gathered my courage and strode up to the door, pulling the door open wider and stepping slowly inside.

This room was well-lit and appeared to be some sort of study, with several bookshelves whose worn wood rose from floor to ceiling and a plethora of comfy-looking armchairs. Two long couches in plush emerald velvet stood in the center of the room, facing each other on either side of a blazing fireplace. I felt as though I had stepped back in time. A handful of people lounged around the room. I slowly realized that all of them were men, wearing formal dress clothes but in various states of disarray. Most of them had removed their jackets. I saw several slung around the room; some had loosened or removed their ties as well. One of them, with unruly blonde, slightly shaggy hair, was laughing in the middle of the room. He held a heavy glass decanter, the dark liquid sloshing back and forth. He jumped onto the coffee table between the two couches and was clearly delivering the punchline to some hilarious story. The room roared with laughter.

A man seated to the right of the fireplace, facing me, chuckled and shook his head. He was wearing all black, even his tie. He pinched the bridge of his nose and shut his eyes briefly, almost as if he had a headache or was secretly annoyed by what the blonde guy said. His nose was noticeably too big, but it gave his face some character. He had dark, slightly curly hair. One soft curl swung back and forth over his forehead, and his eyes flickered towards me. He and I made eye contact before his gaze left my face to travel quickly up and down my body. He took in my plain black dress and black flats. His eyes lingered on my hair, as usual. I had started going gray prematurely; my jet-black wavy hair streaked with silver. I dyed it for years before finally quitting and embracing it. I was used to people staring at me because of it. Meeting my gaze again, he cleared his throat, "Ah, we're all set in here, thanks. You can tell the others they needn't check in again for the time being," he gestured across the room towards the sideboard, "There are some empty glasses you could take though."

I felt warmth growing in my cheeks and spreading across my face. I hoped I wasn't blushing furiously and tried to control it. The room had suddenly gone quiet, and I realized with dismay that everyone had gone still and was now staring at me, waiting for my response. *Oh my god*, I thought, *they think I'm some kind of maid or something*. This was not the way I wanted the week to kick off.

"Oh, um…" I stammered, struggling for what to say, "I'm not, I mean, I don't… I don't work here," I finished lamely. Surely, my cheeks were bright red by now. The man's eyebrows flickered up slightly in surprise.

A handsome man with a strong jawline stepped towards me from somewhere off to my right. His thick brown hair slicked back from his forehead. He had kind, brown eyes. I recognized him immediately from the many pictures Emily had shown me.

"You must be Cassie." He smiled warmly, raising his hand to shake mine. "I've heard so much about you from Emily. I'm Josh. It's a pleasure to finally meet you." Two dimples framed his broad smile and dazzling white teeth.

"Yes." I smiled back, hoping I looked as confident and self-assured as I was trying to project. "I'm Cassie Harper. It's so nice to meet you, too." I reached out and shook his hand.

He clasped my hand between his and turned to nod at the dark-haired man. "And this idiot is Ben Fischer." He grinned, turning back to me. "We mostly ignore him."

I smiled back and made a sort of nervous giggle. Ben was now standing, both hands in his pockets. He had been looking at the floor. He looked up at us, his dark eyes wide and earnest. Josh continued around the room, introducing me to each of his groomsmen. I was terrible at recalling names, especially when meeting a large group like this. All I was able to retain was that there seemed to be literally three different guys named Mike.

There was an awkward silence for a moment after Josh finished the introductions. Ben cleared his throat, catching my attention. I glanced back his way. "Sorry," he mumbled, "my mistake." He turned and walked away, stopping at the French glass doors on the opposite end of the room. He gazed out into the swiftly darkening evening. The sun seemed to have sunk ridiculously quickly. Only a red glow could be seen on the horizon. I was glad to have made it here just in time before dark. The thought of being out in those woods at night sent a shiver down my spine. I could see Ben's face in his reflection in the window. He seemed to stare out at nothing.

"It's no big deal," I said to his reflection. Wanting to move past it quickly, I turned back to Josh. "Where's Emily?"

"Ah!" Josh exclaimed. He had let go of my hands and clapped his together. "She and the girls are upstairs. You just missed dinner a bit ago. We can show you to your room, and I can have something sent upstairs for you."

"Oh no, thank you. That is very kind of you. I had something to eat just before I left, so you needn't bother." I realized I was standing with my hands clasped together in front of me like a nervous schoolgirl. I tried to stand more naturally, whatever that meant, but I just ended up folding my arms in front of my chest, which felt even more awkward.

Josh smiled his dazzling smile again. "Truly, it's no bother at all. It must have been a decent drive out. Are you sure you aren't hungry?" He didn't wait for me to answer but kept going, at the same time turning to take the offered drink from one of his friends. "You don't have any bags; you must have left them in the car. Is it out front? I'll have everything brought in for you, and your car will be moved out to the garage if that's okay."

"Oh, I," I stammered, "I can grab my stuff and move my car as well; really, it's not necessary if you just let me know where to park..."

He cut me off, but in a smooth, polite way. "Nonsense, it's all taken care of already. You just relax and enjoy the evening. Mark can walk you upstairs to Emily and see you are shown to your room." I looked around the room, wondering which one was Mark. There had to be about ten guys in the room. I figured it was going to be a huge wedding. Emily had probably downplayed that, too. I noticed Ben was still staring out the window into the darkness.

Pulling my gaze away from Ben, I turned to see the shaggy blonde guy standing before me with a wide grin. "I'll be your tour guide for the evening, M 'lady," he said with a little mock bow. He swept his arm widely and gestured towards the doorway behind me. "Right this way." I smiled and nodded, thanking him.

As we walked towards the door, I turned back to Josh. "Thank you. It's so nice to finally get to meet you. And thank you for having me stay for the week."

Josh sank into one of the comfortable armchairs. The others were gathered around the mini bar, refreshing their drinks. Ben stood with his back to the glass doors, his tall form slumped against the wall. His arms were crossed against his chest. His dark eyes raked me up and down again. I couldn't blame him for thinking I was the help, let's be honest. Josh smiled easily. "The pleasure is all mine. I know Emily will be thrilled you are here."

I nodded at Josh and smiled as I turned to leave the room. "Have a good night." My gaze wandered over to Ben, to nod to him as well, but his back was turned once more. His eyes appeared to track me in his reflection on the glass doors as I exited the room. I turned, following Mark back down the hallway.

Mark was very talkative on the walk upstairs. I would come to find out that Mark was always talkative, literally always, not just when he was drunk. He had a very pleasant, easy-going way about him that soon made me feel more comfortable. He chatted about the weather and commented on how short the days were getting now; it was getting dark much earlier now than even just last week. I asked him how long he had known Josh. Partially to make conversation but also because I was fishing for information. Emily hadn't necessarily been tight-lipped about Josh, but she hadn't told me much about his past. To be fair, they honestly hadn't known each other all that long, which I'm sure was part of the reason.

It still felt odd to me that I was only just now meeting him for the first time. The whole thing had seemed rushed to me. Emily had been with Josh for about a year or so, maybe a bit longer. I had to hide my surprise when she told me they were engaged.

Mark had met Josh during their freshman year of college, so he at least had known him a lot longer than Emily. It sounded like Mark knew Josh's family well and had been coming out to stay at the Hideaway with them for years. He told me Josh's brother would be joining us as well, but not until mid-week because he had something going on with work. From what I could gather, the rest of the family arrived on Friday. I knew Emily was planning on having her mom join us Friday morning, but that was a compromise. She had wanted to arrive on Thursday, if not earlier in the week. But Josh and Emily had wanted a few days with just their friends to party and have fun before everyone else arrived.

At the top of the grand staircase, Mark led me up a shorter, second set of stairs that branched off the landing to the right. Mark explained that the guys' wing was up the stairs to the left, on the other side of the grand staircase, and that the girls were all staying on the right-hand side. He led me down several turns. As usual, I was focused on taking in my surroundings and our conversation and forgot to note the route we were taking. I always did that in new places and could never retrace my steps to make my way back on my own. I blamed it on my self-diagnosed ADHD, but it was probably just carelessness. I thought about asking him to tell me the way back, but let it go. I would figure it out or ask Emily for help later. I slid my hand into my dress pocket and pulled out my phone. The signal still looked super weak.

"Hey," I asked, "Do you have a signal on your cell? I haven't tried to make any calls or anything, but I'm not sure my text to Emily went through earlier. It looks like it may not be working."

Mark laughed, nodding. "Yeah, that doesn't surprise me. That's one downside of being out in the middle of nowhere like we are, I honestly never have a good signal when I'm here. It works the best out by the road." He gestured with his head over to the right. How he knew what direction the road was from where we were now was beyond me. "Or out back, past the gardens, towards the edge of the property, you can sometimes get a signal. They actually still have a landline phone here for that reason. Isn't that funny? Who has a landline phone anymore, right? But it does come in handy in these situations."

I nodded and made a mental note to ask where the phone was at some point. Not that I needed it or anticipated having to make any calls, but it did feel weird to be cut off from the rest of the world.

"Didn't I see a sign for a town or something nearby on the way here? What's the closest city?" I thought I had seen the sign not too long before turning onto the dirt road through the woods.

Mark nodded, "Oh yeah, there is a town close by." He pointed off to the left of the direction we were heading now. "Although I wouldn't even call it a town, more like a little village maybe. And if you think the no-service thing is bad, those folks down there are really living in the dark ages. I'm not sure many of them ever travel far from home. A strange lot, those ones."

"Mmm." I made a vague, non-committal sound low in my throat. I could hear voices coming from up ahead. Mark stopped at a door and wrapped lightly with his knuckles. The voices quieted, and he called out, "Ladies! Everyone decent, I hope."

The door swung wide, and I saw Emily standing there with a huge smile on her face. "Yes, you dork," she laughed. Then, seeing me standing behind Mark, she let out a high-pitched squeal and launched herself past him.

Emily threw her arms around me and squeezed me, swaying back and forth as she did a happy dance.

"Cass! I'm so glad you made it! I was beginning to think you might ditch us!" I had to chuckle a little internally at that. She knew me pretty well.

"Of course I made it," I replied as she stepped back and twirled for me.

"What do you think?" Holding her arms out, I saw she was wearing a pink silk sash with the word "Bride" printed in rhinestones.

"Fabulous." I smiled. Emily's smile was infectious. She was gorgeous, with wide, innocent-looking hazel eyes and pin-straight, thick, shiny blonde hair that fell nearly to her waist. Emily could easily captivate any audience and always had a story to tell. She always knew just the right thing to say. She understood people in a way that I often didn't. Regardless of how tedious this week may feel, I was here for her. I told myself I could get through it, and I could do so with a smile on my face.

"How was your drive down? Any trouble finding the place?"

"Oh, no. I was able to make it here just fine. You weren't kidding about it being isolated, though."

"What's wrong then?" she asked, studying my face intently.

"What? Nothing, nothing's wrong." I held my hands out, palms open, as though to show I wasn't hiding anything.

"Cassie... what is it?" Emily lowered her voice and folded her arms across her chest. She planted her feet wide, blocking the doorway as though I wouldn't be allowed to enter without giving her the correct answer.

Mark held up a hand, "She had a little run-in with Ben, but no harm done."

"Ben?" Emily raised one eyebrow, "What did he say now?"

"Eh, don't make him sound like that," Mark exclaimed, swaying slightly. He was clearly more than just a little tipsy. "Bens alright. He's just too smart for his own good. Man's a genius," he said as an aside to me. "And sure, he can be a little dense sometimes, but it's not like he's *always* saying something."

Emily rolled her eyes slightly at me. "These guys, it's like a freaking cult, I swear. The way they defend each other."

"What!" Mark slapped one hand on his chest like he'd been wounded, shaking his head in mock outrage. "A cult? We're more like a mafia... some kind of epic crime family."

Emily threw her head back and laughed, "Get out of here, Mark; go back to your boy's club downstairs." Mark started to stagger backward down the hallway.

"Fine, I'll leave you to your... whatever you *girls* do."

"Fine," Emily chuckled, "and tell your leader I said not to drink too much tonight. We have a big day coming up. If he starts now, he will never make it to the end of the week!"

Mark held his hand up, cupping it behind his ear, and squinting at Emily as if he were suddenly having trouble hearing what she was saying.

"Good lord." Emily shook her head at him in disgust, but she was grinning.

Mark smiled back and winked at me before disappearing around the corner.

Emily and I stood in silence for a moment before she suddenly grabbed my arm. "I'll be right back," she called out vaguely in the direction of the room filled with her bridal party. I doubted anyone had heard her. She was already tugging me down the hall in the opposite direction from Mark.

"So, what happened with Ben? Spill," she demanded.

"Spill what? There's nothing to spill."

"The tea! Come on, what did he say? And yes," she said begrudgingly, "Mark is right, it's not like Ben is a complete asshole, but he does tend to say the wrong thing, often at the wrong time. Just a knack of his."

"Em." I shook my head, although she was still stomping ahead of me in her ridiculously high heels and couldn't see me. "It's nothing, not a big deal at all. He just..." my voice trailed off for a moment. "He just thought I worked here."

"You worked here?" She half turned back, "What, like one of the maids or cooks or something?"

"Yeah." I nodded. "Honestly, it's not a big deal, and I can't say I blame him." She stopped now and looked back at me, a puzzled look on her face. I swept my hands down in front of me, indicating my dress.

"Oh, Cass," she sighed, grabbing my hand again and pulling me more gently this time. "You're always too hard on yourself."

"I'm not being hard on myself; I'm just being realistic," I replied, my mouth in a grim line. "Let's just forget about it."

"Okay," she sighed. "Was he rude?"

"No," I said simply, "he wasn't."

"Okay," she said again. "This is me letting it go. But I could tell something was wrong, so it did bother you." Now, it was my turn to roll my eyes. "I'm just saying, Cass, I can read you like a book."

"Fair enough," I chuckled. Changing the subject, I said, "Speaking of letting things go, I'm going to let go that you definitely undersold how loaded Josh is."

She turned and grinned wickedly at me, walking backward down the hallway, still a few steps in front of me. "You mean how loaded Josh's *family* is," she corrected.

"Still... kind of amounts to the same thing, doesn't it?"

Emily shrugged. "I didn't want to make a big deal out of it or freak you out."

"Why would that freak me out?"

"I dunno." She shrugged. "I mean, it's not the kind of thing you brag about, and, well, sometimes you act funny about stuff like that."

"Stuff like what?" I said grimacing. "Like the fact that I'm a poor, struggling writer, and you're..." I trailed off, "Well, you're you?"

Emily's smile came back. "Well, yes, to put it bluntly."

"There's no other way for me." I grinned back.

"I know, Cass." Emily turned and looped her arm through mine. "That's why I like you," she said, her demeanor serious now. "I can always count on you to tell the truth."

"Good to know." My cheeks colored slightly at her honesty. I'll have to make a point of being blunt more often."

Emily laughed. "Well, let's not go too far." She had stopped at a door on our left. To my surprise, a small rectangular laminated sign said *"Cassie"* in golden cursive letters.

"Ah," I said, "well, this must be my room then. I have to say, I appreciate the sign. But I don't know that I'll ever be able to find my way back here again."

Emily nodded. "Ugh, I know. I insisted on the signs. Honestly, there are no room numbers; how would anyone ever find their room again? They all look the same. But don't worry; I know it seems intimidating, but you'll get used to the layout quickly. You can always ask someone for help. Most of the guys have been here loads of times, too."

I nodded. "I think you're forgetting how directionally challenged I can be, but I'll take your word for it."

Emily grinned. "It's not as bad as it seems. On most floors, the place is a big rectangle anyway, so you should always be able to find your way back."

"Hmm." I thought for a second. "I'll have to treat it like a maze. What do they say the trick is? If you keep your hand on the wall to your right and don't let go, you can always find your way out again... eventually."

Emily laughed in that infectious way of hers. "You are such a nerd, Cass. Who even knows random facts like that? Like, how is that worth remembering? When have you ever been in a maze?"

I grinned back. "You never know when random knowledge might come in handy. It might save your life someday."

Emily shook her head, opened the door with my name on it, and led me inside. "So here is where you'll be staying. There's a little welcome basket with bottled water, snacks, painkiller... just some essentials. If you think of anything else you need and forgot to pack, just let me know. The staff keep a stock of various items downstairs somewhere. We probably have it here if you need it." It struck me for a moment how she said "we." Emily and I mostly hung out on our own, and I had never had a chance to see her around Josh. It was a bit odd to see them as a unit. I had better get used to it fast, though.

I scanned the room. It was just as gorgeous as the rest of the house. A large four-post bed with a canopy frame on the top sat in the middle of the room, covered in a plush comforter with multiple fluffy pillows. Sheer-looking white curtains hung from the frame at the corners. Like Emily said, a large wicker basket sat on a dresser, stocked with goodies. I would have to go through it later. I was prone to forgetting things when packing, so that would be useful.

My eyes caught on a small luggage pile on the room's far side. Impressive. They had already brought in my things. I noted my purse lying on top of my suitcase. I made a mental note to ask where my car was parked. I caught my reflection in the double glass doors on the far side of the room. The billowing curtains had been drawn open presumably earlier in the day to reveal a view of the grounds, but it was fully dark outside now, and I could see nothing on the other side of the glass. My waves fell limply to just a few inches past my shoulders. Emily's reflection was mirrored next to mine, her gaze darting around the room. Probably looking for dust. I knew she was a clean freak.

I couldn't help but compare. Her thick blonde locks seemed to extend feet past mine. I struggled to grow my hair longer than my upper back, and how on earth her hair could be so perfectly straight was baffling. Mine grew in unruly faint waves, never consistent from one day to the next and never curly enough to be true, gorgeous curls. I typically gave up and threw it into a messy, frizzy bun. I had brought my styling products of the moment with me, hoping to make my hair presentable for a few days.

Emily was slim and tall. Her figure was made for the runway, whereas I was a bit curvier. I knew she claimed she envied me because of it, but gazing at her reflection, I found that hard to believe. Sighing in resignation, I thought of the mermaid-style gown I had tucked into my suitcase and smiled a bit. I did think it looked pretty fantastic on me. I wondered briefly if there was a place to hang the dress; it was probably already getting wrinkled. I spied doors that looked like they belonged to a closet. I would get the dress out right away once I got settled in.

Emily had followed my gaze to the double glass doors in the meantime and nodded as though I had asked her a question. "Yes, that leads to your balcony." She strode over to the doors, and with a twisting motion, she unlocked them and pulled them open. The doors made a creaking sound as they swung into the room. "Not all the rooms have a balcony, but I figured you would like one. In case you want to sit outside and write in the mornings or something. There's a little chair and table out here." That was how Emily was. She always thought of everything and everyone else. I was pleasantly surprised to find that out about her. As a rich girl, I expected her to be entitled and self-centered. Obviously, that was a stereotype, and it certainly didn't apply to everyone. She was one of the most considerate people I knew. If anyone deserved to be happy, it was Emily.

"Thanks, Em, that was really thoughtful of you." She had already stepped through the doors and disappeared into the darkness of the balcony. A cool gust of fall-scented night air rushed through the open doors. I followed her outside, breathing in deeply. Like the smell just before a storm, the air held a hint of rain, but there was a tinge of something off, almost rotten, beneath it. Like damp leaves and earth, yes, but something else... what it reminded me of I couldn't think of at the moment. I didn't remember seeing that it was supposed to rain. I hoped the rain wouldn't ruin any of their plans for the week. Emily, and Josh, according to Emily, were what I think of as outdoorsy. I was sure they would have some type of outdoor activities, games, or sports even, planned for us this week. I groaned inwardly at the thought of being forced to play group volleyball or, God forbid, golf. If that happened, I hoped we wouldn't be near the house. I would probably break a window.

The only outdoor activity I engaged in regularly and enjoyed was jogging. I had brought my running shoes and workout clothes just in case there was a nearby path or road I could run on. I hated the thought of going a whole week with no exercise. While Emily maintained her slim figure effortlessly, I needed to lift weights and run constantly to maintain being a good ten pounds heavier than I'd like to be. I hadn't noticed a path or anything on the drive in, but maybe some smoother trails through the woods would be okay to jog on if I was careful. Not worth twisting an ankle on a tree root. I shuddered to think of any injury more serious than that taking place out here. Mark hadn't made the local village sound too promising. Any sort of help or medical care would probably take a while to get here. I shook my head to clear my thoughts. Why did my brain always have to go to the worst-case scenario? I could be so morbid sometimes.

Emily was staring out over the balcony into the distance. As my eyes adjusted, I slowly made out the faint glow of the skyline over the trees. I realized that my room must face what I assumed was the back of the house, opposite the drive. I could make out shapes below us, lumps that must be bushes, flowers, and what looked like a stone path zigzagging through the foliage below. *This must be the garden,* I thought. Beyond the garden, which looked massive, I could see a flat stretch, presumably grass, as far as I could see bleeding into the shadows.

Emily and I stood in silence for a few minutes. She seemed to be lost in thought. She probably could use some time to decompress after entertaining her guests all day. Emily was definitely an extrovert. I'm sure that's the only reason we ever became friends in the first place. I once read that introverts don't make friends; an extrovert just finds them and adopts them. I believed that was true wholeheartedly, at least in my case. Even still, I knew Emily liked her downtime, too. As long as this week would feel for me, I had to remember it wouldn't be easy on her either. Especially once her family, her mother, in particular, started to arrive. I would do what I could to help and shield her from the brunt of it.

Almost as though she had read my thoughts, Emily reached over and placed her hand on top of mine on the balcony ledge. She was quiet for a moment, squeezing my hand gently, almost absentmindedly, then she said, almost in a whisper, "I'm really glad you're here, Cassie. I'm just... I'm just really glad you're here. I know this isn't your cup of tea."

I turned my head sharply to look at her. I could barely make out her features in the darkness. Her lips seemed to be pressed together in a straight line, stretched thinly, almost as though she were grimacing. "Okay, it's your turn," I said swiftly, "what's wrong Em?"

She turned to me and seemed to snap out of it. "Nothing's wrong. Can't I just be glad one of my best friends is here? It's going to be an awesome week." She was back to her peppy self again, but I had seen a glimpse of what was beneath it, and I didn't like it. I felt a dull, twisting sensation low in my gut. That ache I had been feeling all week, which had dissipated when I had finally arrived at the Hideaway, was back. Why was I feeling like this? Was it something more than just the dread of social anxiety?

Everything was fine. Nothing was happening. I just needed to suck it up and get over it. I could be social at times; I just needed to be in the right mood. I needed to get myself in the right mood and the week would fly by, and it would be over before I knew it. Besides, I loved Emily; I would surely like her taste in friends. I would be able to find someone else, at least one other person, that I could connect with.

At the very least, it would be interesting, wouldn't it? Getting to meet other people, other couples, and getting to know about them and their lives. I was a good listener, and I filed away those little quirks, the funny little habits that people had. I would bring them out later in my writing when I needed to add a dose of reality. Those were the little details that made a character more believable. This week there would be good people watching, as I liked to think of it. Especially the wedding and reception itself. I had brought one of my notebooks that I liked to use to jot down little thoughts, ideas for stories sometimes, or just a funny or interesting phrase someone used. I always felt a bit guilty using those though, like I was plagiarizing someone else's life.

Emily had gone back to staring out over the vast darkness below. It was so black just beneath us, it almost felt like we were suspended over water. Like we were on the balcony of a cruise ship, with the dark water of the ocean churning below us in our wake. The breeze gusted again, Emily's hair flying back behind her. Perhaps that was the scent I couldn't pinpoint earlier. I could almost smell the sea. It was very faint, but it was there. I wondered momentarily how far we were from the coast. Why hadn't I bothered to check a map before setting out? My sense of being on moving water strengthened. Where were we going? Where would we end up? I wasn't sure I wanted to know.

I pulled myself out of my nonsensical thoughts and studied Emily's face again. She was smiling faintly now. There was nothing wrong, just like she said. I'm sure she was just nervous. How could she not be? She was getting married this week. It was normal to be nervous.

I reached out and squeezed her hand this time. "Josh seems really nice Emily." I had only spent a few moments with him. I struggled to think of something more to add. "He really made me feel welcome here."

Emily's smile deepened. "I'm glad Cass. He's always a good host. His parents taught him that, I'm sure."

I nodded in the dark. "It's going to be a good week. You'll see." I don't know why I added that part. Maybe I was talking more to myself than to her. Emily nodded and took a deep breath. She seemed about to say something else.

"Emily!" A voice shrieked from behind us, snapping me back to the present. I jumped halfway out of my skin.

I could make out movement in the room behind us, but even though the light leaking in from the hallway was dim, it was enough to blind us momentarily after staring out at the darkness for so long. Emily laughed and darted back into the room.

"What are you up to in here?" I heard the unfamiliar female voice call out.

Emily grinned and gestured towards me. "Just showing Cassie her awesome room for the week. Kristy, meet Cassie. She's the one I've been telling you about. She had to arrive a bit late."

Kristy looked me up and down, eyebrows raised, clearly judging my outfit. Then she gave Emily a pointed look, as if to say, "Really?" I gritted my teeth. Emily gave her a warning look back. Begrudgingly, Kristy held out her hand limply to shake mine. Her grip was limp too, her hand damp with sweat. I could tell she was more than a little tipsy. I groaned internally. I was a pretty lightweight drinker, there was no way I was going to be able to keep up with this crowd. I already knew Emily could drink me under the table. It made no sense how much she was able to put away.

"Nice to meet you," Kristy said. "So, you're the writer. Anything I would have read?"

I doubt it. Do you read? I wanted to ask. Instead, I pulled out my usual go to song and dance routine. Not likely anything you've read before, just some small print articles, a few short stories. I was mostly self-published and had held down various jobs on the side, mostly in magazines and articles posted online. Writing about real life was my job, and what paid the bills, but it wasn't my passion. I could tell I had lost Kristy's interest about halfway through my usual spiel. People wanted or half-expected me to say that yes, in fact, I'm actually Stephen King... surprise! Sorry to disappoint.

Shockingly, Kristy wanted to get back to partying, and of course they couldn't do that without the bride. We headed back to the party. Emily took the time to introduce me to everyone, just like Josh had. I probably retained about as many names as I had the first time. It would take me a while to learn and remember everyone's names. I had a week, but with a wedding party of twenty-some people that probably wasn't long enough. I gave myself a mini quiz: I remembered Catherine, Emily's maid of honor. She was tall and blonde like Emily. Rather stoic and reserved. There was Kristy... wouldn't forget that one. The short brunette was Blair; that was different enough to remember. I had to wonder fleetingly whether I would even see any of these people again after the wedding. How much effort did I really want to put into getting to know them?

As could have been predicted, a wine glass quickly found its way into my hand. I sipped the chilled white wine and nodded in acquiescence that it was very good. After a few sips, I decided it indeed wasn't bad. I could stand to sip on this; I just needed to drag out the one glass for the rest of the night. It had to be getting late, although I had no clue how late these people planned on staying up partying. My room was far enough down the hall that I shouldn't hear too much noise. I would probably be able to sleep through it once I made my excuses and headed to bed. Another thing that Emily had perhaps thought of and planned for.

I did my best to make small talk for the remainder of the evening. I chatted with a few of the quieter girls that were lounging near the fireplace. Catherine seemed nice, if not a little severe. I had only met her briefly once before at an event Emily had dragged me along to. I couldn't remember the name of the other girl with her. This room was similar to the one the guys were gathered in when I arrived. No bookshelves, unfortunately, but comfy seating. The couches here sat low to the ground and were a bluish/turquoise velvet instead of emerald. There was a fireplace in the middle of the room, the logs already burned down low. There was a large desk at the back of the room, in front of the French glass doors. It looked like where the duke would sit and open his letters. The age and condition of this place really were amazing. I wondered how much of the furniture was original. It all certainly looked like it.

My eye caught on a large painting to the right of the desk. I made my way over there eventually. Just as I had thought, the house in the painting looked very similar to the Hideaway itself, though clearly not in its current state; the lampposts out front by the drive were missing. Dark green ivy coiled and twined up the face of the house on either side of the grand entrance though, just like it does now.

I noticed something else I thought was different, or at least I hadn't seen it on the drive in. A large, no, really what must be a massive tree, was in the background of the painting off to the right in the distance, back behind and to the side of the house. The painting depicted the sun setting on the horizon, behind the tree line. The leaves of this particular tree almost glowed, with red, pink, and golden tones, reflecting the light from the sunset. There was something odd about it. It looked like something was hanging from the tree, almost like a figure attached to a rope or something. I squinted, leaning in closer, trying to make out what the figure was supposed to be.

"Boo!" A loud voice shouted next to my ear. I jumped a mile, nearly spilling my wine all over myself. I turned with wide eyes to see Mark grinning next to me. The guys had infiltrated our little party. "Jesus Mark," I breathed out with a rush of air. My heartrate returning to normal. "You scared me."

Mark laughed and held up his glass. I caught a whiff of what was probably whiskey. Or brandy. I wasn't really up to speed on liquor. He nodded at me. "Cheers!"

I clinked my glass against his obligatorily. "Cheers," I muttered back.

"Alright everyone, alright," Emily called out from the center of the room. Josh had his arm slung around her shoulders, tucking her into his side. She barely came up to his chin. He was much taller than I had realized initially.

"It's getting late." General groans arose throughout the room at that statement. I, however, breathed a sigh of relief. "We have a big day tomorrow, and the next day, and the next day..." chuckles followed as Emily laughed. "All I'm saying is, let's pace ourselves a little bit. I don't want everyone to be nursing a hangover during horseback riding tomorrow." I groaned a little at that. Accidentally out loud.

Mark definitely heard me and shot a lopsided grin my way. "Ah, you'll be fine, we've picked out a real brute for you to ride," he whispered in my ear.

I looked at him sideways and rolled my eyes. Bringing my attention back to Emily, just behind her, I noticed Ben lurking over by the entryway. He was staring, practically glaring, at Mark and I.

"And before anyone asks, yes, it is mandatory, but I promise you will love it! We are going in groups of ten, just a short ride through the grounds to give you all a tour. We'll have a picnic lunch outside, then time to relax and play some croquet, and time for everyone to change and refresh themselves before dinner."

Josh laughed and gave Emily's shoulders a squeeze. "Your whole week has been planned out for you, down to the minute. Just roll with it guys." Emily shrugged and gave a half-hearted grin. Josh gave her a quick peck on the cheek.

"Happy wife, happy life," someone called out. That garnered a general laugh and cheers from the group. Croquet, huh. I had no clue how to play, but honestly it could have been much worse. Although there was plenty more to come, I'm sure. Emily was a planner; Josh had that part right. I had heard her talking about planning vacations, several trips she had been on with her family over the years, and then with Josh this year. I had no idea how she coordinated it all. My brain didn't work that way.

"The next day is supposed to be a beach day, weather permitting," Emily continued. Well, I was right, we must be near the ocean, just like I had thought. I quickly went through a mental inventory of what I had packed. I was pretty sure I had brought both of my bathing suits. I couldn't decide which one was more flattering so in the end I thought I had thrown both into my suitcase.

"And with that," Josh finished, I realized I had zoned out and missed whatever else Emily had been saying, "it's off to bed for the lot of you." Phew. I checked my watch. It was only 11:00, honestly could have been worse. I was glad not to have to make my excuses to duck out to bed early.

"Don't forget you have bottled water in your rooms for a reason. Drink some!" Emily called out as everyone started to shuffle out. I saw people leaving their empty glasses, in some cases half full, on the sideboard for the staff to clean up. I grimaced a little inwardly, thinking of the interaction with Ben earlier.

I looked up for him, but he was already gone. Probably one of the first ones out the door since he'd barely been in the room earlier when Emily was talking. He struck me as an odd one, that's for sure.

I followed the crowd back to my room. The guys had said good night in the hallway outside our rooms. Catcalling and whistling when Josh kissed Emily deeply on the mouth and whispered something in her ear before turning and leaving. She smiled radiantly afterwards; her cheeks flushed with warmth. I decided I was truly happy for her. I still had my reservations about how fast everything had happened, but Josh did seem to make her happy. They were a beautiful couple.

After I said a general goodnight to everyone and closed my bedroom door behind me, I realized I had forgotten to ask where the bathroom was.

I also realized I had no idea where Emily's room was, though presumably in the same hallway somewhere. I checked my phone and saw that the text I sent her earlier when I arrived still hadn't gone through. So much for that. Before wandering around, I decided to get my dress out of my suitcase before it wrinkled further. I had meant to do that earlier.

I carefully pulled my dress out and checked behind the doors that I had assumed to be a closet earlier. I found that I had been right. A long pole ran on either side of the little walkway, with plenty of extra empty hangers. There were also surprisingly a lot of old clothes hanging in the closet as well. I ran my hand over an old-fashioned fur coat with giant shoulder pads. I realized there was another door on the other side of the closet and froze.

Did Emily give me an adjoining room and forget to tell me? That would really surprise me; it wasn't like her, but she had a lot going on this week. I tip-toed over to the door and pressed my ear against it as quietly as I could. I heard nothing on the other side. After staying that way for a minute or so, I debated taking my chances and opening the door. I felt like knocking would be weird. But then again, so would walking in on someone. I gripped the door handle and gently turned it. As it cracked open, I could see nothing but pitch black. I doubted anyone could have gotten ready for bed and had the lights off that fast. I pulled the door open wider and realized it was actually a small bathroom. I felt somewhat relieved to know I had a private bathroom. Not that it would have been the end of the world to share, but this was much nicer.

I felt around until I located the light switch. I had an image suddenly of putting my hand on a fat spider waiting on the other side of the wall. The lights flickered on. They were super bright, the room flooded with harsh white lighting. Not the soft warm glow that seemed to be present in the rest of the house. The bathroom looked too new overall to be part of the house originally, I decided. That was a bit disappointing, but it made sense that the family had chosen to renovate to add some additional bathrooms, especially if they were used to entertaining large parties like this. I wondered if all the guest rooms had private bathrooms like this. That must have cost a small fortune. I thought then about the master bedroom and what it might look like. I pictured a large, attached bathroom with a clawfoot tub.

I yawned, suddenly feeling exhausted. It must be getting on towards midnight by now. I stretched and examined my hair in the mirror, noticing my black eyeliner was smudged beneath my pale blue-gray eyes. I threw my hair up into a pineapple on top of my head. I quickly fished my PJs out of my suitcase, grabbed a make-up remover wipe, brushed my teeth, and got settled into bed. The mattress felt amazing. It had been a long day and would be an even longer one tomorrow. I realized too late that I needed to turn the lights off first before climbing into bed. There was no bedside lamp, just a small round table.

I jumped back out of bed and remembered to plug my phone in as well. Not that there was much point charging it. At least I could still take pictures with it. The thought of being cut off from contacting anyone outside the house made me feel uneasy for a moment, but then I remembered the landline phone. I reminded myself again to ask where it was.

I found the main overhead light switch next to the door. About to turn it off, it occurred to me the door was unlocked. I quickly engaged the lock and tried to check by turning the handle, like an idiot. Of course, it opened easily; I was on the wrong side of the door. I relocked it while it was open, checking the outer handle to make sure it didn't turn. Focusing on the lock, I didn't hear the soft shuffle and swish of footsteps until they were already upon me. Startling, I looked up to see Mark's head swiveling back my way. He had been coming from the opposite direction of the guy's quarters, from farther down the hall. He didn't look too surprised to see me, but clearly, he was in a hurry. Rushing past, he had almost missed me standing there in the open doorway.

He threw me a quick grin and a wink. "G'night," he said briefly, and continued down the hall until disappearing around the corner to the right.

Hmm. I wondered what he was up to. Shrugging, I jiggled the door handle one more time. Satisfied, I closed the door. I gathered my courage and switched off the lights. I had fixed in my mind's eye where the bed was, and raced towards it as soon as the lights went off. I quickly leaped into bed, my heart thudding, and pulled the blankets up under my chin. Apparently, my subconscious was still scared of a monster hiding under the bed, just waiting for the moment the lights went off to grab me by the legs. I used to sprint back to bed at night like that when I was a kid but hadn't done so since. I wasn't safe until I was back under the covers, my comforter a magical shield that protected me from monsters and ghosts. This house seemed more prone to ghosts than monsters... nonetheless, I drifted off quickly to sleep without too much trouble.

TUESDAY

E mily wasn't kidding when she said we had a big day ahead of us. It all started with a massive breakfast.

I had no idea what to expect for breakfast, and after waking up and tottering around in my room for a bit, I was kicking myself for not asking. She had probably explained to the rest of the group before I had arrived. I checked my watch and saw it was almost 8 am. I had woken up fairly early on my own without setting an alarm. I find I often do that when sleeping in strange places. You're never used to the sunlight streaming into the room differently than at home. I had completely forgotten to shut the curtains over the balcony doors, so it was pretty bright in the room by the time I woke up.

I decided to jump in the shower quickly. Debating whether or not to wash my hair, I got in with my hair still in a high ponytail from the night before, but then decided to just go ahead and wash it. I dressed quickly in a pair of comfy, stretchy jeans and a plain, long sleeve t-shirt. I would bring my light jacket down with me too. With it being a day for horseback riding and lawn games, I figured dressing pretty casually should be fine.

I styled my hair with curl cream and gel and scrunched it to maximize my waves. I realized to my dismay that I hadn't thought to pack my hair dryer and diffuser. I always forget something. You would think at some point I would learn and start making a packing list for trips. I checked the cupboards under the sink for a hair dryer but found only extra toilet paper. I debated for a moment knocking on doors to ask to borrow one. I couldn't imagine with ten girls there wasn't a hair dryer in the house. They couldn't all be as forgetful as I was. I decided it wasn't worth bothering anyone this early. I would just have to go down with wet hair and deal with it taking forever to dry.

I grabbed my phone and stuck it in my back pocket before laughing at myself. I had the habit, like most of us, of bringing it with me everywhere I went, but it really didn't seem necessary at this point. I left it sitting on the bedside table and stepped out into the hall. I realized then that I would have no way of locking my bedroom door behind me once I left, though there wasn't much that I needed to worry about losing. I had a brief chuckle at the thought that any of the other guests would find anything I owned worth stealing. I decided I was being silly and not to worry about it.

I was hoping I would run into someone else in the hallway, especially Emily, but no such luck. After standing in the middle of the hall indecisively, I decided to look for Emily's room. I passed no one in the hallway and read the name on each door as I passed, committing them to memory the best I could. I saw Blair's room and was proud of myself that I recognized at least one of their names. I came to Emily's room towards the end of the long winding hallway. I knocked softly on her door. I knew she was typically an early riser, but I didn't want to wake up the whole floor. There was no response, and no sounds coming from inside the room. I decided the best thing to do would be to just make my way downstairs.

I was somehow able to find my way back to the main staircase. I was very impressed with myself, but it was probably sheer luck that I had made the right turns. Thankfully, when I got to the bottom of the stairs, I heard voices drifting from just down the hall on my right. I followed them easily and found myself entering a massive dining room.

There was an oversized dining table made of dark shining wood that seemed impossibly long. I lost count but realized it could easily seat over twenty people. I was surprised to see about half the guests were already here. Some were already seated, eating at the giant table, and others were piling food on their plates from a buffet set up on the far side of the room. Emily was standing with Josh by the buffet table. She noticed me entering the room and waved me over mid conversation.

She interrupted her thought briefly to say good morning to me, and gesturing at the table told me to help myself. I eyed the coffee at the far end of the table with relief. I didn't think I was going to make it through the day without some caffeine.

I filled my plate with fruit, bacon, scrambled eggs and some toast. It was quite a spread, and all this just for breakfast. I wondered exactly how many people were working down in the kitchen. From what I had gathered putting bits and pieces together last night, the impression I had was that the layout of the house followed the traditional English manor, with the staff quarters, kitchen, and storage areas all on the basement level. They had quite an undertaking feeding this many people for a week, not to mention the rehearsal dinner Friday and wedding reception on Saturday, all of which were to take place on the grounds. I wondered if they were bringing in a catering company for the actual event. They had to be. I had no idea how large the kitchen was, or how many staff they had, but I had gathered there would be over 200 people attending the wedding.

I awkwardly made my way around the table, searching for a spot. I chose to sit on the other side of one of the quieter girls I had chatted with last night. Although I couldn't recall her name for the life of me, she seemed nice. She nodded and gave me a friendly smile as I sat down. Her attention was on one of the guys who was recalling a story of a camping trip, which turned into a disaster when an unexpected early winter squall came through the mountains. It sounded interesting, actually. I busied myself with eating and sipping piping hot coffee with creamer mixed in and listened in quietly. The girl sitting next to me had a funny way of wrinkling her nose when she laughed. For some reason, she reminded me of a little mouse with its nose twitching back and forth. She was cute but had a plain sort of face, not one that would be easily recognizable or remembered. I wondered how she knew Emily and decided to ask her later when I had a chance.

I scanned the room periodically for Mark, but he didn't seem to be downstairs yet. Small wonder. He had certainly been up and about late and had more than his fair share to drink from what I could tell. Thankfully I had managed to nurse my one glass of white wine without anyone taking notice. I planned to do the same thing tonight and get away with drinking as little as possible. I might have a second glass at the wedding, or even the rehearsal dinner, but I wasn't up for that every night for a week straight.

Some of the group finished up with breakfast and decided to head into another room to hang out. Emily mentioned the guy's lounge (I assumed that meant the room they had been in the night before) or the receiving room as good options to move to. I opted to stay in the dining room. I grabbed a second cup of coffee, sat back and relaxed and listened in on the conversations around the table.

Eventually Mark showed up, looking chipper and no worse for the wear from his escapades the night before. His hair was damp and looked freshly washed. Still as shaggy as ever. He found a spot a few spaces down on the other side of the table from me. Josh and Emily wandered over and joined us. Emily had a coffee mug in her hands as well that she sipped from slowly. Josh must not be a coffee drinker, or he had been up even earlier than the rest of us and already finished his. Emily looked around the room as though she was looking for someone, and then craned her neck as though she was trying to see out the doorway and into the hall.

"Where's Ben?" She asked, turning to Josh. "Don't you think you should go check on him babe? I think he's the only one that hasn't come down yet." She checked her watch as she said this last bit. I'm sure she was thinking of Ben's welfare, but also about her schedule for the day. Josh's brows wrinkled for a moment before he responded.

"Oh, no." He shook his head back and forth. "No need. He was up super early, before everyone else. He's not big on eating breakfast, at least not early. Although I did tell him we'd make sure the coffee stays out for him. He went for a run first thing. Although..." trailing off, now it was his turn to crane around the room, glancing at the doorway into the main hall. "Now that I think about it, I am a little surprised he's not back yet. It could only take him so long."

"Hmm," Emily mused. She took another sip of coffee. "Well maybe he is back, and he's upstairs showering."

"Yeah." Josh's brows unfurled. "I bet you're right. If he's not down in a bit, I'll go check his room."

That answered my question on whether there was a trail to run on. I'd get the details on where the trailhead was. I could probably scope it out today horseback riding. I may have lost my chance to run today though, given we had our itinerary laid out for us for the remainder of the day. Emily had referred to the croquet time and "rest" time as though there might be options. I would love to opt out of croquet and sneak off for a run then if I could manage it.

Ben resolved the mystery of his whereabouts for us a few moments later by making his appearance. Still in his running clothes, and damp with sweat. He was wearing a tight black running shirt and black shorts. A sweatband pulled back most of his hair from his face, but the damp curls at the base of his neck had clumped into little ringlets. Ugh. I hated it when guys had better hair than I did. He gave a quick nod Josh's way and grabbed a small plate with bacon and eggs and a coffee. I noted he took his coffee black. Yuck. I didn't understand black coffee drinkers. Although perhaps the bitterness suited his personality well.

At Josh's questioning, Ben shared he had a good run. It was about a four-mile run round trip taking the trail through the woods. He had made it about two miles out and decided to double back, because he knew that the village lay not too far beyond, and he didn't want to run through there.

"What's the condition of the trails?" I asked him, curiosity getting the better of me. He glanced up at me quickly, his dark eyes meeting mine. His expression seemed almost as though he was surprised I would deign to speak to him. I guess he thought I was bitter too.

He swallowed a mouthful of food before responding. "Pretty good actually. Not as bad as I remembered them being." I noted he'd obviously been to the Hideaway before. It seemed that most of Josh's friends were regular visitors.

"That's good to hear," I responded. "I was hoping to go for a run myself. But I'd hate to twist my ankle on a tree root out in the woods alone."

He nodded, considering this. "There are definitely some roots, you have to keep an eye out. But it's doable for sure." He quieted for a moment. "You're right though, I don't think it would be best to go alone. Just in case," he added, almost as an afterthought. "I could go with you actually if you'd like."

I was taken aback by the offer. Maybe he wasn't harboring a grudge against me after all. The way he had been staring at Mark and me laughing last night had made me think otherwise. That and his general moodiness. I struggled to come up with a response, and he was just staring at me expectantly. Josh and Emily were staring at me, too. I took a sip of coffee to buy myself some time. I didn't want to be rude, but I wasn't used to running with anyone else. I had no clue what his pace was, but given how tall and lean he was, I doubted I could keep up with him. I was pretty fast, but still. And I ran too hard to speak without gasping, much less carry on a conversation. It would just be too awkward. I didn't want to hurt his feelings, though. What did he mean by saying it was best not to run out there alone? He had done just that. Or did he mean it was best for *me* not to run alone?

I gulped my coffee audibly. I had stalled long enough. I opened my mouth with no real plan as to what would come out of it and mumbled, "Yeah, that would probably be a good idea." That wasn't necessarily a yes, but it wasn't a no.

Ben nodded and seemed satisfied with my response. I thought he probably took it to mean I was agreeing to run with him. Ugh. Why was I having such a hard time saying no lately?

Emily smiled and rapped her coffee mug down firmly on the table. "Good!" She said, smiling broadly back and forth between the two of us. Ben looked somewhat embarrassed by her enthusiasm, flushing a little. One of Josh's buddies, I think his name might have been Eric, seated off to Josh's left piped up suddenly.

"So, what do you do for work, Cassie?" He asked politely. I smiled back at him. I was pleased to be part of the conversation and to get to know the rest of the group, but I was a little bummed that was the question he decided to ask me. I gave my usual spiel. I made sure to throw in the names of some of the bigger, more well-known periodicals I had been published in. Eric nodded and listened politely while he ate his breakfast. I could feel Ben's gaze on me as he listened intently to my answer. For some reason, I refused to look in his direction. I don't know why I felt like he would judge my response. I had no clue what he did and no reason to think he'd find my answer wanting. But for some reason, his attention made me uncomfortable.

"How about you?" I finished politely. Eric (that was in fact his name) explained what he did at some length—something in investment banking. I honestly couldn't say I understood half of what he said. "Oh," I responded when he finished. "Isn't that similar to what you do, Josh?"

Josh nodded in confirmation. "Yeah, that's right. Eric and I met through work actually." He smiled and clapped Eric on the back fondly.

"Oh, nice." I smiled and nodded. Emily had pulled her phone out of her pocket while we were chatting. She was wearing skin-tight navy-blue pants and a white cable-knit sweater. She was dressed a bit on the preppier side, but I was relieved to see most people were dressed casually today. She was typing out something on her phone. It almost seemed like she was texting someone, but I figured she probably had no signal like the rest of us.

It occurred to me then for the first time to wonder how she was managing to coordinate and communicate anything to do with wedding prep. There had to be last-minute questions and arrangements to be made. I knew she had a massive amount of flowers being delivered, chairs for seating for all the guests for the outdoor ceremony, the cake, who knows what else. Maybe they had a computer hardwired to the internet somewhere here. That must be the case. Good old email would still work.

I glanced over at Ben and felt the conversation had lagged while I mused about the wedding. "What about you Ben? What do you do?" I made an effort to smile politely at him. He didn't meet my gaze this time, pushing scrambled eggs around his plate with his fork in a bored sort of way.

Josh jumped in to answer for him. "Ben is a physicist actually." He smiled over at him fondly. "He doesn't like to brag about it, but he's basically a rocket scientist."

"Wow," I responded. I guess Mark wasn't exaggerating about Ben being brilliant. "That's impressive. I don't think I've ever met a physicist before."

Ben shrugged and glanced Josh's way. "Yeah, well, it's not as cool as he makes it sound."

"He's just being modest," Josh continued. "On top of that, he knows pretty much everything about any random topic you can think of. Ask him something and see, it's like a party trick of his." He grinned over at Ben, who was now fidgeting in his seat. "Hey Ben, how does an air conditioner work?" Ben rolled his eyes. "No really, he knows, like in great detail. Tell her." He reached behind Emily to punch Ben in the shoulder.

Ben sighed and pinched the bridge of his nose between two fingers. Clearly, he did that when he was annoyed. "An air conditioner works basically utilizing compression and expansion. See, air, or gas particles are always moving, vibrating and bumping into each other, and when a gas is compressed the particles bump into each other at a much faster rate causing friction. This friction heats up the air. When the air is allowed to expand, the particles bump into each other less frequently and the gas cools. By cycling between compression and decompression, a temperature gradient can be formed, and heat is absorbed from inside a house and then pumped outside to be dissipated through the condenser coils."

I shook my head. "I'm not following, you're saying an air conditioner cools the air by actually heating it up first? But how does it compress enough air inside such a small space? Enough to cool down the whole house?"

"See!" Josh interrupted Ben as he opened his mouth to respond. "The guy's a genius; he can tell you how just about anything works. He's a history buff, too, knows about everything that happened, ever."

"That is an overstatement," Ben said matter of factly, shaking his head.

"Okay." Emily clicked her phone screen off and set it down on the table with a sharp tap. "As fascinating as this conversation has been," she turned and placed a hand on Ben's shoulder, "and thank you, Ben, for educating all of us; we really need to get going. The horses should already be ready and waiting for us out back. Babe, will you let the others know we'll head out back in about 10 minutes?"

Josh was already standing up. "On it babe." He grinned and winked at her, bending down to kiss her on the top of the head. Babe...something about their pet name for each other grated on me a bit. I didn't know why. Ben seemed relieved he was cut off and spared from trying to explain compression further to me, and I was relieved I had gotten out of having to try to understand it. He made his excuses and ran upstairs to go shower and change.

About fifteen minutes later, Emily had gathered the remaining group in the dining room and led us out back. Our route took us past the lounge area from last night, towards the back of the house, into a massive library. She announced in her tour guide voice that the main entrance into the garden was actually through the library.

I lingered behind the group in the library, my head lifted to gaze up at the ornate painted ceiling, my jaw dropped slightly open. Ceiling high shelves lined every square inch of wall space. There were two floors. There was even a spiral staircase leading to the second level. I was in heaven. I didn't think Emily had any intention of living here after the wedding, but if I were her, I would never leave. I noticed suddenly that Ben had joined us and was watching me geek out over the library. He strode behind me, both hands in his pockets and a broad grin on his face.

"Pretty cool, huh?" Was all he said.

"Yeah, it really is," I replied.

"So, you're a writer?" Ben said. "That's really cool." He cleared his throat nervously, "I know you write mostly print articles." He nodded towards the library shelves. "Have you ever thought about writing a book?"

I gazed up at the shelves reaching to the ceiling. "I would love to, actually," I mused. "I guess I just don't know where to start."

Ben looked thoughtfully at me for a moment. "Hmm... I guess, like with most stories, you should start at the beginning."

I laughed, raising an eyebrow at him. "Oh yeah? It's that simple huh?" I asked grinning.

"Yeah." He grinned back. "It's that simple." We walked together in awkward silence for a minute or so, still lingering behind the group. He definitely looked nervous, I decided. As though he was struggling to come up with something else to say to me.

I decided to put him out of his misery. "So, how long have you known Josh?"

"Since we were little kids, actually," Ben replied. "I've been coming here to stay with him and his family since we were young. He's one of my best friends. I'd do just about anything for him." I watched Emily playing tour guide out in the garden.

"Yeah," I said, "I feel the same way about Emily. Although," I added, "I haven't known her anywhere near as long." He nodded. I studied his profile for a moment. He was a little strange, that was for sure. But maybe he was just socially awkward. "Hey," I said, "You got here before me, has everything been... okay?"

Ben looked at me, an eyebrow raised. "What do you mean?"

"I mean, has everything been going okay with Josh and Emily this week so far? Everything's been fine... with the house?" Ben looked at me thoughtfully for a moment.

"Yeah. I mean, I think so. Why do you ask?"

"I dunno," I said, watching Emily laughing at something Josh said, "It was just... Emily seemed a little... strange last night. I thought maybe something had happened. She seemed like she was worried about something." I turned back to see Ben studying me intently, a solemn look on his face. "I'm sure it was nothing," I added quickly. He stared at me for another moment, his expression unreadable, before nodding.

"Come on you guys!" Emily called, waving us over. We hurried out to join the others. I watched Ben out of the corner of my eye. What had made me ask him that? About the house specifically? I felt oddly like I could trust him, but he was a total stranger.

The garden was gorgeous, of course, but the library was the star of the show in my book. We stopped to admire various flowers as Emily led us on through the garden portion of the tour. There were some type of blood-red roses that I would need to ask the name of. They were such a bright, vibrant red color, they practically glowed in the sun. I wasn't sure I had ever seen anything like them before. They were scattered everywhere, blooming all throughout the garden. I stuck my face into a large clump of them and breathed deeply, closing my eyes. They smelled heavenly too. When I opened my eyes, I saw Ben, back to his typical lurking again at the tail end of the group. He was staring right at me, watching me. His expression was... hungry, almost. My cheeks flushed.

Mark suddenly appeared out of nowhere. He plucked one of the roses a few inches below the bud and tucked it behind my ear. "A flower for you, M' lady," he said, giving another mock bow. Then he lifted my hand to his lips and kissed the back of it gently.

"Mark!" I chided, pulling my hand back, and laughing despite myself. "Don't pick them!"

"What?" He held his arms out. "It's no big deal. I don't think they're going to miss one rose, do you?" He asked, gesturing around us at the massive garden.

"Well, no," I sighed. But still." I glanced back in Ben's direction, but he appeared to be focused on Josh now. He stared at him so intently that it almost looked like he was deliberately avoiding looking at me. I saw a muscle tense, flexing and loosening in his jaw.

Josh was temporarily taking over the role of tour guide, "...and that was added by the first generation. The second generation added on to the gardens and made them into essentially what you see today. We maintain a garden staff that tends to the gardens almost year-round. Obviously, there's less to do in the winter, but you wouldn't believe the amount of effort that goes into maintaining them."

Emily added, "They've been featured in several magazines and documentaries." I really wasn't into gardening. Whatever the opposite of a green thumb is, I have that. I can kill any plant left in my care with a swiftness that is truly astonishing. The thing is though that I do have a fondness for them and often will buy little potted succulents or herbs, thinking this time will be different. News flash, it never is. But still, I could admire someone else's handiwork.

We continued the tour and eventually made our way past the stables to where the horses were saddled and waiting for us. There was a small crew of what I guess would be called stable hands waiting to help us. Harvey, the oldest one who had to be at least in his early 70s, was planning on riding out with us to lead the group.

Emily, naturally thinking of everything, had arranged to have a few small tables and some chairs brought out with a tent slung over them to provide shade. The first group would head out on horseback while the second group hung behind and relaxed. I spied a sideboard with water bottles and what looked like champagne and orange juice chilling. It looked like the festivities would start early today.

It turned out Mark and I were to be with Josh in the first group of riders, while Emily hung back and waited with the second group. Mark wasted no time teasing me that my horse, named Bessie, was in fact the toughest, meanest horse in the stable, and she would throw me immediately the first chance she got. His teasing did make me laugh and made me feel a little less nervous. I had only ridden a horse one other time that I could remember, and I had been about 13 at the time.

We were all given a quick lesson on horseback riding, handling a horse correctly, and communicating where you wanted them to go. Harvey shared that the horses had done this route many times, so the amount of guidance they would need should be minimal. I watched as Mark, Josh, and then Ben, who was also apparently in our group, mounted their horses quickly. Clearly, it wasn't their first, or second, time on a horse.

I felt my cheeks flush as I went through the instructions Harvey had given again in my head. I placed my left foot in the stirrup. It was much higher off the ground than I had thought it was, and that threw me off. I was standing awkwardly with one hip hiked up too high. I put all my weight on my left foot in the stirrup and using my left hand, pulled myself up while swinging my right leg up and over. I managed to just barely make it onto the side of the saddle and awkwardly pulled myself up from there. It wasn't graceful, but I made it. It gave me a tiny bit of comfort to see that Kristy struggled much more than I had. She needed assistance from Harvey and another stable hand to help hoist her up into the saddle. Once everyone was seated as comfortably as possible, we were ready to head off.

We started off in a large group, all clumped together at first. Mark was chatting away next to me, something about a football team he followed. I noticed Ben off to our left. He was eying the red rose tucked behind my ear. I had forgotten it was still there. He looked away quickly this time when he noticed me watching him. The horses eventually fell into a single file line on their own as we neared the edge of the forest. The trees weren't very thick here in this section of the woods, more widely spaced than they had been on my drive in at least. There was a dirt pathway worn through the undergrowth. You could tell the horses must have come through here many times, though it was partially overgrown again, as if it hadn't been used recently.

While we rode, Harvey told the group all about the care of the horses and the house's history. He had worked for the family for most of his life and had grown up in the local village.

"The woods here extend for miles, depending on which direction you go, but there are also pathways through the woods that lead out to open fields," Harvey explained from up ahead of the group. "Historically, the estate maintained large fields of crops that were harvested annually. Back in the old days, the Haverford estate was responsible for growing the crops that supplied most of the food for the town. Many of the villagers worked the fields, and their families were dependent on the crop yield." Harvey cleared his throat. "Now, this was going back quite a ways, well before my time, believe it or not," he chuckled. "They used to hold a festival of sorts, celebrating the harvest. The Haverfords were always generous."

The horses were calm, and we kept a slow, plodding pace. I felt myself relax and started to enjoy the ride. Clearly, they were very tame, and I had been silly to be nervous in the first place. Eventually we came to a ridge that overlooked a massive valley below. The view was absolutely stunning. There was even a picturesque little church with a steeple rising out of the trees far in the distance. It seemed too far away to be in the village itself, but then again, I wasn't sure where exactly the village was. I figured it must mean there were other signs of civilization nearby.

The foliage was nowhere near peak fall colors yet, but likely would be very soon. From this height and distance, you could see the hints of orange, yellow and red, with the leaves on some trees just starting to turn. I could have sat there much longer than we did. Some of the group wanted to get down to take pictures, but we decided it wasn't worth the hassle of having to mount again, especially since the whole group wasn't present anyway. We decided we might take a walk later in the week and take photos then. Kristy asked Josh if they planned to have any wedding photos taken here in front of the view. Josh frowned and thought for a moment.

"Actually, I have no idea. Em could be planning that, but if not, I should suggest it. It really is a gorgeous view."

We moved on from the cliff face and continued on our journey through the woods. We were heading back to the house now, down a continuation of the worn dirt path. This path wouldn't be too bad to run on I mused, but I didn't think this was the same one Ben and Josh had been talking about. I would have to remember to ask them today so I could run first thing tomorrow morning. Correction, I would ask Josh. I didn't want to bring it up again to Ben and prompt him to make plans to meet me.

As we exited the edge of the woods, I realized we were seeing the house from the opposite side we had started from. The tent and horse stables were off to our right now in the distance. Nothing but a massive field of plush grass separated us from the house and gardens. Nothing, I realized, except for a large tree. It took me a moment, but I recognized it from the painting that I had been looking at last night. It was massive, a weeping willow, its branches rising and then hanging down low, the leaves trailing almost to the ground. As we passed by, I peered through the leaves, searching for anything that might be hanging there amongst them. I saw nothing. It was much windier out here in the open than it had been under the cover of the trees in the woods.

A massive gust of wind blew up out of nowhere, shaking and whipping the willow branches back and forth. Some of the horses neighed, sounding startled. I heard a wind chime start to ring; it was clanging loudly. Suddenly, Bessie reared up on her hind legs, neighing and snorting.

"Whoa girl, whoa." I tried to calm her down. I pulled back hard, and then harder on the reins, squeezing her sides with my knees to try to stay on her back. I thought I caught a glimpse of something in the branches. Was it a frayed rope? I gripped harder, I could feel myself sliding backwards with each buck. Without warning, she took off like a rocket, slamming past the other horses, away from the willow tree. She was heading to the left of the house, away from the stables. My heart thundered and leapt into my throat. What the hell was I supposed to do now? Trying not to panic, I kept a steady grip on the reins and tried to run through the list of instructions they had given us at the start. I couldn't remember if digging in with my heels was supposed to slow her down? Or was that to make her turn? Oh my god, what was I thinking of getting on a horse? I had no clue what I was doing.

Over the sound of Bessie's hooves trampling the ground, I heard faint shouts coming from behind me. If they were trying to yell instructions to me, I couldn't hear a thing they were saying. I was starting to panic now. I began to hear hoofbeats that were beating out an opposing rhythm from Bessie's frantic gallop. Swiveling to my left, I saw Ben approaching quickly. He was pushing his horse hard, whipping the reins up and down. He was lifted out of the saddle, practically standing in the stirrups in a low crouch. I did a double take, trying to keep an eye on where Bessie was heading at break-neck speed and keeping my eyes on Ben. I could see the black fence bordering the forest in front of us. What if she didn't see it in time to stop?

"Help!" I yelled at him, not sure he could hear me. "I can't remember what to do!"

He had pulled up parallel to me now and was edging over closer. "Pull back on the reins with both hands, and squeeze with your knees into her side at the same time!" He yelled back at me.

"Whoa," he called over to Bessie now. "Whoa girl, halt, it's okay." I did what he said the best I could, pulling back on the reins with both hands, I leaned my torso back and lifted slightly off the saddle, squeezing with my legs and thighs, I pressed my knees in. I felt Bessie start to slow down beneath me and held on tightly. Ben had brought his horse directly next to me and reached over and grabbed onto the reins. Bessie finally slowed down and then came to a stop.

I took a deep breath and felt myself go limp. My heart was racing. Ben held firmly onto the reins and patted Bessie on the side of the neck.

"It's okay, it's okay," he repeated to the horse. I noticed he was breathing hard, his nostrils flaring—almost as if he'd been the one running after me instead of his horse. He turned his attention to me. "Are you okay?" he asked, concern etching lines between his brows.

"Yeah," I said, my voice trembling a bit. I'm okay. I'm not hurt or anything, just freaked out."

Ben nodded. "That's understandable," he said. He managed to dismount somehow while still holding onto the reins of both horses. Then he reached and held up his hand to help me down. I grabbed onto his hand and shifted my weight onto him while I swung my right leg back over the horse. He waited while I worked my left shoe out of the stirrup. It felt good to be back on the ground on my own two feet.

Josh and Mark, followed closely behind by Harvey, thundered towards us on their horses. They pulled up on the reins and came to a stop a few feet behind us.

"Everyone okay?" Harvey called out to us.

"We're fine," I yelled back, "Everything's okay now."

"Good." He nodded and dismounted quickly, walking his horse over to us. "I'm so sorry that happened," he said to me, but swiveled his head back to address Josh as well. "I've never seen Bessie do anything like that. She's a tame old lady. Something must have spooked her badly."

I nodded. "It was the wind chimes. I could tell they freaked her out." No one said anything for a beat. Mark and Josh exchanged a look.

"What wind chimes?" Ben asked.

"The wind chimes that went off when the wind started blowing through the trees," I explained. "I'm not surprised that awful racket spooked her."

Ben stared at me for a moment and then began shaking his head slowly. "I was right behind you, Cassie. I didn't hear any wind chimes," he said matter-of-factly.

I didn't have any response to that, I just gaped back at him. What was he talking about? He must have just not been paying attention.

"Well." Harvey broke the silence. "We should head back to the others. "Miss, I'm going to walk your horse back alongside mine if that's okay with you? I think Bessie's caused enough trouble for one day."

I smiled at Harvey and nodded my agreement. "Yes, I think that's for the best. Thank you." Ben handed her reins over to Harvey.

"You okay riding yours back?" Harvey asked Ben. "If not, I can walk him back, too."

Ben glanced at me a moment before nodding at him. "I'm fine; I'll ride him back."

"Okay, good." Harvey nodded towards Josh and Mark. "You three go on ahead; there's no need to wait for us. We'll meet you back at the tent. I told the others to head back that way; they should be there by now, waiting."

Ben hopped back on his horse, and the three of them started off at a light trot. I did admire their ease on horseback. It was clearly evident that all three of them had spent a significant amount of time riding and probably had lessons as kids. Who knows, maybe Ben and Mark had grown up owning their own horses, too. I had yet to find out where either of them were from.

When we set off for the ride, I had thrown on my light fall jacket over my long-sleeved tee, and I was glad I had. The breeze held a slight chill whenever the sun went behind the clouds. I stretched either side of the open jacket across my chest and folded my arms tightly across it, keeping it closed.

Harvey spoke up. "So, how long have you been a friend of the Haverford's?" He asked.

I thought for a moment. "Oh! Well, I'm not, really. I mean, not that I'm *not* a friend of the family's, but I'm a friend on the bride's side. One of Emily's friends. I just met Josh for the first time this week actually."

"Ah," Harvey responded. He didn't speak again for a minute or two. I was starting to regret that the guys had gone ahead. He seemed nice enough, but making conversation the whole walk back was going to be awkward.

I looked around the field, trying to get my bearings. I noticed there was no garage anywhere in sight, which was not what I had expected. I figured the cars had to be parked out towards the back, on the right-hand side of the house when facing it. That was the direction I had seen the gravel drive disappear off to last night. Had it only really been last night that I had arrived? This week was going to take forever.

"Where are all the cars?" I asked aloud, looking over at Harvey in confusion. "I figured there was a garage or something back behind the house, but that's obviously not the case."

"No, Ma'am." Harvey shook his head. "The family added a garage at one point, and a nice one at that, but they didn't want it spoiling the view on the grounds." He jerked his head to the left. "It's off hidden in the woods out that way in a big clearing. There's a gravel drive that runs through the woods a bit. That's where we parked all the guests' vehicles."

"Ah, okay. Thanks, that makes sense." He must have helped move the cars over yesterday. With so many guests arriving at once, I'm sure it had been all hands on deck. The thought piqued my curiosity further.

"How many staff are there at Haverford House?" I asked.

"Oh my, hmm..." he trailed off for a moment, "I'd have to think about that one for a bit. Let's see." He squinted off into the distance. "There's the gardening staff, although they aren't here year-round necessarily, nor are all of 'em full time. There's me of course, the stable hands, all local boys that we hire from the village, they're seasonal too, or come and go at least. There's several maids, they're under Mrs. Evans, she manages the household really. There's Cook, and she has one full time girl, but the maids and some of the seasonal staff help to pitch in whenever there's big events, like holidays and things. The maids help with the kitchen duties and serving too. Gosh, there's a few others that come and go as it were too."

I nodded. "And do you all live in the village, or do you stay here at the house?" It was all so old fashioned, it reminded me of a period piece.

"Well, as far as that's concerned, most of the full-time staff at least have a room here at the house. We're down on the lower level. But not all of us necessarily stay overnight full time. I'm here for this week, but I don't... prefer to stay in the house overnight. I typically travel back and forth during a normal week. What with the wedding and all, it's not your typical week, you see."

Yes, that made sense. I wanted to ask how often the Haverfords, Josh's parents especially, came to stay here. As charming as it was, it was so remote and quiet here. I could see it becoming tedious after a while. It felt like a slightly rude, prying question so I let it go. The old man had walked much more briskly than I had expected. I had to keep up a good pace, practically speed walking, to keep up with him. The horses had been quiet and calm the whole walk back. We were nearing the tent and the others now. I started to veer off towards the tent, as Harvey was making his way back towards the stables. I began to turn to thank him for walking me back, when I felt a firm grip on my arm. I jerked my head towards him in surprise.

"The keys are downstairs, too, down on the lower level," he said intently, his voice barely audible.

"Keys?" I responded in confusion; my voice pitched low to match his instinctively, "What keys?"

"The car keys," he replied. "You were asking where the cars are kept. They're off down the gravel drive that branches from the main drive, just like I said. But the keys are kept downstairs. In the hallway outside the kitchen, there's a small office that belongs to Mrs. Evans. You'll find them inside."

It hadn't occurred to me to wonder what had happened to my car keys. I guess I assumed they left them in my purse, in my room with my luggage, though honestly, I hadn't really thought about it at all.

"Okay..." I replied. "That's good to know, but why are you telling me this?"

Harvey released his grip on my arm. "You seem like a nice young lady. I hope you enjoy your stay." With that, he whistled to the horses and turned away from me, heading back towards the stables.

I stood staring after him, trying to process what had just happened.

"Cassie!" I turned to the sound of Emily's voice to see her jogging towards me across the lawn. People lounging under the tent had turned to watch her. "Oh my god!" She reached me and threw her arms around me, pulling me in for a hug. She pulled back away from me, her hands still on my arms and held me at arm's length. "Are you okay? I can't believe that happened. What the hell?"

"I know right." I chuckled a little, shaking my head in disbelief. "It was crazy. But no, I'm completely fine. Just a little shaken, that's all."

"Well, I don't blame you. Gosh I'm nervous to even take the rest of the group out. Maybe we should just cancel the horseback riding." She bit her lower lip in indecision, then glanced up at the sky. Gray clouds were rolling in over the woods in the distance.

Following her gaze, I replied, "Honestly, I think it might rain soon. Was it supposed to rain today?"

Emily shook her head no, concern creasing her brow. "No, it wasn't, but it sure looks like it now."

I nodded in agreement and shivered a little. "It feels like it, too." The air was humid and heavy now. I held my hands up, hovering over my hair. "I can feel my hair getting bigger already."

Emily looked at me, confused for a moment, then laughed, "Luckily I don't have that problem, but I guess it comes in handy to predict the weather."

"Yes," I laughed back, "you are lucky. But, I agree, it's a useful tool."

Emily hooked an arm through mine and started to lead me towards the tent. "Maybe we'll cancel the rest of horseback riding to be safe. I'm not sure everyone wants to go anyway. We can finish up refreshments and start with croquet. We were going to do sandwiches outside for lunch, but we could always move that inside." She was thinking more to herself out loud now.

Once inside the tent, condolences were offered all around for my horseback riding ordeal. Emily announced the second tour was canceled, and I could tell everyone was pretending to be disappointed. She sent Mark to go let the stable crew know we were done for the day. Josh, ever the charming host, came over to check on me and offered me a drink; they had mimosas available as well as ice cold lemonade, both cold and warm apple cider, and water. I chose the warm apple cider. The heavy brown ceramic mug felt comforting in my hands. I was grateful to be offered a non-alcoholic option, and I just couldn't seem to get warm.

I sipped it slowly and watched the others finish their drinks. Kristy downed the remainder of her mimosa from a delicate, long-stemmed glass before getting up to grab another. I wondered absentmindedly what number she was on.

Eventually one of the stable hands brought out the croquet equipment. I groaned internally. I really didn't want to play, but I told myself to suck it up and get it over with. How bad could it be? *Well*, a small voice grumbled in the back of my head, *that's what you thought about horseback riding too*. I sighed and forced myself to get up and follow the group out into the field. The clouds were heavy and dark overhead now, threatening rain. Too bad we couldn't use our phones to check the weather.

I tried my best to focus and listen intently while Josh and Emily gave us all a quick tutorial on how to play. It seemed likely that most of the others had played before, but that was just an assumption on my part. It turned out we were short a few sets of mallets and their matching-colored balls. It was a large group after all. Someone had the idea of having a few people play in pairs. I jumped at the chance. That would give me fewer opportunities to embarrass myself, and my partner could give me tips. Mark offered immediately to be my partner and Ben shot us a dark look as he walked over to join me. I handed Mark the dark blue mallet and matching ball and we broke off into small groups to play.

Unsurprisingly, my swing was awful. Mark was actually pretty good and helped me practice off to the side. I didn't quite understand all the rules, but I felt like I got better as the game went on. I could probably get the hang of it eventually if I kept playing. It was my turn to go on the final run. We had to hit our ball through the final hoop and into a wooden peg to win the game. Basically, a hole in one was needed, there was no way I was going to be able to do it. I begged Mark to take my turn for me, but he crossed his arms and shook his head no at me laughing. "No way man, you got this, you can do it!"

"Seriously, Mark, " I whispered, "I can't make it, come on."

"Nope. I believe in you, even if you don't." He clasped his hands on my shoulders, peering into my eyes intensely. "Just aim and be the ball Cassie... be the ball."

"Oh my god, you are so annoying." I shook my head, resigning myself, and made my way over to line up my shot.

Mark cupped his hand over his mouth. "Like I haven't heard that before!" He called after me.

I took a deep breath and prayed the ball wouldn't go embarrassingly wide. I took the shot. The ball went right through the hoop and clunked audibly off the wooden pole. "Yes!" I yelled, shooting my hands up into the air and turning back towards Mark in disbelief.

He ran over to me, shouting and lifting me up into the air onto his shoulders, cheering, "We won, yes!!! Suck it, Josh!" He yelled over in his general direction. Josh was cracking up. It was actually pretty exciting, I'm not going to lie, but our celebration was a little over the top.

"Put me down, you idiot," I told him, still laughing.

He set me gently back on the ground, and I looked over to see people from the other game next to us laughing and clapping for us. Led mainly by Emily of course. One of the Mikes was chanting "USA! USA!" Which Mark thought was hilarious. Ben stood a few paces behind Emily. He had his hands shoved in his pockets again, and he was absolutely shooting daggers at us with his eyes. That put a bit of a damper on my excitement. I smoothed my shirt down over my hips. It had ridden up when Mark had lifted me up and paraded me around the lawn.

Just then I felt a raindrop land on my cheek. It was just one or two at first, so it was hard to tell if it was really starting to rain, but it soon became obvious. The others decided it wasn't worth finishing their games to get soaked, and we began to pack up to head back inside. Instead of heading straight for the house, some of the girls, led by Kristy, ran under the tent. The whole group ended up following, and we gathered there for a few moments. The boys started arguing with the girls to get moving inside, but a few of the girls, again, led by Kristy, insisted it could clear up quickly, and we might as well hang out under the tent for a bit and have a few more drinks. No one could decide what to do, and I eyed the sky impatiently. I had a feeling this was going to be more than a light shower.

I noticed Ben was staying out of the argument. He kept eyeing a bank of dark storm clouds in the distance, growing steadily closer over the woods. I wound my way through the crowd under the tent over towards him. Not wanting to be too obvious, I pretended I was interested in checking out the drinks on the side table. I cleared my throat as I neared him.

"Hey," I said, getting his attention. "I didn't thank you for helping me with the horse earlier. That was really nice of you. I had no clue what to do."

He gave me a cursory glance and shrugged before turning his attention back towards the gathering storm. "It was no big deal."

"Oh." I colored slightly. Was he angry at me for some reason? "Well, um, thanks, anyway." He nodded without turning back to me. *Okay... message received.* I made my way back over towards the group.

Someone had pulled a Bluetooth speaker out of somewhere and started blasting dance music. Kristy and Blair were grabbing another drink. I sighed and grabbed a chair. It looked like we were going to be out here for a while longer.

I sat on my own for a few minutes before deciding to grab another cider, just to warm myself up. I sipped it slowly while the others laughed and partied. Ben and I seemed to be the only ones not into it at the moment. I would have been tempted to go sit with him, but he'd made it clear he wasn't interested in talking to me. He sat next to the drink table by himself. He seemed to be making a point to not look in my direction now, which was fine by me. That was better than glaring.

Eventually, a song came on with a booming, deep bass line. Some of the others howled. I looked up to see Kristy had climbed onto one of the tables and was doing some kind of *Coyote Ugly* table dancing for the group. I had to admit she was a pretty good dancer, but really, it was a little much. Not to mention, it was only 1:00 in the afternoon. I thought, not for the first time, that this was going to be a long, long week.

Some of the other girls had started dancing, but on the ground, at least. Soon, the guys were joining in, too. Kristy had hopped down off the table to join the others. Suddenly, I saw one of the Mikes push her out from underneath the tent into the rain.

"Michael!" She shrieked. He laughed, pointing at her. She grabbed his arm and dragged him out into the rain with her. Mark pulled one of the girls out to join them after a minute. Before long, the others joined as well. Josh and Emily ran out holding hands, Emily shrieking and laughing. I giggled a little, watching them. It was kind of fun, with the rain and everything. Emily saw me laughing and ran over to me. "Come on, Cass!" She grabbed my hand, trying to pull me up while dripping water on me.

"No." I laughed. "No way Em."

"Yes way," Emily insisted, "live a little, you're moping around under here."

"Well, to be fair, it's a little cold out, and just a little wet." I plopped back on my seat. She pulled me to my feet again.

"Come on! I'm the bride..." She stuck her lower lip out in a fake pout. "I'm instituting mandatory dancing."

I laughed. "I don't think that's a thing... but fine." I sighed, rolling my eyes. I followed Emily over to the others. We spun together, laughing and singing along.

Mark came and danced with me for a few minutes after Emily left me to rejoin Josh. He was a fantastic dancer. We competed to see who could do the best robot, laughing at ourselves and each other. Catherine and Blair were cracking up watching us and eventually joined in. Only the quiet, mousy girl hadn't joined us out in the rain. She was standing under the tent, her arms folded around her, shivering. She was laughing, though. I glanced over and realized Ben hadn't joined in either. Apparently, he had decided to go back to glaring at me instead of ignoring me. We made eye contact for several seconds before he looked away, staring at his feet instead.

Suddenly a flash of lightning lit up the sky over the forest, and a crack of thunder pealed. A moment later, a sheet of rain came down all at once like a curtain being drawn. A few of the girls screamed and squealed. I started laughing. We sprinted, in groups of two and three at a time, to squeals and laughter, and made for the back garden. The closest entrance to the house would be back through the garden and the library.

By the time we made it back inside, everyone was more than soaked, and I was freezing cold to the bone and shivering. I was trying not to be melodramatic like some of the girls, but I was struggling to stop my teeth from chattering. My hair would be wrecked for the rest of the evening unless I got back in the shower and styled it again.

Emily directed us to head back to our rooms, get changed and warmed up, shower, if we wanted to. She let us know we were free to relax on our own in our rooms, or elsewhere in the house, but they would have sandwiches laid out in the dining room and drinks would be in the guy's lounge for anyone who wanted to join. Mark shook his head like a dog, and rivulets of water sprayed off of him. I couldn't help but notice his wet t-shirt clinging to the muscles on his arms. Ben, who wasn't wearing black for the first time this week, happened to choose a white long sleeve t-shirt today. It was naturally see-through now, and clung to his abs. Every muscle was outlined. I tore my eyes away and scanned the room. Josh was similarly built. So was one of the Mikes. What the heck, was every guy here just ripped? It seemed a little odd, but I guess that's what being independently wealthy gets you. They all probably had the best of everything, and all the time in the world to exercise. Plus, good genes.

I shook my head to clear it and joined the other girls who had started to file out and head upstairs. My plan was to take advantage of the break in forced socializing as much as possible. I would have to decide whether to shower or not, and after getting dry, I could run down and grab a sandwich and hopefully sneak back up to my room.

Emily called out suddenly behind us. "Just a reminder, dinner starts at 6:00 sharp tonight, black tie only." There were a few chuckles at that. "Ya'll best be dressed to the nines; we're taking some pictures tonight!" Ah, I was wondering when the obligatory photo taking would commence. Afterall, if we didn't post on social media, how would anyone know we were having a good time? Not that anyone would be posting much of anything from here this week. I froze for a second, one foot hovering over the bottom step of the staircase. Wait a minute... black tie? I had packed some of my nicer dresses, but they were all simple. I didn't have anything that sounded fancy enough for that. After a moment's hesitation I turned around and went back to find Emily.

She was standing in the hallway outside the library, huddled together with Josh and Ben. I groaned and squeezed my way in between the crowd, leaving to head upstairs, and made my way over to them. One of the guys stopped me to congratulate me on my croquet win again. I thanked him and managed to make some kind of response that was apparently funny. The few people left chuckled and continued on their way. I was only half paying attention. What were they talking about back there? Ben had a hand in his pocket, the side facing me, and it looked like he was holding something and rotating some small object back and forth. I hadn't noticed him doing that before. Josh's back was to me so that I couldn't see his face, but Ben and Emily both looked serious. Worried even, like something was wrong.

I approached them and cleared my throat. "Everything okay guys?" They all turned abruptly, as though I'd startled them. Emily's smile seemed to come too readily to her face and be too wide.

"Everything's fine, we were just discussing the festivities this week. You know, there's just so much to plan, so many details for the wedding and all."

With Ben? He didn't seem like the wedding planning type. But I kept my thoughts to myself.

"Well, if there's any way I can help at all, you know I would be happy to. Let me take on some of the details for you, you shouldn't have to do it all yourself."

"Oh." Emily waved my offer away with one hand, "You know how I am, I'm too much of a control freak. But of course, I would love and value your opinion, maybe I can go over some of the flower arrangements one more time with you?"

"Sure!" I nodded. Why did I feel like she was throwing me a bone? "Um, actually, could I steal you for just a moment? I wanted to discuss something with you."

Emily looked surprised for a second, but she walked over to me and reached up and gently tugged on my hair at the side of my face. I realized she was pulling something out of my hair, but until she held up a single red rose in front of me, I had no clue what it could be.

"Oh." I smiled. "Thanks, I forgot that was there."

"I'm surprised it made it through the crazy horseback ride and dancing in the rain." Emily grinned, shaking her head. "What a day. Not at all what I had planned."

I smiled, shaking my head in agreement. "No, but still good though."

"True, but hopefully this doesn't happen on Saturday."

Ah, I thought. Maybe that's what she was worried about. The ceremony had to take place outside. The house was massive, but I was sure there was no one room that could easily fit the wedding ceremony if they needed to move it indoors. Not unless there was a grand ballroom or something. I guessed there could be for all I knew.

"Um, can I talk to you privately for just a second? Sorry." I added the apology, glancing over at Josh and Ben. I felt a little rude, but I really didn't want them to overhear my conversation with Emily and they were clearly still listening to us.

"Absolutely!" She said brightly, tucking her arm in mine. I transferred the rose to my other hand, not sure what to do with it at this point. I watched Ben's eyes, tracking it, like a dog with a stick. What was his deal with the rose? Did he have some kind of problem with it? Or did he have a problem with Mark? I'd seen him staring at us too many times. Almost like he was jealous. He probably saw him pluck it and place it behind my ear. I had noticed him watching me just before that. My gut twisted a little at the thought. Was he actually jealous?

Emily led me down the hallway swiftly towards the main entrance. "See you later Babe!" Josh called. Emily blew a quick kiss over her shoulder.

We soon left the hallway and made it to the stairs. We scaled them quickly. Looking down, I noticed we were still dripping onto the carpet. The poor cleaning staff would probably have a puddle waiting for them in the library.

"What's going on Cassie?" Emily asked me a little breathlessly.

"So..." I said, fumbling with my words for a moment, I just came right out with it. "I was thinking I would just like... skip dinner tonight." Emily froze halfway up the steps.

"What do you mean? Why would you want to skip dinner?"

I stopped as well, but due to my momentum I was a few steps ahead of her. "It's not that I don't want to go, it's just that. Well..." I felt my cheeks flush a little. "I don't have anything to wear Emily. I don't even really know what black tie means, exactly, but I'm pretty certain I don't have it. Unless you want me to wear my bridesmaid dress, I'm going to have to skip it."

Emily stared at me for a moment and then her face fell a little. "I'm sorry Cass, how stupid of me. I wasn't thinking."

"It's okay." I rushed to cover up my embarrassment. "It's not a big deal, really, but I think it's just easier if we make up some excuse. Like just say I have a bad headache or I'm not feeling well or something. I'm sure no one will think anything of it, or care."

"I don't know…" Emily trailed off in thought for a moment. "I do know actually." She held up one finger. "I have the perfect idea, you can just borrow one of my dresses!" She looked excited now. "I brought a ton of extras because I couldn't decide what I wanted to wear. You can take your pick!"

"Emily…" I cocked my head to the side and pointed to my chest. "I think you're forgetting something… or two somethings. We're not exactly the same size. I'm quite confident I won't fit into anything you own."

Her face fell again, and she looked down at her chest. I knew it was something she hated about herself, and I felt a twinge of guilt for pointing it out to her. No matter how many times I told her I'd wished my whole life for smaller boobs, she never seemed to believe me.

"Okay, yeah, you're right." She thought some more. "I know! There are other dresses here, I know exactly where they are. I'll have them brought to your room. Pretty much everyone will be downstairs at lunch, no one will ever know. You can try them on and I'm sure you can find something that fits you!"

"Other dresses?" I questioned, "Whose are they?"

"Oh, who knows." She waved her hand. "They must've belonged to other family members, random cousins and that sort of thing. I'm sure there have been loads of family staying here over the years that kept clothes here. No one will miss them for a night."

"Um, okay…" I felt a little weird about it, but I guessed I didn't really have any reason to object.

"I'll have lunch brought up for you too, you won't have to leave your room at all. It's settled." Emily clapped her hands together and continued up the stairs. "You can't miss dinner Cass; it's going to be such a nice evening." A crack of thunder boomed in the distance, but it sounded much closer than before this time.

I waited in my room, having towel dried off a bit and squeezed the rainwater from my hair over the sink. I debated whether I should get in the shower or wait until after someone came to bring the dresses and lunch. It was almost 2:00 now, and my stomach growled with anticipation.

I was shivering again and noticed goosebumps standing up on my arms. I decided I might as well go ahead and shower while I waited. The hot water felt heavenly. I stood there far too long, thinking.

When I got out of the shower, I wrapped myself in a towel and stepped through the closet. It occurred to me there could be a dress hanging in here that might work as well. I had forgotten about the clothes. I peeked around the closet doorframe and saw a pile of dresses had been laid out across the bed. There was a tray with several sandwich halves cut into neat triangles, along with a steaming cup of tea and a small pot of milk and sugar.

I decided to try on a few of the dresses right away while I waited for the tea to cool. The first two didn't fit quite right, but they were okay, I guessed, given I had nothing else. I examined the others and found a silky, black dress with a sweetheart neckline. It looked like it might fit me. The shoulders and upper back were made of sheer black lace adorned with a pattern of vines and leaves stitched in black thread. A layer of lace overlay covered the rest of the dress with an intricate art deco design stitched with silver thread and tiny silver beads. It had a short train trailing behind it. It was a beautiful dress. It looked vintage, possibly hand stitched. The overall effect reminded me of something straight out of *The Great Gatsby*. Thankfully I had bought a brand-new strapless bra for my bridesmaid's dress. I threw it on and wiggled into the dress, just barely managing to pull the zipper all the way up. Unfortunately, there was no floor length mirror in the room, but I checked my reflection in the bathroom. The dress fit. It was tight, but it fit. The sheer lace dipped low in the back; I hoped my bra wouldn't peek out over the top of the dress as the night went on.

I quickly removed the dress for now, hanging it on a spare hanger in the closet, and after a moment decided to hang the others up as well. I hadn't tried them all on, hopefully another one or two might fit in case we were supposed to dress up every evening. I threw on my PJs for the time being and quickly did my hair. I had wolfed down most of the sandwiches by now and the tea was now cool enough to sip. I would wear my shoes I had brought for the wedding so I would be all set for tonight. I breathed a sigh of relief and decided to relax and spend my time reading one of the new books I'd brought with me.

The afternoon had flown by and was over sooner than I would have liked. After curling up in bed with my book, I felt cozy and sleepy, and had no desire to leave it. There had been cracks of thunder here and there throughout the afternoon, and it had continued to rain steadily. Checking the clock, I decided I had better get dressed. I forced myself out of bed and, donning the black and silver dress again, I went with a quick twisted updo to get my hair off my shoulders. I left several waves curling down loose out of the messy bun. The baby hairs that always escaped at the base of my neck were curled and frizzy. My hair overall was pretty frizzy with all the humidity in the air, but it would have to do.

I almost forgot to throw some makeup on. I did that quickly, adding a retro cat eye in black eyeliner, and decided I was as ready as I'd ever be. For the past half hour or so, I had heard the girls getting ready; voices calling out for this or that, and footsteps running up and down the hall. I stepped out into the hallway and ran into Kristy. She was with the quiet, mousy girl. Kristy eyed me up and down; she seemed to be making a habit of that. After a moment she cooed, "Oooh, I love your dress. Where did you get it?"

I colored immediately. Why hadn't I anticipated someone might ask me that? "Oh," I stumbled, "I can't remember to be honest; I've had it for years."

"Really?" Kristy murmured, pursing her lips, "Hmm..." She started to turn away. "Well, it suits you. I like your makeup too."

"Oh, thank you," was all I managed. That was nice of her to say. Nicer than I had expected from her. The nice mousy girl gave me a nervous looking smile. She was dressed in a silk gown, a pale shade of lavender. Kristy had a short, slinky, skintight little dress on. Both probably cost more than my salary for a week. "You look great as well," I blurted out in their general direction.

Kristy smiled, almost smirked, back. "Emily wants us to head down, the guys are already waiting for us."

"Okay, sounds good."

She turned and led us down the hallway. I guessed Emily must be downstairs already as well. Apparently neither Kristy or Mousy felt it was worth striking up a conversation on the way, which was quite frankly fine with me. I busied myself with attempting to study each painting we passed in the gloomy hallway. I wanted another chance to check out the painting of the house I had seen last night. Maybe it was wind chimes that had been hanging from the tree in the painting. Although whatever it was had seemed much too big given how far away the tree was.

We made it to the top of the stairs without seeing anyone else. As we started down the stairs, I was focusing on not tripping over my dress when I heard a whistle and catcalling from down below. I looked up to see a group of guys and a few girls gathered together. They had all turned to watch us descend. I wasn't sure who had started it, but assumed it was probably Mark as he yelled out, "Looking fine ladies!"

Kristy laughed and posed for him. "Oh, go on," she said, voguing down the stairs, which garnered more whistling and general ruckus. Ben was there, shockingly, all in black. He was staring at me again. A loud peal of thunder shuddered through the walls of the house.

"Okay," Mark said, "I could feel that one. Storm's getting closer."

The group made its way into the dining hall. There was music playing in the background from somewhere. Probably to try to drown out the storm. I never understood why people were afraid of thunderstorms. I happened to love them.

I was surprised to see little cream-colored cards at each place setting. Our names were printed on them in gold letters. Assigned seats... interesting. Were they going to do this every night for dinner? I had missed last night's meal.

I found the card with my name on it and sat down gratefully. My feet didn't hurt exactly, but I wasn't used to walking in high heels. I found myself facing Emily, which I noted appreciatively. Ben was unfortunately seated to her right. Josh on her left. I checked the card to my right and saw Mark was seated next to me. The card on my left read, 'Amelia,' and when Mousy came and sat down, I did a fist pump in my mind. Yes. Now, I wouldn't have to mortify both of us by asking her what her name was again. She gave me a little smile and said, "They tend to be much more formal at dinners."

"I guess so... I wasn't expecting that." I took a sip of my water. The glass goblet was heavy.

"You get used to it. Although it does all get a bit tedious after a while." She shrugged. "Are you having a nice time so far? It must be hard not knowing anyone."

I nodded, appreciating the acknowledgement. "It has been a little," I said honestly, "But mostly everyone has been so nice, that makes it much easier." I inadvertently looked at Kristy when I said that last bit. She was showboating again, practically twerking in the middle of the room. Clearly, she liked attention. Or was she just drunk? Well, if she wasn't yet, there was plenty of time for that. I noticed there were beverage and menu cards placed on each plate.

Amelia had followed my glance in Kristy's direction. "She's not that bad you know, once you get to know her. She just can be a little catty sometimes. And a little annoying," she added as an afterthought.

"Oh," now what was I supposed to say? Perceptive of her to notice my dislike. "Yeah, it's hard getting to know everyone at once with such a big group." A diplomatic response, I guess. Amelia nodded and gave me a sympathetic smile. Waiters had started to make the rounds and were heading our way. I grabbed the drink menu, and we perused it together. Mark sat down a moment later, drink already in hand. I decided to stick with white wine again, it had served me well last night. I honestly sort of preferred a dry red, but it sometimes gave me a headache.

Everyone seemed to be in a great mood tonight. Despite the rain putting a bit of a damper on the day, and the thunder booming and shaking repeatedly, drinks were brought out, and we ordered from the choices laid out on the food menu. For the main course, I stuck with a dish that had chicken and mashed potatoes with green beans; all things I could pronounce. Mark kept up a steady flow of conversation next to me. He started telling me funny stories about Josh and some of the other guys, some of the crazy things they did in college. I couldn't help but notice throughout the meal how often Ben looked over at us. He kept staring at Mark and me. It was really starting to get on my nerves. I tried to ignore him and focus on what Mark was saying. I kept sipping my wine to calm my nerves. A young man came over and refilled my glass, almost to the rim, before I could notice and stop him. I continued to sip absentmindedly while listening to Mark. Ben continued to glare. He must have noticed that I noticed by now, but he kept doing it.

Someone had started asking the girls how we had all met Emily. It started at the far end of the table, and people were taking turns. It was a nice way to get to know who people were better. It came to be my turn when we were nearly done with our food. I paused eating a little early to prepare in my head for what I would say. I didn't have a fear of speaking up in public exactly, but it had never been my favorite thing to do. It was kind of a cute story anyway. I started recounting in my head.

I met Emily by happenstance. I had been shopping, browsing for new books in a little local bookshop, when I noticed a woman out on the sidewalk walking past briskly. She was wearing an outfit that looked like it was straight out of *Vogue*, and I found myself wondering who she was, what she did for a living. I knew the part about how she got absolutely drenched with mud when a delivery truck drove by and just sprayed her from head to toe would get a lot of laughs. After watching her standing completely still, frozen, staring down at her outfit in horror, I wouldn't tell them that I had started to smile, almost to laugh, at how ridiculous it was, like from a cartoon really. Until, that is, I had noticed the expression on her mud-splattered face and realized that she was about to cry.

Without thinking, I had rushed outside, told her that I saw what had just happened, and that I lived in an apartment right around the corner. I offered to take her back to my place so she could get cleaned up and could change into some of my clothes, if she needed them. I had no idea at the time that she had been on her way to an important job interview. She agreed to my suggestion, and the rest, as they say, is history. And she did get that job, by the way, I would add at the end.

When it came to my turn, Emily turned to me and said, "Ah, Cassie, not my oldest, but one of my dearest friends. This is a good one." She held her hands out, palms up, gesturing for me to start.

Ben chuckled into his glass. "According to Nietzsche, women can never truly be capable of friendship."

Emily whipped her head around and stared at him. The look on her face said it all. "Really, Ben. What is that supposed to mean?"

"Nothing, forget about it." He gestured to me. "Please, continue." Why had he chosen to wait until it was my turn to say something like that?

"What made that pop into your brain just then?" I asked curiously.

Ben stilled, looking at me. "I... dunno. No reason, specifically. I just said it without thinking."

"Mmm." I nodded slowly. "So, a Freudian slip then?" I tilted my head, raising one eyebrow. "How interesting." I knew he had some kind of issue with me. So, that was it? He thought I wasn't a good friend to Emily. Why? Ben flushed, catching my meaning.

"What does that mean?" Mark asked, looking confused.

"Freud had a theory that the little mistakes we make when we speak, like saying the wrong name, misquoting, or slips of the tongue, are connected to our subconscious thoughts, or desires, that sort of come out to the surface accidentally," I explained, watching Ben's face. He flushed a bit. "But it doesn't just have to be something you say, it could even be a mistake in your memory or an action you take. They're like... little clues... to how a person really feels." It was quiet for a moment.

"So..." Mark said thoughtfully, "you think Ben saying that just now wasn't random?"

"No, I don't," I said, smiling at Mark. "He clearly said it just as Emily was calling me a good friend." I met Ben's eyes again. He looked at a loss for words.

Mark chuckled. "Wow. Sounds like Freud might have been on to something."

Ben glowered. "Well, Freud was also a cocaine addict, so." He shrugged dismissively. That got a few laughs from the table.

"Yeah, well, Nietzsche was a Nazi, so there's that," I said without thinking.

Ben froze and eyed me over the rim of his glass. "That's not true, actually."

"Yes, it is, actually," I dug in. "Everyone knows Nietzsche was greatly admired by the Nazi regime. His writings were widely studied, taught in their schools, and used to justify their..."

"Huh," Josh interjected suddenly, "look at this Ben, have we finally found someone who is smarter than you?" He was grinning over at Ben, mocking him. "At the very least, someone who can actually argue with you and have a chance at holding their own."

"No, *actually*," Ben looked irritated now. "It isn't true. Nietzsche's work and writings were appropriated by the National Socialist Party, that's true, but his sister was his guardian later on in his life, and after his death, she modified his work to fit her ideals. *She*, was a Nazi." We were all silent for a moment.

"Hmm." Mark shrugged beside me. "Sounds like something a Nazi would say."

I couldn't help it; I snorted, stifled a laugh the best I could, and almost spit out a mouthful of water all over the table.

The look on Ben's face silenced any further laughter. He stood up, throwing his cloth napkin on his plate, and turned to Emily and Josh. "Excuse me," he said and left abruptly.

We all just sat there in awkward silence. No one knew what to say. Emily turned to Josh. "What's wrong with him?" She whispered.

"I don't know." Josh shook his head, still staring at the empty doorway he had disappeared through. "I mean, I do know why he's upset, but I don't know what's gotten into him lately. He's been in a weird mood all day."

"Why is he upset?" I asked curiously.

"He's German," Josh sighed. He closed his eyes and rubbed his forehead in circles at his temples. He looked like he had a headache. "Well, his family is, I mean. From Germany. He was born there, spoke fluent German, and he moved here when he was a little kid."

"Oh..." I said, with a sinking feeling.

"And he got teased sometimes about it. He had an accent at first. Some of the boys at school... they'd call him a Nazi. He used to get really upset about it, at the time."

Well, now I felt awful. Why did I have to bring up Nazis in the first place? It wasn't exactly polite, high society talk.

Emily looked much more sympathetic now. "Maybe you should go check on him babe."

Mark started to stand up. "I'll go check on him."

"No!" I practically exclaimed. Mark stopped mid crouch, freezing at my tone of voice. He was the last person who should check on him. I stood up and pulled my napkin off my lap, setting it down gently next to my plate. "No, I'll go," I said quietly. "It's my fault."

I turned and left the room without waiting for a response. I exited the dining hall wondering how in the heck I was going to find him. He could be anywhere, and the house was massive. He may have gone back to his room. He couldn't have gone outside, at least not in this weather. Another crack of thunder rolled right on cue. The entire house rumbled in its wake. The glass chandelier above my head tinkled, swaying slightly. Good lord, this storm was getting ridiculous. I was surprised to find Ben on the other side of the foyer. He was pacing back and forth, raking his hands through his hair. He hadn't noticed me yet.

"Ben," I called out to him, starting to head over to him. He turned, surprised to see me.

"What?" He asked. He was clearly still upset. He stood with his hands on his hips. This was off to a good start.

"Ben, I'm sorry, I had no idea," I started.

"Don't worry about it." He waved his hand, dismissing my apology.

"No, I feel really bad. I didn't know."

"I know you didn't," he said. "It's not your fault." He paused for a moment. "But you know who did?" He asked, starting to look angry again. "Your buddy Mark. And here's a little tip." He crossed the base of the stairs, moving closer to me. "You might want to take it easy with him. He's got a long history when it comes to women, and as soon as gets what he wants from you, he'll be gone, and you won't hear from him again."

"I don't know what you're talking about," I said, my heart starting to pound in my chest. "He's just being friendly; there's nothing going on between us."

"Oh okay." He nodded sarcastically. "Sure there isn't. Just don't say I didn't warn you."

I flushed. "I'm not planning on sleeping with him, if that's what you're implying."

"Yeah, well, you could've fooled me," he spat at me. I felt my cheeks burn hot. We stood there, frozen for a moment. I told myself to just walk away. I turned to leave momentarily, before turning back to him.

"You know, I don't know where you get off thinking you have the right to comment at all on who I talk to, much less who I sleep with. You've known me for what, less than 24 hours now?" He winced, looking away from me, towards the front door. "And a better question would be: why do you care?" I was raising my voice now. The thunder was loud, and there was music playing, but that would only do so much. I told myself to calm down. We were right outside the dining hall still.

"I dunno." Ben shrugged. "I don't, I guess."

Did he mean he didn't have the right, or he didn't care? "You don't what? What's that supposed to mean?" I demanded.

Ben shrugged again. "It means whatever you think it means."

"What kind of nonsensical, bullshit answer is that?" He opened his mouth to retort, but I continued before he could get a word in. "You've done nothing but lurk around, glaring at me since I arrived. Do you mind telling me what it is about me exactly that offends you so much?"

Ben stared at me for a moment, his chest was heaving as though he was breathing heavily. A muscle in his jaw ticked like he was trying to hold back his words. He composed himself. "Why don't you go back to the party before we say something we regret?" He tipped his head in the direction of the dining hall as he spoke.

"I think it's a little too late for that, don't you?" I said coolly, crossing my arms and standing my ground.

"Fine," he spat at me.

"Fine!" I yelled back over the sound of a thunderclap. Suddenly I felt a stinging in my eyes. Oh god, I couldn't cry in front of him; I refused to. I had the bad habit of crying when I got really angry. I hated that I did it, but I'd never been able to control it. He was blocking my way to the stairs. I couldn't show my face back in the dining room either, not after what they all probably just heard. I turned my back on him and trotted down the hallway to the left of the staircase. I ducked into the guy's lounge room, praying everyone would stay in the dining hall. I knew they were going to serve dessert, that should buy me some time. Time for Ben to leave, to calm down. Then I would head back to my room.

I took deep breaths, tried to slow my racing heart, and stopped the tears threatening to spill. Why did I react that way? Why did I let him get under my skin like that? I replayed the argument in my head. I was trying to remember our exact words. Everything I had said was true. I hardly knew him. Why did I care what he thought of me in the first place? He was clearly a jerk. He hadn't given me any real answers.

I paced the room, back and forth. How embarrassing. All I could do was hope that no one heard us.

I had stopped my pacing in front of a large portrait of a regal looking man. Some old relative of Josh's I assumed. I studied his face closely. I could see the resemblance. How uncanny, I thought, to think that I was looking at a real person, from who knows how long ago. Before there were cameras, possibly. A real person with hopes and dreams, with secrets. I walked over to examine it closer, welcoming the distraction. My eye caught on a strange, rectangular shape at the bottom of the portrait. I stared, trying to sort it out. Then I realized that what I had taken at first to be part of the painting, was actually an object stuck inside the frame. It was a piece of paper. It had been folded and tucked into the corner of the frame. *How odd*, I thought, as I plucked it loose. It was nearly flush with the glass of the frame and was wedged in tightly. The paper looked and felt old. It was yellowed and faded.

I unfolded it gently. It took me several moments staring at it to take in what I was seeing. The top half of the page was covered in hand-written, tiny markings. Crude little symbols, made up of lines. They looked vaguely familiar. I recognized them as some kind of primitive language, but it was nothing I could read. The little markings were in clusters, but didn't flow in straight lines, forming a strange pattern that reminded me almost of tiger stripes, or the irregular pattern of black markings on a birch tree. My eyes scanned the bottom half of the page, which depicted a drawing of what looked like an arm. It was positioned horizontally, so the hand wasn't included and would have been off the right side of the paper. The arm actually had what appeared to be the same strange clumps of writing, in that odd pattern, in patches zigzagging back and forth all over the skin. What on earth was this?

I flipped the paper over to check the back. More of the script was scattered, along with more little drawings, this time haphazardly. At the bottom of the page, another larger drawing, again quite realistic. My brain took a moment to catch up to my eyes. I tried to process what I was seeing. A tree branch arched over the page, and hanging from a rope, by her feet, was a naked young woman. Her arms were flung out beneath her, and she hung limply. What was clearly more of the strange writing covered her body in tattooed stripes from head to toe. I realized with a start that her eyes were either left unfinished or were meant to be missing. Two dark pits staring out. *What the fuck?*

My heart started to pound again faintly. What was this? As disturbing as it was, I was somewhat comforted by the thought that it was clearly very old. But where had it come from? Who had made it, and why was it left tucked into the frame of a painting? I tried to recall if it could have been there the first night. There was no way to know. I had only ever been just inside the entrance of the room, I never made it far enough to have seen the paper, and even if I had, it may have been there and easily gone unnoticed by me and everyone else.

I stood there, unsure what to do next. I guessed I should show it to someone, but who? Emily? The drawings were more than a little disturbing. But it was so old. It was probably harmless. I hated to bother her with it and add more stress to an already stressful week. I tore my eyes from the drawing and studied the rest of the page. I still couldn't make any sense of the tiny script, but I tried to glean what I could.

There were drawings of several different kinds of flowers and plants depicted that I didn't recognize. The drawings had arrows coming off of them, followed by the strange writing; like they were being labeled. One drawing showed what were clearly roses. There were also crops, like corn stalks and various vegetables, growing out of the ground. Some of the arrows pointed to the dirt at the base of the plants. There was a drawing of a deer skull, with antlers branching off the top. I had seen something similar recently in the house. The door knockers on the front door, I remembered. I felt goosebumps rising along with the hairs on my arms. Something else was familiar. The girl, hanging from the tree. Could that be what was in the painting upstairs in the study? Was it meant to show this girl hanging from the willow?

I nearly yelped when the door banged open behind me. Mark walked into the room, scanning. "There you are!" He said, looking relieved. "Are you okay Cassie? We could hear, well, we could hear that the conversation didn't go great."

I sighed. "Perfect. What did you hear exactly?"

"Oh." He shrugged, "We couldn't hear what you were saying really, just that you sounded upset. Are you okay?" He asked again, walking closer to me across the room. I looked down at the paper in my hand, drawing his gaze to it as well for the first time. I started to fold it back up again.

"What's that?" Mark asked.

I attempted to analyze the tone of his voice, studying his face. He didn't look like he recognized it. He just seemed mildly curious.

"It's nothing," I responded back. I tucked the folded piece of paper inside one palm, laying my hands together to cover it up. I don't know why, but I decided then that I didn't want to show it to anyone just yet.

"Okay…" Mark trailed off. "Um, look, I'm sorry for what happened at dinner. I didn't mean to spoil everyone's evening." He looked like he meant it.

Great. My gut twisted a little at his words. That must mean it had put a damper on everyone's evening back in the dining room too. I sighed. "I know. It's okay." Wait, I thought, was it though? Ben had said that Mark knew about him being teased as a child. Well, no, I corrected myself, he wasn't that specific, he just said that Mark knew. That might just mean he knew he was German. Even so, it did seem like a cruel sort of thing to do. Mark didn't strike me as the type of person who would do something like that.

We stood silently for a minute or two, Mark staring into the fire burning low in the grate.

"Where's everybody else?" I asked after a moment. He seemed lost in thought.

"Oh, most of them are still drinking in the dining room. A few went to help look for you. I guess I should head back that way and let them know I found you. Some went up to bed already for the evening. I guess it's going to be an early night, everyone is just going to turn in."

I nodded, and we turned to head back to the dining hall. When we got to the door, Mark told me he would duck in and just let them know I was okay. I really appreciated that. I didn't want to talk about what happened in front of everyone. How embarrassing to be the only new person here and cause a big scene. What was I thinking?

I stood out in the hallway for a moment or two, and then Mark reappeared. I couldn't hear any of what was said inside. The rain and thunder were shockingly still going strong. Was it ever going to stop raining? So much for beach day tomorrow if not.

"I'll walk you back to your room," Mark said, turning and heading towards the staircase.

"That's not necessary..." I started to say.

He cut me off. "No worries, it's not a problem at all; it'll just take a minute."

But why though? Why would Mark feel he needed to escort me to my room? We walked in silence up the stairs and headed right, down to the girl's wing, as I had come to think of it. Was Ben right? I thought a bit nervously. Was Mark just trying to take me back to my room? It didn't feel like it. As friendly and playful as he had been with me, I had the feeling that was just his personality, how he was with everyone. I honestly didn't feel there was anything more between us, and I felt I could trust him. My gut feelings usually weren't wrong, but still, Ben's words echoed in my mind, making me doubt myself, making me feel uneasy. That and the creepy pictures. I still had the paper tucked inside the palm of my hand.

We reached my door in no time, and I realized I knew the way back to my room. I felt more confident that I could make it on my own. Mark nodded to me and said, "Have a good night, Cassie."

"You too." I mustered up a halfhearted smile for him. He smiled back and started to make his way back down the hall.

"See you bright and early for beach day tomorrow!" He called back over his shoulder as he went.

"Can't wait," I called back, watching him go.

I read for a while before switching the lights off and settling down to sleep. Once again, I made sure my door was locked, and I sprinted back to my bed as soon as I flicked the switch. I had studied the piece of paper I'd found for a while but was no closer to understanding what any of it meant than I had been before. I hid the rectangle, now a bit crumpled from being held, inside the pocket of the fur coat hanging in the closet. I couldn't have explained why I felt I needed to hide it, but I did. The sounds of the storm outside helped lull me to sleep.

I startled awake some unknown amount of time later. I felt disoriented and my heart was pounding hard. I sat propped up on one elbow, perfectly still, straining to hear anything over the sounds of raindrops still falling. It was silent at first, but then I heard stirring, then footsteps out in the hallway. I rose to go see what the commotion was about. But at the last moment I grabbed my robe out of my bag, glad that I had thought to bring it. I still felt self-conscious going out without a bra on. Once out in the hall, I crossed my arms over my chest, hugging the fluffy robe tightly to me.

"What's going on?" I called softly to the retreating backs of some of the others heading down the hallway. They were walking toward the stairs.

I had learned last night that Amelia went by Amy. She shook her head, eyes wide. "We don't know. We all thought we heard something. We're going to check it out." She looked frightened.

I followed them down the hallway, the plush carpet soft and luxurious between my bare toes. When we made it to the first set of stairs, I could hear loud voices coming from below. We all peered over the handrails, straining to see what was going on. By the time we reached the landing at the top of the main staircase, I realized some of the guys were headed this way as well, galloping down their flight of stairs that led to the boy's wing. I saw a small group huddled on the main stairs below us, about a quarter of the way up. They were all kneeling around something or someone.

Josh stood up as he saw us coming and held up both hands in the air, in a surrendering type of stance. "It's okay everyone, everything's okay. There's no need to panic. We're sorry to have woken everyone."

"What's going on?" One of the Mikes asked, heading further down the steps. "We heard screaming."

Screaming? Was that what had woken us? I couldn't remember hearing anything, only the feeling that something had woken me suddenly. In the dim lighting, I tried to make out what I was seeing. It looked like they were examining a broken piece of wood or something. I looked around us, trying to spot a section of the railing missing. Or maybe it was from the ceiling. Had someone fallen off the upper level? But I couldn't see any damage to the railing, or anything missing. Despite Josh clearly trying to stop us, we made our way closer down the staircase. I realized suddenly what it was, with a jolt of fear striking through my gut like lightning. It was antlers. What I had mistaken for wood, was a set of antlers, branching off the head of a deer. There was literally a deer head sitting on one of the steps.

I heard someone gasp. The others made their way down to the bottom of the stairs, into the foyer, squeezing past the group huddled there to stay as far away from the thing as possible. I followed them, shaking my head in disbelief.

From the base of the stairs, I could clearly see I was right, a decapitated deer head was just sitting upright on the steps. It's lifeless eyes blank and staring. A dark stain spread in a circle on the carpet beneath it. The air was tinged with an almost metallic scent, combined with an earthy gaminess. What the hell was going on here? Who would have done something like this, and why? It all made no sense.

I examined the group that had found the deer head more closely. People had started to move around, but it wasn't hard to tell who was in which group. Everyone from upstairs was in their PJs, or robes, like me, and everyone who had been downstairs already was still in their formal wear from dinner. Josh and Emily were still dressed, although I hadn't noticed Emily initially; she had been kneeling down in front of the head on the bottom stair. She didn't look so good. Both Ben and Mark were still in their suits. Ben reached up and loosened his tie around his neck as I stared at him. Mark was just staring at the head, one hand over his mouth and chin, his eyes darting back and forth as though he was thinking, trying to figure it out.

It struck me as odd that Mark had made a point to escort me back to my room last night as though the evening was concluded when here he was, along with the others, still fully dressed, clearly not having ever gone to bed yet. Why was that? I wondered if they had said something to him when he went back into the dining room to tell them he'd found me. Maybe they just hadn't wanted me around last night. Maybe Emily didn't.

I shook my head to clear it. I was being silly. They probably would have just assumed I didn't want to socialize after Ben and I had our argument. But that being the case, why was Ben still downstairs with them? Apparently, he had made his way back to the group afterwards. The whole thing just struck me as strange, and I had the sneaking suspicion for the first time that I didn't have the whole story. There was something going on here, but I had no idea what. I made my way over to Emily.

"Hey," I said softly, sliding an arm around her back. "Are you okay? You don't look so good."

"I don't feel so good," Emily sniffed. "Whoever did this is seriously fucked up." I nodded in agreement.

"What happened?" I asked. "Did you guys hear anything? Or…"

Emily shook her head no. "No, nothing at all," she interrupted. "We were hanging out in the lounge, Josh and Mark and me. We went straight there after dinner. Honestly, I sort of just wanted to head up to bed." She lowered her voice a little, looking around, "But Josh was worried about Ben." Emily rolled her eyes a little at me. "And he wanted to wait up for a bit, see if he was okay." Emily sighed. "He still seemed upset when he joined us but doing okay." She shrugged. "We all hung out for a bit longer, while the guys had another drink. Then I said I was getting tired and headed up to bed. That's when I found the... the..." I patted her back.

"It's going to be okay, Em," I said, trying to comfort her. "We'll figure out who did this."

Meanwhile, Josh continued to try to calm everyone down and send them back to their rooms. He said the deer head would be taken care of, and not to worry about it. As though a decapitated animal head was just an inconvenient little mess, like a spilled drink, that could be cleaned up and forgotten about. Ben caught my gaze again; he looked like he wanted to say something to me. He started to move towards the stairs. I turned abruptly and headed back upstairs. If he wanted to apologize for earlier in the evening, he could do it later, without the entire group watching. I wasn't in the mood to speak to him right now anyway.

Back in my room, I paced up and down the floor. I found myself out on the balcony. The rain had finally let up. I checked my watch when I got back. It was around 1:00 AM. Not as late as it had felt. I stared out into the darkness of the grounds. Now that the rain had cleared, I saw it wasn't as cloudy as it had been last night. The sky looked lighter because of it, and I could see a little better than I had the previous night standing out here with Emily. Poor Emily. She really didn't need anything else to go wrong this week. This week was supposed to be happy and carefree and all about her and Josh. I sighed and chewed on my lip. After what had just happened, I felt like I needed to come clean about the paper I had found, but I was reluctant to cause further troubles.

I caught sight of what I thought was something moving out in the open field. It was a dark object, nothing more, in the faint moonlight. I strained my eyes to pick out any details. Was it a person or an animal? I really couldn't say. It moved towards the tree line. Suddenly, it stopped moving entirely and was still. I stared at the spot where I had last seen movement, trying to make out a black shape amongst more black. I felt the hair rising on the back of my neck. Why had it stopped? With a jolt of fear, I realized that I had left the lights on full blast in the room behind me. I would stand out like a sore thumb, backlit from behind. Was it staring back at me? Had it seen me watching?

Whatever it was, it started moving again, just when I was no longer sure it was ever really there in the first place. It disappeared into the shadows of the tree line and was lost from my view. I went back into the room and turned the lights off. Standing out on the balcony for several moments, I waited for it to come back. To start moving again. But I saw nothing further that night.

I did have a strange dream, though. I was walking through the halls of the Hideaway House. I could hear a piano being played from somewhere up ahead. I found the room eventually. A large black baby grand piano sat drenched in moonlight shining through a large bank of windows. A man was seated there, playing, his dark head of curls was bowed over the keys, so I couldn't see his face. I drifted into the room, almost as though my feet weren't touching the floor.

A woman stood next to the man. I realized with a little fissure of surprise that she was wearing the vintage black dress I had worn to dinner. She held a sheet of music in her hands, staring down at it as she swayed to the music. She hummed along a little, then began to sing in a husky voice. I looked again at the man at the piano. He looked familiar...was that, Ben? I drifted closer, peering at the woman's face. She had dark hair. I felt the room darkening, starting to fade. A dog barked in the distance. She looked up at me just as my vision dimmed, and I saw my own face, gazing back at me.

WEDNESDAY

I slept in a little later than usual the next morning, apparently making up for the activities of the night before. After some deliberation on whether or not I wanted to go for a run, I donned my running clothes, slipped on and tied my shoes, and was throwing my hair into a ponytail before heading out when I heard a soft knock on my door. I froze and turned to face the door. I walked over and opened it, figuring it was probably Emily.

To my surprise, Ben stood on the other side, leaning casually with one hand propping him up against the door frame. He was in a gray running shirt this time. How colorful of him. "Good morning," was all he said.

"Morning..." I responded back. When he said nothing else, I added, "What's up?"

He cleared his throat. "I was coming to see if you were ready to go for a run. It looks like you are."

Um... what? Was he freaking kidding me? How could he think I would possibly want to go for a run with him after last night. He must be delusional.

"I'm sorry..." I started, with no clue as to how I was going to formulate a response. This was awkward as hell. "I'm confused... why would you think I wanted to run with you still?" Bluntness for the win.

He grimaced slightly and looked away from my gaze, turning his head down the hall. A muscle ticked in his jaw. Please tell me we weren't about to fight again.

"I don't think that..." he replied, "But I do think that I'm not about to let you go running by yourself. And as I was getting ready this morning, it occurred to me that you might do just that..." He finally met my eyes again. "And it looks like I was right."

I stared him down for a full minute, saying nothing. And he just stared right back at me. Was this guy for real? "Maybe," I said in a quiet voice, "I didn't make myself clear enough last night. What I do, Ben, is none of your concern. So, if I want to go for a run, it's no skin off your back. Now, if you'll excuse me..." I moved as though to walk past him, expecting him to move out of my way. He didn't. He actually moved to his left, blocking me from leaving the doorway. I almost slammed into his chest. He was inches away from me, and I felt a bolt of fire course through my mid-section.

I stifled a gasp and took a quick step back. I glared up at him, my breath quickening. I felt my face flush and a wave of anger swept over me. What kind of game was he playing? Was he really going to try to stop me from leaving my room?

"Are you serious right now?" I tried to control my anger, to stay calm. "You're really going to try to physically stop me from leaving?" He ran his hands through his perfect curls, and putting his hands on his hips, he just stared at me, saying nothing.

I looked him right in the eyes and said, "Move." In as commanding a voice as I could. He looked up and down the hall, like he was hoping someone else would appear to help him. This was unreal. "Move, Ben. Get out of my way."

"No." He wiped his upper lip like he was starting to sweat. "No, I'm not letting you go on your own."

"Yes," I said, starting to get a little hysterical. "You are. You are not in charge of me."

"I know that, Cassie, okay? I know." He was starting to sound a little hysterical now, too. "But I'm not letting you go by yourself, and that's that. So either go back inside, change, and don't run, or you can let me run with you. That's it."

"Oh really, those are my choices?" I said sarcastically. "What am I, a toddler? You don't get to dictate my choices for me, Ben. I don't belong to you." I didn't know why I felt I needed to add that last bit.

"I know!" He was raising his voice now. "Trust me, I know. I..." he trailed off. Closing his eyes, he pinched the bridge of his nose, and took a deep breath. "Please, Cassie," he said in a softer voice. "Just, let me come with you. I'll leave you alone. I won't bother you; I won't even talk to you. Just... please, don't go by yourself." He stared at me now, his dark eyes wide and pleading. I was taken aback. I said nothing.

Suddenly he stepped to the side, clearing a path for me to leave the room. "I'm sorry," he said, "I won't try to stop you from leaving. But I will follow you, if you go. You can't stop me from doing that."

He stood there, waiting for me to make a decision. I just stared at him for a minute, trying to read his expression. "What do you know?" I said slowly. He blinked at me, as though that last bit didn't compute.

"What?" he asked, his brow furling in confusion.

"You heard me," I said. "What do you know? What is so dangerous out in those woods, that you feel the need to try to stop me? That you're practically begging me? What. Do. You. Know?" That was it, I was done. I was done with him, and I was done with the creepy paper and drawings, and the dead deer, and just the general fucked up atmosphere of this whole place. I had had it, and I wanted some answers.

He stared at me, eyes wide, until finally answering slowly. "Other than the fact that someone left a deer head on the stairs last night? I don't know anything."

Okay, he had a small point there, but I was too worked up to let it go. "Really? That's it. You don't know anything else?" He nodded. "Why are you so hysterical over me leaving?"

He shook his head. "I'm not hysterical. I'm just trying to stop you from getting hurt." I folded my arms across my chest, raising my eyebrows at him. "From hurting yourself," he corrected. "I'm not hysterical," he repeated.

"Hmm," I said, "you could have fooled me." It felt good to throw his words back at him.

He colored deeply, his eyes dropping to the floor. "Cassie, about last night, I'm..." he started.

I cut him off. "Save it for someone who cares Ben." He swallowed and nodded, keeping his gaze on the floor. I watched him for a moment. Then I turned and pulled the door shut behind me. I took off at a brisk walk down the hallway. I was going running, that was for sure. Nothing was going to stop me going now, and I was going to see what the hell was out in those woods that had him so spooked.

Ben followed me, just as he said he would. I marched down the stairs, carefully avoiding the stained area that was still visible where the deer head had sat. I turned left and headed down the hallway, not bothering to stop to see if anyone was in the dining hall yet. I continued on through to the library, out the double doors, into the garden. I almost slammed the doors shut behind me, but that felt a little too over the top. I made my way through the garden paths. I didn't remember how to get out of the garden, but thankfully none of the hedges were high enough to reach over my head. I could see I was headed in the right general direction, and that was all I cared about. I noted the rose bush near one of the fountains, where Mark had put the rose in my hair. I had a momentary urge to stop and ask Ben what his problem was again, but I knew it would do no good. I hadn't gotten a straight answer from him yet, and I wasn't expecting one.

I eventually found my way out of the garden. Ben trailed behind me. He didn't say a word. In my head I was daring him to try to tell me I was going the wrong way, but he stayed silent. Once through the gardens, I eyed the stables up ahead to the right. The unbroken line of forest spread out in the distance past the field. It didn't occur to me until that moment that I didn't actually know where I was going. I had forgotten to ask where the trailhead started... I kicked myself internally. Damn it. I figured I could probably make my way back to the general area where the horse trail opened up, but I knew that wasn't the running path they were talking about. I sighed and eventually slowed to a stop. I swallowed my pride, with difficulty, and turned back to Ben.

He pointed off to the far left, in the opposite direction I would have gone to find the horse trail. "The trail is over that way." I didn't bother to respond. At least he had anticipated my question, so I didn't have to speak to him.

He continued in the direction he had pointed, and I slowed to walk next to him but several yards away.

The chill early morning air was genuinely starting to feel like fall. I regretted a bit that I was only in a thin t-shirt, but I knew I would heat up quickly once I started running. I tend to overheat easily when I run, and I would be glad I hadn't dressed warmer soon. It was truly a gorgeous morning. I knew it would probably get hotter as the day wore on, and there were no rain clouds in the sky. Hopefully that meant Emily's beach day wouldn't be ruined.

As we neared the tree line, I spied a plain wooden marker, a few feet tall, that must mark the trail head. Ben was heading straight towards it. Once the gap in the trees and the trail were clearly visible, I broke out into a light jog. Ben followed suit, falling in behind me.

I swiped over on my smartwatch and pressed the button to start tracking my run. All the awkwardness and self-consciousness I would have generally felt from running with Ben were notably absent. My anger at him had relieved me of any feelings of self-consciousness, but it also made me want to leave him in my dust.

I could feel within the first minute or so of starting out that it was going to be an excellent running day for me. I had good and bad days, days when I was able to run at my top pace, and hardly felt I was breathing hard, and other days where I struggled to finish a two-mile run, gasping for breath. Today was one of those good days, and I ran hard, and fast. I checked my pace when we were about a mile out and saw it was even faster than typical. I tried to caution myself to slow down, not to overdo it, but I couldn't help it. I was fueled in part by my anger at Ben, and wanting to show him up, and partially by my frustration in general. I ran out all the nervousness, anxiety, and fear that I had felt over the past few days, and it felt good.

When we hit about the two-mile mark, Ben called out to me that this was where he usually turns back. I noticed with no small amount of satisfaction that it was difficult for him to speak. I slowed to a light jog and turned to face him. I started to head back past him, the way we had come. Part of me wanted to ignore him and keep going, but I wasn't sure I could keep this same pace for four miles and figured pushing to go farther was probably a bad idea.

On the run back, I did slow a bit now that much of the anger and pent-up frustration had dissipated. I started paying more attention to my surroundings, to the forest around us. On the way out, I stared carefully at my feet as I ran. It was a bit disorienting, but the last thing I wanted was to twist an ankle and give Ben the satisfaction of being able to say he told me so. I felt more confident now that I was more used to the terrain. About a half mile back down the trail, something caught my eye through the trees. I peered through the leaves and flickering light. About fifty yards off to my right, I saw an object that definitely wasn't a tree, but I wasn't sure what it was. I came to an abrupt stop, Ben almost plowing into me.

I struggled to control my breathing before I spoke. "I see something," I nodded out towards the object amongst the trees. "There's something over there." I stifled a gasp as I realized it almost looked like something large hanging from a rope. My stomach flipped a little, thinking of the drawing.

"What?" Ben responded, catching my gasp. "Are you okay?" Ben was breathing heavily, hands on his upper thighs, he leaned forward slightly, slowing his breath.

"I'm fine," I snapped. "But there's definitely something there."

"Okay," he said after a moment. "Can I suggest we ignore it and keep going?"

"You can suggest that," I replied, "but I'm going to see what it is."

"Of course you are," he said resignedly.

I headed out into the underbrush. It was slow going; the forest was much thicker here. There were old fallen trees everywhere. It made it difficult to navigate in a straight line. I stopped at one point and gazed back, trying to locate the trail again. It wasn't that much further, but I had a momentary panic at the thought of losing the trail. I guess I saw Ben's point a little bit at that moment, but I wasn't about to tell him that. If anything were to happen out here, we had no cell service, no way of calling for help, or navigating back to the house other than using our own wits. But still, he was absolutely being over dramatic this morning. It wasn't that serious. Unless, of course, he knew something I didn't.

As we drew nearer to the object, it became clear what it was without the need to go any further. It was a deer carcass. It had been strung up in a tree by its back hooves with a rope. And it was missing its head. The body swayed gently in the breeze.

"Oh god…" I trailed off. *What the hell?* The similarity to the way the girl's body was strung up in the drawing was both uncanny and disturbing. I tried to calm my racing thoughts. It was technically normal to string up a deer to process it for venison, I reminded myself. It didn't necessarily mean anything more than that. But this seemed like too much of a coincidence. Besides, no amount of rationalizing could explain why the head had been chopped off and ended up inside the house. In the middle of the night. Was it left as some kind of warning? If so, to who?

Ben had made it to my side and stood staring at the deer. After a moment, he stepped out in front of me and continued to make his way towards it. I decided to further break my silent treatment and called out to him, "Um, is that necessary? It's pretty clear what it is from here, I don't think we need to get any closer."

Ben called back to me, without turning his head. "Just stay there. I want to take a closer look."

"Why?" I called back. Did this man always have to do the opposite of what I wanted him to?

"I want to see if there's anything here that might tell us who did this," he called back, turning towards me this time. "I'll be right back."

Screw that. I followed him over to the carcass. Up close, I was grateful the air had remained cool. There was no stench yet, but I imagined there would be as the day went on. Ben stood staring at the ground beneath where the deer's head should have been.

Oh god, I thought, *now what*. Please tell me he didn't find anything weird. I'd had about as much of that as I could stomach right now.

As I caught up with him, I saw he was staring down at nothing. There was nothing on the ground at all. I breathed a sigh of relief and scanned the forest floor around the base of the tree. I checked the branches above—just a simple rope tied to the branch. There was nothing else. I didn't see any clues, notes, or anything odd at all.

Ben looked over at me, pointing to the ground underneath the body. "What do you see?" I looked at him quizzically for a moment before peering closer at the ground. I moved a little closer and crouched down, getting as close as I felt comfortable being. What was I missing? Did he see footprints or something?

I turned to peer up at him. "I don't see anything," I said, giving up.

He looked at me, an expression of grim satisfaction on his face. "Exactly."

I stood and stared back at him. "So... ?"

He gestured at the blank ground beneath the body. The ground was trampled slightly, as though someone had been moving around in the area, but that was all. He pointed at the ground. "Where's the blood?" I stared at him, and then back at the ground. Why hadn't I thought of that?

"If the deer was killed here," he continued, "it's head cut off, or chopped off, where's all the blood?"

"I don't know," I said, "Maybe the rain washed it away?"

Ben shook his head. "I don't think the rain would wash away all evidence of blood. It looks like there was never anything here."

"I guess that means someone... what, drained it somehow? Into a bucket or something?" The thought of a bucket full of blood made my empty stomach turn slightly.

Ben nodded. "They must have." We stood in silence for a moment. I noted again, as I had on the drive in the first night, the apparent lack of wildlife. I didn't hear any birds chirping or squirrels rustling. But then again, we had made a ton of noise tramping over here and probably scared everything away. I tried to remember if I had seen any animals the day before on the horseback ride.

"The question is, why?" Ben broke the silence. "I'm no hunter, but as far as I understand it, the main reason anyone would want to kill a deer, aside from the sport of it, would be for the meat. But in this case, they left the meat behind, but took the blood?" We met each other's eyes. It was a great question. Who would do that, and for what possible reason?

"And then, that someone left the head in the house, for us to find," I said matter-of-factly.

Ben nodded slowly. "The other valuable part. They left behind."

After a moment, we decided to head back towards the house. I didn't feel like running anymore, but I was certainly up for getting out of these woods as fast as possible. We kept a steady pace on the route back. Ben still hung behind me, but only a few feet instead of a few yards. I felt oddly okay with his closer proximity, maybe even relieved.

When we made it back to the trailhead and out into the open field, I could feel myself relax a bit. I couldn't help but feel a little grateful that Ben had followed me on the run. It would have been a lot scarier finding that carcass on my own. That still didn't make his behavior okay, though.

When we got back to the house, Ben and I headed straight for the dining room. Some of the staff were in there, setting up for breakfast. Emily was sitting at the massive table by herself. She was wrapped in a fluffy robe, and her hair was tied on top of her head in a loose knot. Her eyes widened in surprise when she saw the two of us enter the room together, still in our sweaty running clothes. She and I exchanged a glance, and I shook my head imperceptibly. I would tell her later.

"Well good morning," she said, stretching lazily. More to Ben than to me, she continued, "Wesley just arrived."

Ben nodded. "Who's Wesley?" I queried.

Emily turned to me. "Oh, he's Josh's older brother. He couldn't make it out any earlier in the week." She waved her hand. "I dunno, something to do with work. I'm surprised you didn't hear him arrive. He drives the loudest sports car on the planet." She rolled her eyes.

"We were out for a run," Ben responded. "Must've just missed him."

I frowned a little. That made it sound like we went on a run together, willingly, which was definitely not the case.

Emily saw me making a face and looked like she was about to say something when Ben continued. "Hey, is Josh around?" *Interesting*, I thought. So, he wanted to tell Josh about the deer carcass, but not Emily.

Emily thought for a moment. "Yeah, he's with Wes, but I'm not sure where they went exactly. Maybe check the lounge?"

Ben nodded. He started to leave and then turned back to me. "You okay?" He asked me softly. What was his deal? Now he was worried about leaving me alone in the dining room with Emily?

I looked at him quizzically. "Yes, Ben. I'm fine," I said flatly. He just nodded again and turned and left the room. Why was he suddenly so concerned about my welfare?

Emily waited a moment after he had left before she grabbed my hand and pulled me into a chair next to her. "So? Spill it! You guys went on a run together? Did you make-up already?" I don't know why she was smiling. I didn't find anything funny about it.

"No, we did not make-up, and we definitely did *not* go on a run together." I sighed and slumped back in my chair. I was exhausted already, and it wasn't even 9:00 a.m. And it wasn't just because I had pushed myself too hard on the run, which I realized I definitely had. I could already feel a soreness starting up in my calves.

Emily looked confused. "Okay, well tell me what did happen then."

I had just enough time to explain precisely how shitty my morning had been before we were joined by some of the group heading down for breakfast. I didn't leave the part out about the deer. I don't know why Ben didn't bring it up to Emily, but I wasn't going to hide it from her. Emily said little, her eyes opening wide in surprise. Her gaze flickered back and forth rapidly as she stared off into the distance at nothing. Clearly, she was thinking about something, trying to figure something out. Was she thinking about last night? Did she have an idea of who might have done this? I was debating asking her and telling her about the paper I had found as well. I had just decided I was going to, when we were interrupted by Catherine and Blair entering the room.

People began trickling in two and three at a time. Mark, Josh, and Ben were noticeably absent; I tried not to read too much into that, but my curiosity was piqued. Emily nudged me to grab some food and, more importantly, coffee. Regardless of dead, headless deer, we were apparently still going to the beach today. She wanted me to have a chance to eat and shower before we left.

I had to confess, I didn't quite understand the whole beach day thing. It was the start of fall, and it didn't really seem like the right time of year to go to the beach. I soon found out that "Beach Day" meant bringing a picnic lunch to the beach and sitting out and drinking—all day.

After downing several cups of coffee and a decent amount of food, I headed upstairs. I managed to shower quickly, and with a minimal amount of deliberation, I donned the less revealing bathing suit I had brought, knowing I would be more comfortable in it. I threw some curl cream in my hair and opted for quickly tossing it into a loose braid. There was no point in bothering to style it today. I pulled a loose pair of jean shorts over my suit bottom, and an over-sized, soft, white tee-shirt. I decided to grab my phone from the nightstand, along with my sunglasses and some sunscreen.

It might be nice to take pictures at the beach, but mainly I was hoping I'd have a signal once we were off the property.

When I got back downstairs, most of the party was ready and waiting in the foyer. I was glad to see Mark and Josh were back with the main group. I looked briefly for Ben but didn't see him. Kristy was in a hot pink, tiny, triangle bikini tied with strings. She had an oversized bag with her, and pulling a flask out of it, she took a sip and passed it around to some of the guys. Her tan made me feel self-conscious of my deathly pale skin. I didn't go anywhere without my SPF 45.

Several cars had been pulled around into the roundabout, enough space for all of us to pile in. I learned from Eric that it was about a 40-minute drive out to the beach, even though it wasn't actually that far away as the crow flies. I guessed it made sense that it would take a while to get there, given that it took about 20 minutes just to wind through the woods to the house.

The group in my car continued to pass around Kristy's flask, which I declined, until it was empty. "Don't worry everyone, I brought refills!" she called, pulling a giant bottle out of her bag to general whoops and cheers. I was glad everyone was still having a good time, but the events of last night seemed oddly easily forgotten by the group. No one mentioned the deer head, and no one asked me about finding the carcass. I took that to mean the guys had decided not to share it with the larger group.

When we got to the beach, I was surprised to see that a few of the staff had set out ahead of us. There were giant beach umbrellas, comfy lounge chairs, and a little pop-up tent already waiting for us. There were various beverages chilling on ice under the tent. I opted for lemonade this time. The sun was very warm out at the beach, and if you weren't in the shade, it was too hot to tolerate for any extended length of time. I was surprised given the time of year. I coated myself in sunscreen quickly and made sure to get a spot under one of the umbrellas.

I realized Ben had made it after all. He was sitting about as far away from me as he could get, which was fine by me. Being out in the fresh air with the wind blowing the smell of the sea over us was so refreshing and invigorating. I felt better than I had in days. I leaned back in my chair and closed my eyes, determined to relax and enjoy the beautiful day. I felt slightly anti-social, but no one seemed to mind that I was keeping to myself.

I soon located Wesley in the middle of the group. He was quite loud and boisterous, and I hate to say that I took an instant dislike to him. There was no one reason, but overhearing his conversations, he struck me as particularly pretentious and a bit self-centered. No one bothered to make the rounds introducing him. I figured most of them had met him before. The morning passed without further incident; we ate lunch sitting in our beach chairs and enjoyed the view. After lunch, I remembered suddenly that I had brought my phone with me and wanted to check to see if I could get a signal out here. I grabbed it and made my way down to the water's edge where the gravelly sand was smoother and more compacted, and it was easier to walk. I decided I would walk a ways down the beach searching for a better signal. Maybe I would even walk up to the road and see if it was better up there. I didn't have anything in particular I needed to do online, or anyone I needed to reach, but it just felt odd being cut off.

I was relieved to see I did have a signal out here. My phone had been flooded with notifications. I had forgotten to put my smartwatch back on after showering this morning, so I hadn't noticed the notifications. There were a few work-related emails that I skimmed through, text messages from a friend asking how my "bougie" week was going so far. When I was all caught up, I decided to put the phone away and focus on my surroundings: the sound of the waves, the spray of the surf, the sun on my back. There were even seagulls flying overhead. I was glad to see proof that there was some wildlife about, other than one dead deer.

I realized I had been absentmindedly walking and had traveled much farther than I had meant to down the beach. I looked back at the group and couldn't make out who anyone was from this distance. I noticed Ben wasn't following me, though. I guess he wasn't worried about me "hurting myself" or twisting an ankle or whatever out here. After a while, I decided it would be weird if I stayed off on my own any longer, and I made my way back to the group. I was surprised to see that a bunch of people had actually decided to go in the water. I figured it would be ice cold by now, but maybe I was wrong. It had been pretty warm during the day still lately, just the mornings and evenings held a chill.

As I moved closer, I realized a few of the guys were throwing the girls into the water. There was squealing and laughing and a few screams. I tossed my phone on my chair and moved a little closer watching them. Kristy kept hiking out of the water, only to get tossed back in again. She was laughing though and clearly doing it deliberately. Mike tossed her in again and everyone cheered. Emily walked over and chided the guys, and out of nowhere, Josh swooped in and ran into the waves with her, tossing her several feet away. Everyone was laughing and cheering now. Emily managed to get back on her feet. She looked utterly shocked and freezing cold, but after a moment, she started laughing too, jumping on Josh's back, and forcing him out deeper into the water. I felt arms lifting me up, and before I could even scream, I was swiftly carried a few feet and tossed in too. The water hit me like a shock. Yep, I was right, it was freezing. I had my clothes on and everything still.

I stood up and let out a shriek involuntarily. God it was so cold. I hugged my arms around myself and turned to see who had thrown me in, although I had a pretty good guess. Mark was standing there laughing his ass off. "Damn it Mark!" I yelled at him. He just grinned at me and bounded into the waves himself.

"Figured you should join the party Cass!" he called back.

I would pay him back for this, as soon as my teeth stopped chattering. As annoyed as I was, it did end up being a lot of fun. The water didn't really get much warmer, but we ended up getting used to it. We played chicken, the girls climbing up on the guy's shoulders. Mark made me play of course, with Emily claiming me to battle. After about a half an hour or so in the water, I heard Kristy yelling at someone out of nowhere. We stopped our horsing around to see what was happening. Kristy and one of the Mikes, the one who had chanted "USA", when we won croquet, were having some sort of argument. I couldn't tell if maybe Kristy had gotten hurt somehow, or what the deal was. She seemed upset now about Mike throwing her in the water, but then again, she also seemed pretty drunk, so I wasn't sure if that was really the biggest issue.

Mike eventually gave up trying to reason with her and climbed out of the water. He headed back and grabbed a beer and flopped down in one of the beach chairs. Emily managed to persuade Kristy to get out of the water too, although she was still upset. After that, the rest of us decided we were done and followed suit. While we were heading back up the beach, I noticed that Ben hadn't joined us in the water. He was still sitting in one of the farthest chairs at the edge of the group, with his chin propped on his hand. It was hard to tell where he was looking since he had sunglasses on, but he was staring out at the water in my direction. I had pulled off my wet shirt and shorts at some point and just thrown them on the beach; far up enough that the waves wouldn't pull them back in. I grabbed them on my way back to my chair, wringing them out. I felt suddenly self-conscious walking back soaking wet in just my bikini.

I hung my wet clothes up to dry on the back of the beach chair and laid out in the sun to try to dry off as best I could. We stayed for another hour or so, maybe more. I tried to close my eyes and relax again, but all I could hear was Kristy whining and complaining about Mike to Emily and Catherine. I felt bad for her if he'd done something inappropriate, but I couldn't help but feel like she was being a bit melodramatic, especially given the look on Emily's face. I could tell she was feeling the same. I felt somewhat relieved when she said it was time for us to think about heading back. Although, I wasn't exactly eager to return to the Hideaway.

On the drive back, I felt that familiar feeling of dread start to creep back over me. The drive felt like it took forever, and I was too hot sitting crammed into the back of the car. We were all crabby and hot and tired, like little kids who had played outside in the sun too long. When we entered the forest that marked the start of the property, I could feel it immediately. Something just felt different. It was like my body could tell when we were getting closer to that house. I told myself I was being silly, but I felt it, just the same. The little break away from the house had allowed me to feel it. My mind kept returning to the strange writing and drawings on the paper I had found. To the deer head sitting on the stairs; its dull eyes. I stared out the car window at the trees flying past and wondered what we would find waiting for us when we got back. Part of me wished I had just kept walking on that beach. Just taken off and left, without looking back.

Our arrival back to the house was uneventful. Although, by that point I was feeling off, a little nauseous even. I chalked it up to the too hot car ride, but I felt that ache of dread in the pit of my stomach that told me otherwise. Emily told us all to go clean up and relax. There would be a few lawn games in the yard for anyone who was interested (I couldn't imagine who would want to be out in the sun any longer) and billiards in the game room. I didn't know where the game room even was, but I wasn't up for any games anyway. Dinner was to start around 6:00 again tonight and, you guessed it, formal wear was expected. How many dresses did these women own? I wasn't sure what the guys did. Was it okay for them to just wear the same suit every night, or were they expected to wear something new? I figured I probably wasn't observant enough to notice either way.

I headed back to my room, showered and washed my hair again (thanks Mark) and dressed in casual clothes for now. I really wanted to relax and rest in my room, maybe even take a nap, but it occurred to me that this could be a good opportunity to sneak back into the study to take a closer look at the painting of the house. Before I left, I checked the pocket of the fur coat to make sure the piece of paper was still there. I don't know how it would be possible for anyone to know I had it, much less find its hiding spot. Although Mark had spotted me holding it, I didn't think he had any clue what it was. I was clearly starting to feel a little paranoid.

Thankfully I saw no one on my way to the study. I practically tip-toed down the hall but felt stupid about halfway there and started walking normally. It wasn't like I needed to hide where I was going, I wasn't doing anything wrong. The study was empty too. I made my way straight over to the painting and peered at the willow tree in the background. There was very clearly a large object hanging from the branches of the tree. It was hard to say for sure, but I thought I could make out what might be two arms hanging down. But then again, if it were meant to be a deer, it would look similar. I sighed in frustration. There was just no way to tell for sure what it was. It was basically just a blob on the canvas.

I turned my attention towards the massive desk behind me. For some reason I felt tempted to check the drawers. I pulled them open, one by one. Many of them were empty or contained just a few old papers. Records and receipts. Nothing that seemed to be of particular interest or importance. I didn't know what I was looking for anyway. Maybe a book that conveniently explained what was going on and what the strange writing and drawings meant? No such luck. I came to the last drawer on the right-hand side of the desk, and went to pull it open, but it was jammed tight. No, it was locked. There was a small, golden, ornate keyhole. I checked the other drawers and confirmed they didn't have locks. No amount of pulling or jostling would make it open. I gave up eventually and returned to my room. I scanned each picture frame as I went, just in case.

When it neared 5:30, I decided it was time to change and get ready for dinner. I had forgotten to even give a thought to what I would wear tonight. I rifled through the dresses Emily had brought for me and found a bright red evening gown that looked possible. It was long-sleeved and had a skirt that widened as it fell, the bottom billowing out in soft folds. The neckline, though, was plunging. I eyed it warily. I doubted I could make that work, but my options were limited.

I managed to slide into the dress and take stock in the mirror. There was some built-in support in the bust, and while it wasn't something I was typically able to do, I thought I could pull it off going braless. There was no bra I owned that wouldn't show smack in the middle of the neckline as it came to a point just below my bust. I opted to leave my hair down this time, as I had taken the time to style my waves, and they had actually decided to turn out decent looking. I pinned one side of my hair back in a twist and called it good enough. I felt a little daring wearing this dress, but why not live a little.

I headed down the stairs on my own this time, surprised to find it relatively quiet and the house still. I crossed the foyer and entered the dining hall to see I was running a few minutes late. It looked like most of the group was already seated. A handful of heads whipped around to look at me when I walked in. Someone let out a low whistle, and I colored slightly.

"Dang, Cass!" Mark exclaimed.

Emily smiled broadly at me. She was practically glowing tonight, in a slim white gown that was plain but elegant. "You look beautiful Cassie." Emily beamed at me.

I smiled back, her encouragement giving me the courage to stop blushing. "Thanks, Em. You do, too. White suits you."

Josh smiled broadly at me, his dimples appearing, and wrapped an arm around Emily, kissing her on the top of the head. "It really does, babe," he said, smiling down at her. She tilted her face up to his and he kissed her deeply. The group clapped and cheered. Someone started clanging their flatware on their glass, and others joined in.

Emily laughed and reprimanded them. "Save it for the wedding people!"

My eyes had locked onto Ben's. He ignored the commotion and stared at me. He didn't look angry this time—just sad. He looked at me like I had hurt him somehow, as though I had just punched him in the stomach. I blinked at him in confusion, feeling an ache start in my chest. Why did he always have to spoil everything?

I tore my gaze away from him and made my way to my seat, which, unfortunately, was still in the same place as last night. It seemed that for once, Emily hadn't thought of everything, I mused. It might have been a good idea to move Mark and me away from Ben, or better yet, to separate all three of us as much as possible.

The dinner progressed much in the same way it had the night before. I almost felt a sense of déjà vu. We ordered drinks; I opted for red wine tonight, headache be damned. We then made our meal selections for each course. Light piano music played in the background tonight, as though it were a reminder to everyone to keep it classy.

I felt oddly restless throughout the meal, as though I just couldn't relax. Partially, I thought it was the dress, but I also was bothered by the fact that Ben didn't seem to be speaking at all tonight, to anyone. He made a few half-hearted attempts to murmur or make "mmhmm" sounds back when Emily or Josh spoke directly to him. He did, however, find it within himself to glare at us every time Mark opened his mouth to speak to me. I found myself wishing he would just stop talking, and I felt less and less at ease as the night went on.

After a while, Emily seemed to notice I was left out of the conversation and made an effort to pull me back in. The conversation at the other end of the table had taken a philosophical turn. While I was understandably wary of the subject, I listened to Emily's explanation. "So," Emily said, "It's almost like, if you were fated to live your life over again, and what if it were exactly the same as it had been previously? Like living the same story over and over. Like the movie *Groundhog Day*, only, it's your whole life versus just one day."

"Hmm," I responded, thinking for a long moment. "Well, interestingly enough, that reminds me of a theory of Nietzsche's actually." I looked sideways at Ben for a moment, gauging his reaction. He just stared down at his plate and pushed food around with his fork. He appeared to be back to pointedly ignoring me. "He believed, based on a misunderstanding of physics, that because there were finite atoms in the universe, they could only assume finite configurations. In short, he believed the laws of physics, as they were understood during his time, meant that the world would repeat itself endlessly, with everything occurring exactly as it already had before."

Ben nodded slightly, raising an eyebrow at his plate. Had I actually impressed him?

"And what was his answer to that?" Josh asked curiously.

"Well," I shrugged, "the response he arrived at was something called *amor fati*, in Latin, which translates to 'love of one's fate.' It's sort of an attitude of acceptance. Embracing all of life's experiences, even loss or suffering, as necessary or good, or, at the very least, inevitable. The concept is tied into Stoicism, and, frankly, wasn't a new concept when Nietzsche wrote about it. I can't recall his exact words, but he wrote something to the effect of saying that his formula for greatness for any human being is to accept your fate. That you should want nothing to be different, not forwards, not backwards, for all eternity." The room fell silent for a moment, as we contemplated living in an existential loop of fate.

Ben was still avoiding looking at me. I cleared my throat. "It's a general theme, I think, maybe not always obvious, but present in many movies, and novels. You'll see the characters sort of accept their fate, almost lean into it, even when it's not necessarily something good. They just give in and accept the pull... sort of embracing the inevitability of their destiny."

Catherine asked me quietly, "Where did you learn so much about philosophy?" She looked impressed, at least.

I laughed a little. "I took a class in college." She nodded politely. "And my professor was hot," I added.

Emily laughed. "You slut!" she said jokingly. Mark laughed loudly at that one.

"Right..." Josh said sarcastically, chuckling a little. "Cassie doesn't exactly strike me as a closet hussy."

"Oh please," Emily said, laughing, "she gets around her fair share." She grinned wickedly at me. "It's just those big blue eyes." She fluttered her eyelashes rapidly. "Trust me, she's not as innocent as she looks."

"Em!" I exclaimed at her in mock horror. My cheeks flushed slightly, and my gaze flickered towards Ben involuntarily as I thought back to his words last night.

"I could've told you that," Mark said, pretending to roll his eyes. Everyone was laughing now. Well, everyone except Ben. I turned to look at him, and sure enough, he was in full on glowering mode.

He finally looked up from his plate at me. "Good to know," he said sneering. And then he added, "I take it your history professor was ugly then? Seeing as you didn't retain much about the Nazis." I stared at him. He met my gaze, a smirk on his face. My cheeks burned.

"Technically our conversation yesterday was about Nietzsche, and that would clearly fall under the web of philosophy too, Ben, but nice try." I sent a fake smile his way.

"Ooh, burn," Mark chuckled next to me.

"Okay, can we not?" Emily said, "Do we really need to start this up again?"

"I'm not trying to start anything up," Ben replied, "I'm just trying to get through a meal without gagging, but it's difficult."

"What's that supposed to mean?" I asked quietly. I felt those seated nearby at the table still.

He looked me dead in the eyes. "It means whatever you think it means." Clearly a favorite asshole response of his. Or he just knew that it got to me before.

I snorted air out my nose and tilted my head back, looking up at the ceiling. I was trying to stay calm, but I was getting irritated now.

"Why don't we just move on?" He suggested. "Emily is right; I don't want to start an argument."

"Well," I said, my head starting to buzz a little. The wine was getting to me. I had a bad feeling I was well on my way to a headache later. "I would be more inclined to believe that if you hadn't been glaring at me all day."

Side conversations had picked up again momentarily on the other half of the table, but now I could sense heads turning towards us, realizing something was wrong.

Ben snorted and sat back in his chair, crossing his arms against his chest. "I wouldn't call it glaring," he said.

"Oh no, what would you call it then?" I asked archly.

He shrugged. "Staring. Does that make you feel any better?" He actually looked angry. So, he was mad at me for calling him out on his bullshit behavior?

Josh, realizing what was happening, attempted to intercede now, holding up a hand between us. "Guys, why don't we all just take a breath, there's no need to argue."

"I don't want to argue," I insisted. "I'm just trying to understand what Ben's problem is."

"Oh," Mark chuckled, "I think it's pretty clear what his problem is." We all turned to stare at Mark now.

"Shut up, Mark." Ben turned his glare onto him.

Mark paused, looking at him carefully for a long moment. "You know what, no, I don't think I will, Ben," he continued, a cheeky grin on his face.

"What?" I demanded. No one responded to me. My heart was starting to pound. I looked from person to person around the table. Did they all know something I didn't?

"I said, shut the fuck up, Mark," Ben said quietly. Everyone in the room had stopped their conversations to watch us. I saw two of the waiters freeze and look at each other. Probably wanting to duck out and leave.

Mark was starting to look pissed off now too. He met Ben's angry glare. "You're such a chicken shit sometimes. Why don't I tell her for you then." He turned to me and opened his mouth to speak, but he never got that far. Ben shot up from his chair and looked like he was practically about to leap over the table at Mark. Josh was clearly anticipating this already and was at his side before I could process what was happening. He placed both hands on Ben's shoulders and held him firmly in place.

"Come on man, take a seat," Josh said calmly. The rest of us were all frozen. Was there really about to be a fistfight in the middle of dinner? And over what? I still didn't understand what was happening.

"That's enough. He's drunk. Let it go," Josh said, his tone still calm. Ben shook his shoulders slightly, and Josh let go of him. He sank into his chair, eyes downcast on his plate.

Then he looked up at Mark and said, "You're a real piece of shit sometimes, you know that?" It was silent for a long moment. No one seemed to be moving.

Then Catherine broke the silence. She turned to Kristy. "Where did you get your dress? It's stunning." Kristy was wearing another slinky little dress, this time in all black. She looked sideways at me for a second before she launched into a loud, long-winded explanation of where she had found her dress. And could anyone believe who she ran into that day trying on Chanel dresses... I stopped listening, grateful to her for capturing everyone's attention away from our dysfunction.

"What's going on, Ben?" I asked him, keeping my voice low and as calm as possible. I didn't want to catch anyone's attention again.

"Nothing," he mumbled at his plate, refusing to meet my eyes. He pushed his food around for a minute. It hardly looked like he had eaten anything. Then he picked up his glass and downed the rest of his drink in one long chug.

He set his glass down, and turning to Emily and Josh, he got their attention and whispered something inaudible before quietly leaving the room. Well, I wasn't going after him this time, that was for sure. I took another sip of my wine, then set my glass back down in disgust. I'd had enough for one night. The remainder of dinner passed by peacefully.

After dinner ended, Emily looped her arm through mine and led me down the hall with the rest of the group to the guy's lounge. Apparently, I wasn't going to get lucky and be escorted to my room early tonight. I was dismayed to see that Ben was in the lounge, sitting in the chair he had been in the night I first arrived. He was staring into the fire and drinking alone. He looked like he was still in an awful mood. Why didn't he just go to bed and leave the rest of us in peace?

We started the evening's entertainment with Never Have I Ever... one of my least favorite party games. Being a bit of an introvert and a wuss, it turns out there are a lot of things I haven't done, and I don't really love being forced to admit to them in a group setting. I opted out of playing. I thought Emily was going to make a stink about it, but her gaze swung briefly in Ben's direction, and she let it go. I guess she figured I had endured enough public humiliation for one night. Ben was ignoring the rest of us, and no one bothered asking him to join in. I sat next to Catherine and Blair on one of the couches. I decided I would make a point of ignoring him for the rest of the evening. Make that the rest of the week.

Wes took it upon himself to give a toast at one point. He grinned his charming but slightly off-putting smile and ended the toast with, "To Josh and Emily, and continuing our noble bloodline." From my perspective, the speech was mostly about how great the Haverfords were and how Josh and Emily were carrying on the family name. This guy was something else. It made me very glad Emily was marrying the younger Haverford brother, and it also made me somewhat apprehensive to meet his parents in a few days.

After that, people broke off into small groups, drinking and chatting. I glanced over to see Mark and Ben standing alone by the French glass doors.

They seemed deep in conversation, and it looked like they were starting to get into it again. I watched them wearily, trying not to make it too obvious.

Kristy and Emily had joined us on the couches. Kristy was talking about what a jerk Mike was, apparently still supposedly pissed at him for throwing her in the water earlier. Although it sounded like they had some previous history between them, that I suspected was the real issue. Still, I found myself feeling much more sympathetic since she tried to rescue the conversation on my behalf at dinner. "Look at this," she said, twisting her calf to the side, to show us something. There was a mark on her leg... I stared at it for a moment. It almost looked like one of the markings on the piece of paper I had found. "He did this... scratched the heck out of me." I listened half-heartedly, nodding, while still trying to keep an eye on the guys.

At one point, Mark reached out and clasped his hand on Ben's shoulder. Ben smiled at him and nodded, saying something back, and then they shook hands. Were they finally making up? I wasn't sure over what, but it seemed to be the case. I breathed a sigh of relief. Good, maybe we could get through one normal dinner now.

I had to pee and realized I had no idea where a bathroom was located, other than up in my room. I asked Emily and she gave me directions. "But you better come back!" She said, pointing at me, "Don't you try to slink off to bed early!"

I smiled and promised her I wouldn't. Ugh, so much for that.

On my way back from the bathroom, which was down a particularly narrow hallway towards the library, I was looking down at my dress when I almost slammed into someone coming in the opposite direction. I realized at the last second that it was Ben.

I felt him grab my arm gently, but firmly, stopping me from continuing forward. I jerked to a stop and stared up at him in surprise. "I'm sorry

Cassie..." he spoke in a low hushed voice, his face close to mine, "about tonight, and, and how I've been in general. I know I've been an asshole, and I truly am sorry. I hope you can forgive me."

I was startled, and overwhelmed by how close he was to me. I could smell his cologne, something spicy and dark but with a hint of vanilla. I swallowed; his eyes dropped to my lips.

"It's okay," I murmured a little breathlessly; it was all I could manage at the moment. I felt a sudden throbbing deep in my core. I started to pull away from him and head back down the hallway to the group. This was too much for me to handle.

"I'll see you around," he said softly, almost forlornly, from behind me.

"Wait." I whipped back around at his tone of voice. "You aren't leaving, are you?" I cringed inwardly. I hated how panicked I had just sounded.

He looked confused for a second, brow creasing. "No, I... well, I was thinking about it, yeah." He paused, then said in a deep voice, "Do you want me to go?" He stood there, waiting for me to answer.

I thought about it for a moment before responding. Would he leave if I said yes? I was oddly sure for some reason that he would. "No," I said softly. "No, I don't want you to go." And I realized as I said it that I really didn't. I couldn't explain it, but the thought of staying alone in that house without him made me feel a little sick. "Afterall," I continued, "who would save me from runaway horses and twisted ankles?"

He smiled broadly at me. A genuine, real smile, and I realized I had rarely seen this smile from him. He nodded and said, "I'm not really leaving. I wouldn't do that to Josh. I'm heading up to bed in a minute..." he grinned a little sheepishly at me. "I just wanted to see what you'd say."

I couldn't help but laugh. "You really are an asshole; you know that right?"

Ben laughed. "Yeah, I'm working on it."

I rolled my eyes. "Sure..." He just smiled at me. "Hey," I said, "do you...happen to play the piano?"

He gave me a strange look. "Yes...why?" He asked, his brow furrowed.

"No reason," I said, shrugging. "I was just curious."

"Okay," he said, still looking confused. "Have a good night, Cassie."

"Thanks, you too." I smiled back and turned and headed back to the lounge.

After rejoining the party for a while, I started to yawn uncontrollably. I checked my watch, but it was only 9:30. Ugh. I got up from the velvet couch and began to walk around the room. Sitting and relaxing was putting me to sleep. I came to the French glass doors at the back of the room and decided some fresh air would do me some good. I opened the doors and stepped out onto the stone patio. I stood for a few moments, breathing deeply, taking in the cool night air.

My eyes scanned the fields and tree line automatically, searching for the dark figure I had seen moving around the night before. It occurred to me then that perhaps I had seen whoever left the deer head on the stairs. It was time to tell someone about the paper with the weird markings that I had found. I gave a little involuntary shudder. All the tension with Ben had distracted me from everything that had happened.

"Goose walked over your grave?" Mark quipped from over my shoulder.

I jumped slightly. "What?" I asked, still distracted by my thoughts.

"I saw you shiver," Mark explained. "You know, people say that means someone just walked over your grave." He cocked his head to the side and said, "Actually, saying grave doesn't really make sense... but saying the place your grave will be takes too long."

I smiled distractedly at him. "Mark, can I ask you something?"

He looked serious for once and sighed, running one hand through his shaggy hair. "I can't tell you, Cass. I'm sorry, but it's just not for me to tell." I stiffened and blinked at him in confusion. So, he did know something.

He continued without noticing me staring at him. "I never should have said anything in the first place. It's just that he's normally so confident all the time, and he can be a know-it-all prick. I couldn't help but give him shit when I had the chance." He held up the glass in his hand and tilted it slightly to the side, indicating the liquid inside. "And then, there was *this* involved. Not my finest hour."

My shoulders relaxed. Of course, he was just talking about Ben. Naturally, he assumed that was what I wanted to ask him.

"No," I said quietly, glancing back into the room behind us. There was no one anywhere close to us. The nearest group was over by the dart board across from the fireplace, and they were hooting and cheering. "That's not what I wanted to ask you about. Although I am slightly pissed at you and everyone else here quite frankly for not telling me what's going on."

Mark looked at me with his eyebrows raised. He shook his head and chuckled. "I like you Cassie, but you're kind of clueless, you know that?"

I just gave him a look back. I was starting to get a clue, but I didn't really want to think about that right now. "What I wanted to ask you is," I continued, ignoring his last comment, "you mentioned visiting the Hideaway before, have you been here a few times?"

"Yeah, sure." He nodded in the affirmative. "I've been here a handful of times, heck maybe even a dozen or more. We've mostly come out around this time every year in the fall to hunt with Josh and Wes and the family. You know, mostly weekend deer hunting trips." He caught himself for a second, clearly remembering the gruesome deer head, and cleared his throat. "But sometimes pheasant."

"We?" I asked, nodding. "Like you and some of the other guys here?"

"Yep," Mark confirmed. "Ben pretty much always, Mike C. and Mikey H. have come out a few times, but not as consistently." He scanned the room, thinking. "Yeah, actually I think most of the guys here have all been out with us before." He frowned for a second, "Maybe not Eric though, Josh met him through work, and he hasn't known him as long as the rest of us."

I nodded to myself. A little voice nagged at the back of my mind, *Ben said he wasn't a hunter, yet he came out here for a hunting trip every year?* I'm sure it meant nothing. Maybe he didn't enjoy it, just came to hang out. *Yeah*, the voice said, *because he's so social...*

"And did anything..." I tried to think of how best to phrase this. "Did anything weird ever happen?" I asked him. He raised one eyebrow, his eyes darting back and forth across my features. Was he suddenly looking more wary?

"Weird? Weird like what?" He asked slowly, then continued before I could respond. "Define weird, Cassie. I mean..." he laughed now looking more at ease. "We've been coming out for the hunting trip for years now. We were pretty young when we started so, I mean, yeah, we probably got up to some weird shit at times." He caught the expression on my face. "I mean," he held up his hands in a don't-get-mad gesture, almost spilling his drink, "nothing too crazy, just stupid stuff guys do. You know how it is."

I didn't, and I'd quite rather not. "Not like that," I said quickly, "I mean anything strange. Like..." I thought for a moment, "like the deer head last night."

He stopped smiling and stared at me for a long moment. "What is it, Cassie?" He asked slowly. "Did something else happen?"

Suddenly, Emily walked up to us. She gripped my arm above my elbow, and, placing her mouth near my ear, she whispered, "I can't find Kristy," in an urgent tone.

I pulled back from her slightly so I could see her face. "What do you mean you can't find Kristy?" I repeated back quietly. I turned to look at the velvet couches. She had just been sitting right there earlier with us—she'd been there all night from what I could remember—but she wasn't sitting there now.

"She's not in here," Emily hissed back. "And from what I can tell, she's not anywhere. I checked her room already, everywhere I could think of upstairs, on our floor, and even the pool."

I blinked for a second. "There's a pool?" What else did I not know about?

"Yes, Cass, there's a pool." Emily sounded a little exasperated. Why was she so worried?

"Well, I mean, it's a massive house Em, I doubt you were able to check every room all by yourself," Mark interjected.

Emily turned to Mark, including him in the conversation. "No, I haven't checked every room yet. But why would she be sitting in some random empty room by herself? She isn't anywhere it would make any sense for her to be."

Mark nodded. "Well, let's not panic, I'm sure she's somewhere." He thought for a moment. "How many bathrooms are there in this house? Twenty-five?" He hazarded a guess. "Did you check all the toilets? That seems like a likely place she'd be, too." Emily's expression wiped the goofy grin off his face.

"It's not funny Mark." She turned and scanned the room again, making sure no one was listening. "It's not just that," her voice barely a whisper, "I found something in her room." She looked really scared. Jesus. If it was another dead animal, I was going to lose my shit.

"What is it?" I asked, not sure I wanted to hear the answer.

"Come on." She grabbed my hand. "I'll show you."

Mark came with us, which made me feel slightly comforted, but my sense of foreboding grew as we made our way up the plush staircase and past the blood stain that almost just, but not quite, blended into the red carpet.

We made our way swiftly down the girl's corridor, running into no one on our way there.

It turned out Kristy's room was on the far side of Emily's. She swung the door open without hesitating and ushered us into the room. The room was a mess. I looked around for a minute in confusion. Had there been some kind of a struggle? A large floral suitcase was thrown wide open in the middle of the floor. Clothes were tossed all over the floor and on every available surface. Makeup, perfumes, hairbrushes, all sorts of random beauty products littered the dresser top and bedside table. There were four or five different purses, for what? I couldn't help but notice the designer labels clearly visible on them. No, I determined, no signs of a struggle, the room was just a complete mess.

Mark was scanning the room just like I was. "Jesus..." he muttered. "I don't know how you could find anything in this mess." My thoughts exactly.

Emily extended an arm and pointed up above the head of the bed. Mark and I turned to look.

Hanging against the wall above the bed, secured around the middle of the four-poster frame, was what I could only describe as an odd-looking upside-down bouquet. There was a thin piece of brown twine tied in a loose bow around several different types of plants, including, I swallowed, a small bunch of the blood-red roses from the garden. There was something else, a smaller object, tucked into the middle of the bundle.

"What is that?" I asked, my voice barely above a whisper.

'I'm not sure," Emily said. "But it's weird, isn't it? Who put it there?" She shook her head, her brows creased in concern. "It doesn't seem like something Kristy would have done, that's for sure. And why would any of the staff do something like that without me knowing?"

I nodded in agreement. It was definitely strange. "Yeah, I agree. But I mean what is *that*?" I pointed towards the bundle now myself. "There's something else in there, in the middle."

Emily squinted at the bundle. "I... I'm not sure. It looks like something... furry," Emily gulped audibly. She looked over at Mark, her eyes asking the question for her.

Mark sighed and climbed up onto the mattress. He had to step gingerly around the various objects scattered all over the surface of the bed. It occurred to me then to ask if Kristy was always this messy. Maybe this wasn't from her. Was there a chance someone had come into her room and dumped the contents of her suitcase and several large bags out on her bed? If so, what were they looking for? I thought of the piece of paper hiding in the fur coat in my room. I stared at the bundle of plants. How many of these were drawn on there? I knew the roses were.

He was just tall enough to be close to eye level with the weird bouquet. He stood there for a moment, staring at it, moving his head around to see it from different angles. Clearly, he was reluctant to touch it. Eventually, he turned to look back at us, a grim expression on his face. "I think it's a rabbit's foot. And I don't mean the kind you buy at a gift shop."

"Oh god..." Emily murmured under her breath. "What the fuck is going on?"

"There's something else in here," Mark called over his shoulder. "But I'm going to have to take it apart a bit to see what it is." He reached up and started to fiddle with the bundle.

Looking over at Emily, I saw she looked pale, almost like she was going to pass out. I grabbed her arm. "Are you okay, Em?" She didn't respond to me. "Why don't you sit down." I led her as carefully as I could around the piles of clothes scattered all over the floor to the accent chair next to the French glass doors. I realized that the layout of Kristy's room was almost identical to mine.

Once I had Emily seated a bit of the color started to return to her cheeks. "Where's Josh?" I asked gently, rubbing her back. "I'll go get him."

She looked up at me, and I was startled to see her eyes looked slightly wet, almost like she was about to cry. "I don't know," she mumbled. "The last I saw him, he was with Wes." I thought back. I couldn't remember seeing him in the lounge just before we left, but that didn't mean he wasn't there.

"Okay." I nodded, keeping my tone light. "I'll go find him."

Mark cleared his throat and hopped down off the bed. He made his way over to us, holding something out in the palm of his hand. I peered down at the object he held. It was brown, so it had blended in with the twine and the stems. I saw as he came closer that it seemed to be a tiny, crude little figure in the shape of a person. It was made of wicker and tied with a smaller bit of twine wrapped around its middle. It was in the shape of an 'H' with both its arms and legs sticking straight out. It had what looked like a tuft of blonde hair made out of yarn. My stomach twisted. Jesus Christ. It was supposed to look like Kristy. Who would take the time to make something like this? Was it some kind of effigy?

Emily made what sounded like a strangled sob. I looked up at Mark. "We need to find Kristy."

We quickly headed downstairs and gathered everyone together. It was easy enough, as most people were still in the guys' lounge. I asked one of the other Mikes, not Kristy's Mike, and Eric to go find Josh and Wes. They thought they had mentioned something about the game room, so they headed there first. I sent Mark up to Ben's room to wake him up. It seemed like he was the only other person missing from what we could tell, aside from Kristy, of course.

Josh and Wes made it back with Mike and Eric first. Josh rushed over to Emily to check on her and make sure she was doing okay. I watched their conversation from across the room. Josh pulled her into a hug and stroked her hair. I stood next to the window. I was debating how much I should tell them. About the dark shape I had seen heading into the woods during the night? That could have been anything. I had the piece of paper. The painting. Which was little more than a smudge really. The deer head. Now the morbid little bouquet. What were the actual facts though? Strung together, it was an odd sequence of events, but was I grasping at nothing? The most likely explanation was that someone was messing with us. The real question was why, and, more importantly, who?

The feeling of dread that had settled comfortably back in my gut like an old friend eased slightly when I saw Ben enter the room. His hair was disheveled. He was wearing his running clothes. That struck me as odd for a moment, but then I rationalized he likely would have been in his PJs when Mark woke him up and it wouldn't have made much sense to put his suit back on. The running clothes were probably the easiest thing to throw on quickly.

I watched him search through the crowd in the room. My heart lurched. Was he looking for me? His eyes found me by the window, and he nodded at me from across the room. I gave him a half-hearted smile back.

Josh cleared his throat loudly from over by the fireplace and raised his hands up to get everyone's attention. People started to notice nearby and quieted down. Eventually an expectant hush fell over the room. "Okay everyone," Josh began, his voice steady and even, "I know everyone is feeling a little freaked out right now, but we're sure Kristy is going to be just fine. We are asking for everyone's assistance, whoever is willing..." he paused there for a moment to let us think, "to systematically search the house." He nodded towards the doorway, and we all turned to see Harvey standing there, his back ramrod straight against the wall just inside the doorway. He held a large, ancient looking flashlight in both hands. He nodded solemnly back at Josh.

"We've enlisted the help of some of the staff. We are going to do this in a logical, orderly fashion," Josh continued. "We don't need people rushing around, getting hurt or lost themselves. Remember, this is a big place, and I'm sure there will be a logical explanation shortly." I felt the level of collective anxiety in the room drop a notch; at least there was a plan in place.

Wes spoke up from a few paces off to Josh's left. "We think there is a good chance Kristy is missing on purpose," he added, lifting his chin in the air. "We understand she was somewhat upset this evening... and she had been drinking."

"As we all have," Emily spoke up suddenly, eyeing Wes begrudgingly.

"As we all have," Wes agreed. "I'm just trying to say that there's a good chance she's upset and has gone off somewhere. Let's try not to overreact."

Sure, and that would explain the creepy bundle with the weird little wicker voodoo doll left hanging over her bed. I tried not to roll my eyes.

The rest of the staff were waiting out in the hallway. They had brought some flashlights in case people wanted them. They told us to divide up into pairs and stay together. If anyone found Kristy, they were to head back to the main foyer. One of the stable hands would wait there with a radio so he could contact the rest of the staff and spread the all-clear.

Mark sidled up to me and nudged my arm. "Wanna be my partner, partner?" He said in a terrible impression of a cowboy, tipping an imaginary hat my way.

"You are such a dork." I shook my head, but I couldn't help but chuckle. We both saw at the same moment that Ben had stopped short a few feet away from us. *Here we go again.*

"Actually," Mark said, "I spy with my little eye, Amy, all alone." He nodded across the room. "I think I'll go see if she needs a partner." He winked at me and left. Subtle.

Ben approached me slowly once he was gone. "Hey," he said, "Are you okay?"

"Yeah," I said, "I'm fine. I'm just worried about Kristy." Ben nodded and sighed. I felt a little pang of guilt. Kristy wasn't my favorite person, if I were being honest, but I'd really hate to think anything bad had happened to her.

"Did you hear about what was left in her room?" I asked him, my voice pitched lower.

He looked at me and nodded again. "I did. Mark filled me in when he came to get me."

I nodded. I thought about the piece of paper in my room again. "I want to help look for Kristy," I said, "But there's something I think I need to show you first."

He gazed back at me with a slightly puzzled expression on his face. "Okay..." he said slowly, "lead the way."

People were queuing up to leave the room as Josh and Emily stood with Harvey assigning groups to search specific areas of the house. When it was our turn, I asked if we could cover the girl's wing.

Emily looked back and forth between Ben and me curiously for just a second and then nodded in agreement.

We headed up the staircase in silence and made our way down the winding halls. When we reached our section of the hallway, I led Ben straight to my bedroom and held the door open. He looked at me with raised eyebrows for a moment before entering my room.

I walked over towards the closet/bathroom hall, scanning the room. Nothing seemed out of place. Naturally, my eyes landed on the four-poster frame above the headboard. There was nothing but an empty, blank stretch of wall.

I went into the closet, rifled around in the pocket of the oversized fur coat, and grasped the paper in my hand with a flood of relief. I had half expected it to be gone. I turned back to find Ben standing outside the closet, watching me.

I walked back over to him, unfolding the paper as I went. I handed him the piece of paper. He looked at me for a moment and then began to study the yellowed sheet.

When he flipped it over and saw the figure hanging from the tree, he froze and looked up at me.

"What is this, Cassie? Where did you get this?"

I told him about finding it in the corner of the picture frame in the guy's lounge.

"It looks really old..." he trailed off, turning the paper over in his hands.

"I can't read the writing, so I have no clue what it says. It looks like it's written in some old, more primitive language," I told him. "Do you think it's related to everything else going on?"

He didn't respond for a moment, peering intently at the script covering the page. He said after a moment, "These are runes. It's a form of writing used primarily by the Norse and the Celts." I stared at him blankly. "Also known as pagans," he added. He handed the paper gingerly back to me. "I don't read runes so I can't tell you what it says either, but it's freaking creepy, that's for sure."

I nodded and sighed in agreement. He hadn't answered my question earlier. "But do you think this is all related? It seems like too weird of a coincidence. There is a deer skull on the paper, and there was the head on the staircase. I noticed the door knockers on the front doors are in the shape of a deer skull and antlers too," I said as I pointed in the general direction that I thought was towards the front of the house. "And these roses." I pointed to the drawing. "They look just like the red roses from the garden."

Ben shrugged slightly. "Well, I mean, all roses look alike, don't they? The shape of them at least. These are just in black ink; they aren't necessarily red."

"No," I agreed, "you're right. They could be any color, sure, but there were also red roses from the garden in the bundle-thing hanging in Kristy's room. There are too many coincidences."

"So, what does it all mean?" Ben asked me simply, shrugging again, both hands in his pockets.

I stared at him. I had expected more of a reaction. "I don't know," I said, throwing my hands up in exasperation. "Why don't you tell me Ben?"

He looked at me in confusion. "What does that mean, Cassie?"

I was tempted to say it meant whatever he thought it meant, but I restrained myself. "It means..." I fumbled for the right words, "it means that you're close with the family, you've been here how many times? I know you come out every year in the fall for a guys hunting trip." If the fact that I knew about that fazed him, he covered it up well. "You're telling me in all the times you've been here, you've never seen anything like this." I held up the paper. "You've never seen any dead animals laying around? Any creepy wicker figurines? All of this is new. And you know nothing about it."

I stared him down until he broke eye contact first and looked away. "Look, Cassie," he sighed, "I don't know what you expect me to say, but no, I haven't seen any dead animals lying around, other than the ones somebody shot with a shotgun right in front of me. And I don't know anything about what's happening right now. My best guess would be that someone is messing with us, deliberately. I mean, there's nothing supernatural about any of this." He held his hands up, gesturing around. "And in reality, it all sounds like a lot of weak, tenuous connections you've drawn to be honest." I stared at him in disbelief. Was he kidding? "Trust me, there's going to be a perfectly logical explanation to all of this."

I wanted to scream in frustration. I wasn't drawing tenuous links, or whatever he had called them. I was noticing things. Noticing patterns that told me, in my gut, that something was very wrong with this house.

Ben sighed, sensing my frustration. "Look, the best thing we can do right now is to keep looking for Kristy. When we find her, I'm sure you'll feel a lot better."

Oh, so now he was patronizing me like I was some hysterical girl caught up in the melodrama of the evening. I studied him for a minute, taking in his running clothes. My eyes drifted to his feet. He had his shoes on.

I hadn't noticed it until just now, but he was wearing his running shoes. Why would he have put his shoes on to come downstairs?

He saw me looking at him strangely.

"What?" He asked, holding his arms out to the side.

"What were you doing tonight, Ben?"

He just stared at me uncomprehendingly for a moment. "What do you mean?" He asked. I didn't respond. My heart rate was starting to rise. "I was in bed, asleep." He grew more agitated when I still didn't respond. "Are you trying to ask me if I had something to do with Kristy's disappearance?" He demanded. He shook his head in disbelief and ran both hands through his disheveled hair. He turned his back to me and started pacing back and forth across the room. "Just when I was starting to think you didn't hate me after all," he mumbled.

"I don't hate you, Ben," I said quietly.

"No," he snapped back, "You don't hate me, you just think I'm some kind of serial killer," he said, his voice rising.

I glared at him, my voice flat and ice-cold. "Who said anything about Kristy being dead?"

He froze and stared back at me. "Are you fucking kidding me Cassie?" He looked genuinely hurt now. "I've been doing everything I can, to try to–"

"To try to what?" I interrupted him. "Make me feel welcome? Because you really did a great job of that, from the second I arrived." His face flushed at that, whether in anger or embarrassment, I couldn't tell. "And it's been nothing but sunshine and rainbows from you ever since."

"Forget it, Cassie. Okay? I don't know why I bother." He sighed. "Let's go start looking for Kristy and get this over with." He started to leave the room and turned back to me. "Unless, of course, you want to go back downstairs and request a partner who's not a psychopath."

I rolled my eyes, brushing past him and back into the hallway. "I agree; let's just get this over with."

We spent the next half hour searching each and every room along the hallway, checking every bathroom, under beds, closets, anywhere we could think of that could fit a person. We came up empty handed. On a positive note, we didn't find anything else that shouldn't be there either. That was something at least.

Eventually, we gave up, having combed our section of the house, we headed back downstairs to the foyer. A few other groups had beat us there, and others were still trickling back in. Josh made the final call to end the search for the night. Someone asked about searching outside, and there was a chorus of voices at that. Some were clearly in favor of moving the search outdoors, and others, not so much. Josh and Emily clarified that they had several of the staff members, who were the most familiar with the grounds, outside searching already. Still, it was difficult at night, so they planned to continue tomorrow morning. I could tell everyone was exhausted and burnt out at this point. Just as we were wrapping up for the night, Harvey entered the foyer, through the front doors.

He walked up to Josh and whispered something in his ear. Josh looked at him in surprise, asked him something, which Harvey nodded in response to. Josh turned to Emily. "Kristy's car is gone," he told her. A cacophony of voices rose, and he raised his voice, once again holding his hands up. "Everyone, Kristy's car is missing. We just confirmed it." There were general groans. "I know, I'm sorry we didn't think to check that in the first place. We're obviously guessing she decided to leave, though we don't know why. Let's get some sleep and we'll figure things out in the morning."

The guests started to shuffle up the stairs. I could hear murmurs and words like "inconsiderate" and "waste of time," and "drama queen." I stood there, lost in my own thoughts, chewing on my bottom lip. She left all her luggage, her clothes, her perfume, her designer handbags... Had she taken anything with her at all? I was about to say something, stop everyone and yell out that this made no sense. Then I stopped myself. That must mean she was coming back. Obviously. God, I was more tired than I realized. And maybe Ben was right; perhaps I was jumping to conclusions, or looking for things that weren't really there.

I dragged myself to my room and got ready for bed as quickly as possible. I didn't bother to wash the makeup off my face. I triple-checked the lock on the door and climbed into bed. I didn't bother to run this time when I turned off the lights. I felt exhausted and defeated all at once.

I tossed and turned for what felt like hours, my mind spinning, running over the same tracks over and over. Kristy, the painting, the drawing, the strange symbols. Had that been one of the runes on her leg? No, it was just a scratch. Then there was Ben, his running shoes. Before finally, finally drifting off to a fitful sleep.

In my dream, I walked the corridors of the Hideaway House. Past a room I recognized as the dining hall, then further down, past the library. I continued to make my way through the darkened hallways, as though I were searching for someone. Down a narrow corridor, I heard a voice behind me, a man's voice. "Cassie." Was all he said, before coming up behind me and sliding his right arm around my waist. I felt his warm breath on the side of my face. He kissed me, right at the base of my neck, sending shivers up and down my body. I felt an aching in my core. I pressed against him, arching my back, turning my head, so his lips met my mouth. As he kissed me, I felt his hands move up to my chest. I wanted him to touch me. I wanted him to–

A sound, like thunder, crashed through the corridor. He pulled away from me and was running, heading back down the hallway. I knew that if I didn't stop him, something awful, something horrible, would happen.

I followed him, running as hard as I could, starting to sob. The hallway turned left, then right, then back again. Turns I hadn't taken on the way here. I came out eventually onto a landing, a wooden railing stretching off to my left. I was on the main landing at the top of the stairs. Even in my dream I was confused. How had I ended up upstairs? I heard a scratching, ticking sort of sound coming up from the darkness. Then a light *click, click, click,* that reminded me of the sound of a dog's claws on a tile floor, echoing from the foyer below.

The sound grew nearer, with a dragging *thump* that followed behind it, in a rhythm now. My heart pounded, threatening to burst out of my chest. I stared at the top of the stairs, frozen in horror. All I could do was wait.

It scaled the railing. One horribly long appendage, like a pale spider leg, ending in some kind of deformed hoof, unfurled itself over the top of the railing. It was followed by others... too many others. Its skin was almost white, but it was covered in black tiger stripes of writing. Its body followed, sliding, and landing with a thump on the carpet. My stomach twisted and churned. It had a body that was human-like, with legs and arms that were unnaturally long. Its head was twisted upside down, with the face of a woman, mouth open impossibly wide, as though in a silent scream of pain. Her long hair was tangled and twisted in knots with sticks and leaves caught in her filthy tresses. Antlers rose impossibly out of its back. Her eyes rolled in terror. The thing started to walk slowly towards me, the legs at unnatural angles. I could hear its bones cracking, breaking, and reforming with every step. It scuttled sideways, shuffling like a crab, heading closer. I opened my mouth to scream, but no sound came out.

Finally, willing my body to move, I turned to flee back down the hall the way I had come. A gorgeous woman with a head of red curls in an old-fashioned maid costume stood directly behind me. She tilted her head to the side and gave me a sympathetic smile. She unfurled her hand, palm facing out to me, and whispered, "Run."

Right as she blew a palmful of powder in my face, I breathed in involuntarily, coughing and sputtering. I heard the sound of the wind chimes ringing clear as a bell and a dog barking in the distance. I remained conscious just long enough to feel my eyes rolling back into my head as I collapsed to the ground.

It was dark, but the moon was visible just over the treetops, bathing everything in pale light. I was barefoot, I could feel the damp grass sliding over my feet, tickling my ankles as I walked. There were fires all around me, tall piles tied together, corn stalks, the tips burning. I approached at a steady pace. There were voices chanting up ahead. A tall figure loomed in the darkness, a man, made out of branches, the fires were already being lit at his feet next to the great tree, its leaves swaying back and forth in the breeze. I could smell the scent of fall, of mystery, of change, in the night air. I breathed it deeply, my blood singing, my pulse pounding. The figures around it danced in the moonlight, in the firelight. I came closer, joining them. They pulled me in. I swayed, chanted with them, and sang. I felt alive, and close to death, all at once.

I wanted to stay here forever, in this moment, with all of them. They painted our foreheads, the old ones, dipping their thumbs in the bowl of blood. It was warm on my skin. A wreath of flowers, the blood-red roses gleaming in the flickering light, was set on my head like a crown. I drank deeply from the cup they offered us, one at a time, like my sisters. The girl next to me turned, her red curls shining, as though streaked with threads of fire. She cupped my face in her hands, kissing my forehead. Her lips came away red with blood. She looked at me and we laughed, her green eyes sparkled with starlight, and the blood in my veins sang. "Dance with us," she whispered. "You're home now." And I knew she was right. I was. I was finally home. Tears of joy tracked down my cheeks as she took my hand and led me into the circle.

I saw the bodies then. They were hanging, swaying with us, to the sound of our voices. I looked up at the sky, throwing my arms wide. I laughed, and she laughed with me. We danced together for what felt like an age, a lifetime. I twirled, spinning faster and faster, until the dizziness took me. Then I slept and remembered no more.

I woke up hot, covered in sweat, the tail end of a scream leaving my throat. I gasped for air, throwing the blankets off me. I heard footsteps out in the hallway, pounding towards my door. The door flew open and slammed against the wall.

"Cassie!" I heard a voice exclaim. I scrambled backwards in my bed instinctively, as Emily bounded across the room, her blonde hair streaming behind her, shining in the pale moonlight.

"Cassie," she repeated. "What's happened? Are you okay?" She clambered onto the bed, grabbed my hands, and huddled next to me.

"I– I'm okay," I said in a shaky voice, my throat feeling raw. "It was just a dream. Just a bad dream."

"Oh, Cassie." She hugged me with one arm. "It's okay, let me get the lights."

She left me and made her way back to the doorway, flipping on the lights. They blinded me momentarily, so I squeezed my eyes shut. That was when she screamed. I screamed back, moving backwards and hitting the headboard. My eyes flew open, and, seeing her expression, I scrambled, practically falling off the bed, frantic to get away from whatever she stared at behind me.

I made it over to her by the door, and grabbing her arm, I clung to her, turning to look back at the bed. A bundle of plants hung over the head of my bed, just like the one in Kristy's room. I saw a piece of corn stalk in the back, hanging down past the bunch of blood-red roses. Something furry was visible from here, in the center of the bundle. Rivulets of red ran down the wall beneath. For a moment, I thought there was blood all over the comforter on the bed as well, large, scattered gobs of it. It took me a second to recognize what they were: rose petals.

Emily pulled me backwards out of the room. I was barely able to think straight as she led me quickly down a long winding hallway, to a door marked 'Josh.' She banged loudly with her fist on the door.

Josh emerged seconds later, eyes wide, his perfect hair disheveled and hanging down limply rather than slicked back like usual. "Emily," he breathed, "What is it?"

"In her room," Emily half sobbed, falling into him. He wrapped his arms around her and looked over her head at me, questioning. I shook my head.

"The same as it was in Kristy's," I told him. His eyes widened in surprise.

"But there's blood," Emily whispered into his chest, her voice muffled. "We're not sleeping there tonight. We're not."

Josh's brow creased. He looked angry. "Enough is enough. This is getting out of control."

The door next to us swung open into the room, sucking a rush of air out of the hallway. Mark's head peaked around the doorframe. "What's going on?"

"They found a bundle of creepy shit in Cassie's room," Josh explained. "Just like in Kristy's." Mark frowned, looking at me.

"It wasn't there when I fell asleep." I stared at him, my eyes widened, unfocusing, until I wasn't really seeing him. "I'm sure it... it wasn't there when I went to bed. That means... that means..." I couldn't continue. I started to tremble. I was freezing cold now. The damp sweat on my body had left me shivering, covered in goosebumps.

Mark walked over to me and reached up to wipe my forehead. "You have something on your forehead," he said. He lifted his fingers gingerly to his nose, sniffing them. "I think it's blood." Hot tears born out of fear started to trickle down my cheeks. He pulled me into his arms. "Hey, it's going to be okay," he murmured against my hair. "This ends tonight; it's going to be alright." I buried my face against his bare chest, sobbing. I remembered the blood on my forehead in my dream. How is that possible? Was that part real? Then I remembered the bouquet and the blood trickling down the wall above my bed. Of course, it must have dripped on me.

In between my sobs, I heard footsteps behind us in the hallway. Then Ben's voice asked in a low, urgent tone, "What happened?"

Josh explained to him in a hushed voice. I couldn't make out their words. They were both whispering. I reached an arm over Mark's shoulder, wiping my eyes, trying to dry up my tears. Their voices rose a little higher like they were arguing.

I finally turned around to face Ben. He saw my face and stopped; he looked horrified and furious all at once. I could only imagine what I looked like: tears and blood streaked all over. He turned back to Josh. "Yes," he said firmly. "We are." His jaw clenched, his chest rising and falling rapidly.

They stared at each other for a long moment before turning back to the three of us. *What was that about?* Josh turned to Emily and me, "The two of you will sleep here tonight." His tone left no room for arguing. "You can sleep in my bed; I'll sleep on the floor." We all started to protest at once. He held up his hands.

"Josh," Emily said, her voice steadier now. "Don't be ridiculous. You can't sleep on a hard wooden floor. You'll wreck your back. How many beds are there in this place? Don't be silly."

"I'm not being silly Em," he replied, "And I'm not letting you out of my sight. I'll sleep on the floor, in front of the door." We all looked back and forth at each other, unsure what to do next. The boys ended up arguing for another five minutes or so. Ben kept looking at me searchingly, like he was about to say something. I thought for a moment he was going to suggest I sleep in his room, but in the end, he said nothing.

After a few more moments of deliberating, most of which I tuned out for, the group somehow arrived at the solution of dragging the mattress from Mark's room into Josh's room. The guys would sleep on the mattress on the floor, giving the girls the proper bed. I guessed it was the quickest solution, if not the easiest. The three of them made quick work though of dragging the mattress, still covered in its fitted sheet, onto the floor of Josh's room. Emily and I helped bring the bedding and pillows over. I ducked into the bathroom in Josh's room to clean the blood off my forehead.

Ben and Mark left to go investigate my room, returning about ten minutes later. Ben's jaw was clamped shut tightly in anger. They spoke with Josh out in the hall for a while, what seemed to take forever, while Emily and I settled into bed. We huddled next to each other. I lay there, eyes wide in the darkness, straining to make out any words in their low rumbling murmurs. They had left the door cracked open. I could only make out fragments here and there. "... don't know anything... that can't be..." I could tell they were all angry. Ben was clearly furious.

Josh and Mark returned to the room, closing and locking the door, they settled in to sleep. I lay awake, listening to the calming cacophony of the others breathing. I didn't know how I was going to fall back to sleep tonight. I thought of Ben, alone in his room and wondered if he was back to sleep yet. I pictured him awake, pacing back and forth as he seemed to when he was upset, or thinking. I thought of the other girls, sleeping in their rooms on the other side of the house, unaware of what had happened. Should we have woken them all up too? Where would we all sleep then? We should leave, I thought, my eyes starting to get heavy. We should leave this house, and not come back.

THURSDAY

Somehow, I did manage to fall asleep, although I had no memory of it when I awoke. Sunlight filtered through the curtains. It took me a moment upon waking to remember where I was. I felt a momentary schism in my brain. I knew I wasn't quite where I belonged but couldn't remember why. I rolled over and saw Emily, sitting next to me, propped up against a stack of pillows. She smiled when she saw I was awake. "Hey," she said.

"Hey," I replied, "good morning." I sat up and stretched, looking around the room, getting my bearings. The blankets on the mattress on the floor by the door lay in a crumpled heap. The guys had already woken up and left the room.

Emily yawned and stretched. "How long have you been awake?" I asked. I hoped she hadn't been waiting for me for very long.

"Not too long," she replied, "I asked them to bring up breakfast for us because I thought you might not be up for heading downstairs right away."

I smiled at her. "Thanks, Emily, that was really nice of you."

Emily smiled back, "A little sustenance will do us both some good. And more importantly, coffee."

I laughed a little and nodded in agreement. I didn't want to think about what had happened last night, but it was hard to think of anything else at the moment. "Emily," I said thoughtfully, "I've been thinking..."

"In your sleep?" Emily interrupted, she looked amused. She climbed out of bed, pulling a silk scrunchy from around her wrist, she tipped her head upside down and started pulling her hair into a bun on top of her head.

"Yes," I chuckled, "in my sleep..." I had done a lot more than that in my sleep last night, I thought darkly. "Something was bothering me. I couldn't think of what at first, but then I realized what it was."

"Was it the creepy bundle of roses covered in blood? Cause if so, same," Emily responded.

"No," I said, getting a little exasperated. She seemed to be in a much more lighthearted mood than I was this morning. "It was my door. It was locked when I went to bed last night. I'm 100% sure of it. In fact, I checked it multiple times. But obviously someone came in my room last night, and when you heard me scream, you ran to check on me and opened the door yourself."

She'd finished messing with her hair and stood looking at me, waiting for me to finish. "That means," I continued, "whoever is doing this has a key."

Emily thought for a moment, chewing her lip. "Yeah, I guess you must be right. But what does that tell us?"

"First of all, it tells us this is an inside job. Meaning it makes it almost impossible for it to be someone sneaking into the house somehow, trying to mess with us. It's someone inside the house, someone who has access to a key to my room, to Kristy's room possibly, to," I threw my hands up, "who knows where." Emily nodded thoughtfully. "Are they different keys?

135

The keys that would open, say, my door and someone else's in the same hallway?"

Emily thought for a moment before responding. "I honestly don't know Cassie. I hadn't thought about it before, but I guess they could all be different keys or the same key. Sort of like a master key? I don't know, but we can find out, or Josh can. If he isn't sure, we can talk to the staff. Mrs. Evans, someone must know the answer to that, I'm sure. Although," she said, pausing for a moment, "I'm guessing Kristy's door would have been unlocked, right? If someone went in there while she was gone, while we were all downstairs, it's not like she could have locked her door behind her."

"No," I said slowly, "you're right. Not unless she had a key, too." We sat, lost in thought for a moment. "Well, in any case, that sounds like a good plan; let's see what Josh can find out." There was a soft knock at the door, and Emily went over and opened it.

A maid, a young woman in a plain, simple black dress and black flats, walked into the room, smiling and wishing us good morning. She set a silver tray piled with dishes on the dresser. A second girl carried in a second tray, balancing a huge carafe filled with what I assumed must be coffee and two heavy mugs. The first girl asked us if we needed anything else, and Emily told them no, we were all set for now, and thanked them. I thought of the maid in the old-fashioned uniform I had seen in my dream last night. She certainly wasn't wearing the same dress as these maids were. And why had the same girl been in the last part of my dream, taking part in the ritual with me? None of it made any sense; what a crazy dream. I thought of how she had said I was home and shuddered visibly; a thrill of dread mixed with exhilaration flooded through me.

Emily gave me a strange look before turning to pour me a coffee. She added cream, stirred it, and brought it to me in bed. We ended up bringing the trays over, too, and we ate a feast of waffles, sausages, and various fruits. We sipped our coffees, and we chatted; our conversation turned towards lighter things, like the wedding festivities, what time family would start to arrive tomorrow, who would avoid who, and who would get drunk; Emily told me what her cousins were up to lately, and the drama between her Mom and her Aunt. I forgot all about the events of last night for a moment and ended up feeling grateful we got to spend this time together. With everything going on, I felt I had hardly spoken with Emily this week.

Eventually, Josh and Mark came back to the room to check on us. They escorted us back to our wing. Mark checked my bedroom first before I entered, and then he waited outside my room while I quickly showered and dressed. I told him he didn't need to, but he insisted it was okay. I was grateful to see the bundle and the rose petals had been removed. The wall behind the bed had been washed clean. There were fresh linens and a different comforter on the bed, too. As I dressed, I bent down to pull on my sock and froze. Balanced on one foot, I started to tip over and had to catch myself on the bed. I swung my right foot onto the bed and peered closely at it. I ran a finger over the mark on the top of my foot. It was slightly raised. It looked almost like a pointy letter 'B.' *What on earth? How had I gotten a scratch like that?* I thought of the scratch Kristy had been complaining about. She thought it had been from Mike scratching her horsing around in the water. What was happening here? I felt a shiver go down my spine.

Before leaving the room, I checked the fur coat. The note was still there, tucked into the outer pocket. I breathed a sigh of relief. Only one person knew where that note was hidden, and I really didn't want it to have been him in my room last night. I unfolded the paper and scanned it, searching for anything that looked like the pointy 'B' on my foot. I found it easily in several places. It was scattered throughout the writing. I folded the paper again, placed it back in the coat pocket, and went out to meet Mark in the hallway.

Mark and I were walking down the corridor towards the stairs when I suddenly stopped. He kept going a few paces before he realized I had stopped behind him.

"What?" He asked, coming back over to me. "Cassie, are you okay?"

I stood there for a moment, thinking, and then said, "Yeah, I'm fine; I just remembered I forgot something in my room. I'll be right back." I went back to my room, grabbed the folded piece of paper out of the coat pocket again. Slipping it into my front jeans pocket, I ran back to meet him.

I could've kicked myself. What was I thinking? It hadn't even occurred to me this morning that I should tell Emily about the paper. She knew about the deer Ben and I had found in the woods and obviously all about the deer head, but not the paper. Unless Ben had told Josh, I supposed, then she might know about it. But if so, it seemed odd she hadn't mentioned it to me. I would find a moment today to bring it up and show it to her. Maybe I could pull both her and Josh aside and share it with both of them. I thought it should be pretty obvious now, to everyone, that there was something very wrong going on here.

We made our way downstairs and found the dining hall and the guy's lounge empty. Mark frowned, scratching his head, trying to think of where everyone might be. Finally, he decided we should check the game room next. He led me back upstairs to the side of the house that held the guy's wing. He turned down a different branch of the hallway and led me through a set of double doors.

We had entered what could only be a large ballroom. I stared in awe up at the ceiling covered in gorgeous paintings. The scene on one half of the ceiling depicted a field overflowing with an abundance of some sort of crop: I'm guessing wheat, with workers out in the field, cutting the wheat down with large handheld scythes. The other half of the ceiling showed a party on horseback; they were hunting, their dogs running ahead of them, scenting the air. A stag ran out in front of them; its head twisted back as though watching his doom approach. I shuddered.

Mark didn't seem to notice, or care about the ballroom. I remembered he had probably been in here many times before. He led me on through and out a set of double doors on the other side. Down a narrow corridor to the right, we entered a large space. The room felt dim and cozy. The walls were painted a dark, rich emerald. It was full of oversized leather armchairs, with small round tables scattered throughout. There was a billiards table in the middle of the room and what looked like a full bar against the wall off to the left. There were several games of darts hanging on the walls. There were also heads. A lot of them. Stag, elk, even a black bear. I avoided the dull, dead eyes staring down at us. The far wall was filled from corner to corner with built-in wooden cabinets, glass-faced, containing more shotguns than I had ever seen in one place at a time.

A small group was gathered on the far side of the room, in front of the gun case, around a circle of armchairs, clearly having a tense conversation. Emily, Josh, Wes, and Ben were all there. I was a little surprised to see Mike and Amy as well. We approached the group, and Josh and Wes stood up when they saw us coming. There weren't enough chairs in the circle. Wes offered me his, insisting I take it. He and Ben remained standing, along with Mark.

"So." Mark swung his arms back and forth. "What's the plan for today? How do we root out who's doing this and put a stop to it?"

Josh frowned. "I really don't know that we can," he sighed, "We don't have much to go on."

Emily said, "Cassie, tell them your idea about the key." I nodded and repeated our conversation from that morning.

Josh looked pleased. "That's something I can easily find out," he replied, "It will give us something at least, a clue to who could be doing this. There must be a limited number of people who have a key."

"Or have access to one," Ben spoke up.

We all digested that in silence for a moment. "And there's this," I said, pulling the paper out of my pocket. I handed it to Josh first. He studied it in silence, eyebrows raised. He passed it to Mark next, then Wes, and finally Emily. Ben handed it to Amy when it was his turn. I watched everyone's reactions as they studied the paper, exclaiming over what was on it, pointing to the drawings. Emily stared at me in shock.

"Cassie..." her voice trailed off. "What is this?" I told them all about finding the paper.

"I think the markings are runes," Ben explained. He told us about the Celts. "Runes have their root in Germanic peoples, the Norse, and, eventually, the Celts used runes. They were a form of writing, but they were also believed to contain power or magic. A Norse legend claims that Odin hung upside down, by his feet, from a tree," he cleared his throat, "for something like nine days, and that's how he harnessed the power of runes."

"That's an odd coincidence," I mumbled. Ben nodded.

"There are definitely some... pagan themes to all of this," he added. "Not just the runes, the dead animals, they could be reminiscent of animal sacrifices. The..." he struggled for a moment, "the girl," he nodded toward the paper, "could also be a sacrifice. The deer in the woods... the blood was missing. The crops drawn here; they could be writing about the harvest. There was a holiday, a celebration of sorts, but it traditionally takes place in the spring. They called it Beltane. It was a celebration of the coming of spring, but it was also about fertility. They would light bonfires, usually two. They believed the fire was purifying and would promote fertility.

140

Sacrifices of animals were common back then. They would sacrifice an animal to appease the gods." I thought back to the horseback ride with Harvey. He had mentioned something about a festival being held here at the estate to celebrate the harvest.

"In the hopes of being fertile?" Mike asked.

Ben nodded. "Pretty much. Fertility of the land, as well as people." We sat, contemplating. I stared at him. Everything he said made sense to me and was along the same lines I had been thinking, especially after my dream last night.

"So, what," Mike said after a moment. "Someone is trying to sacrifice animals to the gods? Why are they leaving this shit in the house for us to find?"

A few people shook their heads. No one had any answers.

"Was there a holiday that took place in the fall?" I asked Ben curiously. I recalled the night air smelling like fall in my dream. He thought for a moment.

"There are two that I can remember. There was Samhain, which is the holiday our modern-day Halloween is based on. That's at the end of October, though, obviously, and involves communion with the dead. There's also a holiday called Mabon, which celebrates the autumnal equinox. So that takes place towards the end of September, right around this time, actually. It was mostly a celebration of the harvest, giving thanks. It was also tied to the Oak King."

"Who the fuck is the Oak King?" Mike asked.

"He was sort of a god, a deity of the woods. He was also known as the Green Man." I felt a chill go down my spine. I thought of the dark figure I had seen disappear into the woods. "He symbolized the cycle of life: death and rebirth. He represented several things: vegetation, wine, madness, and fertility. He was a horned god, often depicted with deer antlers, but sometimes they were shorter, more like devil horns. Think of him as like the pagan version of Bacchus, the Roman god of wine, but his mythology is also loosely related to the Christian devil."

Mark was still looking at Ben. "You seem to know a lot about all of this, Ben." Ben met his eyes. An uncomfortable silence fell over the group.

"Ben knows a lot about a lot of things," Josh said in a dangerously quiet voice.

We sat there for a few minutes, no one knew what to say or do next. My mind was racing. This had to all be related. Why hadn't Ben told me more about all of this earlier, when I'd shown him the paper? I thought of the scratch on my foot. Maybe I would show it to him later and see if he knew what it meant. He told me he didn't know how to read runes, but he certainly also seemed to know a lot more about them than he had originally let on. Surely though, the scratch must just be a weird coincidence.

Finally, Emily stood up and clapped her hands together. "Right, well, I think we have two options. We either call off the wedding and send everyone home—"

"Babe!" Josh exclaimed, staring at the back of her head in shock.

"Or," she continued, ignoring him, "we continue on as we have planned. As far as I see it, no one has gotten hurt. The worst that has happened is we've all had a few scares. I, for one, don't feel comfortable sleeping alone from now on, but we can come up with a solution for that." She gazed around the room, her eyes meeting each of ours, waiting for our response.

"Did they ever sacrifice humans?" I asked.

Ben turned to find me looking at him. He met my eyes. I flushed momentarily, thinking suddenly of the first part of my dream last night. I had never seen the man's face in the corridor, but I knew it was meant to be him.

"Yes," he said simply, "they did." Silence fell again.

No one seemed entirely up to the task of telling Emily and Josh to cancel their wedding. I thought over Emily's words and realized she was right. Technically, no one had been hurt. That we knew of, anyway. There was still the mystery of Kristy's flight in the middle of the night.

We left the game room with more questions than answers. But Josh had a plan to follow up with the staff about the keys. For now, we all agreed we would go nowhere alone. We would only travel around the house in groups of at least two people. Josh and Emily spread the word to the others, explaining what had happened last night and that everyone should be on the lookout for anything odd and report it back to the group.

The plan for that day was to spend some time in the morning lounging in and around the pool. Then, a light lunch was planned in the dining hall. Ironically, the afternoon's activity was hunting. Emily and Josh had figured mainly the guys would want to go hunting, but that the girls might either choose to join or to lounge outside.

I sat curled up on a lounge chair near the wall, away from the pool. My arms wrapped around my legs, I stared into the water, thinking. I couldn't help but glance occasionally at the odd scratch on my foot. I was able to convince myself it was a coincidence, until I looked at it again, that is. It was just way too deliberate and purposeful looking. But when could it have happened?

I recalled the feeling of damp grass tickling my ankles during my dream. The feel and smell of the chilly fall air. How everything had been drenched in moonlight. Moonlight shone through the bedroom window when I woke up; I remembered Emily's hair shining in the dark. Had I somehow gone outside? Walked through the damp grass to the willow? Maybe I scratched my foot on a stick or something outside. Then there was the blood on my forehead. The details of the dream had just felt too real. But how did I end up back in my bed then?

I tucked my marked foot underneath the other one, feeling self-conscious as Emily came over and took a seat on the chair pulled up next to mine. She slumped down in the chair with a loud sigh.

"It's going to be okay, Em," I said softly. Most of the others were playing and horsing around in the water. It reminded me of the beach. I looked around the room. Ben was notably absent. I realized then, with a little jolt, that Josh and Wes were nowhere in sight as well.

"I guess," she said glumly.

I glanced at Emily sideways for a moment. "Em, what were you worried about? That first night, right after I arrived?"

"What do you mean?" She asked, whipping her head to me. "I wasn't worried about anything."

"Out on the balcony," I said gently. "I saw your face; you were definitely worried about something." Emily met my eyes for a long moment before shrugging nonchalantly.

"I dunno," she said, "I don't remember feeling worried about anything then. Maybe I was thinking about something about the wedding. It's been a lot," she finished simply.

I nodded, watching her. "Yeah, okay, that could have been it. But if it were something else...if something else strange happened earlier in the week, I hope you would tell me. You can trust me, Emily."

She looked at me sharply, studying me for a moment. Then I saw her shoulders relax. "I know that, Cassie. I do trust you. It's..." she paused, lowering her voice and looking around the room. "It's not anything like that. Nothing else strange, I mean, like what happened last night. The head, or the bouquet things...nothing else like that has happened. It's just..." she trailed off. I grabbed her arm, leaning in closer as she stared into the distance, thinking. Finally. I knew she knew more than she was willing to admit.

"It's just a…feeling that I have. I…I can't really explain it." She turned to look at me, her eyes wide. They looked green at the moment, freckled with gold. Her eyes were like that, always changing color based on what she was wearing and her surroundings. "You'll think I'm crazy," she whispered.

"No, Emily," I said in a rushed whisper. "Trust me, after what I've seen, and felt this week, I won't." She studied me again for a moment before nodding. Then she looked around the room again.

"Have you noticed anything strange with the guys?" she whispered.

"Like what?" I asked, my brow furrowing.

"Like…" she smiled and laughed a little uncomfortably. "I told you it's going to sound crazy…but remember how I was joking the other night about them being like, a cult?" I frowned, thinking back. The first night, with Mark in the hallway, she had mentioned they were like a cult. I nodded slowly. And he had said no, they were more like the mafia.

"Yeah," I whispered back. "I remember now. You were joking around about it with Mark."

"Yeah," she said, biting her lower lip. "I was kidding. But…sometimes, it does feel like that. Like, I don't even know, Cass…but like, maybe they are all…involved in something. Something I don't know about. Does that sound crazy?"

I watched the guys playing in the water with some of the girls. One of them lifted Blair and tossed her a few feet away, muscles bulging. They did all seem to be in oddly good shape, I mused. Most of them were built; I had noticed that after horseback riding the other day. "What's made you think that?" I asked.

"I don't really know," she continued, "it hasn't been any one thing, but I've just been getting this weird feeling, especially lately. This week…once we were all here together. Like they all know something I don't. I trust Josh, obviously." She bit her lower lip again, frowning. "But I've just had this weird feeling. It's probably nothing. I mean, a bunch of them were in a frat together in college...maybe it's just like, the leftovers of that whole mentality, you know?" She looked at me hopefully. I nodded slowly. "They've all been out here before, I think. Loads of times for most of them. You don't think..." she trailed off again, looking worried, "you don't think they know more about all this weird stuff than they're admitting, do you?" We looked at each other for a long moment. Was she telling me everything she knew? I had seen her whispering with the guys, too. I took a deep breath.

"What's the tea ladies?" We both jumped slightly, startled by Mark standing a few feet away from us, dripping. He grinned and ran his hands through his wet hair, slicking it back. How long had he been there? Had he heard what we were saying?

"Nothing!" Emily said brightly, smiling up at him. "Just silly gossip about people back home." She gave him her most dazzling smile. She lied so easily, I thought uncomfortably. Mark nodded, grinning back.

"What time is lunch?" He jerked a thumb back towards the group in the pool. "The natives are getting restless. And hungry," he added, grinning. Emily laughed and nodded, standing up. She helped to pass out towels to everyone. I was still completely dry, having never gotten in the pool. It was odd that Josh, Wes, and Ben were still missing. I hadn't seen Josh and Wes leave the pool, but they had been here at least. I didn't think Ben had ever joined us.

We made our way past the guy's lounge on our way upstairs to change, and Emily peeked inside. I followed her as she ducked into the room. We found Ben sitting alone by the fire. "Hey," Emily said, "have you seen Josh and Wes?"

Ben shook his head. "No, I haven't. I thought they were swimming with you?" He eyed me grudgingly. So, he was in here alone, sulking this whole time.

"Okay," Emily mused. "Thanks. We're heading up to change. Lunch will be in about a half hour." Ben nodded, and Emily turned to leave. She stopped and turned back to me. "I'm going to go check the game room; I want to ask Josh something. I'll see you at lunch."

"Okay." I nodded. "Sounds good." She gave me a weak smile and left. I looked back at Ben. His face was like storm clouds. Clearly, he was still upset with me for suspecting his involvement with Kristy's disappearance. I felt slightly guilty about that, although after the conversation I had just had with Emily, it seemed even more warranted at this point.

"Ben..." I started before trailing off. "I know you're upset with me..." I didn't know what to say to him. This was all too complicated.

"It's fine," he said flatly, "I'm over it."

"Are you?" I asked, eyebrows raised. "You don't seem like it. Is something else bothering you then?"

He looked up at me, his dark eyes wide. His expression suddenly looked more sad than angry. "You don't need to worry about me, Cassie." He sighed. "I don't deserve it." I started to shake my head, but he nodded. "No, really. Just...I just wish you could trust me. But it's clearly my fault that you don't."

I stared at him. This was the most honest he'd been with me all week. "Can I?" I asked slowly. "Can I trust you, Ben?" He nodded at me solemnly. "Okay..." I started, thinking rapidly, "tell me what you were whispering about with Josh last night."

He raised an eyebrow. "Last night?" He asked, eyes flickering back and forth.

"In the hallway last night," I prompted him. "After we found the...thing, in my room." He stared at me for a long moment before responding.

"I just..." he licked his lips. Was he nervous? "I just told him I thought we were in danger."

"In danger?" I asked, my eyebrows raising in surprise. "In danger from what, Ben?" He looked away from me, off to the back of the room. Was he looking over at the painting of Josh's ancestor? Where I found the paper? I felt a chill go down my spine.

He looked back at me. "I wish I knew, Cassie."

"What kind of answer is that, Ben? Tell me why you think we're in danger."

"I don't know. The bouquet things...the deer head. The carcass strung up, with the blood missing. The paper you found...I just have a bad feeling that someone is...planning something."

I nodded slowly. "Oh, so I'm not just grasping at straws now? Being melodramatic? What changed your mind?"

He stared at me in frustration. "Your face last night. Covered in blood."

I shrugged, looking away. I thought of the look he gave me when he saw my face; when he'd found me in Mark's arms. I blushed slightly. I wondered which he had been more upset about.

He continued. "There are too many things happening at once for it to all be a coincidence."

I nodded. "I agree." I thought back over my conversation with Emily. "Did you go to the same college as Josh?" I asked him. He seemed startled by the sudden change in topic.

"Yes..." he said slowly. "We both went to Duke for undergrad, and then I went to Harvard for grad school. Why?"

I ignored his question, nodding. "And you met Mark there?" He nodded slowly. Did he seem uneasy about my line of questioning? "And were you in a fraternity together?"

He gave me a quizzical look, his brows wrinkling. "Well, yeah, we were. I mean," he rolled his eyes slightly, "Josh made me join with him...I never would have gotten in otherwise." He licked his lips again. "But I don't see what that has to do with anything."

I nodded, thinking. "And did you...did your frat have any...traditions or rituals? Anything odd like that?"

Ben stared at me now. "Cassie, no. Our frat didn't have any pagan rituals if that's what you're asking me." He rubbed his hands over his eyebrows, sliding them down his face. "Jesus...I mean, there was some hazing, some stupid shit. But it was your run-of-the-mill, stereotypical fraternity stuff. Not anything like this."

I flushed a little. "Okay, well, fine then. And how many of the guys here this week were in your frat?"

He thought for a moment. "I dunno, let me think..." He was silent momentarily, counting in his head. "Six of us...Mark, Josh and me, obviously. Then Mike, and Mike H., and Jack. But he joined later." He looked up at me earnestly again. "But Cassie, this has nothing to do with the frat."

"Okay." I nodded, sighing. Well, that was a dead end, then, assuming he was telling the truth. "And you guys aren't...part of anything now?" I asked, crossing my arms over my chest. "You aren't doing anything...involving any of this stuff?"

Ben just stared at me for a moment, then he stood up suddenly and started pacing back and forth. "Cassie, I don't get it. Why are you insisting I know something about all this? What did I do to make you think that?" He sounded exasperated again.

"You didn't do anything, Ben. I just...I dunno. You're close to Josh, and you know the family well. You've come here how many times? Since you were a kid, you said. Something odd is happening here, and it's all tied into this house..." I trailed off. I had been about to add *to this family*, but the thought made me uncomfortable.

"So, you think Josh has something to do with this stuff?" he asked incredulously. "Josh is just as baffled as I am," he insisted.

"And his family?" I asked, staring back at him. He met my eyes for a moment before looking away uncomfortably. "I don't know anything about that, Cassie."

I stared at him in disbelief. He was lying to me. I knew it in my gut: he was either lying or withholding something. "Yeah," I said, rolling my eyes. "Okay, Ben."

"Seriously?" he said, holding his hands out palms up. "You still don't believe me?"

I looked him right in the eyes. "No, Ben. I don't. I think you're hiding something from me. I'm not sure what. But you let me know when you're ready to be honest with me."

He flushed deeply, his chest rising and falling rapidly now. He ran a hand through his hair. "Yeah? Well, trust takes two people, Cassie." He glared back at me.

"And what have I done to betray your trust, Ben?" I asked him quietly. We glared at each other. He continued to breathe rapidly. Eventually, he dropped his eyes to the floor. He was clearly frazzled. So, there was something, then. Something I'd done that hurt him? My gut twisted, my heart started to race, as I watched him. Why did he have to look so...hot, when he was angry? God, this was so stupid, what was I doing?

"Huh," I said. I was angry now, too. Angry at myself more than anything. I couldn't seriously be falling for this guy. "Big surprise... you won't tell me, will you?" He met my eyes only briefly, before turning and pacing away from me, further into the room. I gave up in frustration, heading upstairs to change out of my bathing suit; I left him alone in the lounge.

Lunch was in the dining hall. Most of the group seemed to be in a light-hearted mood, laughing and chatting. Ben kept to himself, not speaking to anyone. Emily seemed to be back to her usual, cheery self; back to playing hostess. She laughed and joked with the others.

Before we left to head outside for hunting, I grabbed Emily by the arm and said, "Hey, has anyone heard from Kristy today?"

She sighed, pulling her cell out of her pocket. "Nothing yet," she said, "I've been keeping an eye on my phone, but then again, I'm not sure I'd get it anyway."

I nodded. "Maybe when we're out hunting? If we go far enough away from the property, towards the village, maybe you can get a signal out there and try calling her?"

Emily's brow lifted; she looked relieved. "Yeah." She nodded. "That's a great idea. I'll bring my phone with me."

A tent had been set up again out back, with plenty of drink options and some snacks. We had a gun safety lesson from the grounds crew and Harvey. They had even set up target practice on the back field. Josh and Wes walked around, giving everyone pointers. I hung back at first, projecting an air of aloof disgust that I didn't try very hard to hide. The last thing I wanted to see right now, or ever again, quite frankly, was another dead deer. Given everything that had happened, I thought it was honestly a little tasteless not to cancel.

But, as I cradled the shotgun open over the crook of my arm, I thought it might not hurt to learn how to shoot a gun. I had no intention of actually shooting at any animals today, but a little target practice might not be bad. I lined up at one of the targets when it was my turn. Josh came over to help; he adjusted my stance and my grip and explained again how to aim correctly.

"You'll want to brace yourself," he explained, "it's going to kick back more than you'd expect. Your shoulder might be a little sore."

I aimed the best I could, and when everything felt right, I squeezed the trigger. I actually hit the target on my first try, off to the far-right edge, but still. The stock had kicked back hard, just like Josh had warned me. I could already tell my shoulder was going to be sore tomorrow. I took several more practice shots before admitting to Josh reluctantly that this was kind of fun.

He laughed, clapping me on the back. "That a girl!" He exclaimed. "She's a natural!" He called out to Emily. She laughed and gave us a thumbs-up. I grinned back, glad we could still have a few moments of fun.

"Hey," Eric said, turning to Josh, "don't we need hunting permits to do this?"

Josh chuckled a little, patting him on the back as he passed, making his way over to help Catherine. "We don't need to worry about things like hunting permits." Eric frowned. "The local law enforcement is pretty minimal out here. Besides, they pretty much let us do whatever we want; as long as we stay on our own property."

When it was time to head out into the woods, we broke up into small groups. I made sure Emily was in my group. I wanted to be there when she tried to call Kristy to see if she could get through. I still had a nagging feeling in the pit of my stomach that something wasn't right.

Mark somehow ended up in our group. He was trying to help me correct my aim; I kept pulling to the right. He stood behind me, wrapping his arms around me, adjusting my grip on the gun and helping me aim. I could feel Ben's glowering presence and his eyes on us. He walked away from the group a few feet, running his hands through his hair. I looked away, my mouth in a grim line. I was going to ignore him. All he had to do was talk to me; be honest with me. But clearly, he wasn't able or willing to do so. He continued to watch us as we prepared to leave. I was a little surprised when he made no effort to join us, but really, I couldn't have cared less.

On our way out through the woods, I couldn't help but scan the trees at eye level. I saw nothing unusual. Mike and Amy were with us as well. Mark was giving Mike shit about something a few paces behind me. Amy was her usual quiet self, but she walked beside me, keeping pace.

I turned to her, "You know, I'm pretty sure the deer are going to hear us coming from a mile away."

She laughed a little at that, looking back in the guy's direction. "Yeah, no kidding. They aren't exactly quiet, are they? Although," she said thoughtfully, "this isn't really likely to be a successful trip in the first place, is it?"

"Why's that?" I asked curiously, then couldn't help adding, "Because we all literally just learned how to shoot five minutes ago?" I noticed then that she wasn't holding a shotgun.

She giggled. "True, there is that. But also, I thought the best time for deer hunting was first thing in the morning. Right?"

I thought about that for a moment. "Hmm, I have limited experience, but that does sound right. I remember my dad going hunting once with a buddy of his. He left super early that morning before we even woke up."

Amy nodded. "I'm pretty sure it's around sunrise, or maybe also in the evening around dusk, which are the best times." She looked up the trail towards Emily and Josh. "I don't know why we're out here in the middle of the day. It doesn't make much sense." She shrugged and seemed to move on to think of other things, falling silent again.

I watched Emily and Josh now. They seemed deep in conversation, not necessarily arguing, just having some kind of intense discussion. Neither of them seemed to be paying any attention to their surroundings at all. Amy was right; it was a little strange. There certainly didn't seem to be much hunting going on during today's hunt.

We continued down the running trail at a steady pace, tracing the route Ben and I had taken the other morning. I thought again of Ben wearing his running shoes last night. There may be a perfectly good reason. Deep down, I didn't honestly believe he could have anything to do with whatever happened with Kristy, but at the same time, I reminded myself that I hardly knew him. While he somehow felt weirdly familiar to me, I had only known him for what, not even four days now? Part of me wanted to trust him, but how could I really be sure about him? How could I really be sure about any of them? Other than Emily, I technically couldn't trust anyone here. I felt a shudder go down my spine as my gut twisted slightly. It was Thursday. That meant I just had to get through the remainder of today; tomorrow would be the rehearsal dinner, and the wedding would take place on Saturday. Then I could leave. I could leave this horrible, dreadful house. And I would never come back.

We had reached the point that branched off to the right, where I remembered us turning around on my run with Ben. We hadn't seen a single deer. Or anything else, for that matter. Again, I was struck by the apparent lack of wildlife in these woods. Josh and Emily continued to the right, leading us closer to the village. I was getting bored and sick of traipsing through the woods. The humidity levels in the air seemed to have been rising steadily since this morning. It wasn't hot under the shady cover of the trees, but it was definitely sticky. I was about to call out and ask if we should turn around and head back when I remembered we had planned to get as close to the village as we could to call Kristy. Reluctantly, I kept silent, and we continued on.

I soon began to notice a change in the forest around us. The trees were becoming thinner, more widely spaced out, and there were more pine trees than there had been before. I wondered if we were finally approaching the edge of the forest. There was suddenly a clearing in the trees opening up on our right. Mike pointed it out and said this would be the perfect spot to sit and wait for deer. He explained we could choose a spot on the edge of the clearing and wait for the deer to wander through, and sometimes they slept in clearings like this too. The group agreed this was a good idea and we approached the edge of the clearing, looking for a spot. I stopped dead in my tracks. The others around me came up short as well, and we all just stared.

In the middle of the open clearing, which was about ten yards or so across, there was a large wooden frame built in the shape of a man. Dried corn stalks were tied around the base, around his legs. Bundles of cornstalks lay off to the side in piles.

"What the fuck!" Mike yelled. "Are you shitting me?" He looked away from the clearing pointing to where the trees became even thinner about 50 yards away from us. I could see what looked like open space through the branches. "It's the villagers," Mike exclaimed, "it has to be! They've been out here, building this freaking..." he fumbled for the right term, "burning man in the middle of the woods. They're trying to hide it here in the clearing." He turned to Josh. "Look, man, I don't know what the fuck is going on, but it has to be them. It's the only explanation that makes any sense."

Josh sighed, eyes closed, rubbing his temples. Emily stood there, shaking her head in disbelief. She looked up at Josh. "I can't believe this. He's right, Josh. It has to be them. You told me they were sort of living in another century out here. Clearly," she gestured, "they're living in the century of whatever the hell this is."

"How did they get in the house?" I piped up. Everyone turned to me. "If it's really them, if people in the village are involved, then how did they get inside the house? Into my locked bedroom? Into Kristy's room? It doesn't make any sense."

Mark looked thoughtful for a moment. "Well, I'm sure they found a way, Cassie. I mean, where do the staff come from? Most of them probably live here." He pointed in the direction Mike had. "They probably opened the front door for their neighbors, and let them walk right in."

I stared back at him. He was right. Harvey had told me as much. He said most of the staff were locals and had grown up in the village. Even he himself was a villager. He had also said he preferred not to sleep up at the house. I wondered briefly why that was, a shiver going down my spine. Harvey. I had to find him and speak with him. I nodded slowly, keeping my plan to myself. "You're right, Mark," I admitted, "that could be what's happened."

Mark nodded and put his hands on his hips. "Do we go down there now? Confront them?"

"What?" Josh said, "Just start knocking on random doors, asking if anyone's chopped off a deer's head lately and left it as a present for us?"

Amy snorted. Emily slid a hand over her face in frustration. "Look, we aren't doing anything right now. I'm going to the edge of the woods to try to call Kristy, if I can get a signal. Then we head back to the house."

Josh nodded. "I'll speak with Harvey and Mrs. Evans when we get back. Maybe we can set up some sort of watch tonight with the staff who are willing to. Maybe in shifts? I'll see if they have any ideas..." he trailed off.

Any ideas for what? Keeping us safe at night? Or who might be doing this?

We all followed Emily to the edge of the woods and waited while she called Kristy's cell. It rang repeatedly but kept going eventually to voicemail. The fact we got her voicemail at least was encouraging. At least we knew the calls were getting through. I craned my neck, peering down into the village that was now visible below us. I was tempted to suggest we follow Mark's suggestion and head down there to see if anyone might be willing to talk to us, maybe just about the burning man; we didn't have to mention anything about the house. But Emily was on the verge of tears by the time she hung up for the final time. She'd left Kristy a rambling message asking if she was okay and asking her to please call as soon as she could. The sky above us had been growing darker, and the wind was picking up. I thought I felt a raindrop or two as we stood and waited. Finally, Emily turned and stalked angrily back into the woods, and the rest of us turned to follow her.

Luckily, it was only just starting to sprinkle by the time we made it back to the house. Some of the girls who had opted not to go on the hunt had already abandoned the tent and headed back inside, not wanting to be caught out in a downpour again.

I stalled in the foyer. Unsure of what to do next. I wanted to ask to speak with Harvey myself, but now that Josh had shared he was already planning to, I didn't want the others to think it was odd. I certainly felt like Josh could be trusted, and Emily trusted him. Mark seemed harmless, if not a little bit of a loose cannon, especially when he had been drinking, but hadn't there been several times that I questioned whether he might know more than he seemed?

I tried to think back, remember the times I had seen them whispering quietly amongst themselves. Who had been there? Once it had been just

Josh, Emily and Ben. Mark wasn't there that time. Josh and Ben had been arguing back and forth about last night; but Ben claimed he had just been trying to convince Josh we were in danger. Then the three guys had all talked out in the hallway after that, while Emily and I were lying there waiting for them to come in to go to sleep. I had to agree with Emily. I had a sneaking suspicion that they all knew something I didn't. But maybe that was just my anxiety...my paranoia, talking.

I sighed in frustration, pacing back and forth now across the floor at the base of the staircase. I just felt like I needed to be doing something. I needed to take some sort of action, anything, to try to figure out what was really happening here.

I thought of the piece of paper covered in runes. That was really the most concrete piece of evidence we had at this point. I realized it was still in the front pocket of my jeans. I quickly reached my hand in to double-check and felt the rough corner of the paper. If my phone were working, I could look up what some of the symbols meant. Maybe there was a computer here somewhere that was hardwired in and had internet access.

I searched around the lower floor for Josh or even Wes, thinking they could help me, but they were nowhere in sight. One of the maids, I recognized her as one of the girls who had brought up breakfast for Emily and me, passed by me in the hallway, smiling shyly.

"Can I help you find anything, Ma'am?" she asked politely.

"Actually." I stopped short, "Yes, maybe you can. I'm curious if there might be a computer or something somewhere that has internet access. I just need to look something up really quickly, and my cell phone hasn't been working."

"Ah," she said, "yes, phones are always an issue here, unfortunately. Mrs. Evans has a computer in her office." She chewed her lip, suddenly looking a little nervous. "But it's kept locked. She isn't here at the moment."

Shoot. "Okay, well, that's okay. Do you know when she might be here?" Come to think of it, I hadn't seen Mrs. Evans yet, that I knew of.

She looked at her watch. "She should be back later this evening, Ma'am. I can let her know you might need some assistance."

"Thank you, that's very kind of you," I replied. "I really appreciate your help." I turned to go, continuing on my way, when she called back to me.

"Is it something that could be in a book, Ma'am?"

"What?" I turned back, confused for a second.

"What you need to look up. Is it something that could be found in a book?"

Having profusely thanked the maid for her suggestion, I raced down the hallway towards the library. Why had that not occurred to me?

My enthusiasm waned quickly after entering the library. The sheer number of books was completely overwhelming. I didn't see how I could ever hope to find what I was looking for, not unless someone had left a convenient guide to ancient runes lying out for inquisitive minds to find. But the library was peaceful and calming, and I felt somewhat safer here than I did in the rest of the house.

It had begun to rain steadily at some point while I perused the shelves. I heard the low rumble of thunder in the background, each successive boom creeping steadily closer. I scanned as many titles as possible and grabbed anything that looked remotely related or interesting off the shelf to investigate closer. I tried searching for a book about pagan rituals. I wanted to read more about Beltane and Mabon, about the Oak King, but I was coming up empty.

I heard a light knock coming from somewhere below me, I had made my way to the second level by now and looked down to see Ben standing in the doorway, watching me. How long had he been standing there, I wondered?

"What are you up to in here?" he asked.

I sighed and shoved the book in my hand back on the shelf. "I'm trying to find... I dunno, some kind of guide to deciphering ancient runes or something."

He looked like he wanted to laugh for a moment. His lips stretched out briefly at the corners before he quickly subdued his expression. "Cassie," he said seriously, "even if there were a book like that here, and I doubt there is, I'm pretty sure you have to be, like, an expert, to interpret runes. I don't think it's a word for word translation." I glared at him. Well, I felt pretty stupid. I hadn't thought of that. "But what do I know," he gestured around at the shelves, "maybe there's a runic dictionary somewhere in here."

"Okay," I said, folding my arms, "you don't have to be a jerk about it." I couldn't help but smile, just a little.

He smirked. "I'm sorry, it would have been a good idea otherwise."

"Yeah, other than the part where I'm an idiot." I plopped down on an accent chair. "I just wanted to feel like I was doing something, you know?"

Ben nodded. "Yes, I know the feeling."

"I just wish we had heard from Kristy today. I have this bad feeling that something happened to her."

Ben looked wary suddenly. Clearly the topic made him uncomfortable. "Well, I mean, her car is gone Cassie. I think it's safe to assume that means she left on her own accord, right?"

"I guess so," I sighed. There was that inconvenient fact. "But all her stuff is here. She left her purses, her suitcase, all her clothes, her perfumes... everything. So, she was upset about Mike and just decided to, I dunno, grab her car keys, head to her car empty-handed, and leave? It just doesn't make any sense."

"Purses, plural," he said, "there's no way to know, but maybe she had another purse she took with her?" He shrugged.

"Mmhmm." I nodded. "And why did you have your shoes on last night Ben?

He chuckled, swinging his hands onto his hips and looking away from me. "Annnddd we're back on that again."

"Yeah, Ben, we are back on that again. Care to give me an explanation this time?" I stared down at him, eyebrows raised.

"Oh, you're actually going to give me a chance to explain myself this time?" He held his hands up to his chest, "How kind of you."

I rolled my eyes. This was not off to a good start.

"I do in fact have a perfectly good explanation for that. When Mark came and pounded on my door, waking me up, to tell me that Kristy was missing, I was in my boxers." I tried not to picture that. "So, I got up, and got dressed as fast as I could. And the first thing I thought to grab were my running shorts. And then, my sleep-addled brain decided putting on a running shirt, made the most sense next. And then," he held up a finger, "it occurred to me that Kristy might have gone missing," he paused and gestured animatedly out the window, "*outside*. And if that was the case, I decided it would be logical to put shoes on. Naturally, the shoes I chose were..." he gestured for me to fill in the gap for him, which I did not. "You guessed it, my running shoes. But trust me, I really, really, wish I had just walked downstairs barefoot, so as to avoid your suspicion that I might be an ax murderer."

"Okay..." I sighed, "fair enough."

"Thank you." Ben smiled, folding his arms across his chest.

"But it did look pretty suspicious," I added.

Ben smiled graciously. "Yes, I can understand that. Can we move on now from the whole murderer thing?"

I set my mouth in a begrudging smile. "I guess so."

"Perfect." He clapped his hands together. "Now, for the reason I'm here," he began.

"Oh, it wasn't for the pleasure of my company then?" I asked sarcastically.

"Nope." He grinned. "Although it's always a pleasure, of course. And, I should add, you aren't supposed to be wandering off on your own. But no, the reason I'm here is to remind you that you are summoned to dinner, in about," he checked his watch, "one hour."

"Duly noted," I replied. He smiled and nodded. I expected him to turn and leave, but he stood awkwardly for another moment. He stared up at me, licking his lips nervously and sighing loudly. He looked like he was trying to decide something.

"Um," I said expectantly, "was there something else you wanted to tell me?"

"No!" He looked surprised. "No. Like what?"

"I don't know, Ben." I shrugged, amused. "You looked like you wanted to say something else."

"Oh." He frowned. "I, no, there wasn't... there wasn't anything else."

"Okay, weirdo," I said under my breath as he turned to go.

"I heard that!" he called from the hallway.

"See you at dinner, freak!" I called back. I heard him laughing as he made his way down the hallway. I smiled to myself for a few seconds after he left. It was nice to see he wasn't serious 100% of the time.

Once more, I found myself in the position of needing to fit into a dress. I was starting to think that Emily had seriously dropped the ball by not warning me that I would need a different designer gown to wear every night of the week.

I opted this time for a simple, flowing, romantic-looking, pale pink gown. It was a shorter dress rather than floor length, and it left my ankles feeling a bit chilly, but that was probably the least of my concerns. I pinned my hair up in a loose bun and called it a day. I dunno, somehow the whole creepy pagan-ritual atmosphere wasn't really making me feel motivated to dress up. Call me crazy.

I made my way down to the dining hall, meeting a few of the other girls in the hallway. Overall, the mood of the group seemed very subdued. The storm was still raging outside, giving me a strong sense of déjà vu yet again. It almost felt for a moment like I was trapped here, forced to live out the same formal dinner in an elegant backwoods hell night after night.

We entered the dining room right on schedule. I eyed the place cards warily, seeing that, yet again, our places at the table hadn't been moved. When I sat down, I turned to Mark and said, "Can we be on our best behavior tonight, please?"

That wiped the grin off his face for a moment. He leaned towards me and whispered suggestively in my ear, "I will if you will."

I shook my head. He had a point in a way, but really?

Ben straightened his tie across the table, watching us. Had Mark whispered to me on purpose, to make Ben jealous? What kind of game were these two playing? I warned myself to calm down. The last thing anyone needed right now was another argument. It would honestly be laughable at this point. We had to be able to make it through one dinner without blowing up at each other. I made a point to smile right at Ben. He raised one eyebrow and nodded and smiled back at me, if not a little wearily.

Unfortunately, this meal seemed to be doomed for other reasons. The topic of conversation at the table abruptly swung to the strange goings on that had been taking place, and no one seemed inclined at any point to change the topic. There were different wild theories being thrown out, some of which made no logical sense, but the general consensus in the end was that this must have something to do with the villagers, perhaps with help from the inside. We quieted as staff entered the room to bring our drinks and then food. Forcing a change in topic, if only for a few moments.

Emily tried several times to change the topic permanently but was having no success. I hated to make it worse, but my curiosity got the best of me. I turned to Josh. "Did you get a chance to speak with Harvey yet? Or Mrs. Evans?"

Josh paused, his fork halfway to his mouth. "Harvey didn't have any ideas about who could be involved with all this. Maybe kids from the village? Teenagers or something, pranking us?"

I nodded thoughtfully. "And Mrs. Evans?" I asked.

"She, ah, I haven't had a chance to speak with her yet. I guess she's not feeling well tonight."

"Oh!" I raised my eyebrows at that.

"What is it?" Emily asked. "You look surprised."

"Oh, no, it's nothing," I replied, "it's just that I had been hoping to use her computer tonight."

"For what?" Emily asked me. She was looking down at her plate. Did her voice seem too nonchalant somehow? I sighed internally. This was getting ridiculous. Now I was suspecting Emily was involved in all this? I thought back to the night I had first arrived. Why did my brain keep returning to that moment on the balcony? I watched her cutting her food and waiting for me to answer. Because she wasn't just worried. She was scared. That had been fear on her face that night. Was there more she hadn't told me? She had opened up to me at the pool, but had she told me everything she knew? Or was she still holding something back?

"Cassie?"

I snapped back to the present. "What?" I asked.

"Why did you want to use the computer?" Emily asked, watching me now.

"No reason, really," I said, "it's just something for work." I chuckled. "I can't get anything done this week without cell service." Emily nodded, looking satisfied with my response. I noticed Ben watching me carefully. I met his eyes for a brief moment before looking away.

"So, are plans all set for the wedding, then? Are there any last-minute issues?" I asked. Emily sighed.

"Just stupid little frustrating hiccups." She laughed. "You won't believe the snafu with the lawn chairs. They called and left a message for me, confirming the order was for 150 chairs to be delivered. Can you believe that? What an awful mix up that would have been." I nodded. I could tell she was more than relieved to have the subject finally changed.

"Left a message, how?" I asked curiously.

"With one of the staff," Emily replied easily, "they usually try to answer the phone right away if it rings."

"Especially this week," Josh added, chuckling.

"Yes." Emily nodded in agreement. "Luckily, they took the message, and I was able to get through to them right away to correct the issue. I had said from the beginning we needed 200 chairs, at least, if not more. In fact, I'm positive I made it clear we needed extras. You never know when some random relative is going to show up with an extra guest tagging along."

Mark turned to me and said, "You know, Cassie, speaking of plus ones, I just realized it never occurred to me to ask, but are you bringing anyone?" I stared at him, confused for a moment. "You know, like a plus one, to the wedding?"

"Oh," I said, "no, Mark, I don't have a plus one for the wedding. Why?"

"Oh," he responded nonchalantly, "no reason, really." Looking over at Ben, he lifted an eyebrow. "I was just curious. So, no boyfriend, or anything, back home then?"

"No," I responded, sighing, "I'm single, Mark. Thank you for clarifying, and for pointing it out to everyone."

Mark laughed. "Hey, I just wanted to be sure, you know? Didn't want anyone to assume anything." Ben stared at him in irritation.

"Okay," Emily said, "yes, thank you Mark. Moving on…"

Ben looked over pointedly at Josh. Their eyes met, and Josh shook his head.

"Okay," I interrupted. "What's with the line of questioning? Hmm? And the little looks?" I saw all three men freeze. "Between you two," I gestured between Mark and Ben, "and you two." I gestured from Josh to Ben.

"Me?" Josh said, his eyes going wide. Putting a hand over his chest, he asked, "What did I do?"

"Seriously," I said, calmly but firmly, "Someone is going to explain to me, right now, what everyone keeps joking about and hinting at." I looked around at all of them. No one moved. "No one is leaving this table until I hear the rest of the joke that I'm clearly the butt of."

Mark chuckled. "Cassie," he set his silverware down, "come on, we're just messing around, being idiots. No one's laughing at you."

"No, Mark." I shook my head. "I'm done. I want to know what's going on."

"Okay…" Mark said, looking at Ben as though unsure what to do next. Ben sighed and pinched the bridge of his nose, closing his eyes for a moment.

"Okay… um, Cassie, can I speak to you outside then?" Ben nodded towards the door.

"Seriously?" I looked at him with raised eyebrows. "You can't tell me in here?"

"No," he said incredulously, starting to look flushed now, "No, I can't tell you in here." He began loosening his tie. Mark chuckled, turning it into a cough when Emily turned to glare at him.

Emily was staring back and forth between him and Mark. She looked irritated now too. "You know what, the two of you have interrupted dinner for the last time. Ben, I think you owe us all an explanation. Anything you have to say to Cassie, you can say in front of the rest of us." Ben turned to stare at her, wide-eyed. "Go ahead Ben," she gestured at me, "answer her. Enlighten us all."

I heard a choking sound next to me and looked over to realize that Mark was trying to cover up the fact that he was laughing hysterically now.

Ben glared at him. "Shut it, Mark." He was fully blushing now.

Even Josh had started to chuckle. "Yeah, go ahead Ben, we're all waiting."

"I hate you guys," he mumbled. Then he cleared his throat, attempting to regain his composure. "Cassie, can I please speak to you in private." He addressed me directly. "Please."

I stared at him. Part of me wanted to make him tell me in front of everyone. I sat back in my chair, studying him. I decided he deserved to be tortured, just a little bit. "I agree with Emily, actually."

Emily gave Ben a smug look.

Ben just stared at me in horror. "I can't…I can't possibly, Cassie, come on." He looked like he was starting to panic now. Both Josh and Mark were shaking with silent laughter. I was beginning to suspect what it might be, and it was a conversation I would rather have in private, but before I could speak, Ben stood up.

"Okay. Well, I'm not going to be forced to answer, okay?" He shrugged. "So, just, forget about it." He walked out of the dining room without another word.

Josh and Mark erupted, booing loudly as he exited the room.

"Oh my god," Josh shook his head. "How many times is he going to walk out this week?"

"Thank you, ladies," Mark laughed, shaking his head, as he started slow clapping, "seriously, thank you both. That was exquisite. A round of applause. Did you see his face?" He asked Josh.

"Priceless..." Josh said, shaking his head, still chuckling.

Emily looked at me, shaking her head as well. "You three are all idiots." She looked thoughtful for a moment. "Come on, Cassie." She stood up, putting her napkin on the table. "Catherine, Amy..." she interrupted the conversation going on at the other end of the table, "Blair," everyone stopped to look at Emily, "Come on ladies, I've had it with the men for tonight. We're going up to the ballroom. Let's go."

We all hesitated for a moment before getting to our feet one by one. Emily ushered us swiftly out of the room.

"The ballroom?" Mike called out. "Why?"

"Don't worry about it!" Emily called back over her shoulder. "You're not invited. Girls only."

"I know what they're doing." I heard Josh say behind me as we exited out into the foyer. *Well, that makes one of us*, I thought. Emily led the girls upstairs, into the grand ballroom. She disappeared into a little door that was hidden in the wall. The waist high trim and the crown molding were built in, right over the door, causing it to blend into the wall. I gazed up at the ceiling, my eyes lingering on the deer hunt, waiting for her to return.

Was there a clue hidden in this painting? I couldn't help but wonder. I had found the piece of paper in the frame of a painting; maybe I needed to study the artwork in the house. A moment or so later, we heard loud club music start to pump out. I began to grin. The music was so at odds with the look of the formal ballroom, it was pretty funny.

Emily danced out of the closet, making her way over to us. We started laughing and cheering, and pretty soon we were all dancing too. Someone decided we needed more alcohol before too much time had gone by. I begged to differ. The combination of dancing and what I'd already had to drink was making me feel a little light-headed, but in a good way, I decided. I was probably already squarely on my way to being drunk, if not at least tipsy. A few of the girls left, and returned with a convenient cart on wheels, filled with bottles and glasses.

It didn't take long before some of the guys trailed in. "No!" Emily called out from across the ballroom, making a shooing motion with her hands towards them. "No! No men allowed!" I laughed and spun.

The guys complained and got into a fake argument with Emily and Catherine as they tried to push them back out the door. Josh and Mark showed up a few seconds later. A slow song happened to come on, just then. Josh walked over to Emily, holding his hand out to her. I couldn't make out what he was saying over the music, but I could see his lips moving. She shook her head no and folded her arms. He got down on one knee and spoke to her again. She grinned and finally relented, allowing him to stand and take her in his arms. He led her out to the middle of the floor, and they danced together as everyone cheered and clapped. Blair, returning from getting herself another drink, had taken it upon herself to get me one too.

"No." I laughed. "I have had more than enough."

"Come on!" She yelled over the music. "Live a little!" She held up her glass and clinked it against mine. I lifted it to my lips and drank. We danced and drank. Until eventually another slow dance came on. Mark made his way towards us. "Well, the men have infiltrated us at last," Blair said, "here we go," rolling her eyes at me, as Mark approached.

Mark bowed deeply to me. "May I have this dance?"

I giggled and shook my head. "You're not supposed to be in here."

"Well, Josh is." He laughed, taking the glass from my hand, he walked over to the side of the room and set it down on the floor. Then he walked back and grabbed my hand, leading me out to the middle of the floor. He slid an arm around my waist and pulled me to him. "This is more like it," he said to me, "it finally feels like a party. What a downer most of this week has been."

I sighed. "You're right. I can't say this week has been at all what I expected."

Mark nodded. He watched Josh and Emily, dancing and laughing together.

"It's good to see the two of them having some fun, at least." I smiled, watching them for a moment as well.

"That's for sure," Mark replied. "Although, that one," he tipped his head towards the doorway, "not so much." I knew who would be standing there before I turned. Ben stood just inside the doorway, leaning up against the wall, his hands in his pockets. He glowered at Mark and me. He didn't try to hide it either when he saw me looking at him.

"You know," I said to Mark, "I'm sick of your little games."

Mark chuckled. "I don't know what you're talking about. I just saw a pretty girl without a dance partner, that's all."

"Mmhmm," I said into his ear.

"If he was smart, he'd cut in," he said, grinning at me, as he stepped back and spun me around. I was somehow a much better dancer with him leading me; I couldn't help but enjoy it.

I laughed as he spun me close to him, and then pushed me back out, dramatically. "Somehow, I don't see that happening." The song came to an end, and Mark released me, taking a step back and bowing low to the ground. As the next song began, a few of the girls let out whoops and shrieks. *I guess this is turning into a real party,* I thought.

I turned to look over at the door, and saw Ben still standing there, watching me. My head was buzzing. *Oh no,* I thought, I was more than tipsy. What was in that last drink? The one Blair had brought me? I hadn't even bothered to ask. Somehow, my feet were already walking over to Ben. He watched me approach, crossing his arms over his chest.

"Well?" I said to him expectantly.

"Well, what?" he asked sullenly.

"Are you ready to tell me what you guys keep laughing and joking around about?"

He just glared at me. "I don't think so."

"Why?" I asked him, feeling irritated again.

"Because I don't think it matters anymore." His gaze flickered over to Mark momentarily.

"Well, I think it does. I want to know."

He looked at me. "No, not right now. You're drunk."

That ticked me off. "I'm not drunk, Ben. I had a few drinks, there's a difference."

"Not if you aren't used to having a few drinks, then there's not much of a difference at all."

I flushed, glaring at him for a moment. "Okay." I looked around the room. "Do you want to dance with me then?"

"No," he scoffed. He was practically chuckling, shaking his head.

"No?" I raised my eyebrows at him, my cheeks burning at his rejection. "Really? You're such a jerk. Fine then."

"Fine," he said back, shrugging, like he didn't care what I thought of him.

"Fine," I replied. Abruptly, I turned and left the room. I stalked down the hallway, trying to calm my racing heart. He hadn't just refused to dance with me, he had actually laughed about it. Like it was ridiculous. It stung more than I wanted to admit.

After a moment I could hear footsteps behind me. I turned to see Ben following me down the corridor. I somehow made it to the top of the stairs without getting lost, and then I did my best to step carefully down them without tripping.

Out in the foyer, I walked out to the middle of the room and turned back, standing with my arms crossed, waiting, as Ben trailed behind me. He moved slowly down the steps, looking like he was walking to his gallows.

"Why are you following me?" I asked him. I kept my voice even, blinking rapidly, keeping my eyes dry. I refused to tear up in front of him. I wouldn't give him the satisfaction of knowing he affected me at all.

"Did you forget that we aren't supposed to wander around the house alone?" He asked. "I'm not going to let you traipse around by yourself at night."

"Yeah? Well, you aren't invited to come with me. And I'm not traipsing around, I'm looking for something." I wasn't going to sit around, waiting for something else to happen. I was going to start systematically searching the house. I was going to look for any clues that might help me figure out what was happening here.

"Okay, what are you looking for?" Ben asked.

"None of your business," I replied. I turned around and set off down the hall towards the guy's lounge.

"Come on, Cassie," Ben said, "stop messing around."

"I'm not messing around," I snapped, whipping back to face him. "I don't want you here, Ben. Not until you grow up and tell me what's going on."

Ben rolled his eyes. "Okay." He put his hands on his hips. "Fine, if I tell you, will you stop playing games?"

"Playing games?" I chuckled. "*You* are the one playing games." I pointed at him. "You and Mark. I don't know what your problem is, but I'm not kidding, Ben. This is the last time I'm asking. After this, I'm not going to care what the answer is." I glared at him. "Go ahead."

He looked around the foyer. "Here?" he asked incredulously, holding his arms open. I looked around us at the empty foyer.

"What's wrong with here?" I asked, exasperated. "What kind of room do you need to tell me what's going on?"

Thunder crashed loudly, and I saw a flash of lightning through the large stained-glass skylight above us.

"I don't know." He looked around, starting to panic a little. "I can't do it here."

"Can't do what, Ben? What the heck is it? Just spit it out."

"I can't, Cassie, I can't just..."

"You can't just... what? Be honest with me? For once? Since I've arrived here, you've given me completely mixed signals. You acted like you hated me for the first two days–"

"I never hated you, Cassie; come on." He ran his hands through his hair.

"No, you did, Ben. You glared at me, at Mark, for two days straight. At times you have been a complete, utter asshole." He stared at me, clenching his jaw. "On numerous occasions, actually."

"I know..." he said, "I know, I–"

"You what, Ben? Finish that thought." I stopped talking, waiting for him to answer. I refused to speak again until he told me the truth.

"I can't take it, Cassie! Okay?" He was practically yelling now. "I can't take watching you flirt with him and joke around, and, and he... just, was able to connect with you so easily. Like it was just effortless for him. Like always. Meanwhile, you thought I was an asshole from the beginning. You wanted nothing to do with me. And I..." he stopped, trailing off. Then he just looked at me, waiting for me to say something, his chest rising and falling rapidly. I met his eyes.

"I haven't been flirting with Mark," I said slowly.

"Then what would you call it, Cassie? I saw the two of you with my own eyes, over and over again. In the garden, when he put the rose in your hair. Horseback riding...at the beach, when you played chicken. Playing croquet, target practice...for fuck's sake, you were crying in his arms while he was... half-naked last night!" He stopped and slid a hand over his face, taking a deep breath. "He has been all over you."

"There's nothing between us, Ben, nothing," I insisted. "He's a nice guy, okay? He's funny. He's easy to talk to and joke around with. We're just friends. There was no flirting."

"Well, it sure looked like it to me." He lowered his voice. "When I saw you, just now, dancing with him? It made me want to..." he trailed off again, looking away from me and shaking his head.

"Want to what?" I asked breathlessly.

"To... to rip him apart with my bare hands," he admitted. "And we've been friends for years." He looked at me, bitterly, as though it were my fault.

I just stared at him in shock, frozen for a moment. "Why?" My heart was starting to beat faster now.

"Why?!" He laughed darkly. "Why do you think, Cassie?" He ran his hands through his hair again and looked up at the ceiling for a moment at the skylight. "I haven't slept... in days. Since you got here. I can't..." he started pacing. "I can't sleep. I can't eat. I can't..." he stopped and met my eyes, his cheeks flushed. "I can't think..." he paused, looking at the ground, taking a deep breath. "I can't think about anything but you."

I felt my cheeks flush deeply, and my heart pounded in my chest as his dark, fervent eyes met mine. I struggled to speak for a moment. "Why didn't you just tell me?" I managed, faintly.

"Tell you how?" He asked, a pained expression on his face. "Just stop you in the hallway and tell you that I'm, what... obsessed with you? After knowing you for a day? Not even a day?" I blushed deeper, recalling how I had thrown that in his face at one point. "Meanwhile," he continued, "you and Mark...it's been driving me crazy. And he knows it, too." He shook his head. "It's like he can't help it."

I thought back to their conversation in the lounge. Had Ben asked him to back off? Why was Mark acting like this if he knew Ben liked me? Maybe he was right; perhaps he couldn't help himself. But I didn't think Mark had feelings for me... I was sure of it.

I didn't know what to say or do next. Ben was just standing there, watching me. Waiting for me to respond. I was quiet for a long moment. "Well, thank you," I said, "for telling me."

He shot me a devastated look, then dropped his head to the floor, nodding slowly.

"What?" I said, moving closer to him. "What did I say?"

He chuckled wryly, refusing to look at me. "I just told you," he said slowly, "that I'm in love with you, and your response was, 'Thank you for telling me.'" He wiped a hand over his brow. "So, thank *you*," he continued, turning away from me towards the staircase, "for making it abundantly clear to me that you don't feel the same way. And for the record, this is why I didn't want to say anything."

"Ben!" I said, walking over to him. "That's not what I meant."

"It's okay, Cassie," he said, walking up the stairs, "just forget about it. Forget I said anything, okay?"

I followed him up the staircase, grabbing his arm and attempting to turn him towards me. "Ben, please wait." He stopped walking but still refused to look at me. I took another step up. I cupped the side of his face in my palm and turned him towards me. He finally met my eyes reluctantly.

"It's okay, Cassie, really, it is. I understand if you don't feel the same way." His eyes scanned back and forth over mine, over my lips. He reached up and tucked a stray lock of hair behind my ear, "I won't bother you anymore," he whispered, "...and I won't let anything happen to you."

Happen to me? What did he think was going to happen to me? I looked at him and felt a jolt of something like apprehension in my gut. Mixed with what I couldn't deny any longer was desire.

I slid my hand to the back of his neck, pulling him slowly towards me. I kissed him. He didn't react for only a split second. Then I felt his lips part, and his arms wrapped around my waist. He pulled me close to him, kissing me deeply. His tongue swept over mine. I leaned into him, pressing against him. He pulled me tightly to him, and his kiss became more urgent and hungry.

He broke off and trailed down to the base of my neck, kissing and tickling me. I let out an involuntary little moan. He responded with an answering sort of low rumbling growl in the back of his throat. I felt a throbbing deep in my center. He returned to my lips, kissing me again. "Cassie," he whispered against them. He caressed my cheek lightly with his thumb. He met my eyes and then kissed me once more, slowly, deliberately.

My legs had gone limp; he was basically holding me upright at this point. I had melted completely for him in seconds. I felt my cheeks flush again in embarrassment. Why was I so attracted to him? He had been such a jerk at times. And I couldn't even trust him fully, yet here I was, somehow in his arms and completely at his mercy.

Pulling back to look at me, he studied my face. "You are so beautiful." Just then, thunder crashed, the house shook, and we heard a massive boom, like an explosion, from somewhere outside. Then the lights went out.

I heard screams from upstairs when the power cut off. Ben and I stood there frozen for a moment in near-total darkness, both panting and breathing heavily. Eventually, my eyes started to adjust, and I could begin to see by the faint light leaking in through the skylight high above us. "You have got to be kidding me," Ben murmured, "perfect timing."

I giggled a little at that. I could hear raised voices. It took another moment for people to get their bearings. Someone emerged onto the landing. They were holding up a cell phone, using it as a flashlight. Ben released me as the light from the phone shined right in our faces. I tried to steady myself on weak legs, holding on to his arm still to balance myself.

"Oh, hey guys!" I heard Mark call out, "How's it going?" in an annoying sing-song voice. The light lowered, away from our eyes, flipped to point up at the ceiling, and I saw it was Josh holding the cell phone. He was followed closely behind by Mark, and Emily stood off to his side, I could see from here she had a death grip on Josh's other arm.

"Great, until you got here," Ben retorted. Aside to me, he said softly, "If you hadn't guessed, they've been torturing me all week."

I grinned. "I can only imagine." My heart still pounded slightly; I hadn't recovered from the kiss.

Josh called down to us. "I'm guessing with the timing of that, there's going to be nothing we can do inside the house to get the power back on."

Ben responded, nodding. "Most likely it's a blown transformer." He thought for a moment. "I mean, we can go check the panel and make sure we didn't just blow a fuse, but from the sound of it I'm not optimistic."

Josh nodded at Ben. "Sounds good. Let's get some flashlights and candles first for everyone."

In no time, we had help from the staff to bring out a few flashlights, and candles were lit in the guy's lounge. Ben and Josh left, with Wes joining them, to go check the panel. I assumed it must be somewhere down in the lower level. The girls hunkered down in the lounge, mainly on the couches. The surface of the large coffee table was littered with candles, and a fire burned in the grate. Ben winked at me from the doorway before ducking out with the others. My stomach did a somersault.

I sat there quietly while the girls chatted. I had to stop myself from sitting there grinning like an idiot. In spite of the power outage, and everything else going on, I couldn't help but feel a little giddy. I was definitely still tipsy as well.

Emily, on the other hand, looked miserable. She sighed loudly. "This entire week is a disaster."

"No, it's not Em," I said quickly. The others all murmured similar platitudes at the same time.

"No." Emily held up her hands. "It is. It's been a complete and utter disaster. What on earth are we going to do if we can't get the power back on?"

"We'll call for help, they'll send a crew out," Amy started to say.

"With what phone?" Emily responded. "We can't even call for help!"

"We'll go out to the road," Blair said, "we can call for help from there."

I felt the butterflies in my stomach lose a bit of their gusto at Emily's words. *We can't even call for help.* Our only connection to the outside world was the landline phone, and we just lost it. Was this done deliberately? Of course not, I thought, shaking my head to clear it. The outage had been timed perfectly with the thunder and the booming sound.

"I'm pretty sure landline phones still work, even without power," Catherine mused thoughtfully. I made a mental note to ask Ben when he got back, he would know.

"Even so, who knows how long it will take a crew to get out here, in the middle of nowhere, to fix it," Emily continued, "I can't believe this." She shook her head.

I sighed, unsure what to say. It wasn't an ideal situation, that was for sure. I knew the whole thing with Kristy was still weighing heavily on her mind too.

We sat together awkwardly, quiet for a few minutes. I realized I really needed to use the restroom. I put it off as long as possible, before announcing where I was going, and grabbing a candle to bring with me.

I thought I could easily remember the route to the bathroom and set out on my own. About halfway down the hall, I passed a young man, one of the waiters, carrying an ornate silver platter in one hand, with a carafe of something balanced on top. He had a white towel folded over his arm. I noticed absentmindedly that his outfit looked extra fancy and formal tonight. Perhaps this is what they would wear for the wedding rehearsal dinner tomorrow. He nodded, tipping his upper body towards me in a half bow before continuing on his way. A moment later, I paused, realizing the mistake I had made.

We had said we weren't to go anywhere alone, yet here I was, traipsing off in the dark to the bathroom all by myself. I was lucky the only person

I had run into was the waiter. I turned around and headed back down the corridor to the lounge. When I got there, I was surprised to see the guys were back from checking the breakers. They must have just walked in.

"Where is she?" Ben asked, sounding a little panicky.

"I'm right here," I announced from the doorway, feeling sheepish. He whipped around. "I forgot about not going anywhere alone…" I trailed off, looking around the room.

"God," he sighed, covering his mouth with his palm.

"Where is it?" I asked, confused.

"Where's what?" Ben asked.

"In the hall, I just passed a waiter bringing something to drink, a big carafe, on a tray. Where is it?" They looked at each other, confused expressions all around.

"Well, he didn't come in here." Emily shrugged. She looked despondent.

"Okay…well who else would he be bringing it to then?" My eyes widened. Did that mean there was someone else here? Someone in the house we didn't know about?

"Are you okay Cassie?" Ben asked, looking concerned.

"I'm fine," I reassured him. I turned to Emily. "Em, will you come with me?"

She nodded, and started to get up, but struggled for a second, given how low and deep the sofa was. Josh helped pull her up to standing. She joined me, tucking an arm in mine, and we started back down the hall.

"What's the verdict?" I asked, already figuring I knew the answer.

"They weren't able to do anything," Emily grumbled.

"I'm sorry Em. It'll work out somehow." She nodded glumly. "I really like the waiter's new uniforms," I said cheerfully. "They'll look extra snazzy for the wedding." She frowned a little at me. I continued, "I'm sure everything will look much brighter in the morning Em."

"Yeah, literally..." she quipped, "like when the sun comes back up so we can see where the hell we're going." I laughed. "So," her tone changed swiftly, "did we interrupt something? I saw you standing there with Ben."

I laughed again, blushing in the dark. "Um...he confessed his undying love for me."

"What!" Emily smacked me, "Get out! Are you serious? And it took you this long to tell me?"

"Yes," I laughed, "I'm actually serious."

"What the heck?" Emily laughed now too. She held up her hands. "Okay, okay. I take it back; this week hasn't been a total waste."

I smiled at her. "No, I guess it hasn't."

"Wow..." She shook her head, "Ben in love. Never thought I'd see the day."

"I know," I conceded, "he is kind of an old curmudgeon, isn't he?"

Emily giggled. "This is true, but we still love him anyway." She glanced sideways at me. "He's a good guy, Cass. Really." I nodded, feeling a little reassured by her words. She skipped a little down the hall. "Oh, Cass, this is going to be so much fun! We can go on double dates now."

I couldn't help but smile widely at that. My cheeks were going to be sore tomorrow from grinning so much.

Emily and I made it safely to the bathroom and back without being accosted. Once back in the guy's lounge, we all agreed there was little else that could be done to remedy our situation for tonight. The guys decided to play "darts in the dark," undoubtedly led by Mark, I would imagine. They broke out the liquor and we all settled in for the remainder of the evening. I couldn't help but steal a few looks in Ben's direction and caught him looking my way a few times as well. At least he wasn't glaring anymore.

I got up at one point from the couch, where I was ensconced with the girls, talking about all things wedding, to grab some water. The dark look he shot me from across the room as I made my way back made my stomach flip again.

When the night was winding down, we realized we still needed to decide on sleeping arrangements. Emily and I ended up back in Josh's room, and Mark ended up either stuck with us as well, or without a mattress. Some of the girls decided they were comfortable sleeping a few to one room back in the girls' wing. Others chose to pair up with a few of the guys and drag mattresses over. It occurred to me how odd this would all seem to Emily and Josh's parents when they arrived tomorrow. Tomorrow was Friday, finally, I thought with a sense of relief. Maybe the chaos would be over once the real adults arrived and sorted everything out.

We headed upstairs all together. We carried candles with us so we could see. The guys walked us to our rooms and waited for us to change for bed. I changed into a wireless bra, an oversized sweatshirt, and PJ pants. I threw my hair into a pineapple. It was hard to get used to the power being out. I walked into my bathroom and flipped the light switch, completely forgetting. I thought again of the waiter and the mysterious carafe. Where was he going? I could already tell I wasn't going to be able to sleep tonight. I slipped my phone into my pocket, checking to confirm it was charged. I ducked back out into the hall. Ben was waiting for me, arms folded, leaning against the wall and chatting with Mark. He grinned at me, taking in my messy bun. Josh and Emily emerged from her room, and we all headed down the hall to the guy's wing.

Everyone called out goodnight to each other. Ben slipped past me in the hallway. I felt his hand brush mine as he went past. "Goodnight," he whispered to me, before disappearing into his room. I was both relieved and a little disappointed that he didn't try to invite me inside.

We settled down to sleep, but I lay there, wide awake, staring at the ceiling. I flipped back and forth, trying not to disturb Emily, but I couldn't get comfortable. I could feel the alcohol finally wearing off. I just prayed I wouldn't end up with a pounding headache.

Finally, I gave up trying to sleep. I got up quietly and tip-toed to the door, turning the handle with a soft click, and shutting it gently behind me. I made my way, barefoot, down to Ben's room. I knocked softly on the door, waiting to see if it was loud enough to wake him. The door swung open faster than I expected.

Ben peeked out, shirtless, using the glow of his phone screen for light. Raising his eyebrows when he saw me, he swung the door open wider. "Cassie?" He smiled a little. "What are you doing?" I tried not to stare at his abs.

"The waiter, was taking a tray to someone, and it wasn't any of us. I think there could be someone else here in the house that we don't know about. I want to go look for them."

"What?" Ben's eyebrows rose again in the dark. That was clearly not what he was expecting, or hoping, I would say. "You've gotta be kidding me right now. You want to wander around in the dark, in the middle of the night, searching for someone who is supposedly hiding from us in the house?" He shook his head and ran a hand over his face. "Do you realize how insane that sounds?"

"I can't sleep," I told him, ignoring that last bit. "And if the waiter just brought them something, that's a good sign that whoever it is, is still here—in the house right now. We've probably already waited too long. This may be our only opportunity to catch them."

"Fine... fine," he sighed. "You know what, I can't sleep either. I guess I should just be glad you didn't go by yourself. Give me a second." I waited, peering up and down the hallway. I could only see so far in either direction before the hall was swallowed by darkness. *Okay, I thought, this is creepy as fuck.* Ben stepped out into the hall, wearing a white t-shirt and PJ pants. He was barefoot as well.

"Didn't think to put your running shoes on this time then?" I whispered.

He stopped dead, peering at me in the dark. "Are you being serious right now?"

"I'm kidding, only kidding," I said, holding up my hands. "Come on, let's get going."

"Where is it we're going exactly?" Ben asked with a sigh.

"The third floor," I whispered back.

"Dare I ask why?"

"It's the only floor we haven't been on at all this week, right? Well," I shrugged, "that and the basement level. But it doesn't seem like that would be a good hiding place."

Ben didn't respond for a moment. "So, aside from this mysterious waiter, what makes you think there's someone else here?"

"Well, besides the deer head and the creepy bouquets, I think I saw someone the other night. I happened to be looking out my window and saw something moving across the field, away from the house. They headed out into the woods. I thought it could have been nothing at the time. It could have been an animal. But what if it was a person? What if I saw whoever has been doing this? I mean, given the stuff they've been leaving for us, they must be going outside at some point, right? Maybe they're moving around at night."

"So naturally, you picked the night we don't have power to decide to go looking for them," Ben concluded. I chuckled a little at that. I thought for a moment.

"Why didn't you tell me any of that stuff earlier? About the pagan holidays? The Oak King? All of that?" I could feel more than see Ben shrug next to me in the dark.

"I dunno, I didn't think it was that relevant. All those things are ancient traditions. Sure, some people still practice a form of modern paganism, but their practices are pretty tame comparatively."

"Hmm," I said, "so they don't involve chopping off deer heads?"

"Not that I'm aware of." Ben chuckled.

"Well, maybe that's what we're dealing with. In a more extreme form."

"It could be," Ben agreed. "I'm still more inclined to think this is someone just messing around with us. What do you expect to use for light, by the way? I don't know where all the flashlights went, but we could go check in the lounge. A candle wouldn't be ideal." I pulled my phone out of my pocket and turned on the flashlight mode. "That'll work," Ben said.

We made our way out to the second staircase landing at the entrance to the guy's wing. Instead of heading left, towards the main staircase and the girl's wing beyond, we turned right. The hallway led us down a ways before we hit another curving flight of stairs. From the looks of it, the red carpet also extended up to this level. "Is there a set of stairs on the other side, too?" I whispered to Ben.

"Yeah." He nodded. "There is. I know that much. I haven't been upstairs in ages, since I was a kid. But we used to run up and down on this level, chasing each other. We'd play hide and seek and ghost in the graveyard." He smiled fondly. "I used to love those nights. We'd scare the shit out of each other."

I smiled, thinking of similar summer nights spent outside, playing with neighborhood kids. "Nothing to make you feel more alive." Ben laughed.

"This is true. Although, if someone jumped out now and yelled boo, I'd probably pee my pants." We both cracked up, trying to stifle our laughter.

"Okay," I said, "we need to shut up, or whoever is up there will hear us coming from a mile away."

"Cassie," Ben said, stopping and turning to me. "Come on, this is a little nuts. If you really believe someone is up there, we should stop. We should either come back in the morning or go wake up the others and bring them with us. Let's not be stupid about this. Besides, it doesn't even make any sense in the first place. Why would the staff not tell Josh and Emily that someone else was here in the house? Instead, they're what? Bringing them food?"

"Look, I don't know, okay? Maybe it doesn't make much sense, but where else was he going with that tray? And if we're willing to believe the staff could be involved with all the other weird stuff that's happened, why isn't it possible they're also helping someone hide in the house?"

Ben stared at me for a long moment. "Okay, fair enough. Let's go hunt down the boogeyman."

We made a better effort to be as quiet as possible as we reached the third-floor landing. I swept the phone back and forth, trying to peer down the hall in both directions. In the end, we opted to head to the right. We passed through a wide hallway with multiple doors on either side. We stopped at each, turning the door handle slowly before peering inside. I was starting to feel majorly creeped out. With the power being out, a dark room was no indication that someone wasn't potentially inside. But over and over, the light from my phone swept over empty rooms and empty beds. Most of the furniture was covered in sheets. This didn't look very promising, and I was starting to feel very relieved by that.

At the very end of the hall, we came to one more door that faced us in the corner, before the hallway turned to the right. I recalled what Emily had said on the first night about each floor just being a big rectangle. We pushed open the last door and entered a larger room than I had been expecting. This looked to be a library and sitting room. I noted a round window on the far wall, with a cushioned window seat underneath.

"Cassie." Ben breathed next to me, staring at the wall to the left. I turned, following his gaze. A massive painting hung on the wall. From here, I could make out a figure, standing in the woods. I stepped closer, holding up the light. He was shrouded in darkness, his features indistinct, but on his head, were a set of slim, curvy antlers. The painting gave me chills. I stilled, turning to look at Ben. He met my eyes.

"The Oak King?" I asked.

Ben nodded slowly. "It sure looks like it could be."

"See!" I whisper-yelled at him. "You want to tell me again that I'm making this all up? There is something weird going on with this house, Ben."

"I never said you were making it up, Cassie. I just..." He looked back at the painting, studying it the best he could in the dark. "I just think there's some explanation. We just don't have all the facts yet."

I stepped up to the base of the painting. I didn't see any markings that looked like runes in the painting. Or anything obvious stuck inside the frame. "We should come back here during the day. See if there are any other clues."

"Okay, Cassie," Ben replied. "Can we go back to bed now? Do we really need to search the other side of the house?"

"We're already here," I said, "and this side didn't take us that long really."

"Okay." Ben sighed. "Let's get this over with." He headed towards the door.

"Are you in such a hurry to get away from me then?" I asked him. He turned back to me and closed the few steps between us.

"No," he whispered, "I'm not." He pulled me to him, kissing me gently at first, then more frantically, walking me backwards as he slid down to my neck again. I stifled a moan. Clearly, he learned fast. He pressed me against the wall, next to the painting. One of his hands slid up the curve of my back, beneath my sweatshirt. I shivered. A boom of thunder rolled; a flash of lightning briefly brightened the room.

"Ben," I breathed. He pulled away from me.

"Come on," he said, his voice rough, "let's keep going. This place is giving me the creeps." I nodded in the dark, calming my breathing.

We crept back out into the hallway and made our way down an empty corridor. I was surprised to see there was a handrail to our right that overlooked the staircases and foyer below. Of course, I thought. You could see the stained-glass skylight from the foyer, there had to be an opening on this level. We passed through it swiftly. I thought, with a little twist in my gut, this would be the perfect spot for someone to watch us coming and going. I had never even thought to look up.

I had gotten ahead of Ben and entered the hall on the other side. There was a door to my left, at the very end of the hall, just like the room with the painting of the Oak King. I put my hand on the handle, waiting for him. Just then, I heard a creaking sound, slight at first, then growing louder, as a set of double doors at the hallway entrance swung shut, blocking Ben from my view. I gasped, taking a step back. There was no one in sight.

I ran up to the door, twisting and yanking on the handle. "Ben!" I cried out in a hoarse whisper. "Ben?"

"Cassie!" I could hear him calling for me on the other side. He was loud at first, but then his voice seemed to grow fainter—no, not fainter...farther away. I heard the clang of wind chimes that was now becoming familiar. I started to sway, my eyes closing against my will. I was gone before I hit the floor.

We ran. Down the corridor. The red carpet sinking beneath our feet. I told myself not to look back. We were so close. I glanced to the side. But it wasn't Ben's face I saw. I recognized him, though, as the waiter who had bowed to me in the hallway. He gripped my hand in his. "Come on," he told me, eyes wide with fear. We were panting, our breaths coming in gasps. I felt myself starting to tire. How much longer could I run? We would never make it. We hit the top of the third-floor landing and jogged down the curved stairs. We sprinted down the next hallway, heading for the second staircase. We were down in a flash. Just one more, and we would make it. Just one more, and a few yards, and we would be out the front door. And I would never, ever step foot inside this house again.

We hit the landing above the main staircase, and I felt my heart leap into my throat. "No," I cried out, falling to my knees.

"Get up," he begged me, yanking on my arm, "we can't stop."

They were waiting for us down below. Their faces hidden in shadow. How many of them were there? I saw the gleam of a shotgun barrel. Why were they hunting us? Was this fun for them? A game?

"No!" I cried out again. Tears streamed down my cheeks. I turned to him; he started to pull me to my feet. That was when I heard the gun go off. "NO!" I screamed as his body slumped to the ground next to me. He stared at me, his eyes unseeing. "No... ohhh," I sobbed. I leaned over his body, my red curls falling over my face as I cried. I didn't have the strength left in me to run anymore. Suddenly, everything went black, with a resounding crack.

"Cassie!" I felt hands on me, shaking me and trying to lift me off the floor. "Cassie!"

I opened my eyes and screamed, "No!" trying to push him away. It was Ben, staring down at me and cradling me in his arms.

"It's me," he gasped, "Cassie, it's Ben. It's okay; I'm not going to hurt you."

"What-what happened?" I asked.

"What happened?" Ben asked, still breathing hard. "You tell me," he said. "The door slammed shut out of nowhere. I couldn't open it; the handle wouldn't turn at all."

I looked around us in the dark, confused. Next to me, the set of double doors was still shut. "How...how did you get over here?"

Ben pointed down the hallway to the left. "I ran," he said, "I ran around, down the stairs, over and up the other set. I came as fast as I could. You were on the ground when I got here. What happened?"

"I-I don't know," I gulped, thinking of the dream. It was so vivid. So real. "I must have fainted or something. I had a... a nightmare. I've had a lot of them, this week."

Ben stared at me. I couldn't make out his expression in the dark. "Okay, Cassie," he said finally. "It's been a long night. I think we should head back. Besides, if anyone is up here, I think they know we're here now."

I nodded in the dark. "Okay," I said weakly. "Let's get out of here."

We found my phone lying face down on the carpet. I scooped it up and turned the flashlight back on. We made our way quickly down the stairs to the second floor. My heart started to pound in my chest. I realized we were following the same route from my dream. I peered over the railing into the foyer, scanning the staircases and the foyer below for shadowy figures. They were empty. I followed closely behind Ben until we returned to the door to Josh's room.

Ben reached out and stroked the side of my face lightly. "Goodnight, Cassie," he said softly. "I want you to go inside and lock the door behind you. And don't come back out until morning this time." I smiled weakly at him. "You promise?"

I nodded. "I promise. I think I've had enough adventures for one night."

Ben grinned and leaned in, kissing me briefly. "I'll see you in the morning."

I opened the door and slipped inside. "Goodnight," I whispered. I shut and locked the door. I heard the handle jiggle once from the other side, then Ben's soft footfalls as he headed to his room.

I meant to keep my promise to Ben. I really did. But some indeterminate amount of time later, I was startled awake. I sat up in bed, my heart pounding. Once again, I had the distinct impression that a sound had woken me. I sat there, straining, but could hear nothing. I looked over at Emily's sleeping form. She looked undisturbed. The men on the floor were two lumps in the dark, but they were still. "Emily?" I whispered. She didn't move. I nudged her back a little. Still nothing. "Em!" I pushed her a bit; she grumbled and stretched out an arm, then turned over and continued to sleep.

I stood up and made my way over to the bedroom door. I would just peek into the hallway and make sure there was no one out there. I stuck my head out, looking up and down the corridor in both directions. Turning to the left, I saw someone walking away down the hall. Her back was to me, but I recognized the slinky black dress.

"Kristy?" I called out softly to her; my brows wrinkled in confusion. I saw her pause, flinching for just a second, before she took off rapidly down the hall. She disappeared into shadows. "Kristy!" I called out loudly now.

"Josh... Mark!" I yelled, "It's Kristy, wake up! Hurry, I'm going after her!" I took off down the hall, pausing long enough to pound my fist on Ben's door as I passed. *What on earth was she doing*, I wondered. Had she just arrived back at the house? Maybe she went to find Emily and, realizing she wasn't in her room, had come looking for her in Josh's room. But why didn't she knock then? Maybe she did, I thought. Perhaps that was what woke me up. I was sure she had heard me call her name. Why did she run away from me? It hit me then. Kristy. Could it have been Kristy the whole time? Was she the one doing this?

I jogged down the hall, turning to the right. I saw her again, up ahead, just for a second before she disappeared around the next corner. "Kristy! Wait! Where are you going?" I called out to her. I couldn't imagine Kristy somehow killing a deer or chopping off its head, then lugging it into the house. The thought was a little ridiculous. Had she left the bundle in her room? In mine? She was certainly capable of that. Maybe she was working with someone else in the house.

I rounded the next corner and came to a stop. The corridor ended in front of me, forming a 'T,' continuing to my right and left. I reached the end of the corridor and scanned quickly in both directions, not knowing which way she had gone. I saw her then, to my right. She was at the far end of the hall. A bank of windows lined the left side of the hallway. Faint moonlight filtered in through the clouds. A crack of lightning flashed nearby, temporarily illuminating the hall brightly. Even still, I could barely make her out from this distance in the dark. It looked like she was standing there, perfectly still, with her back to me.

"Kristy," I called out, heading towards her. "What's going on? Where have you been?" She didn't respond. I approached her, "We've all been worried about you. We looked everywhere for you. But then your car..." She started...convulsing. Her back shook, shoulders jerking, with some type of inner spasm. Was she about to puke? I stopped, my heart starting to thump loudly in my chest. "Kristy?"

Why was she still wearing the same dress? I was sure it was the one she had been wearing the night she disappeared. I looked down at her feet. Her feet were bare, and...they looked...dirty. Caked with dried mud, up past her ankles. "Kristy..." I croaked, my voice barely a whisper now. Where were the others? I yelled out to them and banged on Ben's door. There's no way I hadn't woken up at least one of them. And I'd left the door to Josh's room open, I thought. Any minute now, they would realize I was gone and come to look for me. Oh god...I didn't even know where I was right now. I had followed her mindlessly, not paying attention. I didn't know if I could find my way back to them. I took another tentative step towards Kristy.

I heard a creaking, cracking sound...almost like a door swinging open on squeaky hinges. Kristy was convulsing harder now. She lifted her arms from where they hung at her sides, and her right arm snapped, shifting down at an awkward angle. Her left cracked and hung limply behind her back. She twisted her legs oddly, bowing them...before one of them cracked loudly. Then she scuttled, scrambling forward, at a run. "Kristy!" I yelled; I darted forward, following her around the corner.

But she was gone. An empty corridor stretched out before me. She must have turned, I thought, into a branching hallway. I took a few steps further down the hall after her and stopped. My heart was in my throat. I decided to run back, try to find the others first. Clearly, there was something very wrong with her. I turned around to head back, to try to retrace the turns we'd made. As I started to turn, I heard it— a faint creaking sound above me. I felt the hairs on my arms standing up, goosebumps rising beneath.

Kristy hung upside down in front of me. She wore a crown of roses on her head. Her face was even with mine. Her eyes were missing. Two black holes gouged from their sockets. She screamed. I could feel her hot breath on my face. "RUN!" she cried. As splinters of bone split the surface of her skull, rupturing her skin. Horns, pushing out... blood dripping, running in rivulets off the tips. Ivy curled, curving and growing, winding down her neck. Leaves were sprouting as I opened my mouth wide. We screamed together.

After what felt like an eternity, my limbs obeyed me, and I turned and ran. I sprinted as fast as I could, sobbing, my breath coming in gasps. Tears streamed down my cheeks. My heart slammed against my ribcage. I launched myself around corners blindly.

I fell, tripping over my own feet, stumbling on all fours until I could find my balance. I sprinted past several doors before recognizing there were signs on them— the girl's wing. I realized with a tiny sliver of relief that I had made it to our hallway. I hadn't realized the guy's wing met up with ours coming around from the other direction. If only I could make it a little farther, before the...thing, that was, but wasn't Kristy caught up to me. I sprinted now, legs and arms pumping, until I burst out onto the landing at the top of the stairs to the girl's wing. I started to descend, taking the stairs two at a time and nearly landing on my face. I grabbed the railing, catching myself at the last moment.

"Cassie!" Someone called out from up ahead of me. "She's here! This way!" I heard running footsteps and saw lights bobbing up and down in the dim light filtering through the skylight above.

"I'm here!" I called back, sobs of relief wracking my chest. I collapsed in a heap on the ground at the top of the main staircase.

Someone ran up to me before slamming to their knees and sliding to a stop at my side. I felt Ben's arms wrapping around me, pulling me to him. I put my face in my hands and wept. I couldn't hear or couldn't understand what he was saying to me. He ran a hand down the back of my head, over my hair, soothing me. After a few minutes, I quieted. "Shh, it's going to be okay," he murmured. "It's okay. You're safe now."

I lifted my head slowly. He peered at me, trying to make out my features in the darkness. "Cassie?" He reached out, tucking a now damp lock of hair behind my ear. "What happened?"

I looked around and saw the others: Mark...Josh, with his arm around Emily, his body half in front of hers, as though he was trying to shield her from whatever had happened to me. Mike and Amy were there, and behind them was Catherine. They were all wide-eyed, staring at me, waiting for me to speak.

"K—" I started, but my throat was raw from screaming and sobbing, my voice coming out a croak. I cleared my throat. "Kristy." I managed.

"Kristy?" Emily replied, her voice sounding small. "She's here? Did you find her?"

I nodded. "Yes, y-yes." I saw the others react, eyebrows raising. Mike looked behind me, back the way I had come.

"Where is she now?" Mike asked. "What happened to her?"

"It was... it was Kristy..." I continued, "but, it wasn't her, it wasn't her..." I began to cry softly again, trembling. Ben gripped me tighter, his hand squeezing my upper arm. I took a deep breath. "She wouldn't answer me, wouldn't say anything. She had her back to me. I followed her, but she ran away... I..."

"It's okay," Ben said, taking a deep breath.

"I found her," I continued, "but then... she changed."

"Changed? Changed how?" Josh asked, his voice apprehensive.

"Her face..." I said, a sob escaping me again. "She had no eyes. It was horrible. I screamed, and she was, she was screaming too."

"God..." Catherine muttered, crossing herself.

I grabbed Ben's shirt, turning to him. "She was wearing the same dress she had on that night, the night she went missing. And her feet... her feet were dirty like she'd been running in the mud outside."

"Okay." Ben nodded. "Okay..." his voice gentle, "I think maybe," he looked reluctant to continue. "I think maybe...do you think maybe you had a bad dream? A nightmare again?"

"No!" I sobbed. "No, Ben, it was real. It really happened, I swear..."

"Okay." He nodded, like he was agreeing with me. "Okay then. Well, she's gone now. It's going to be okay." I nodded, wiping tears away. "Why don't we, um," he paused, looking over at the others, at Josh and Emily. "Why don't we head back now, okay? Let's head to bed."

I took a big, deep breath, trying to calm myself down. I nodded again in agreement. Catherine and Amy looked relieved. Mike looked questioningly at Josh. "Are we going to go look for her?" Josh looked over at us. At Ben, I realized, and then shook his head no to Mike, waving his hand. They didn't believe me. And really, I couldn't blame them. I was an incoherent, rambling mess.

Ben pulled me gently to my feet, supporting me as we returned to the guy's wing. We arrived at the door to Josh's room, and Emily came and stood next to me, wrapping an arm around my waist and helping to hold me up as Ben stepped aside to speak to Josh. They whispered back and forth to each other for a minute before Ben returned to me, supporting my weight again.

He told Emily, "I think Cassie should come with me for the rest of tonight. I'll make sure she's okay."

Emily looked at him momentarily, then at me, eyebrows raised. I nodded weakly, and she let him lead me down the hall.

I felt completely numb as he brought me through the door to his bedroom, helped me climb into bed, and lit several candles on the dresser.

Then he locked the door, double-checking it, and came to lay on the other side of the bed. He pulled the covers over me, tucking me in. I stared at the candles on the dresser opposite. There was a Harvard pennant on the wall hanging over the dresser. A photo in a frame hung beside it. I couldn't quite see the details, but I thought I could make out Josh and Ben's faces. It looked like they were wearing graduation hats.

"I won't be able to sleep," I said quietly to him. He was propped up on one elbow, watching me from across the bed. He had left a big distance between us. "Can I lay with you?" I asked.

"Of course," he said, opening his arms and lifting the covers as I slid over to him. I settled down against him, and he wrapped his arms around me. After a moment, he began to stroke the back of my head, running his fingers gently through my hair. I lay with my head on his chest, my eyes open, for a long time.

FRIDAY

I woke to sunlight streaming through the open curtains early the next morning. Ben seemed overly quiet and thoughtful. He didn't bring up last night, or try to ask me anything further about what had happened. He stroked my hair until I fell asleep. I woke up to find him sitting in the chair out on the balcony. The French doors stood open, cool, crisp morning air flooding the room and clearing my head.

From the general mood, I guessed I wasn't the only one relieved that last night was over. The skies were clear of rain clouds, and there was a buzz of excitement in the air. The wedding rehearsal and rehearsal dinner would take place this evening.

Ben had offered to head downstairs on his own to try to scrounge up some coffee for me, but I insisted I was up to the task of joining him. While I appreciated his concern, it was starting to feel like he was treating me too delicately. As though he thought I was fragile and might break at any second. I glanced at my reflection briefly in the mirror in Ben's bathroom. I had dark circles under my eyes, and my skin looked extra pale. My blue eyes were tired and dull. I sighed. Maybe I shouldn't blame him. I felt and looked awful this morning. He smiled brightly at me when I exited the bathroom, and we headed down together early for breakfast.

The breakfast spread was lackluster, no doubt because of the power. But the kitchen staff had managed to make coffee somehow. I blessed them as I held a steaming mug in my hands and breathed in the comforting aroma.

True to her word, Emily's mother, Anna, showed up practically at the crack of dawn. She had agreed begrudgingly to arrive on Friday but had told Emily she would be here "first thing." She strode into the dining hall during breakfast, like she owned the place, eyeing the massive dining table, the drapery, and the carpet skeptically, with her eyebrows raised.

"Mom!" Emily yelled, bolting out of her chair. She ran around the table and launched herself into her mother's arms. I had to try not to laugh at the look of shock on Anna's face.

"Well," she said, smoothing down her coat, eyeing her daughter up and down as well. "I'm glad I'm here, too." Emily led her mom swiftly out of the dining hall; I presumed to go find Josh.

I enjoyed a few moments of peace before Mark joined us downstairs. He saw me sitting at the table and made his way over to me, rubbing his hands together. "So, you and Benny Boy, huh? Who would've predicted that?"

"Oh my god, Mark..." I groaned. "It's way too early for that."

Mark laughed and patted me on the back, making his way over to get some food.

After breakfast, we were left to our own devices for a while. I decided to hang out and read in the girl's study upstairs. Ben had been dragged into helping with something wedding-related by Josh and Wes. Catherine was downstairs with Emily. But Amy and Blair announced they had decided to join me. More like they were asked to join me, to keep an eye on me and not let me out of their sight. I had overheard Ben talking to them in the hallway outside the dining hall. They were sitting on the other couch, chatting.

Their heads together as they giggled, gossiping about mutual friends. I heard a bit later when Catherine wandered in that some of Josh's family had arrived—his parents, his uncle, and some of his cousins.

Eventually, Ben walked into the study, looking for me. He was wearing his running clothes again.

"Hey," he said a little shyly.

"Hey," I said, smiling. I suddenly felt weirdly self-conscious as well.

"Um, so, it's getting kind of crazy downstairs."

"Oh really?" My eyebrows raised. "What's going on."

Ben shrugged. "Family arriving...everyone freaking out about the stuff that's been happening this week. Freaking out about the power being out. Although it sounds like Josh's Dad is already pulling strings to get a crew out here stat."

"Hmm." I nodded "Well, that's good, at least. If there's a time to use your influence, I guess it would be now."

Ben nodded. "True. And I have no doubt he'll get the power back on in no time."

"Should I go check on Emily?" I asked him. I remembered thinking to myself the first night that I should try to shield her from the family drama if I could.

Ben shook his head. "I wouldn't if I were you. I practically got dismissed just now." He held up both hands. "Although, trust me, I didn't mind one bit. Add to that, there's a bunch of stuff being delivered."

"Oh yeah?" I turned backward, leaning on the top of the couch. "Like what?"

"Like what appears to be an insane amount of flowers for starters. They're storing them in coolers or something downstairs tonight to keep them fresh. I don't know why they couldn't deliver them tomorrow, but that's stressing everyone out."

"Yeah, I did hear about that. I know Emily was not happy they had to be delivered Friday instead of Saturday."

"There's also a van with a bunch of other decorations, tables for the ballroom, God knows what else. That thing." He tipped his head towards the French glass doors, indicating something out on the lawn.

I hopped off the couch and jogged over, opening the doors and stepping onto the small balcony. I was surprised to see a low fog had settled in. I could see what I assumed was a giant wooden pergola being assembled in the distance. Men and women nearby were carrying white chairs, two at a time, setting them out on the lawn.

"Wow," I murmured, "this wedding is really finally happening."

Ben looked at me sideways. "Don't speak too soon. We still have another night to get through. Let's hope someone decides to stay in their room tonight." I gave him a look and smacked him on the arm. "Ouch," he joked, rubbing his arm like it hurt. "Sorry. Too soon?"

I sighed. "I'm okay, Ben, really. You don't have to keep walking on eggshells with me." He turned to gaze at me as I stared out the window at the fog creeping through the woods. I felt him studying my profile.

"I'm just worried about you, Cassie. But I know you're tough, okay? I'm not trying to...to treat you like you can't handle things."

"I know," I said, turning and making an effort to smile. "I know you're not. That's not what I meant. I appreciate you looking out for me."

Ben nodded. "Are you up for going for a run?" He asked. "Or too tired? No worries if so. Maybe the fresh air would be good."

I contemplated for a moment. We'd eaten breakfast not too long ago, but my appetite hadn't been great. I thought I'd be okay to run.

"The general stress levels in the house are too stressful for me right now," Ben added. "None of it has anything to do with me, but I'm sucking in the energy around me like a sponge. I gotta get out of here."

I laughed. "I can understand that." I'd forgotten how stressful weddings could be, especially with Emily's family involved. Who knows what kind of drama Anna would get up to. And it's not like we were coming off of a relaxing, peaceful week. "Sure," I said, smiling at him. "Why not? You're right; it might be nice to get out of the house for a bit."

I went back to my room and changed quickly into my running gear. We met again at the top of the staircase. I almost asked Ben to wait outside my door for me, but I felt more than a little silly. In the light of day, I realized that as terrifying as last night had been, there was no way any of it had been real. I didn't need to be nervous to walk down the hall alone. Still, I found myself looking up and down the hallway as I went, checking the ceiling.

We descended the stairs just in time for Ben to introduce me to Josh's parents. Josh's Uncle, his dad's brother, and a few male cousins weren't far behind. I felt a little intimidated meeting them all at once. They were an intimidating group, but they also made a point to thank me for coming and make sure I felt welcome.

I could see where Josh got his looks from. Josh's father, Martin, clapped Ben on the back before pulling him into a hug. "I swear, you still get taller every time I see you, son."

Ben, laughing, replied, "It's been a while! It's so good to see you." He turned towards me and said, "This is Cassie, one of Emily's bridesmaids."

Martin grasped my hands in his. "I'm so pleased to finally meet you, young lady." His brown eyes were warm and kind. "Have you been enjoying the house so far?"

I mustered my best smile and replied, "You have a beautiful home."

He seemed pleased by my response. The lines next to his eyes deepened. "Ah well... while the Hideaway, or Haverford Home, as is its proper name, is not our home year-round, it is certainly our ancestral home." He released my hands. "And we are very proud of her and her history."

I was tempted to ask if he could share a few details of that history with me, specifically regarding any human sacrifices that might have taken place on the property, when Ben, seeming to read my mind, placed a hand on my shoulder. He gently guided me towards the front doors.

"We were just heading out for a run, actually. We wanted to make sure we got some exercise in before the rehearsal starts."

Martin nodded. "Enjoy your run." We turned to leave. "Just watch your step out in those woods. They can be treacherous."

Ben nodded to him. "We'll be careful." He nudged me as we made our way out the front doors. "You have a beautiful home," he mimicked me. "What a diplomatic answer!"

I chuckled wryly. "That was the best I could do."

Our run was the calmest part of our day. We set off at an even clip, significantly slower than the last time, and we took our time, neither of us rushing to get back to the house. Despite the fog, it was a beautiful morning. The air felt slightly chilly and refreshing. As we ran, I felt that it was truly a new day. The events of the past week were starting to feel more distant and a little fuzzy. Perhaps I had been overreacting all along, my imagination running out of control. We rounded a curve, and on the trail up ahead, a large buck was visible in the fog. He had heard us coming and was standing frozen in place, looking right at us. We slowed to a stop. I stared into his large, soft eyes. Why did I feel like he was looking right back at me? I don't know how long I stood there before Ben's voice broke me out of my concentration with a start.

"Cassie." Ben grabbed my arm. "Are you okay?"

"Yeah." I shook my head. "Of course I am I'm fine."

He gave me a strange look.

"Come on, let's keep going." I shrugged his hand off my arm, and we picked up our pace. The deer was gone.

Thankfully, nothing eventful happened on the way back. We turned around, where the path jogged off to the right towards the village and made our way back. When we got back to the trailhead, we could see the pergola and chair setup had come a long way.

"Come on," Ben said, still breathing heavily. We better head in."

I nodded, then turned to look off to the left toward the willow tree. I couldn't see it from here because of the fog. "Hang on," I replied, taking deep breaths myself. "I kind of want to go check out the willow tree for a minute."

Ben stared at me for a long moment. "You don't know when to quit, do you?" He said.

I looked at him, raising an eyebrow. "What's that supposed to mean?" He started to respond, but I held up a finger. "And don't you dare say, whatever you think it means." Ben grinned, chuckling. "I swear to god, Ben..."

"No." He laughed. "I wasn't going to say that. I just mean... haven't you had enough yet?"

"Enough of what?"

"Of all of this." He held his hands out gesturing around us. "The creepy bouquets, the deer, the paintings, the inexplicable vision of Kristy you had when you wandered off alone last night?" I sighed loudly, placing my hands on my hips. "After last night, I would have thought that you'd had enough. That you were done...with trying to figure out what's happening. But you're not, are you? You just don't seem to know when to quit."

I looked at him, a slow smile breaking out over my face. "No, I'm not done, Ben. Not even close."

He rolled his eyes, throwing his hands up.

"Yeah, I got the crap scared out of me last night, but I'm not going to just give up. Something is very, very wrong here. And don't tell me you don't feel it."

He had turned away from me to momentarily gaze back at the tree line before turning to face me again.

"I do, Cassie. I do. Something feels...off, for sure. This whole week has felt... ominous. Like, it's building up to something. Like something is about to happen, but I just don't know what."

I nodded, agreeing completely. That was exactly how I felt. That something was coming; something awful was about to happen.

"But," he continued, "I think the best thing, at this point, for your own sake, would be just to let it go. The rehearsal dinner is tonight; the wedding is tomorrow. We are almost done with this week. Let's just get through the rest of it and leave."

"Hmm," I said, nodding. "So, you're not even a little bit curious about who's behind all of this? About figuring out why someone would go to the trouble of making those creepy bouquets, making little voodoo dolls of us, running around chopping off animal heads, feet, and whatever other appendage you found in my room?"

Ben shook his head, tight-lipped. "You don't want to know. Trust me." I stared at him for a long moment.

"Yeah, okay then. I'm going to check out the willow tree to make sure we aren't missing anything. Are you coming with me or not?"

"Of course I am, Cassie," he said, exasperated. "But I want you to promise, for real this time, that you won't leave your room alone tonight. I'm not kidding. If there is someone out there moving around the house at night... it's reckless and dangerous."

"Okay, okay," I said, "I get it. Trust me, I'm not in a hurry to wander around at night again any time soon."

We decided to head over to the willow at a light jog. We headed in the general direction of the tree. Eventually, it loomed out of the fog in front of us. Undoubtedly, the fog added to the general feeling of mystery and apprehension I felt approaching the willow. But I knew it wasn't just the fog, either. We slowed simultaneously. Neither of us spoke for a moment. I peered through the thick hanging branches. There was certainly nothing obvious visible, but the tree was massive.

"You know," Ben murmured in a soft voice, "to the pagans, the willow tree was magical; it was closely associated with water, the moon, and the goddess. It sort of represented feminine power."

"Hmm," I murmured back, gazing at its hidden depths. I thought of my dream, how I had danced around the willow with my sisters, all women. I reached out, brushing my hand against the hanging leaves, moving them gently aside like a curtain. I slipped through the opening. Ben followed closely behind me.

We walked slowly around the base of the tree. I couldn't have fit my arms around it, not even with four of me. I wondered how old this tree was to have grown so huge. Had they really danced around it? Just as I had in my dream? I couldn't shake the feeling deep down that that part of my dream had been real somehow. Especially standing here now. I half expected to see the maid walking amongst the leaves. We didn't speak; I scanned the branches for a wind chime, the piece of frayed rope I thought I saw that day during horseback riding or anything more sinister that might be hanging there. I eventually gave up. There was clearly nothing here.

"What did you hope to find?" Ben asked.

"I wasn't hoping to find anything," I replied, thinking involuntarily of Kristy's face—her missing eyes. I shuddered slightly. I had wanted to make sure she wasn't here, but I wasn't about to admit that to Ben.

We hurried back to the house, wanting to make sure we had plenty of time to shower and change. I could only imagine Em's reaction if we were late for the rehearsal.

At the top of the stairs, I said bye to Ben and headed for my room. "Hey," he called out. I turned back to him. He reached up and tucked my flyaway, frizzy hairs behind my ear. I guess he was making a habit of that. "We still need to finish what we started last night before all the craziness happened," he said in a low voice. "Don't think I forgot."

"Ben." I colored as he leaned in to kiss me. "Gross, I'm all sweaty."

He chuckled against my lips. "I don't care." He kissed me briefly before letting me go and jogging off down the hallway.

I showered as quickly as I could. I just remembered that I should've checked with Emily about what we should wear for tonight. I chucked my useless cell phone onto the bed. I had picked it up, forgetting momentarily that I couldn't just text her to ask. Wrapping myself in my fluffy towel, I peeked out into the hallway. Seeing no one around, I quickly tiptoed to Amy's door and knocked softly.

"Who is it?" I heard her voice call out.

"It's me, Cassie!" I replied. A few seconds later, I heard the lock click, and the door swung inward.

Amy was wearing a long, formal-looking evening gown. I sighed. "That answers that question."

She looked confused for a moment. "What, is someone looking for me?"

"No, sorry." I shook my head. "I just got out of the shower and realized I didn't know what to wear for tonight. I guess I should have assumed it was formal wear again. I'm running out of dresses." I grumbled that last part more to myself.

Amy tilted her head to the side, looking a little sorry for me for a moment. Of course, I thought. Wearing all these borrowed dresses, whoever they belonged to, probably did little to hide the fact that I was the poor girl to these people. I scolded myself instantly for thinking that. Amy had been nothing but kind to me. She thought for a moment, then turned to look back into her room.

"What about my closet?" she asked. "I saw a few dresses in there earlier that might fit you. "They looked really nice," she added helpfully.

I smiled. "Sure, that would be worth checking out."

She swung the door open wider for me to enter her room. We sifted through the dresses in the closet together. She was quiet at first, then she asked me, "Why do you think those... bouquet things were only left in your room and Kristy's room?"

I looked over at her sharply. It was the first time she'd really mentioned anything about the stuff that had been happening to me. "I don't know," I said slowly. "It does seem strange, doesn't it? It hasn't happened again since that night." She was staring at the empty space above her headboard now. "You know," I started, "I never got to hear how Kristy and Emily met."

She looked over at me. "What do you mean?"

"You know, the other night at dinner. We were all going around the table saying how we knew Emily. How did Kristy know her? Did she ever tell you?"

Amy stared out her window for a moment, thinking. "I'm pretty sure they met in a class at college," she said after a moment. "Kristy was there on scholarship if I remember correctly. She lost both her parents fairly young." I raised my eyebrows at that. I didn't know that about her. Amy nodded, seeing my expression. "She didn't..." she trailed off, looking at the floor. "She didn't have much. But she was really smart."

"Really?" *Wow*, I thought. "And how did you meet Emily?" I asked.

Amy smiled easily at that. "Oh, our families are old friends. Our dads actually went to Oxford together." Oxford. Huh. "Emily and I played together all the time when we were kids." I pulled a silver-blue corset-style ballerina dress out of the closet with one hand, keeping my towel closed with the other and held it up for her. Amy smiled warmly. "It's perfect. I bet it looks beautiful on you. It'll match your eyes. And your hair."

I smiled back. Thanking her, I headed back to my room. It wasn't until the door shut behind me that it occurred to me that we had been referring to Kristy in the past tense.

I made my way alone down the hallway towards the grand staircase. As I disturbed the freshly vacuumed carpet, my black flats left a visible trail of light footprints. I had debated over wearing my high heels again. But the dress reminded me of something a ballet dancer would wear and seemed to call for ballet flats. Plus, if I were going to spend the evening walking up and down the aisle a billion times, I would rather do it in comfortable shoes.

When I made it to the top of the stairs, I saw everyone was starting to gather in the foyer. I breathed a sigh of relief; thankful I wasn't late. Ben was standing below, near the entrance to the dining hall, wearing his all-black suit again, of course. How appropriate for a wedding, I thought, rolling my eyes internally. Although I had to admit, he did look good in black. I saw him notice me descending the stairs and do a double take. The look he gave me made my core melt. I focused on trying not to trip over my own feet. Emily and Josh stood with their parents at the base of the stairs, speaking with an older man dressed like a minister. Emily's face lit up when she saw me. She excused herself and came over and took my hand, squeezing it in hers.

"Where did you find that dress? It looks fabulous on you. Did you notice the power is back on?" She jumped up and down excitedly. She was radiant in a white silk bodycon dress. Her hair had been curled and pinned back like she would wear it tomorrow. I remembered they were doing a practice run of her makeup and hair today.

"Yes," I responded, mirroring her excitement. "Just in time! You look gorgeous, by the way. Your hair is perfect; I wouldn't change a thing."

"Why thank you." She smiled and curtsied a little. Anna, Emily's mother, had approached us along with Josh's parents and the minister. Josh's father introduced him to me as Father Thomas. He looked at me with baleful eyes, stepped in front of me, crossed himself, and then proceeded to do the same to me.

"Bless you, my child," he said solemnly.

"Thank you..." I said awkwardly in a small voice, unsure how I was supposed to respond. Emily gave me a funny, confused look like she was about to laugh. I shook my head slightly, keeping my face still as a stone. Father Thomas lost interest in me as he was led on to meet someone else.

"What the heck?" I mouthed to Emily. She laughed before being pulled away by one of the staff to weigh in on a question about the table settings.

"Boo!" I heard a voice whisper-shout in my ear. I jumped a little, leaning away and turning to find Mark laughing at me. "Awe, don't look so disappointed," he said, "it's just me, not your new boyfriend."

"What are you, five?" I asked Mark, shaking my head. "So, are we having fun yet?" I asked him, scanning the room. Come to think of it, where was Ben?

"Oh, loads," Mark replied. "But I'll be having a lot more fun when this rehearsal ends, and we can get something to drink."

I shook my head again. "One track mind." Mark winked at me.

Josh's Dad, Martin, I recalled his name after a moment's forgetfulness, announced that we were to head outside to start the rehearsal. Mark offered me his arm, and we followed the group down the hallway. I guessed it made more sense to head through the library than the front doors, but it made for a slow procession, given we all had to crowd together and shuffle down the narrower corridors to get there.

The day had warmed considerably. Which I was thankful for, given I hadn't thought to grab a sweater or anything to ward off the chill. The dense fog, which had lingered for most of the morning, had finally cleared. We went through a basic run-down of events, interspersed with jokes from the guys here and there. Overall, the group was in a happy, festive mood. The stress of the morning seemed to have melted away now that plans were set and in place. I was a little disappointed to learn that Mark was to be my partner walking down the aisle. I guess I just assumed I would get to walk with Ben. But it was based on height, which made the most sense. It could have been worse; poor Mike had to walk all by himself since Kristy hadn't returned. I suppressed a shudder as the image of her face flashed before me again.

I was right about walking up and down the aisle a billion times. It seemed to me we could have been done much earlier than we were, but they wanted everything to be just right. Watching Emily and Josh practice their vows made me surprisingly a little teary-eyed.

When even Emily and Anna were finally satisfied, we concluded for the evening and made our way back through the library into the house. I was surprised at first to learn that the rehearsal dinner would take place upstairs, in the grand ballroom. But when I thought about it, I realized the dining table downstairs probably wouldn't be large enough to seat everyone present.

The staff had done an excellent job. Round tables were set up on the sides of the room for guests, with a long table against the middle of the far wall for the wedding party. Family were to be seated at tables on either side. The middle of the ballroom floor was left open for dancing. It made sense that they set it up for the wedding tomorrow so as not to have to move everything again. For tonight, they had seated the group at the round tables only. A bar had also been set up in a corner of the room. I was shocked to see a live band playing light music in the background. In true Emily fashion, our places at the table had been marked. I found my seat and was pleased to see Mark, Ben, Amy, and Mike at my table. Unfortunately, Ben was seated across from me rather than next to me.

We sat through a brief string of toasts and cheers. The big speeches would be saved for tomorrow night. The servers brought us drinks to our table. We were all settled in and waiting for the food to be served. A cacophony of lively conversation took place all around when I saw Josh's Dad get up from his table and make his way over to the door. Harvey was peeking through the doorway. He must have called him over to speak to him. They concluded a brief exchange, and Harvey left. I watched Josh's Dad return to his seat and decided to take my chance. I swiftly got up from the table and made my way out the door. I could see Harvey retreating down the hallway, disappearing around a corner. I thought, not for the first time, he walked fast for an older man.

I broke into a light jog to keep up with him, grateful I had chosen my flats. He must have heard me coming because he stopped and turned towards me. "Everything okay, Miss?" He asked.

"Yes." I nodded, calming my breathing. "I've been meaning to find and talk to you, but I didn't have a chance."

He nodded amicably. "What about, Miss?" I thought for a moment, suddenly at a loss. I didn't know what to ask him. Where did I even begin?

"That day," I started slowly, "with the horses," I struggled to remember her name for a moment. "With Bessie." He nodded, grimacing slightly. "Did you hear the wind chimes?"

Harvey thought for a moment. "No, can't say as I did, Miss."

I nodded thoughtfully. "But are there wind chimes somewhere near there?"

"Near the old willow tree?" He looked off to his right side, at the ceiling. "Not that I know of." I nodded, considering. "Not unless someone put 'em there without anyone knowing."

I nodded again. "And do you remember if wind chimes were hanging there, say, a long time ago, in the past?"

He looked off to his right again, thinking. "Now that you ask, it may be as if I can vaguely remember wind chimes at one point. But yes, that would have been a long time ago now."

"And..." I paused momentarily, considering. "Can you ever remember anything else, hanging from that tree... a long time ago?" Harvey stared at me. I waited expectantly.

His eyes flickered back and forth over my face, taking in my features. "I'm not a young man," he sighed, "I know; I'm old as the hills to you. And you look as young as a child to me, Miss. I'll tell you what I do know." He lowered his voice. "If you," he pointed a gnarly finger at me, "know anything, about anything, hanging from that tree... my first piece of advice to you is to keep it to yourself. And my second piece of advice to you, is to leave." With that, he turned away and left me alone in the hallway— a lump in my throat.

I made my way slowly back to the ballroom, my shoulders slumped. I wanted to run after him, force him to tell me more, tell me what he knew. But I felt a shiver down my spine, recalling his words. Perhaps he was right, just like Ben had said earlier. Maybe I should just mind my own business. Keep my mouth shut and leave this place in my dust the second the wedding was over.

I entered the ballroom to see that Ben had been roped into giving a toast. He saw me enter the room, and the relief on his face was visible.

When he finished, we cheered and sipped our drinks. I had opted for white wine again tonight, but the taste of it made my stomach churn.

The conversation was kept lighthearted throughout dinner. Mark and Amy were a big help in that department. Ben and I sat rather silently, only speaking when necessary. He gave me a look that asked me what was wrong with his eyes. But I shook my head no. I would have to wait to tell him later. I was surprised when dinner concluded, and the music changed to become more lively. Emily and Josh got up at their families' prompting to dance. We all clapped and cheered, the guys catcalling as they kissed. Eventually, other couples started towards the middle of the dance floor to join them. I smiled to see Josh's parents dancing together. Anna had brought her new boyfriend. Not to be outdone, she led him out onto the floor. Mark stood up and turned to Amy, bowing and asking her to dance. She flushed slightly and agreed, smiling. I smiled broadly, watching them go. Ben got up and slowly walked around the table to me. He held his hand out. "Do you think you can spare a dance for me tonight?"

I smiled, already taking his hand. "I guess I can save *one* dance for you." He chuckled and led me out to the middle of the floor. He pulled me close to him, tucking one arm around my waist and holding my hand aloft with the other. He whispered close to my ear, "You look absolutely stunning tonight. That dress was made for you." I blushed slightly.

"You don't look so bad yourself. Although, what's with the all-black thing?" He just laughed, offering me no explanation.

"Where did you disappear to earlier?" he asked. I quickly recounted my conversation with Harvey in a hushed tone. When I got to the last part, I felt him stiffen in my arms.

"He actually said that?" he asked incredulously. I nodded, my chin brushing against his shoulder.

"Jesus," Ben sighed. "I don't believe it."

"I know," I whispered back. I wish he would tell me more, but I have a feeling that's all we'll get out of him. Maybe it's best to just take his advice and leave well enough alone. Nothing else has happened lately—well... other than me losing my mind last night. Maybe whoever was doing this is done."

Ben nodded. "I think that's for the best at this point. Let's just get through tonight and tomorrow, and we won't have to worry about any of this anymore." He pulled me closer to him. I leaned my head on his shoulder and relaxed, enjoying swaying with him to the music, feeling his arms around me. I wondered for the first time what would happen to us after the week was over. I realized that I didn't know much about Ben's life. I had no clue where he lived. Would I ever even see him again? What if we lived too far apart? The thought made my gut twist. I noticed Martin was watching us, his eyes tracking us as we danced, and he had a thoughtful look on his face. I decided it wasn't the time or the place to bring up the future. It was a discussion that would have to wait for another time.

Not wanting to be up half the night tonight and starting to feel worn out, the lack of sleep finally taking its toll, I made my excuses after about an hour and a half of dancing and partying. Ben wasn't quite ready to turn in yet. He had promised to play a round of billiards with Josh, Wes, and their cousins. I had a feeling they were planning on smoking the big cigars Wes had pulled out of his pocket earlier.

Ben walked me to my room and kissed me goodnight at the door. Even my toes were tingling by the time he left. When he turned to go, I was half tempted to ask him to stay. I had to work hard on the walk here to convince him I would be safe alone in my room. From what I had gathered, Anna and Josh's mom, Patricia, I think, had overseen putting all the mattresses back where they belonged anyway. It seemed everyone would be back to sleeping in their own rooms for tonight. Even still, he had offered to sleep on my floor just in case. He hadn't suggested he spend the night in my bed, though I had a feeling he had been hoping I would be the one to suggest it. I smiled faintly at the thought.

I made quick work of undressing and getting ready for bed. I carefully hung the silver-blue dress up in my closet. I double-checked that my door was locked, although a remote part of me thought there was little point in that. Flicking off the lights, I skipped lightly, jumping into bed. I may have been asleep before my head hit the pillow.

I awoke hours later and, checking my watch, saw that it was just past two in the morning. It seemed unlikely that partiers would still be stumbling to bed at this hour. I sat listening for several seconds, and hearing nothing; I closed my eyes and attempted to go back to sleep. A moment later, I heard a faint scratching sound out in the hallway. I sat up quickly, scooting back against the headboard while pulling the comforter to my chin. I waited. But all I could hear was the sound of my own breathing and my heart pounding in my chest. Then I heard it again: a scratching sound at the door and whining...it almost sounded like a dog. Had someone brought a dog with them?

After several more minutes of this, I became sure it was a dog I was hearing. I cursed myself for being stupid while at the same time deciding I had no other option. Ben was going to kill me if he found out I left my room again. I got up and made my way to the door. Twisting the handle and slowly pulling the door open, I peeked out into the hallway with the door open a crack and saw nothing. Sighing, my heart in my throat, I pulled it open wider and stuck my head into the hallway a bit.

There it was. A friendly-looking dog was to the left of my door, about halfway down the hall. I felt an immense wave of relief. It looked like a sheepdog, I thought; no, a border collie—one of those black and white dogs that herd sheep. The dog was standing there, wagging his tail back and forth, his mouth open and relaxed, panting slightly. He watched me watching him.

Then, abruptly, he turned and headed a few feet down the hallway before stopping and turning back to look at me. I didn't move. He stared at me for a few seconds, tilting his head to the side, and the look on his face was as though he was trying to talk to me. He turned and went a few more feet down the hall. Then stopped and looked back at me again, tail wagging still. He wanted me to follow him, I realized. Sighing, I disappeared into my room for a second; grabbing my robe and slinging it on, I followed him down the hall, pulling my door shut behind me.

He led me down the hall, always staying about the same distance ahead. We came to what I recognized as the study door, which had been left cracked open. He stopped and looked at me once more before going inside. I approached the door and saw a fire going in the hearth. I peered around the edge of the door, not wanting to disturb anyone inside. A man was seated at the large desk at the back of the room. I could see only the top of his head as he looked down at the desk. He appeared to be writing in a leather-bound journal or ledger. The dog had curled up next to the desk and was watching me.

I cleared my throat, not wanting to startle him. He didn't react at all. Realizing I hadn't been loud enough, I repeated the sound louder, and still, nothing. I took a tentative step into the room. He lifted a page of the journal, and I froze. Even from this distance, I thought I recognized the runes on the page. I made my way closer to the desk, curiosity getting the best of me. He continued working studiously, giving no indication that he knew I was there. The dog gave a warning growl, causing the man to pause and look up from the desk, searching for the dog.

I gasped involuntarily. I knew his face. He looked almost exactly like the man in the painting downstairs. Josh's great-grandfather, or whoever he was. I took in his clothes and his hairstyle. I glanced around at the furnishings in the room. The curtains were different from the last time I was in the room. I swung my head to the wall next to the desk. The painting of the house was missing. There was only a blank wall. I felt the hair on my neck rise and prickling tears gathering at the bottom of my eyes. I crept cautiously closer to the desk, starting to suspect that he couldn't see or hear me in the room.

I realized I had been right; the journal pages contained runes, but not just runes. I saw what looked like a large cursive script as well. Drawings dotted the pages. Had this been the man who drew the page I'd found? Was it ripped out of this journal? I realized with a start that several photos were lying on the desk next to the journal. I crept as close as I dared. I could see from here that the top photograph showed a girl dancing with her arms raised above her head. I realized with a start that she was naked. And she wasn't dancing...I realized with a start. She must be hanging upside down, but the photo was facing him, making it look to me like she was right side up. Her eyes were missing. I stared, starting to tremble.

There was a small pile of photographs there...a pile, I thought. How many? How many girls had he done this to? Why? I clenched my fists. I wanted to strike him, wanted to hurt him. Stop him from ever hurting anyone else ever again. The dog growled again, raising on all fours. He was watching me, his tail still wagging. I had a feeling, though, that this was as close as he would let me get.

The man stopped abruptly, watching the dog nervously, peering around the room and looking towards the door to the hallway. "What is it, boy?" He murmured. His voice was smooth but strangely accented. I watched as his gaze swept over me, lingered where I was standing, where the dog was staring. He couldn't see me, I reminded myself, heart pounding.

Abruptly, he scooped up the photographs and shoved them into the pages of the journal. He put the journal into a drawer on the top right of the desk, shutting it and turning the key in the lock. I saw it was a tiny golden key on a long chain. He looped it over his head, tucking it into his shirt. The dog started barking at me, making an awful racket. I heard the wind chimes again, faint this time, in the distance. I felt weak, almost lightheaded. I turned to leave, stumbling towards the door. I made it about halfway to the door before I collapsed.

SATURDAY

I woke slowly, sunlight streaming into my eyes. Why was I so sore? I couldn't move a muscle without my limbs screaming in pain. I felt as though I hadn't moved in years. I opened my eyes and forced my body into a seated position. I scanned the room, confused. Why was I in the study? I remembered with a pang of fear what I had seen last night. My head swiveled to check the wall. The painting was there. I breathed a sigh of relief.

I stood stiffly and made my way slowly over to the desk. I noted that the French glass doors that led onto the balcony were open. How odd. I tried the locked drawer again, although I knew what the outcome would be. I wondered if I could try to pick the lock with a bobby pin.

Mike's head peeked around the doorframe, scanning the room. He saw me by the desk and yelled down the hall to someone. "She's in here!"

I heard running footsteps coming down the hall. Emily, followed by Ben, burst past Mike into the room. "Jesus," Emily said. "What the hell, Cassie? Where have you been?" She looked really upset.

I stared at them in confusion. "What do you mean? I just woke up." I turned and looked outside. "Why, what time is it?"

Ben was breathing heavily. He slid one hand through his already disheveled hair. He leaned forward, his hands propped on his knees, head hanging. Was he going to be sick?

"What time is it?" Emily asked incredulously. "Cassie, it's almost 9:30 in the morning. We've been searching for you for over an hour."

Ben stood up and paced a few steps. He ran his hands through his hair again. He was taking deep, calming breaths. I looked back and forth from Emily to Ben and then at Mike.

Mike said, "Woke up from where? You weren't in your bed this morning."

I stared at the approximate spot on the floor where I had fallen and apparently spent the night. "I...I was in here," I said.

Emily shook her head. "No, you weren't Cass. This is one of the first rooms we checked."

"No, I was; I was here the whole time. I...I heard something in the middle of the night. I came in here, and I...passed out." They stared at me uncomprehendingly. "I fainted," I said. "Right over there on the floor. I must have spent the whole night there. I literally just woke up."

Mike and Emily looked back and forth at each other. "Maybe the couch was blocking the view of her from the doorway?" Mike mused. "It might have been possible to miss her lying on the floor like that." Emily's brow furrowed.

"I thought I..." Emily started.

Ben interrupted her, "I'm sorry...you heard a sound in the middle of the night, so you left your room and went to investigate it? Alone?" He looked angry.

"Ben..." I sighed.

"No, Cassie! Come on!" he yelled, flinging his arms out wide. "What were you thinking?" Correction. He was furious and almost looked like he was going to cry.

"I'm sorry, Ben, okay?" I felt terrible. Emily had spent the morning of her wedding searching for me, and I had scared the shit out of Ben.

"No, it's not okay. I thought you were..." he trailed off. "I need to get some air." He left the room abruptly.

"So, I'm guessing you don't know... but someone messed with your room," Mike said evenly, eyes wide.

"What do you mean?" I asked wearily. My heartbeat started to drum faintly.

"They wrote all over your bedroom door. They look like those runes... or whatever. And we're pretty sure they're written in... in blood." *What the hell?* I felt my veins go ice cold.

"They also left roses, and...candles, and..." Emily trailed off.

"In my room?" I asked. She just nodded gravely.

Josh walked in a few seconds later. He looked back and forth between Emily and out at the hall. "Is he okay?" He gestured out the door with his thumb. Emily just shook her head no.

"I'm so sorry to have scared everyone; I shouldn't have left my room and gone off alone. I thought I heard a dog in the hallway..." I shook my head. "I don't know what happened."

Emily shook her head again. "It's not your fault you passed out."

"You passed out?" Josh asked. I quickly repeated the story for him. The version that left out all the details. "Well," Josh replied, "We're all just glad you're okay. You had us going for a bit there. Especially with all the...all the..." He drifted off, gesturing vaguely down the hall. Then he shook his head at us, chuckling a little. "My god, though. He was losing his mind.

I've never seen him like that." He gazed at me like he was oddly impressed. I flushed slightly at that. Poor Ben. What a mess.

I mumbled a string of further apologies, and we headed down the hall to my door. Wes, Catherine, and Amy were all standing there, staring at the door, speaking in hushed tones. They stepped aside as the four of us approached. I came to a stop in front of the door. Someone had covered the white door in reddish-brown runes from top to bottom. They formed clusters, I realized, my heart pounding. They zigzagged back and forth across the door in the same irregular pattern from the paper. "Who is doing this?" I heard myself whisper in a soft voice. I turned to face the others. "Who is doing this?" I demanded loudly. Emily looked miserable. She shook her head at me, one tear slipping down her cheek. She reached up a hand and hastily brushed it away. Part of me had assumed all of this would just stop once everyone else started arriving. Clearly, I was wrong. Whoever was responsible still had an agenda.

I pushed the door open into my room, trying to touch the doorknob as little as possible. I gasped as I entered. There were bright red roses... everywhere... bunches tied to all four bedposts. Petals were scattered all over the bed, all over the floor. A bouquet sat on the bedside table. There were three more on the dresser. There were also dozens of lit candles. They littered the dresser and bedside table but were also placed in the middle of the floor. It looked like they were in a circular pattern on the floor. I stepped into the room. The outer ring of candles was connected by a ring of what I assumed was more blood. The center of the circle held a star, also painted in blood. It was a pentagram.

I was pretty sure the pentagram was a symbol for the devil, but who knew what it symbolized in paganism. No wonder Ben was so upset. Slowly, I turned to face the group in the hall. A tear streamed down my cheek involuntarily. They just stared back at me. Josh's brows were creased in anger. Mike was shaking his head. He cracked his knuckles. "When I find these assholes, they're going to pay."

Mike and Amy waited outside my room for me, guarding my door while I quickly showered and changed. My mind reeled while I stood under the hot water. When was this done? I couldn't imagine any of it had been there when I woke up during the night; how could I not have noticed? Obviously, there's no way the candles were lit. Maybe being out of the bedroom had protected me from whoever did this. Then a sudden thought occurred to me. Had I ever even seen my room last night...or did I somehow sleepwalk out of my room, down the hall, and into the study. Did I walk right past all of it? Maybe the entire thing, from the moment I woke up, was just part of my dream...vision...or whatever the heck they were. Maybe there was something seriously wrong with me. My mind rejected that idea. It was the house; it had to be. I could feel it in my gut. That sense of dread was always there in the background. It just got...quieter at times.

We all headed downstairs and gathered in the guy's lounge for a while. Naturally, the theories started back up again. "Why are they targeting your room?" Catherine asked me at one point. Her eyebrows raised. She looked at me thoughtfully for a long moment. "And you didn't see anything? Hear anything?" She eyed me suspiciously. Emily shot her a quick sideways glance. Was she trying to imply I had something to do with this?

"What? You think I planted all that crap in my room myself? Wrote runes on my own door in blood? Where the heck did I get the blood from, exactly?"

Catherine flushed slightly. She pursed her lips and looked away from me. "I'm not saying that... it just... seems strange," she finished.

"Yeah, well it seems pretty strange to me, too." I sighed, folding my arms across my chest.

"No one is saying you did this Cassie. We're all just trying to understand what's happening." Emily patted my knee absentmindedly.

I sat sullenly, silent throughout the rest of the conversation. Did Catherine think I was doing all of this? What would be my motive? Attention? I watched the others as they debated. Who else sitting here might be thinking the same thing? Anna eventually came in search of Emily. She told me she had been relieved to hear I was found safe. She pulled Emily out of the room to continue wedding preparations. Ben still hadn't returned.

I set out to find him when no one was paying attention to me. It was no easy task. I ended up finding him in the pool of all places. It took me almost half an hour wandering the halls. I felt fairly safe doing so, however. Various family members were milling about; the extended family had started to arrive a little early, along with a slew of waiters, maids, and other staff roaming the halls on various missions. I was beginning to feel irritated that I couldn't find Ben. But I guessed I deserved it for leaving my room in the middle of the night.

"Why are you in here?" I asked him. He was sitting on the edge of a lounge chair, staring at the water. "And what happened to not wandering off on our own?"

He sighed. "I wanted to be alone. I figured this was the least likely place for anyone else to be. And besides, I'm quite certain I'm not in any danger."

I sighed and plopped down next to him. "I'm really sorry about this morning, Ben. Truly."

"I thought you were dead, Cassie," he said flatly.

"Well, I wasn't," I said gently. "But I think I did see a ghost." That got his attention. I recounted exactly what had really happened last night. He just stared at me in disbelief.

"It's not that I don't believe you, Cassie, but I'm having a hard time accepting that's even possible. Are you sure you weren't dreaming? Or sleepwalking or something? Doesn't that make more sense?"

"I don't think so Ben. I felt fully and completely awake." He shook his head, apparently at a loss for words. "It's... it's happened a few other times, actually. I thought those were all dreams, but now I'm not so sure."

Ben just stared at me. "Do you have a history of passing out like that? I'm worried you're having some kind of...episodes."

"Episodes?" I asked, confused.

"Seizures," Ben clarified, studying my face. "Has anything like that ever happened to you before?"

"No, Ben." I raised my eyebrows in surprise. "I've never had a seizure, and I can't remember ever passing out like this before."

"Sometimes the person having the seizures doesn't even know they're happening," Ben said gently. "Do you...have any kind of warning before they happen? Like, some people see colors or lights, sometimes people hear things." I just stared at him for a long moment.

"I've heard the wind chimes a couple of times," I admitted, "a few times, just before it happens or sometimes during it." Ben nodded solemnly. "But, I don't think they are seizures, Ben. I think...I think it's the house. It's somehow affecting me." Ben watched me with wide eyes. "Look," I said, lifting my right foot onto the chair, I pointed at the scratch mark. The pointy letter 'B' was still clearly visible. In fact, it looked just as fresh as the first day I noticed it. Ben gazed at it with raised eyebrows. He ran a finger gently over the scratch.

"This is new? Since you got here?" He asked quietly. His brows were furrowed now, and he looked worried. I nodded. "You're sure?" He asked me intensely.

"Yes, Ben, I'm sure. That's what I'm trying to tell you. Something strange is going on here. Kristy had a similar mark too. The night before she left. I can't remember what hers looked like, but it was different. She thought Mike had scratched her that day at the beach." I sighed. "If only we could get that drawer open. I want to go back and try to force the lock. We need to finish checking the rest of the third floor, too."

He shrugged. "I don't think you're going to find anything, Cassie. But heck, I've got nothing better to do right now."

I expected him to fight me more, tell me to let it go. But it looked like what had happened this morning had left him feeling a little numb. I kicked myself again for leaving the room last night. I could only imagine how scary that had been for him—to find my room like that and have me be missing.

We had zero luck with the drawer. We tried everything we could think of, but the lock held. The desk was far too solid to break into. I finally showed Ben the painting with the object hanging from the willow tree. He studied it intently for a few minutes but said nothing. After that, I insisted we head back upstairs to check out the rest of the third floor.

Once again, Ben and I walked up the winding staircase to the third floor. It was much less spooky in the light of day. We started at the far end of the opposite wing, working our way towards the door in the corner that I had been about to open before the double doors slammed shut. We found nothing unusual or out of place. About halfway down the hallway, we came to a vaguely familiar room. A baby grand piano sat in front of a large bank of windows. There was a bar on the other side of the room. Several plush armchairs were scattered nearby. I looked over at Ben. "Play something for me?"

He looked at me for a moment, his eyebrows raised. Then he chuckled a little and walked slowly over to the piano. "Okay..." he said, his back to me. "What should I play?"

I shrugged. "I dunno, just play anything." He turned and looked at me, settling on the bench. He cracked his knuckles, then ran a hand over the keys, wiping off the dust. He stared at me for a moment, thinking. "Hm," he said, pressing the keys lightly; he played what I assumed must be a quick warm-up. It sounded like a chord progression of some type. "Have you ever seen *La La Land*?" He asked me. I smiled slowly, nodding. He smiled back. "Okay then." He stretched and, after a moment, began to play.

I couldn't have said the name of the piece, but I recognized it. One of the themes from the movie. It was the one Sebastian played for Emma Stone's character at the end. I sank into a nearby chair, watching him. He was good. Really good. I smiled slightly, mesmerized by the music. The looks he gave me while he was playing made my core melt.

But after a few moments, I couldn't help but think of the music in the context of the movie. I felt a tightness in my chest, and my eyes stung. Would we end up being able to stay together? Had he chosen to play this piece, in particular, for a reason?

I shook my head to clear it and wiped beneath my eyes. I was being silly. I tried to focus on the music itself, to just enjoy it. I felt myself relax, and for a few moments, I felt almost transported away from here, out of this house. When he finished, he looked up at me shyly. I stood up, clapping. "That was amazing, Ben. I can't believe you can play like that." He flushed slightly, clearly pleased.

"Well," he said, clearing his throat, "if anyone is hiding up here this morning, I'm sure that ruined our chances of surprising them."

I laughed. "True, but I doubt they are in the house today, not with all the extra guests and staff running around everywhere."

"No," Ben said, nodding in agreement. "Not unless whoever is doing this is hiding in plain sight, right out in the open."

I stared at him for a moment. "Do you really think it's been one of us all along?" I asked him.

Suddenly, I was tense and nervous all over again. It was what I had been thinking for some time now. I was afraid it was one of us, maybe more than one of us.

He met my eyes briefly before replying. "I'm not sure anything else makes much sense, Cassie." I chewed my lip for a moment, thinking. "Come on," he said, standing up and pushing the bench under the piano. "Let's get going."

When we finally came to the last door in the hallway, Ben walked ahead of me to open it, eyeing the double doors to his left with caution. They were open now, I noted, no longer mysteriously locked of their own accord. We entered the room and found it was practically empty. What looked like a small writing desk sat in front of the round window. I scanned the walls, but they were bare.

"Look," Ben said, moving close to the far wall. "I'm sure of it..." he said a moment later. "See these lines? Here, and here." He pointed them out to me. They were faint, but I could see a line in the paint. I took a step back. "A large painting, or a photo, used to hang here. You can see the lines, see where the paint was covered up. It didn't fade the same as the rest of the room."

I nodded, sighing, "I wonder what it was. It's in exactly the same spot as the painting of the Oak King in the other room."

Ben scanned the room. "Well, I don't see anything else in here."

I walked over to the writing desk and pulled open the drawer. "Ben!" I waved him over. He peeked over my shoulder into the small drawer. Inside, lay a ball of rough, brown twine and a pair of scissors.

"Could easily be a coincidence," Ben said after a moment.

I nodded. "That's true, but it could also mean whoever did this was up here. It's a practically empty room; probably a safe bet that no one would have much of a reason to come in here."

"For sure," Ben replied. "Honestly, I'm glad we didn't find anything else. I've had enough. I just want this wedding to happen so we can leave."

I nodded in agreement. "And... after that?" I asked hesitantly. He paused, looking at me curiously.

"What do you mean? After what?"

"After the wedding, what happens next?" I asked quietly.

"You mean with us?" Ben asked, an eyebrow raised. I nodded. He looked out the little round window thoughtfully for a moment. "We leave this place." He grinned. "And I'm taking you with me."

"Oh yeah?" I said, chuckling a little. "Taking me with you where?"

"Where do you wanna go?" He grinned wider, walking over to me.

I started laughing. "Ben, I'm being serious right now."

"So am I," he said, chuckling. Then he pulled me into his arms, leaned in, and kissed me. I kissed him back, feeling my limbs start to weaken again. "Ben," I said, pulling away momentarily. He ran his hand lightly down my cheek, then he pulled me closer to him, sliding one hand up my shirt as he kissed the base of my neck again. In irritation, I remained still for a moment, but he was far too effective in distracting me. I gasped a little in spite of myself. He cupped a hand under my breast, moving his lips back to mine. "Where do you want to go?" He asked me again, breathlessly this time. He pressed against me. I felt the solid length of him against my thigh.

"I..." I was struggling to think, much less put a coherent sentence together.

"Name a city," he whispered in my ear, his breath tickling me, chills running down my spine.

"Ben," I said, chuckling, pulling away reluctantly. "I'm trying to have a serious conversation with you right now."

"Okay, Cassie," he said, taking a step back, a self-satisfied, smug smile on his face. He could tell that he'd rattled me. "But I'm not joking. I'll go wherever you are, wherever you want to be."

I swallowed, my chest still heaving, trying to calm my breathing. He just watched me. "You're being serious, aren't you?" I said slowly. He nodded. "Ben, I don't even know where you live. I hardly know anything about you."

He shook his head, frowning slightly. "Not relevant. I'm not tied to where I am now. How about France," he said flippantly. "No? Greece?" I shook my head. "Too hot? Chicago?" I took a step backward. He squinted at me. "More of an East Coast girl?" He moved closer to me again. "Hmm..." he cupped a hand over his chin, studying me intently. I walked several steps backward, away from him, and he followed me across the room.

"Ben..." I started laughing. I had so rarely seen this side of him. He could be pretty funny when he wanted to be.

"Ah ha!" He held up one finger, eyebrows raised. "New York! Huh, I didn't peg you as a big city type, but New York it is."

"Ben," I said, forcing the smile off my face. I folded my arms across my chest. "Are you really saying you'll make an effort?" I licked my lips. Why did I feel so nervous? "You're saying I can count on seeing you again after this week is over?"

He stopped smiling, walked over to me, and lifted a hand. He gently cupped my chin, tilting my face up to his. "Yes, Cassie," he said, meeting my eyes. "I'm saying you won't be able to stop me." He kissed me once more, deeply. My stomach flipped, and the feeling of dread in my gut eased. He kissed me until it disappeared.

We headed back down to the second floor and spent the rest of the morning in the study, lounging on the couches and spinning theories. I lay down with my back against Ben's chest, his arms wrapped around me. I told him about my dreams in detail, leaving out only the part about him. I had a hard time even describing taking part in the pagan ritual. I didn't understand how my brain could even come up with all of that. I was starting to question whether the dreams could have all been real somehow. Clearly, Ben thought I was having some kind of seizures or something. And could I be sure he was wrong about that? I tried to think rationally about everything we knew so far. Everything I had seen and heard this week. I felt the pieces were all there, right in front of me, but I couldn't put them all together properly.

Eventually, duty called. We were summoned to a light lunch in the dining hall. Family members shared funny stories about Emily and Josh. It was actually a lot of fun. Afterward, the girls returned to our wing to spend the afternoon having our hair and makeup done. Emily had brought in a professional hairstylist and a make-up artist. Both had their own assistants. We had fun getting ready together, too. It was turning out to be a pretty pleasant day after all. Even Emily's mom was in a good mood and was actually behaving herself for once. She and Emily posed for photos together, pinning the veil and smiling at each other. Emily was having a great time now, and that was all that mattered. I hoped the remainder of the day would make up for this morning.

I donned my slinky mermaid dress. It had a deep V-neck with a sheer lace back. It was a dark blue color, almost navy. Emily had been kind enough to select the bridesmaid dress color but left it up to each of us to choose which dress style we preferred. I loved how the dress looked, but it was slightly too restrictive on my legs when walking. I could move around in it okay but couldn't walk too quickly since it limited my stride.

Emily had hired what seemed to be a fleet of professional photographers and videographers. They took photos documenting us all afternoon and of the group finally heading downstairs.

They posed Emily in several places, descending the grand staircase. We waited for her at the bottom. She was stunning. I knew I was probably biased, but I couldn't recall when I had ever seen such a beautiful bride.

More photos of Emily and the bridal party waiting to walk outside were taken downstairs. It would be a long walk down the aisle, given we had to make our way from inside the house all the way to the pergola. Music played from the live band near the seats, and the staff cued us using walkie-talkies on when to start walking. We paired up with our respective groomsmen. While we waited, we craned our necks to see all the guests and Josh, in the distance, waiting under the pergola.

Mark and I stood arm in arm. I anxiously surveyed the scene until it was our turn to go. We set off towards the pergola. I mumbled under my breath, "I should have practiced in this dress yesterday. I can hardly walk in this thing."

Mark looked down at my legs for a moment. "Yeah, I can see why that would be a problem. It does make your ass look fantastic, though." He shrugged. "Probably worth it."

I snorted. "You are such an idiot, you know that? Have I told you that yet today?" He just laughed, as usual. "But seriously, Mark, I can't walk very fast," I said anxiously. "You have to go slower with me."

"I got you... don't worry." He grinned at me. "I'm pretty sure we're moving at the same pace everyone else was," he added.

I breathed a sigh of relief as we continued steadily on our way. I was starting to relax when suddenly I noticed something was off. I froze.

"Well, Jesus," Mark said, jerking back towards me. "You can't just stop walking either, Cass."

"The flowers," I said, a note of horror in my voice. "What happened to the flowers?"

Emily had chosen a blend of cream and white blooms with mixed greens. I was positive. We had discussed it in great detail, agonizing over the decision.

I stared at the pergola. It was covered in what appeared to be bright red roses at this distance. I knew from here they would be the same ones from the garden. Mark tugged me gently forward, forcing me to move again.

"Oh, yeah," he replied nonchalantly. "I did hear something about that this morning. I guess the flowers they delivered yesterday didn't keep well. The cooler must have malfunctioned or something. They were all...rotten."

"Why, for the love of god, would they use the roses?" I murmured.

He eyed me strangely. "Well, the wedding was in just a few hours. There was probably no time to do anything else. Where would they get that many flowers on such short notice? Especially out here."

I nodded reluctantly. All perfectly reasonable points. But the fact the roses had been used absolutely repulsed me. They may as well have hung a deer head and a bunch of rabbits' feet up there, too.

We finally made it to the aisle, where the guests sat. Past the smiling faces, we went over to where Josh waited patiently for his bride. We broke off and went our separate ways. I took my place on Emily's side, while Mark stood behind the other men. Wes and Ben were already there waiting. I made eye contact with Ben and looked pointedly at the roses and then back at him. His lips set in a grim line.

Emily made her walk down the aisle last, looking magnificent. Her father kissed her on both cheeks before placing her hand in Josh's. He had tears in his eyes. Anna was rolling hers in the front row. They had split up several years back, and it was still ugly. I couldn't help but smile a little at her reaction.

As Emily took her place beside Josh, Father Thomas lifted a crown made primarily of red roses and set it on Emily's head. A chill ran down my spine. My brows creased. It was too similar to my pagan ritual dream, to the crown Kristy had worn. I felt a sense of impending horror in my gut. Something wasn't right here. I glanced over at Ben to see if he noticed. But he was just watching the ceremony, seemingly unbothered. I remembered then that about 200 people were watching us right now, and I fixed my face, trying to calm my heart pounding in my chest.

Emily seemed unfazed by the crown. She beamed at Josh. They proceeded to listen patiently to Father Thomas until it was time to exchange vows and rings. The rest of the ceremony went off without a hitch. I teared up a bit at the end. Emily and Josh walked down the aisle to the sounds of celebration. We made our way behind them, breaking off into pairs again. This time, we headed out back, near the stables. We would make our way through the woods to the lookout to take photos against the backdrop of the valley below. Thankfully, this time we would ride in little carriages pulled by the horses rather than on the horses themselves.

It was a bumpy ride, but we all made it there in one piece. The photographers arranged us in groups for pictures. Someone had brought a bottle of champagne and two glasses for Josh and Emily to celebrate with their first glass of champagne together. This was another photo op, of course. We all cheered for them again.

We all had to squeeze together to take the larger group photos. Someone, I think it was Mark, made a joke about falling over the cliff face behind us. Or maybe about being pushed. The next thing I knew, I heard one of the guys in the back say, "*What the hell?*" And then the screams started.

Catherine let out a blood-curdling scream first; the other girls who were tall enough to stand in the back quickly followed suit. People started pushing to get away from the cliff edge. Those of us in the front scrambled forward. Someone knocked over a photographer and their camera crashed to the ground in a heap. It was complete chaos. I pushed my way past. I needed to see.

But part of me knew what I would find before I looked. "Oh my god, Kristy." I heard someone exclaim. And my stomach leaped into my mouth.

Kristy's body lay at the base of the cliff below. Her arms and legs sprawled out at unnatural angles. Her left arm was pinned underneath her. Her right arm looked like it was broken, her legs bent at odd angles. Her eyes were open, staring up at nothing. My heart pounded in my chest. *How was this possible?*

The chaos continued all around me as I stood unmoving, staring down at Kristy's lifeless eyes. I heard someone behind me mention the police. Someone was running into the forest to retch. Eventually, I turned and found Ben. He was standing with his hands on his hips, staring off into the woods with a calculating expression. He put a hand on his chin, one finger over his mouth, lost in thought. He started to pace back and forth. He turned and finally saw me watching him. He shook his head at me. He looked upset, but also...something else. Something more. Was he scared? Angry? I couldn't read the expression on his face.

I scanned the crowd for Emily and found her sobbing against Josh's chest. I made my way numbly over to them. When I reached her, I put my arm around her back. She turned away from Josh and grabbed my face in her hands, sobbing uncontrollably. "She was dead the whole time. She was dead the whole time, Cass."

"I know," I managed to croak back. "I know." I patted her on the back as she collapsed onto me, sobbing onto my neck. "It's going to be okay, Emily. It's all going to be okay."

What else could I say?

Eventually, it was determined that we should pile back into the carriages and return to the house. The police were called immediately. How, I don't know. Perhaps on the landline, or someone had to run out to the road. We sat in shock, gathered in the game room, with Emily and Josh's parents. Looking around, I suddenly realized it felt like we were at a funeral rather than a wedding.

Ben sat with me, holding my hand in his. He stared at the floor, chewing his lips. The muscle in his jaw ticked repeatedly. I wanted to talk to him, alone, about what had happened, but there was no opportunity. We heard sirens approaching and waited for the police to make their way to us.

Harvey led them into the game room. The man who was clearly in charge, with a golden star on his chest that read 'Sheriff,' spoke at length with Josh's Dad and his uncle in the doorway. He seemed to send several officers away, but a few others stayed.

He turned to the group and announced in a drawl that they would be taking statements individually from each of us who were staying at the house when Kristy went missing. He added at the end of his speech that this would be done in a timely manner.

We were called out into the hallway one by one. When it was my turn, they called my name, and I started to get up. Ben didn't release my hand right away. He squeezed it. I turned to look at him, and he shook his head slightly at me—just slightly. Then he eyed the police officer waiting at the door.

I was escorted down a narrow passageway to what looked to be a small sitting room attached to a large bedroom. This must be the master suite, I thought numbly.

I sat down on a floral couch across from the Sheriff. Two other officers sat in the room and took notes. He told me this conversation would be recorded if that was alright with me. I told him I didn't object.

Nodding as though that was a given, he proceeded with his questions.

"Was the victim a close friend of yours?"

"No," I replied shortly, adding, "I just met her this week for the first time."

"Did she have any altercations the day of or leading up to her disappearance?"

I hesitated momentarily before explaining how she had been upset with Mike at the beach. I didn't think Mike had anything to do with this.

"Had she been drinking that day that you were aware of?"

Again, I hesitated. "Well, yes..." I started, "but I don't know that she had too much to drink."

He ignored that part. "Who first told you her car was gone?"

I really struggled with that one. "Honestly, I can't remember. I remember someone announced it...I think maybe it was Josh. But I don't remember for sure."

"Did any of you check to verify her car was missing?" I paused for a full minute. I wanted to say yes to that, but the answer was no.

"Was her car not actually missing?" I asked.

"No," he replied, "it was. Someone removed it from the premises." A shiver ran down my spine.

"Listen," I said, "There are a lot of... things... that happened this week. Things that I think you should know about that could be related to Kristy's disappearance."

"Ma'am, we'll judge what's relevant and what's not."

"But, you should hear," I started.

He snapped off the tape recorder and cut me off abruptly. "I've heard it," he said, "you're not the first person we questioned today." Like I was an idiot. "Look, it's pretty clear what happened here. Sounds like she was upset, worked up over some disagreement. She had too much to drink. She walked off into the woods, either to cool down or maybe even to punish whoever she was upset at…"

"Mike," I interjected.

"…so, they would have to go looking for her," he continued, ignoring me. "There were no signs of a struggle at the site. There's no evidence of foul play."

"So, she just threw herself off the cliff then." I stared at him, disbelieving.

"My guess, Ma'am, is that she fell. It was an accident. Maybe she just walked off the side of the cliff in the dark. Didn't even know it was there."

I stared him down for a full minute before standing. "I think we're done here, don't you?" I said coldly.

He gave me a long, hard look, then nodded his agreement. "Get her out of here," he said over his shoulder to one of the deputies.

I was escorted back to the game room promptly. Ben's name was called out next. He eyed me as he passed, trying to read my expression. I waited impatiently for him to finish. He wasn't gone long. Staff came around with water bottles, and one of the officers announced we would be finished shortly, and we could return to our "activities".

I closed my eyes and massaged my temples. I couldn't believe this was happening. Were we all supposed to just go back to the wedding? Like nothing had happened? How much did the guests know of what was taking place here today?

Emily stared numbly at the floor, Josh next to her, holding her hand. This was not how this day was supposed to go. I couldn't help but think of everything we had done, everything that had happened since Kristy disappeared. And all that time, her body was lying there. And we had stopped looking for her. We had tried to call her, I rationalized. And her car...But I had known something wasn't right, hadn't I? Deep in my gut, I knew. Even before that night in the hallway.

I thought back to yesterday with Amy, how she had spoken of Kristy in the past tense, almost sadly. Had she known too? Like me? Or did she know, because she *knew* she was dead? I watched Amy from across the room, her head close to Mike's, as they spoke quietly.

Finally, the last of the wedding party had given their statements. Some interrogation that had turned out to be. Clearly, they would be making no real effort to figure out what had actually happened. The Sheriff stood with his hands on his hips. He shared that the victim's family would be notified. I recalled that Kristy's parents were no longer living. At least they wouldn't have to hear this news.

"None of you are to leave the premises for the time being." He gave us all a stern look, his gaze sweeping around the room over us. No one moved. He tipped his hat at Josh's Father, who nodded back. Then he took his officers and left.

The girls, Emily included, were taken back to our rooms, escorted this time by Wes and Mike. We were told we should take a few minutes to freshen up before heading on to the reception. I shut the door of my room behind me and leaned against it, blowing a long stream of air through my mouth. I walked over to the bed and ripped one of the bouquets of roses off. It was tied with what looked like the same brown twine we'd found upstairs. I tossed it against the far wall in anger. Then I pulled the others down too. Afterward, I stood there for several minutes, breathing heavily.

Trying to prepare myself to get through the rest of the night. This was just so bizarre and surreal. I couldn't imagine how anyone could expect Emily to return to the party like nothing had happened.

I took two seconds to fix my makeup and turned to head to Emily's room. I knocked softly at the door, and it opened almost immediately. "Oh Cass." Emily reached for my hand and pulled me inside. "What am I going to do?"

"I know Em," I said. "This is not okay, and this is not how this day should go." She nodded in agreement. "Do you want to call off the reception? Because if so, I will let everyone know. I won't let anyone else make the decision for you." She gave me a small smile at that. "But if you don't, because you only get one wedding day…well, hopefully," I added, shrugging, and she giggled a little, "and this one is yours. Well, then, that's okay too."

"You are a good friend; you know that Cass?" She pulled me into her arms and hugged me for a long time. When she pulled away, she held me at arm's length. "You're right, we'll never get this day back." She blotted her eyes with a tissue. "Let's go to the reception. I might need some help with fixing my make-up though."

I smiled at her. "I think we can manage that."

I sent Amy to gather the other bridesmaids. We started fresh with Emily's make-up. I recruited a few of the other girls to help me, and we fixed some stray hairs.

Before too long, we were all making our way to the grand ballroom. We formed a line outside the door in our pairs again and led the way into the room. The guests were all standing, smiling, and clapping for us. I could tell from their faces that they hadn't been told. Some excuse must have been made for the extra delay. Or maybe they truly thought Emily had made us take photos for hours. I smiled a little at that thought. She could be a bit extra sometimes.

Josh and Emily were announced as a couple, entering the room behind us to loud cheers and applause. Someone in the crowd whistled loudly. Emily looked as radiant as ever. I really hoped she could move past this for now and make the most out of the evening.

We made our way, winding in between the round guest tables. I swallowed, my mouth a little dry. There were large bouquets of the red roses at the center of every table, surrounded with a circle of small white votive candles, that floated in little glass bowls filled with water. Once again, I couldn't ignore the sinking feeling that something wasn't right here. Why would Emily let them use the roses? We found our places at the head table and took our seats. Ben was seated kiddy-corner from me, on Josh's left-hand side. Wes was on his right, as the best man. Mark was seated on the other side of Ben, directly across from me. Amy sat to my left, and then Emily. Catherine, as the maid of honor, sat to her left. The men were seated with their backs to the wall.

I found the arrangement a little odd, not just because it meant that Emily and Josh sat across from each other, rather than next to each other, but this also meant the girls' backs faced the rest of the room, which felt a little awkward. I was puzzled by it for a minute, but then realized it would have been difficult to seat all 20 of us in a row facing the room, the wedding party was just too large. *Well, 19, now,* I thought.

Wes stood up and pulled out some notecards with his speech he had prepared. I thought how lucky it was that everyone had written out their speeches in advance. I'm more of a wing-it type myself, but I couldn't imagine having to come up with something on the spot right now. The night had taken on a sort of surreal, dream-like quality for me. I felt the warm, low lighting and the hundreds of candles in the room had something to do with it. I stared at the roses on our table while Wes spoke. The flickering firelight from the candles shone on their velvet undersides. I flashed back to the pagan ritual, the firelight gleaming on our crowns of roses. Streaking the maid's hair with strands of fire.

I couldn't shake the claustrophobic feeling of déjà vu that had descended over me. I was starting to feel a little lightheaded even. The last thing they needed right now was for me to pass out at the table in the middle of a speech. I started to sweat a little. I reached for my water glass and took a sip. The ice-cold water helped to cool me a little. Maybe I was getting sick? I didn't think what Ben had said about the seizures was right. Although it did make sense... I hadn't had that much to eat today either, when I thought about it. I had inadvertently skipped breakfast, although Emily managed to scrounge up some coffee for me later on. I hadn't had much at lunch either. All of that, combined with the stress of the afternoon, it was no wonder I was feeling off.

I was startled out of my reverie by the sound of applause. Wes raised his glass of champagne high into the air. "A toast... to the happy couple!" I picked up my champagne glass, half a beat behind everyone else.

I heard Ben clear his throat and swiveled my gaze to him as I lifted the glass to my lips. He stared at me over the rim of his glass, and gave me a swift, subtle head shake. My eyebrows creased to show my confusion. He shook his head no again. I let the champagne hit my lips and fall back into the glass without taking a sip.

My pulse picked up. What was happening? Why didn't he want me to drink the champagne? Ben was ignoring me now, almost making it a point not to look at me. I took his lead and pretending nothing had happened, I set my glass back on the table.

Amy turned to me smiling. "Mm, it's good champagne, isn't it?"

"Y-yes." I nodded, smiling back. "Really good."

"Nothing but the best for the Haverfords," Mark quipped.

Catherine had risen to her feet now. I could tell she was feeling a little nervous. She gripped her notecards a little too hard. A waiter brought the microphone over to her. I frowned as he walked away to stand at the side of the room. He wasn't wearing the snazzy outfit I had seen the other night, just their regular plain black shirts and pants. That was a little odd.

Catherine started her speech, her voice trembling a little at first, but she gathered strength as she went on. I zoned out again about halfway through. I could feel my heart was still working a little harder than it should. I really needed these speeches to end so I could eat something, and hopefully feel better. I eyed my water glass and then thought better of it. Maybe whatever Ben was worried was in my champagne, was in the water, too.

Josh's father gave a brief speech next. Anna rose to her feet afterwards to say a few words as well. I cringed a few times during hers. She made sure to get a few digs in about Emily's Dad. He sat smiling pleasantly through the whole thing. That man really was a saint. Emily had a smile that was slightly fake-looking plastered to her face now. I groaned inwardly for her.

After what seemed like an eternity, the speeches came to an end. Our meals were brought out promptly, carried above the server's heads on massive silver platters. Being at the head table had the advantage of being served first. I watched Ben as the food arrived, but he gave me no further signs or headshakes. Once he had started eating, I decided it was safe and dug into my food too. As the meal went on, I could tell I was starting to feel better already. Hopefully, that meant it was only a blood sugar issue.

But the food did nothing to change the surrealness I felt. I hardly spoke throughout dinner, unable to trust myself to do so. I watched the others eating and chatting and making polite small talk as if this were just a normal, happy wedding. As if we hadn't just found a dead body.

Ben looked up suddenly, doing a double take, almost like he recognized someone. "I'm going to go use the restroom," he announced to the table.

I watched him go. I had to turn my head as he headed to the exit. Harvey had clearly just entered the room. I watched as Ben intercepted him, grabbing him by the upper arm for just a moment, he spoke into his ear. Then they made eye contact, exchanging a look. Harvey said nothing, but I thought he gave Ben an almost imperceptible nod, his expression grim. Then they both continued on their way.

Turning back to the table, I saw Amy was staring at me. "Is everything okay, Cassie?" She asked, her brows creased.

I mustered a smile for her. "Of course, everything's fine."

She nodded slowly, turning back to her plate with a half-smile. Unconvinced.

I waited patiently for Ben to return from the restroom. When he did, he gave me only a cursory glance before taking his seat. I noticed Mark was watching us.

Mark looked at me, then back at Ben. "What's going on guys? Trouble in paradise? You've hardly spoken to each other all day."

Ben looked up at me, giving me a brief pointed look before responding. "Yeah, just a bit. Thanks to you, dickwad."

Mark froze, staring at Ben. "What? What are you talking about?"

"I'm talking about you, not being able to keep your hands off of her." Ben inclined his head towards me.

Mark's eyes grew wide. "Look, I don't know what you think happened, but dude, I did not..."

Ben cut him off. "Oh please, shove it, Mark. You've had your hands all over her all week. We all saw it." He was getting louder now, gesturing up and down the table. "Do you think I'm blind or just stupid?" Heads were turning to look at us now. Catherine's eyebrows went up in surprise. "I let it go earlier...I told myself it wasn't right to bring it up today, but you know what, I don't give a shit anymore. I'm going to kick your ass..."

"Ben!" I yelped as he got up from the table. *What the hell?*

People were starting to turn now at the guest tables. Josh's father was watching us, starting to stand up. I turned to look at Josh. He was just watching Ben warily.

I got to my feet. "Ben, what the hell," I hissed. "Stop it. You have got to be kidding me. You cannot be doing this again."

Ben looked at me in disgust. "If you have an explanation, I'd love to hear it."

"Come on." I threw my napkin down on the table. "We are not doing this here."

Ben looked around the room and nodded begrudgingly. I turned to Emily and Josh, blushing furiously and said, "I am so sorry. We'll be right back."

Emily just stared at me momentarily, looking like she was about to say something. "Okay, Cassie." She nodded.

I turned and left the room, noting Martin had sunk back into his chair. My heart was pounding in my chest. What the hell was Ben doing? I didn't look back to see if he was following me.

Out in the hallway, I walked several paces down the hall, slamming my heels into the soft carpet. I stopped and turned to face Ben, my hands on my hips. "What the hell, Ben?"

Ben walked up to me, speaking rapidly, and put his hand on my cheek. "Don't be upset; I made the whole thing up. Cassie, we have to get you out of here. Now."

I just stared at him. "I'm not following."

"We don't have much time," he said urgently, looking back towards the ballroom. I just bought us a few minutes. We need to find our car keys, and we need to leave—before anyone realizes we're gone."

He grabbed my right hand in his, pulling it off my hip, and started dragging me down the hallway.

"What the hell are you talking about Ben? Why? The police told us no one was allowed to leave. Why would we do that?"

"Cassie," he said, his voice lowered and somewhat breathless, "you are in danger. You can't stay in this house."

"In danger? Me? I don't understand. Danger from who?"

"Think about it Cassie, think of everything that has happened this week. The paper you found, the deer head, the painting, the bouquet that you found in your room, the runes and everything this morning..." he drifted off. "Especially that night, with the bouquet. Think about that. What actually happened that night?"

I said nothing, my mind racing to catch up. We were speed walking now. I could barely keep up with him because of my dress.

"We found the bouquet with the voodoo doll thing that looked like Kristy in her room. That was the same night she disappeared. We all thought she left in her car..."

"I know all that," I interrupted, "so what?"

"Then we all went to sleep," he continued, ignoring me. "Later, that same night, you have a bad dream. You wake up Emily. She comes into your room and finds another bouquet, again with a creepy voodoo doll that was obviously meant to be you."

"Okay..." I paused for a moment. I hadn't realized until just now that I never actually saw what was in my bouquet. The guys had gone back and gotten rid of it for me. "What does that all mean?"

"By that time, clearly Kristy was likely already dead." I stared at the back of his head. "We didn't know it at the time, but she probably died almost immediately after leaving the house that night."

"And...?" I still didn't see where he was going.

"I'm assuming she died after the bouquet was placed in her room. But granted, that's definitely an assumption on my part. Then, just a few hours later, after she dies, a new bouquet appears, this time in your room."

"Okay," I murmured, my heart racing. I thought I was starting to see what he was getting at now.

"What if the journal...what you saw, the...ghost, or dream, or whatever the heck that was, is true? What if women are being chosen to be...sacrificed? Remember the burning man we found in the woods?"

I looked at him sharply. "You weren't with us when we found it," I said swiftly.

"The guys went back later to check it out," he told me hurriedly. *I didn't know that...when?* I wondered to myself. But Ben continued. "It's exactly like what the pagans would have used in their fertility rituals. And it looked to me like it wasn't finished yet. Like someone was building it, getting it ready. What if they were getting it ready because they're about to hold some kind of...pagan ritual. What if they are about to sacrifice someone else? And what if that person is you now that Kristy is dead?"

"What?" I pulled him to a stop, planting my heels in the carpet. "You're telling me, you were thinking all of this, this whole time, and you never said a word to me? What is your deal, Ben? Why can't you ever just be honest with me?"

"I haven't been thinking this all week, Cassie!" Ben looked behind me down the hallway, exasperated. "Not this... this cohesively at least. I just started putting the pieces together slowly, a little at a time. I had a bad feeling for a while that you seemed to be at the center of all of this. But

I didn't want to freak you out. It wasn't until we found Kristy's body this afternoon that I put it all together, and I knew. You're their next target. We have to get you out of here, far away from here. You can't spend another night in this house."

"No." I stared at him, shaking my head. "No. If you're right, I can't leave. I'm not leaving. I refuse to leave without Emily."

Ben ran his hands through his hair, looking hysterical now. "Cassie, that's not possible. They are never going to let Emily leave right now. But she's not the one in danger. You are."

"Who's they, Ben? Who is doing this?" I put my hands on my hips.

"I don't know...Cassie." He was getting hysterical now. "I don't know. Does it even matter? Someone is clearly getting ready to freaking... human sacrifice somebody, and it's you!" He exclaimed. "It's you, Cassie! It was going to be Kristy, but something must have gone wrong. Instead of being sacrificed, she... she must have gotten away, or something. Ran away into the woods and fell. And now it's you. You're next" He was breathing heavily as he walked over to me, taking my chin gently in his hand, he turned my face to his. "Look, I told you I wouldn't let anything happen to you. This is how I do that. You have to trust me." He met my gaze, his chest rising and falling as he breathed rapidly. I studied his eyes. He was telling me the truth.

"Okay," I said after a few seconds went by. "And you're sure Emily's not in any danger?"

"I'm positive," he said, nodding and looking relieved.

"What about the other girls?" I frowned, thinking of Amy, of Catherine. "How do you know they won't just pick one of them next? We can't just leave them here without warning them."

"Obviously, I can't be 100% sure, but it doesn't add up. My theory is that you and Kristy were both... were both..." he flushed a little. I remembered my dream of running with the waiter boy down the staircase. It was hard now to remember the details, but I was pretty sure I had been the red-haired maid in that dream. At one point, I caught a glimpse of red curls and the black dress I was wearing.

"Poor." I finished for him. "Lower class?" I raised an eyebrow. "You think that's why we were chosen."

Ben nodded silently.

"Okay..." I said again. I thought of the scratch on my foot, and the one on Kristy's leg. Had they marked us somehow? As being chosen?

"Look, Cassie, we have to go though. We have to go, now. We've wasted too much time already. For all we know, they've already sent someone to look for us."

I studied him carefully again. Was any of this actually real? Or was he the one jumping to conclusions now? Drawing links that weren't really there?

"Come on," he said, taking my hand again and leading me down the hall. "We need to find the car keys; we're running out of time."

"I know where they are," I said.

Thankfully, Ben was familiar enough with the lower level of the house to get us to the kitchen. It hadn't ever occurred to me before that it might be a good idea to be familiar with the layout of the lower level of the house. Seeing what the lower level was like, I was grateful that he had a clue where it was.

The basement level was like a maze. The hallways were narrow, plain corridors, with offshoots branching in all directions. They were all the same size, too. There didn't seem to be a main hallway. There were none of the fineries present upstairs. The floors were scuffed bare wood, and the walls were plain.

He managed to lead us to what he thought was the entrance to the kitchen. He poked his head briefly inside to confirm. My eyes scanned the walls up and down the corridor from there. A few yards down the hall, I saw a door off to the right. Hopefully, that was Mrs. Evan's office. I trotted over to the door the best I could. I cursed myself again for choosing such an impractical dress.

A bulletin board was on the wall right outside the door, with little notes and things posted. A large paper that looked like some kind of shift schedule, and next to it, a large brass pin protruded from the board. A ring with a set of keys hung from it. I grabbed it, turning my attention to the door handle. I recalled the young maid saying the office was kept locked. It seemed a little silly if the key to the office was left hanging right next to the door, but I prayed it would be one of the keys. I jiggled the knob first, confirming it was locked, and started trying the keys, one at a time.

"Hurry," Ben said next to me, peering anxiously up and down the hall in either direction.

"That's helpful," I quipped. "I'm already going as fast as I can."

Ben expelled a stream of air. "I know, sorry," He mumbled.

"Actually, here." I turned and handed him the key ring. "I'll be right back."

"What?" Ben sputtered, grabbing the key ring from me and fumbling with the lock. "Where are you going?"

I pointed to the kitchen door. "Just in here, hang on." I peeked through the door and saw no one, so I ducked inside the kitchen before he could respond. I scanned the room for what I was looking for. Thankfully, I quickly located a large rack of knives on the far side of the kitchen. I ran over, grabbed a hefty-sized knife, and ran back out of the room to the hallway. I frowned a little. Why was no one in the kitchen right now? It seemed odd with the reception going on. They must have had it catered though, like I figured. Maybe all the food was upstairs already and being brought in from another room down the hall. There had been vans coming and going all day.

Back in the hall, I saw Ben still working his way through the keys on the ring. I suddenly noticed, with a start, a small golden key that was shorter than all the rest. My heart skipped a beat. It was the key to the drawer in the desk upstairs. Ben glanced up at me, doing a double take for a second as he noticed the knife. "What's that for? Are you going to fight your way out with a butcher knife?"

I rolled my eyes, gesturing up and down the hallway. "Fight who Ben? I don't exactly see anyone trying to stop us." I held up the skirt of my dress, pulling the fabric away from my legs, and then I carefully inserted the knife point through the fabric of the dress. Cringing a little, I started to cut, and eventually tear the fabric, in a rough circle all the way around, until the bottom half of the skirt fell away.

I looked up to see Ben watching me. "Okay, that was kind of hot."

I rolled my eyes again. "Shut up... how have you not found the right key yet?"

"I'm almost through the ring," he replied, focusing again. Just then, I thought I heard a sound echoing down the corridor in the distance.

"Shh," I whispered. "Someone's coming." Ben tried to wipe a lock of hair out of his eyes with his upper arm, not taking his hands away from the door. The door handle clicked, and he pushed it open. We rushed inside, immediately noting a set of little hooks on the opposite wall filled with our car keys. I rifled through them quickly, running my hands over the rows of keys. "What the hell," I was starting to breathe fast. "I can't find my keys." I scanned the rows again, making sure I hadn't just missed them. "My keys aren't here."

"It's okay." Ben shot an arm out, grabbing a set of keys on a red leather strap. "Mine are, let's go." We turned and rushed back out into the hallway. Ben stopped and turned back, entering the office again to grab the door and pull it shut.

"What are you doing down here?" A voice called out from down the hall. I jumped, whipping my head around, and my heart started to thump.

It was Wes. I froze. Now what? Thankfully, the knife was in my right hand, and I figured it was already partially blocked from his view. I brought my hand further behind my back. He was approaching at a brisk walk from down the corridor to my left. Ben stepped out into the hallway, clicking the door shut. Wes slowed for a moment, eyeing him. They stared at each other for a moment. My mind raced, trying to come up with an excuse. Why would we be down here? In Mrs. Evan's office?

"Oh, um..." I looked at Ben. He looked back at me, clearly at a loss. "I had asked one of the maids earlier if I could borrow the computer in Mrs. Evan's office for a few minutes. She arranged it for me. I... we... she found Ben and I when we were talking upstairs, and so we headed down here."

"Mmhmm." Wes nodded. He had slowed his pace now. "Okay, well, I came to get you guys. You're wanted back upstairs." He glanced up at the ceiling.

"Okay," I said, stalling for time. What did we do now? "We'll be there in a minute; we just... we didn't get to finish our conversation earlier."

Wes just stared at us, looking back and forth between us, his expression not changing. "Okay," he said evenly. "But you know how Emily is." He chuckled. "I need you to come with me. Now." We stood there without moving, at a standstill. I looked at Ben. "There'll be hell to pay if I don't get you guys back in time for the first dance." He gestured down the hall behind him. "Come on, I'll show you guys the way out." He chuckled again. "It's a maze down here." Ben and I looked at each other for a moment. He met my eyes pointedly and started to move backward down the hall in the opposite direction from Wes.

Wes raised his voice. "Wait," he said, "that's the wrong way." He was starting to sound angry now. "Cassie, come back!" Ben turned and started jogging down the hall. Wes immediately broke out into a run.

I only made it a few staggering steps before realizing I had to take my heels off. I reached down and pulled them off, one at a time, dropping them on the floor. I scrambled to follow Ben. We ran down the long corridor, eventually passing through a set of double doors, the corridor widening in this section. My heart was hammering. I had no clue where to go. I prayed that Ben did. We had entered the basement from the other direction, the way that Wes had come from. I wasn't sure if Ben knew how to find his way out from here.

I turned to look back at Wes and saw, to my surprise, the red-haired maid from my dream. She seemed to step out of nowhere into the hallway between Wes and me. His eyebrows raised in surprise, and he abruptly stopped, fumbling backward a few steps. She just looked at him. Then, the double doors between them slammed shut with a bang, blocking Wes. I slowed, staring back at her. She gave me a casual little wave with one hand before walking across the hall and out of sight. I could hear Wes pounding on the door behind us, yelling something incoherent.

"Do you know where you're going?" I called out to Ben. He shook his head in the negative. Great. I thought. "Okay, so stick to the right side of the hall...make only right turns..." I panted, "that should lead us eventually out of here. I think," I added the last bit. Would that really work? It was worth a shot.

Ben nodded his head in agreement. "Sounds like our best option at this point. Let's just hope we don't end up looping back around and running into Wes again."

We made a right turn at every junction, eventually coming to a long corridor with a single door at the end. We ran towards it, hoping it would lead us to a way out of the lower level. Ben threw the door open. "Oh, thank god," he breathed. We had exited into a dark stairwell. I followed him up the stairs, trying not to trip.

We exited into an empty hallway, plush red carpet beneath our feet. There was a painting of a rabbit on the wall across from us. I saw Ben eyeing it. "I think I know where we are," he rasped, trying to catch his breath. "This way."

He led me down the hall to the left, taking various turns. Eventually, I realized we were back in one of the main hallways leading towards the library. Luckily, we saw no one on our way there. We entered the library, which was dark and ran to the double glass doors at the back. Ben shut them behind us, trying not to make too much noise.

Once outside in the garden, we jogged through the garden path. I winced slightly. Having no shoes was going to be a lot harder out here. We made our way through the garden as quickly as possible, heading around the house to the right; we made our way to the gravel drive that branched off the main drive.

I stopped at the edge of the drive. Ben sensed I wasn't following and turned back. "I can't," I breathed, "run on the gravel," pointing down at my feet, "no shoes." Ben sighed audibly. We stuck to the grass, jogging along the edge of the gravel drive. When we hit the entrance to the woods, Ben stopped short.

"Can you walk on the gravel?" He asked. "If not," he breathed, his chest rising and falling rapidly, "I'll carry you on my back."

I snorted a short laugh. "Yeah...I don't think that's a good idea." I stepped onto the gravel path, taking a few steps. "I can make it," I breathed,

"I just can't run." Ben looked back at the house. I followed his gaze. There was no one in sight.

"Okay," he nodded, "Let's just try to make our way as quickly as possible."

We walked steadily down the gravel drive, Ben keeping pace evenly with me. My breathing finally slowed enough that I could talk more easily. "So, it was Wes," I said to him. "At least, he's clearly involved." I thought back. "He wasn't even here the whole week..." I tried to remember the sequence of events. "He arrived the next morning after we found the deer head on the stairs. Right?" I looked over at Ben.

He thought for a moment before nodding his agreement. "Yeah, you're right. I remember it was the next morning. He was there the day we went to the beach. After we got back from our run that morning, do you remember? Emily made a comment about how she was surprised we didn't hear his car."

I nodded slowly. "Yeah, that's right. We assumed we didn't hear it because we were out in the woods." We both fell silent for a few moments. "But maybe that was on purpose?"

Ben looked my way in the dark, "What do you mean?" He asked. "You think Emily told us that on purpose?"

I paused; I hadn't meant that. Hadn't thought of that at all. But it struck me for a moment. Could that be? Had Emily invented the loud car to throw us off about when Wes had arrived?

"No." I shook my head. "I meant maybe Wes pulled up to the house that morning, in his loud car, on purpose, to make everyone think that was when he first arrived. He could have actually arrived the night be-fore...maybe hid his car in the woods or out by the road. Or heck, even at the garage." I pointed ahead of us. "It's not like any of us ever came out here."

Ben shook his head. "But why would he do all of that?"

I shrugged. "To throw us off, so none of us knew he was here. Maybe he was the one who planted the deer head. Maybe that gave him time to shoot the deer, and bring the head into the house, all without any of us knowing. Think about it...who else could it have been? None of the rest of us were missing that night, were we?" I tried to remember back. That was right; that was the night Mark had taken me back to my room early. I had been asleep...I recalled Emily had given both Mark and Josh an alibi for the entire evening. Ben was silent.

"I...I don't remember anyone missing for any length of time that evening. But people went to bed at all different times that night. I don't know...I think it couldn't have been Josh or Mark. I was with them basically the whole night..." he left off for a moment, thinking. "That was the night we had argued... I was upset... I was only alone for a little while. Otherwise, I'm sure of it; I was with Josh, Mark, and Emily the rest of that night. We found the head on the stairs when Emily went to bed. And there's no way one of them would have had time earlier in the evening to sneak out, shoot and string up a deer, and bring the head back to the house."

I thought over his words for a moment, something nagging at me. He was upset after we argued, I thought. He was alone for a few minutes after I had gone up to bed. I thought back. Obviously, he wasn't in the foyer anymore when Mark escorted me upstairs. So where had he gone before he rejoined the others? And how long was he gone?

I watched him in the dark, out of the corner of my eye. Could it have been him? He might have had time to shoot the deer, bring the head inside...then join the others. They wouldn't have thought anything of it. They would have chalked it up to him needing time to cool down. I kicked myself internally. Why did I keep questioning his involvement in all of this?

For god's sake, he was trying to save my life right now. I knew he couldn't have anything to do with this. But a small part of me, in the back of my mind, still wasn't 100% sure.

Besides, I thought. We had walked through the woods for half an hour the other day. We hadn't seen a single deer... it's not like it was that easy to find one. Much less shoot one. There's no way he would have time to do all of that. It wasn't logical. No, I thought... not unless he had already shot the deer earlier. Killed it somewhere else, then dragged it out, and strung it up in the woods for us to find later. There was no blood, I remembered.

I looked at him again, trying to make out his features in the dark. In the dark. Here I was, willingly walking alone with him into the dark woods at night. No one even knew we were out here. Except for Wes, I thought. Who had tried to stop us. I thought of him calling out my name, trying to stop *me*... leaving with Ben. I felt a chill go down my spine as goosebumps pebbled my arms. And I was out here without my car keys. He had grabbed his. And I had only his word for it that I was in any danger at all. Maybe I was in danger. Maybe I was in danger from *him*.

I slowed to a stop. Ben noticed I was lagging behind a moment later. He stopped and turned back to me. "Cassie? What is it? Did you hurt your foot?" He started to walk back to me. I took a step back. He froze in place. I couldn't make out his face at all in the darkness surrounding us. "Cassie," his voice lowered, "what are you doing? We have to go." I stayed quiet, stalling for time. He took another step towards me, and I stepped back again. I was cursing myself for not wearing more practical shoes tonight. It hadn't necessarily been easy for him to keep pace with me the first time we ran together, but I had been particularly fast that day, and I wasn't barefoot. Who knows how difficult it had actually been for him. Maybe he was capable of running much faster than that. I wasn't sure I had any hope of outrunning him, if it came to that. My heart was pounding again.

"Cassie," he breathed, sounding hurt. "You still don't trust me? After everything..." I saw his shoulders slump in the dark. "Cassie...I would never hurt you; you have to believe me." I said nothing, my mind racing. Maybe not. I wanted to believe that part was true. But had he killed that deer? Had he killed Kristy? He had come downstairs already dressed, wearing his running shoes. And like an idiot, it had never occurred to me to ask Mark if Ben had been dressed like that already when he went to wake him.

"Ben," I breathed, "I want to believe you..."

"Then believe me," he interrupted. "What do I have to do to prove it to you?" I stood there in the dark, my heart in my throat now.

"If it wasn't you," I started, "that killed the deer that night... then the most logical explanation is that it was Wes. And that's assuming he arrived at the house the night before without anyone realizing." I thought back through the events of the week, stringing them together. Everyone else had been in their PJs that evening. They had come downstairs with me when the deer head was found. If one of us was involved, it was either Wes or Ben.

"Yes." Ben nodded, moving a step closer to me. "And who just tried to chase us?" He pointed up at the house, exasperated. "Cassie, we have to leave." He turned to look up the trail. "We are so close; my car is right there." He pointed up the path. "Please, let's go. We can talk in the car."

"But if it was Wes," I continued, "then I can't leave."

"No!" Ben moaned, "No, Cassie, don't do this...we have to go. I'm telling you; you can't stay here."

"No." I shook my head at him, feeling more confident as I thought out loud. "If it was Wes, that means Josh's family is obviously involved. At the center of all of this. That's the only explanation that makes any sense."

It was what a part of me had known all week but hadn't wanted to face. It wasn't just the villagers or the staff trying to carry on old traditions from the past...it had to be them, The Haverfords. This was their property, their home. They were the ultimate be-all, end-all. Out here, they were practically God. It was them. There was no other explanation. And I wouldn't leave Emily to them. I wouldn't abandon her here, to whatever fate they had in store for her. Even if it were possible Josh wasn't involved... didn't know about all of this somehow... his family history... how long could he protect her from them?

I thought about the red roses at the wedding ceremony. About how Father Thomas had placed the crown of roses on Emily's head. In my dream... my vision... of the ritual by the willow tree, they had placed a similar crown on my head. I hadn't been part of the sacrifice, though. At least... not up to the part before I had passed out. Who knows about afterward. Did that mean Emily was safe from being chosen? I decided I couldn't take that risk. Ben stared at me in the dark, waiting for me to finish. I took a deep breath.

"Let's go, Cassie," he said softly, his voice pleading. "Please, we are so close."

"I'm not getting in the car with you, Ben."

I heard him let out a sound, almost a strangled sob. "Cassie, please, do not do this. Don't go back in that house." He started towards me. I held up a hand. He stopped mid-stride. "I'm not going to hurt you. I love you, Cassie. But I can only do so much to protect you. If you go back in the house, I don't know what will happen."

I stared at his features in the faint moonlight just before a cloud passed back over the moon above us. He looked crushed. I paused. I couldn't make up my mind if I could trust Ben fully or not. But I was sure of one thing: I wasn't leaving this house tonight without Emily. I nodded at him, swallowing, making up my mind.

"Okay," I replied. That's a risk I'm willing to take. You want to prove to me I can trust you?"

He eyed me warily for a long moment, and I saw the muscle in his jaw ticking. Eventually, he nodded. "Yes," he responded simply. "I do."

I nodded back. "Then here's what we're going to do."

We made our way as silently as possible, my feet sinking into the plush red carpet of the stairs once more. We had entered the house the way we left, through the garden, back through the darkened library. Ben had led me down an alternate route I had never taken from there. Rather than following the familiar hall past the guy's lounge, out through to the foyer, we had turned left out of the library and taken winding twists and turns for several minutes; we had eventually exited the maze of corridors out into the foyer, this time, entering from the right of the grand staircase. I could hear the distant sound of music drifting down to us from upstairs.

We had passed more paintings I had never seen before, having never been on that wing of the main floor. I scanned them as we ran past until I did a double-take and came to a stop. The last one looked like a photograph. "Hang on a second," I called out to Ben. I moved closer to the framed photo. It showed a group of people at what looked like a party. Some held drinks and cigarettes in their hands, glasses raised to the camera in a salute. I peered more closely at the girl standing off to the side. She stood next to a man seated at a grand piano, one hand on his shoulder, a piece of sheet music in the other. She must be a singer. Did she look vaguely familiar? No, I realized with a start, but her dress did. She wore the black and silver Gatsby dress I had worn to dinner the other night. I was positive it was the same dress. I stared with my mouth open, thinking of my dream that night.

"Come on, Cassie," Ben whispered from up the hallway. "We're wasting time!'

261

When we'd entered the dimly lit corridors, Ben had given me a look that was both forlorn but resigned. He looked like he wanted to cry. Either he was telling the truth, and he had nothing to do with the events of this week, or he was a really good actor, I thought. If I was wrong to doubt him, I felt slightly guilty for putting him through all this. And more than a little scared. I knew he was hung up on the idea that I didn't trust him, but I could do nothing about that right now. And if anything, what we were about to do should tell him that I was gambling on him telling the truth. Because if it wasn't him, it was the Haverfords. And if that were the case, I would prove it to everyone.

I tore myself away from the photo and followed Ben through an open set of double doors. We swiftly surveyed the foyer and peered up the staircase. Thankfully, no one was in sight still. I had removed my bulky smartwatch for the wedding photos, and there was nowhere on my dress to carry my phone, so I had no clue what time it was. Not that it would have mattered anyway; there was no scheduled time for the wedding reception to end. But I wondered how long we had been missing from the ballroom now. Long enough to raise further alarm? Obviously, we missed the first dance, at least. It felt like we had been gone for ages with everything that had happened, but in reality, it had only been what? A half an hour, maybe a little more, if I had to guess. I felt a little pang of irrational guilt and regret that I was missing Emily's wedding. No scenario now saw me back in that ballroom, enjoying the party. My dress being torn in half alone made that impossible. I found myself wondering what Wes had done after we ran from him. That answer would probably give me all the information I needed to know once and for all what was really happening here.

Had he gone back and raised the alarm? That he thought I might be in danger, having run off alone with Ben? Or had he returned to the ballroom and whispered in someone's ear that we were missing. That we needed to be found for other purposes?

We made our way quickly up the stairs. Our luck held as we made our way through the turns towards the girl's wing. We saw no one. As we passed my bedroom door, I slowed for a moment. "Hang on," I called to Ben softly. I ducked inside and quickly grabbed my running shoes. I set the knife down on the bed and sat on the edge of the bed to tie them with fumbling fingers, adrenaline causing me to slip up several times. I forced myself to slow down and tie the shoes properly. Ben had stepped into the bedroom and was watching me from the doorway. I finished and stood up.

"Nice outfit," he smirked.

I realized he was trying to get me to smile at him. I shrugged. "The better to run from you with, my dear."

He lifted his head to the ceiling and released a stream of air through his nose in frustration. "You're killing me, Cassie, you know that?" He stared at me, shaking his head in disbelief. "What did I ever do to you to make you think I'm even capable of any of this?"

"It's not anything you did, Ben," I told him, taking pity on him just a bit. "It's just..." I trailed off, thinking for a moment. "I'm just trying to be logical here. I just met you. Not even a week ago. And yes," I fumbled for a moment, "I do have feelings for you, but I am trying to be objective. There are several ways this could have played out. And it could've been you in some of the... permutations... whatever you want to call them. It could have been you all along."

He stared at me, taking in what I had said. Finally, he nodded. "Okay. I get it." He turned to leave. "But it just as easily could have been Wes, or Josh, or heck, even Mark." He turned back and looked at me sadly. "I just hope the way you find out isn't by getting hurt by one of them."

With that, he stepped back out into the hallway. I stared after him for a moment, thinking. Then I turned to the closet and shoved my hand into the fur coat. The piece of crinkled paper was still there. I breathed a sigh of relief. Ben was still the only one I had ever shown the hiding place to. If he had planned to lure me out of the house tonight, to kill me. Would he have left the paper here as potential evidence in my room? It wasn't enough to prove anything. But it tipped the scales slightly in his favor. I met him back in the hallway, and we continued on our way.

We entered the dark study, fumbling to find the light switch momentarily. When the lights came on, I scanned the room, verifying that no one was waiting there in the dark for us. I noticed that once again, the balcony doors had been left open. A cool breeze billowed the curtains out, the movement startling me momentarily.

I quickly made my way across the room to the desk. Ben still had the key ring gripped in his hand. He handed it to me glumly. I pulled the golden key out of the bunch as I approached the desk. Please let this be the right key, I thought, inserting it into the lock in the drawer. It slid into place and turned easily with a click. I pulled the drawer open and with a flood of relief, found the journal. Its cover was a worn brown leather, just like the one I had seen. I picked it up, running my hand lightly over the soft cover before opening it. It opened naturally to the page with the photographs. I took the stack of photos in my hand, flipping through them, one after the other. It was like going back in time. The most recent photos on top looked fairly modern. At the bottom of the stack, the first photos were without color and obviously very, very old. My gut wrenched in horror as the images of the girls' faces flashed before my eyes. It was sickening.

I paused, flipping back to the last photo. My breath caught. I recognized the tumbling mass of red curls... her face. It was the maid who had helped us escape from Wes earlier in the evening, the one from my dreams.

She was so beautiful. I felt tears threatening to gather in my eyes. It wasn't fair.

I returned to the top photograph, flipping it over to check the back, hoping to find a date and time stamp. I sighed, no luck. Flipping it back to the front, I realized with a jolt that a date was stamped on the front. I did the math roughly in my head. This photo was from almost 30 years ago. I looked up at Ben excitedly. "There's a date and time stamp on this one," I said, holding it up to him. These photos and the journal...this is proof we can use."

"So, what's your plan now?" Ben asked. "Burst into the ballroom waving the photos around?" I looked up at him and froze, my heart leaping into my throat.

Josh's Dad and Uncle walked into the room, followed by Wes. I gasped audibly, causing Ben to turn around.

"That won't be necessary," Martin said as he strode into the room. Coming to a stop, he stood with his legs spread apart, his hands looped casually behind his back. "We'll be taking those photos now. And the notebook."

"I can't let you do that," I said, hoping my voice wouldn't start to shake in rage and fear. "You... I knew you had to be involved."

"Did you, though?" Ben asked nonchalantly. "I guess you aren't as smart as everyone thinks you are. If you were, you would have left immediately, as soon as Kristy's body was found."

I turned to stare at him, my jaw dropping open.

"This one," Ben looked at Martin and gestured to me, "has been running around, playing amateur detective all week."

What the fuck. Was he bluffing? Acting? Like he had been in the ballroom earlier? Was he trying to make them think he was one of them? Or had I been right to doubt him all along?

"Ah." Martin raised an eyebrow. "How charming... and just what do you think you know?"

I swallowed, trying to stay calm. "That you murdered these girls. All these girls." I held up the stack of photos. "For years... or at least, your family did." I thought of the knife I had been carrying and realized with dismay that I had left it on the bed when I put my shoes on.

Martin chuckled at that. "That's right. I wasn't around for most of them."

"Why?" I sputtered, "Why would you do something like this?" I glanced at the photos again, spreading them out like a grotesque fan in my hands. "For years, generations of your family, going back, they were all murderers? What possible reason..."

Martin cut me off. "To you, it may be murder, but to our family, they were a necessary sacrifice. One we had to make if we wanted our bloodline to continue." I just gaped at him, open-mouthed, in shock. He continued, nodding, "That's right. Every generation, going back as long as anyone could remember, a sacrifice was necessary for our family to bear children."

Was he insane? What the hell was he talking about?

Josh's Uncle cleared his throat. "Healthy, children," he added.

Martin tipped his head forward. "That's correct, to bear *healthy* children. There have been babies conceived without the sacrifice, sure, but none that ever made it anywhere close to full term. A miscarriage, every time. The ones that made it long enough to be... delivered prematurely, were... malformed. Grotesque."

"God," I spat out, "So you think murdering... sacrificing... innocent women has somehow allowed your family to... to have children? How can you possibly actually believe that?"

Josh's Dad was starting to look frustrated now. "Because I've seen it, you stupid girl. What, do you think we all just believed it without question? That none of us ever tried to just get on with our lives, leaving this awful... curse... behind us? We tried! Of course, we did. You don't know how many..." he stopped then, his emotions getting the best of him. Wes looked uncomfortably at the floor. "I've seen it first-hand. So, no, we don't like it. We don't enjoy having to do this. But this is what is required for our children, and our children's children, to live. To thrive. To be able to have a... a happy life. So, we do what we have to. For them."

I stared at him, at them, in horror and disbelief. This couldn't really be happening. There was no logic to any of this. My train of thought stopped abruptly. "Does Josh know?" I heard myself ask in a tiny voice.

Martin and Wes exchanged a quick glance. "Josh is... Josh has always been soft-hearted."

I stared at him. "That's not a real answer."

"Well," Martin paused momentarily, "it's the only answer you'll get." He pulled a gun out from behind his back, and he pointed it directly at my chest. Ben made the slightest of movements out of the corner of my eye. "Don't even think about it, Ben," Martin growled. "You're like a son to me. But I will shoot you dead where you stand." My gut twisted. I could feel myself starting to tremble. "And you, Missy, you're going to place those photos, each and every one of them, back in the book. Then you are going to close it, place it back in the drawer, lock it... and you're going to toss the keys over to Wes here." My gaze left the barrel of the gun to find Wes' face. He wouldn't look me in the eyes. "Do as you're told now."

"No." My voice trembled a little. I cleared my throat. "No, I won't let you get away with this."

"Do it, Cassie. Don't be stupid," Ben directed me, his voice calm and firm.

"You don't have a choice, sweetheart. It's too late." I stared at them, trying to think furiously. The opening at the end of the gun barrel was like a black hole about to suck me in.

"There's no way you'll keep getting away with it." I shook my head at him. "Not anymore. Maybe back then... years ago... sure, things were different. But you can't possibly think you won't get caught. One dead body was already found on your property today. What do you think the cops will do when another woman goes missing?"

Martin glared at me for a moment. "What do I think they'll do? Nothing." He replied calmly. "I think they'll do exactly nothing. Which is what they did about the other girl found today." I stared at him in horror. "That was a shame." He shook his head sadly. "A complete waste. But no, I'm not worried anything further will come of it. See, the Sheriff knows what side his bread is buttered on. So does the District Attorney's office, for that matter. Say I let you walk out of here right now." He gestured towards the door with the end of the gun. "You can head straight down to the county courthouse and tell them what you learned here today. And you know what will happen? Absolutely nothing." My gaze drifted towards Ben. I couldn't believe this was happening.

Martin followed my gaze, then pivoted his arm, pointing the gun at Ben. He didn't so much as flinch. "Do as I asked now, or I shoot him first," he said calmly. "He doesn't need to die tonight..."

I met Ben's eyes. He shook his head no, imperceptibly, once. What did he mean? No, don't do it, or no, don't let them shoot me? I stood there another moment, my heart thundering in my ears. I decided to stall for time. "Why was it a waste? Kristy? Why wasn't her death enough?"

Martin sighed deeply. "That was very unfortunate. It's not just about someone dying. It has to be done a certain way. We have to follow the ritual exactly, for it to work. The sacrifice must occur this time of year, at the height of the autumnal equinox. The blood needs to be..." he trailed off. "Kristy's body was found too late to be of any use to us."

I nodded, thinking. "I do have one more question," I said slowly, "why did you choose Kristy? Why did you choose her?" I held up the photo of the red-headed maid. "Why are you choosing me?"

Martin's brow creased. He studied my face. "You aren't one of us." He gestured to the other men, Ben included in the sweep of his arm. "You want to know what you all had in common? You're lower class. The help. We don't poach amongst our own," he finished. "Now, that's enough stalling."

I stared at him for a long moment. Then, with shaking hands, I put the photos back inside the journal.

"Good girl," Martin said smugly. I placed the journal in the drawer, locking it, and threw the keys at Wes, not caring if he caught them. He fumbled for them, dropping them on the floor before quickly scooping them up again.

"Good girl," Martin repeated, smiling at me. "Now, we can do this quickly and quietly. And it will be painless. You won't feel anything. It will be just like falling asleep. We are deeply grateful for the sacrifice you are about to make."

My jaw dropped open. "You... you cannot be serious." I stumbled a few steps back.

"Oh, I am, trust me. I truly wish it weren't the case, but unfortunately, you won't be leaving this house tonight— not alive, at least. But I will let him live," he said gently, tipping his head towards Ben, "if you come with us quietly." I was shaking now.

Martin nodded to Wes. "Go on now." Wes was putting the keys in his pocket. He fumbled with a hand in his other pocket, pulling out something white—a handkerchief, I saw—and a little glass vial of something liquid.

269

I stumbled several steps backward. *Think...think*, I screamed at myself. The heel of my shoe hit the lip on the floor where it switched to the worn wood of the balcony. The balcony. In fear, I continued to stumble backward until I had moved a few paces onto the balcony. I was starting to panic now. The balcony was too high up; there was no way I could jump down from here, was there? Not without breaking my legs. Martin gave me a warning look. Wes was pouring the liquid from the little glass bottle all over the handkerchief. They were going to drug me.

Martin gestured towards me with the gun. "Go on, Wes. Hurry up and get this over with."

"Wait," Ben said, speaking up suddenly, his voice still unnaturally calm and cold. "I'll do it."

I froze. My heart took a stuttering stop in my chest. We all turned as one to stare at Ben. "W-what?" was all I could manage.

"I'll do it," Ben repeated. His voice was calm and even. He stared back at me. "I want to be the one to do it. It should be me." He looked over at Martin. They stared at each other for a long moment.

"Ben..." I gasped. I could feel my mind starting to come apart at the seams. Hot tears of terror streaming down my face. "You're... you're really one of them?" I began sobbing.

Martin gave Ben a slow nod. "Go on then. Take care of it," he said, "but don't try anything funny."

Ben gave him a firm nod and held out his hand to Wes. Wes handed him the rag, covered in what I guessed was likely chloroform. Ben took it from him and made his way towards me. Martin trained the gun on him the whole time. Ben approached me. I was sobbing loudly now.

"How..." I cried to him; my limbs were feeling weak. I could barely manage to stay standing. I stumbled further back and felt my back hit the railing. I grasped it with one hand, propping myself up. "Why..."

Ben moved closer. His face was without emotion; his features were like stone. He held the rag in his left hand. His right hand hit my arm. Without looking down, he quickly slid something cold down the length of my arm to my hand, pressing it into my palm. My fingers closed around it reflexively— his car keys.

He lifted his now empty right hand and grasped my chin gently, as he had before, upstairs. Tilting my face up to his, he kissed me once as I continued to sob loudly. Then, pulling away from me slightly, he whispered against my lips, "Run." And then he tossed me off the balcony.

I think I landed essentially flat on my back on the ground below. The force of the impact knocked the air out of my lungs. My entire body screamed in pain. I felt the car keys fly out of my hand. *No...* I moaned. I had to move. I had to get up to find the keys. My ears strained for the sound of a gun going off, but there was nothing. After a few seconds, I managed to roll over from my back to my side and from there onto my stomach. I ignored the pain, the shaking in my limbs, and the pounding of my heart. The tears still streaking my face were cold in the night air. I felt around blindly in the grass, my arms and fingers fanning out in all directions. I moved a few feet further away from the spot where I had fallen, still crying softly. No, this couldn't be happening. Finally, I felt the underside of my arm brush against cool metal. Oh, thank God, I sobbed harder with relief. I grabbed the keys, scrambling to my feet. Then I ran.

Thankfully, I had cleared the garden when I fell. I ran around the corner of the house, trying to get my bearings; I saw the circular drive at the front of the house and started to head that way. I slipped once, sliding on the grass. I scrambled to my feet and began to veer off to my left, avoiding straying into the light from the lamps in front of the house as much as possible. I ran as fast as I could through the grass.

My shoes felt weird without socks. I felt the grass tickling my ankles. I flashed back to my dream for a moment. I thought of all the women who had died before me. Of my picture joining theirs in the journal. And I ran faster. Eventually, I hit the gravel drive. I took off like a shot down the path. The muscles in my legs and arms burned in protest. Thank God I was a runner, I thought. At least I had a head start, and I had a chance. I could get away if I could just make it to the car. What about Ben? I thought suddenly. Could I try to swing back towards the house and pick him up somehow? I decided to focus on getting to the car first.

A terrible, horrible thought occurred to me as I sprinted down the dark gravel path. There were so many cars here now, all the guests for the wedding, in addition to those of us who had stayed here this week. How stupid of us. How utterly, mind-numbingly stupid could we be? I would be parked in. There was no possible way I wouldn't be. I wasn't getting that car out of there. There was no way. Not only that, I realized with a start, but it was Ben's car...I didn't know what it looked like. Didn't even know what model car he drove. I could feel the tears starting in my eyes again. No. I told myself. No. I wouldn't cry, and I wouldn't give up. Not yet. Not until I was left with no other options.

After another minute or two running, I could tell I was about to enter a clearing. There was the glow of lights up ahead. I stumbled to a halt in a huge clearing. I saw an oversized garage directly ahead of me. At least six or seven garage doors faced me. Parked in front of the garage were what I estimated to be about fifteen or so cars. Only enough to be from the wedding party, not even... maybe some people had decided to drive down together. My car was notably absent. But where were all the cars from the wedding guests? I frowned. While it was a big clearing, there was no way they could have fit everyone's car back here. There were over 200 wedding guests. I realized with relief that they had parked the guests' cars somewhere else. They must have driven them off onto the lawn somewhere.

I scanned the cars in front of me. Now what. I looked down at the keys in my hand. It was an electronic key, I realized, on a red leather strap. There was a little button on the strap with what I recognized as the Mustang logo. I looked up and scanned the lot again. There it was. A black Mustang, the image of the horse running on the back, also in black. Of course, I thought to myself, I should have known. I examined the electronic key more closely, trying to calm myself. I flipped it over, saw the panic button, found the button with the open lock symbol, and clicked it to unlock the car. I saw the lights flash. It looked like my luck had held. It wasn't parked in. I ran over to the car, pulled open the driver's side door, and climbed in. I glanced around me, getting my bearings, raising one eyebrow at the car's red leather interior. It had a push-button start. My seat was way too far back. I slid forward, slammed down the brake, and pushed the button to turn on the car. I adjusted the seat forward to reach the pedals from a seated position. I took a second to buckle my seatbelt, switched the gear to reverse and backed out of the spot, swinging wildly. I shifted back into drive and took off through the break in the trees, back down the gravel path towards the house.

I pulled out into the roundabout in no time. Unsure what to do next, I made a loop around the drive. Scanning the front doorstep and windows as I passed. I peered around the sides of the house. I made another pass. There was no sign of Ben. What now? I thought. I made a third sweep, then drove off onto the grass on the right side of the house. I made my way behind the house, carefully avoiding driving through the garden. I scanned back and forth, but it was difficult to see much outside the cone of the headlights. Ben was still nowhere in sight. Maybe he wasn't out here, wasn't looking for me. I was approaching the opposite end of the house when I saw movement. I realized it was Wes, and he was running and heading towards the car. I saw other figures running behind him. Damn it, I couldn't see them well enough. I slowed slightly, waiting for them to move closer. Satisfied none of them were Ben; I hit the gas again as I saw they were all carrying shotguns.

So, that's where they had gone. They went to the game room to grab shotguns. To hunt me. Clearly, they hadn't anticipated me being in a car. I pressed down hard on the acceleration; the car shot forward like a rocket. I drove, swerving around the corner of the house, and shot back out onto the front drive. I followed the gravel drive now towards the gate. I had no choice, I told myself. I would leave, and I would find help and come back. I would come back for Ben, for Emily. And I would bring the police with me. I didn't care about what Martin said. I would make them listen. If not, I would drive to the next town over. Or the next. Until I found one that had never heard of the Haverfords.

My headlights hit the black gate in front of me. I screeched to a halt. "No," I gasped out loud. "No. No. No!" I slammed my hands against the steering wheel repeatedly. This couldn't be happening. The gate was shut.

I got out of the car. I ran over to the gate. Looking for a lock, a chain. Maybe I could pick the lock. Or break the chain. Or ram the gate. Or... I stopped, examining the gate closer; I realized it was one continuous unit attached to an electronic mechanism that must be controlled remotely. There was no lock to pick and no way I was busting through. I scanned the area at the sides of the gate. There had to be... a manual override, a switch or something, to open it from here, on this side. I could find nothing. I felt the tears starting to prick in my eyes again. I stood there for a long moment. What would I do now? The car was basically useless, I decided. I couldn't fit it down the running path through the woods to the village. It wouldn't make it down the horse path...and that ended in a cliff anyway. There were no other options. I turned back to stare at the car in frustration. At least, I thought, I could drive it back across the lawn and use it to get as far as the running path safely. From there, I would be on my own. I would have to run to the village on foot and hope that someone there would help me. I didn't love my odds.

I paused for a moment. Or, there was one other possibility. If I could make it back inside the house without them catching me...if I could make it all the way upstairs to the ballroom, then I could get to safety there, in the crowd. I could tell Emily and Josh, tell everyone, what had happened, even without the journal. I could make them listen to me. Either way...there was no way they could kill me there, not with an audience of over 200 people. I refused to believe everyone in that ballroom was drinking the Haverford Kool-Aid.

My head whipped around as something dinged off the back of the car. It happened again and then a third time. Then I heard a whoosh of air, and the car buckled. With a jolt, I realized they were shooting at the car. That was the sound of them hitting one of the tires.

I scanned the field in front of me. I could see them now, grouped together. They had stopped momentarily to shoot at the car but were starting to move again. I was screwed. I ran. I took off to the left, along the edge of the black fence. I moved away from the car's headlights as quickly as I could. But unfortunately, I had crossed through the beams of light. That may have been a stupid move, I thought, as I heard one of them cry out. I could have gone to the right, but that would have been the long way around. I didn't know how long I could outrun them, especially with shotguns factored in.

I stuck to the fence and the tree line, hoping the darkness at the forest edge would provide a backdrop and shield me from their view as much as possible. I turned to look back. I could see them running towards me now, following behind me. How many of them were there, I thought with confusion. Definitely more than three. They must have recruited some more distant, crazy relatives to join in their chase.

I ran through the dark, pumping my legs and arms as hard as I could. I decided to stick to the tree line for now, even though it wasn't the shortest path; I had a feeling they couldn't see me. They were still shouting out to one another in the distance. I dared to slow to look behind me and get my bearings again. They were fanning out now, forming a more or less straight line, attempting to span the length of the field towards the house. They were cutting me off from the house. I knew at that moment they would intercept me if I tried to head that way. That left me with only the running path as my option.

I heard shots ring out again. Then a volley of thuds as the shot hit the ground several yards away from me. Either not a great shot or they were still unsure of my exact location. I continued to run as fast as I was able. My whole body was in pain, not only from the fall but from the exertion. I hiked my bra up; it was starting to slide down. Not for the first time that night, I cursed the inconvenience of female fashion in general.

I could feel myself starting to slow, to lag already. I turned to look behind me again. They were fanned out in a long line now behind me. The lawn sloped down here, in this part of the field. I was running downhill from them now, I realized, using the slope to help me pick up momentum. I could see their silhouettes against the pale night sky behind me when I turned my head. See their arms pumping. Their guns held out in their hands.

I realized I had strayed from the edge of the woods. But I would need to head further out into the field anyway. Clearly, they were gaining on me. I would need to shorten my route, or I would never make it to the trailhead. I heard more shots booming behind me. How were they not hearing all of this racket back at the house, I wondered? But then I remembered the live band. They were probably completely unaware.

This time, they struck just a few feet away. Far too close for comfort. I remembered how hard it was to hit a moving target. Especially one that moved erratically. Especially while *they* were moving as well, that would make it almost impossible. They would have to stop, at least for a few seconds, every time they wanted to take a shot. The problem was there were so many of them. The others could keep chasing me while they took turns aiming.

I stopped running in a straight line and started to zig-zag, changing directions slightly as randomly as I could, but still heading towards where I thought the trailhead was. I knew that would be my next barrier, even finding it in the dark. If I couldn't, I would plunge directly into the woods and make my way the best I could. Suddenly, I heard a noise behind me. It sounded different, almost a beating, rhythmic sound. What, did they have a freaking machine gun out here now? I swiveled my head to look and saw something big, moving fast, heading towards me from behind and slightly off to the right. With a second of shock, I realized it was a horse galloping straight towards me. If one of them had gotten a horse...it was over. I was done for.

"CASSIE!" I heard a voice yell out. It was Ben. My heart lurched. I started zigzagging on a diagonal, still moving forward but to the right, towards the horse. "I'm going to try to pull you up without stopping," Ben called out to me. The horse approached behind me, slowing.

"Okay!" I yelled back to him.

"Hold up your right arm," he called back as the horse began to pull up parallel to me. I heard a volley of shots ring out. Ben grabbed my arm. I scrambled to grip onto him. He lifted me off my feet; I was hanging briefly, starting to twist sideways in the air. I grabbed on with both hands and somehow, he lifted me onto the horse into the saddle behind him. I'm sure he had slowed considerably to do so. "Ya!" He yelled at the horse, grunting and pitching forward. I wrapped my arms around his waist, holding on tightly. The horse took off with a burst of speed.

Shots continued to ring out behind us. I squeezed my eyes shut, breathing hard. Trying to slow my breathing. I prayed the horse wouldn't be hit. We took off, flying through the darkness, towards the trailhead. The horse putting distance between us and the shooters.

As we neared the far tree line, Ben reached down and pulled something out of the top of his sock. It was a small flashlight, I realized as he clicked the light on. He shined it up and down the tree line, the ring of light bouncing in time with the horse's stride. I scanned the tree line, straining. "There!" I yelled, pointing off to our left. Ben saw it and clicked the flashlight off, handing it back to me.

"Here," he said, can you hold this?" I took it from him quickly with my right hand before passing it to my left in front of his chest. I tried to find a way to hold the flashlight comfortably while still gripping on to him. He grunted as I moved around.

"Sorry," I told him, "Just don't want to fall off and slow us down."

"It's okay," he replied back over his shoulder. I passed the flashlight back to my right hand, and as I did, I realized my left arm felt warm and wet. I held it out to the side, peering at it.

"Oh my God! Ben, you've been shot!" I cried.

Ben grunted again. "I'm aware," he said dryly.

"Oh my God," I repeated, "What are we going to do?"

"I'm fine," Ben replied. "We're going to get the hell out of here; that's what we're going to do." The horse raced through the tree line, entering the trailhead. It was nerve-wracking riding in the dark like this through the woods, especially at such a fast speed. I peered up at the sky above.

Thank God it was a full moon tonight. I prayed there weren't any clouds. I thought about it for a moment and figured we could probably switch the flashlight on soon to help light the path ahead. There was really only one place we could be at this point; it's not like we needed to try to keep our location a secret. But we also shouldn't make it any easier for them to shoot us. For now, though, the moonlight alone seemed to be enough to see by.

I turned to look behind us and was startled to see a figure step out onto the path. I could see her face in the moonlight. She was draped in a dark cloak. Her red curls were loose, cascading down her back and over her shoulders like a mane. It was the maid. She was crowned with a ring of red roses, and antlers sprouted from her head, rising high into the air. She stared back at me, her green eyes wide. She gave me no signal this time, nor did she speak. I trembled slightly, half expecting her to try and stop us. She had helped us before, with Wes. But the pit of dread in my gut set off warning bells. She gave me a slow, knowing smile, the corners of her lips curling up. My breath caught in my throat at her expression. I turned forward briefly, opening my mouth to tell Ben, but when I looked back again, she was gone.

After about five minutes, Ben started to pull up on the reins, slowing the horse down considerably. "What are you doing?" I asked frantically. Do you need to stop?"

"No," Ben replied, "I'm okay still. I don't think they hit anything major."

"How do you know?" I asked.

"Because I'd probably already be dead by now if they had."

"Oh my God," I said, shaking my head. "Well, that's comforting. I guess." Ben chuckled a little. "Why are we slowing down then?" I asked curiously. I turned around to recheck the path behind us.

"I don't think we need to worry about them catching up to us at this point. At least not on foot," Ben responded. "If they were smart enough to turn around and get their own horses, that would be another story. The horse is probably getting tired, though. Most people don't realize, but a horse can only run about two or three miles at a time before they need to rest. We've gone almost two miles now. A little more than that," I saw we were coming up to the branch that led to the village.

"Why didn't I think of that?" I asked out loud. "Of course, they'll go back and get their own horses. Why wouldn't they?"

"Well," Ben replied, "even if they do, it will take them a while to get them all saddled up and ready to ride. I asked Harvey to have just one horse saddled up, ready and waiting for us. The rest are bedded down for the night." I thought back to the reception when he intercepted Harvey.

"You asked him at the reception?" I asked curiously. Ben nodded. "So... you were already anticipating possibly needing to escape on horseback," I said incredulously.

"Yeah," Ben replied, "I was. I was planning on us escaping tonight. I wanted to have a backup plan in case something went wrong with the car." After a moment, he said, "Wait, what did happen with the car?"

"It almost worked out," I said. "You're going to need a new tire. Probably some body work done." Ben laughed out loud at that. Then bent forward slightly, groaning in pain.

"Ben, we need to get you to a hospital. What's our plan here?"

Ben nodded, silent for a moment. "We're heading towards the village, obviously. I think our best bet is to stop there, head out into the street, and make as much noise as possible when we get there so there are a lot of witnesses. I know where Harvey's wife lives, and I'm pretty sure she would help us. But we can't risk going there. I don't want anyone to know they were involved at all."

I shook my head. Then, realizing he couldn't see me, I said, "I don't like that idea, Ben. How do we know the villagers won't just turn us over immediately? Isn't it in all of their best interest? Otherwise, who do you think they'll go after next? Besides, remember the burning man in the woods? What if they're all part of it?"

Ben was silent for a moment, debating. "I'd like to think there's a good chance they would help us." He sighed. "But you're probably right. The only other thing I can think of is to ride as far out as we can, past the village. Maybe find a gas station or something. We rode in silence for a few moments. "Wait," he said a moment later. "Hopefully my cell phone is still in my back right pocket. We can use it to call for help."

Remembering what Martin had said about walking right into the courthouse, I hesitated. Debating. We could risk trusting the villagers or going to the cops. What was our alternative? In the end, I decided we should call the police. Maybe Martin was bluffing or exaggerating. But at the end of the day, we needed a hospital, fast. And that was our best chance of getting to one. I chewed on my bottom lip for a moment, formulating a plan.

"I know," I said suddenly, "here's what we're going to do..."

Ben chuckled. "You know, the last time you said that, I got shot."

I laughed. "Okay, fair point. But I think my plan is going to work this time."

We made it just a mile or so beyond the village, out to a more major road, before Ben needed to stop. I was able to help him down off the horse, but it was a little difficult. I helped him over to a nearby tree, and he sat against it. He was clearly getting weaker. My heart was starting to race. I had been checking his phone for a signal for the past mile. It looked strong enough that we should be able to call.

I quickly dialed 911. When the operator picked up, I told them I needed an ambulance. My husband and I had attended a local wedding. We decided to head home, and as we were driving down the road, we saw a man on horseback. He waved us down and asked us for help. My husband got out to help him and was shot. The man had threatened to shoot me, but I gave him our car, a black Mustang, just like he asked, and he let me go. I explained roughly where we were located and that we were stranded here with the horse the man left behind. I was worried my husband wasn't doing well, and we needed him to be rushed to a hospital immediately. It wasn't hard to make sure I sounded hysterical on the phone.

I thought my plan would work well. It would hopefully get us to the hospital without involving the police, at least initially. It also gave the Haverfords an out, as much as I hated that, without ever mentioning them being involved. If the whole county really was in Martin's pocket, this might just let us slip past his grasp. I figured the shot-up Mustang would be found later on and might corroborate our story.

I stuck with at least mentioning the wedding because I decided it would be obvious we had come from there. Ben was still in his suit, although he had lost his jacket at some point along the way. Just as I was still in my bridesmaid's dress. My story to the operator certainly wouldn't explain why my dress was torn in half, or the running shoes. Or the fact that I was probably filthy and looked like I'd run several miles tonight. But I kept my fingers crossed that all of that would be overlooked for now, in the moment. And if it wasn't, oh well. The important thing was making sure Ben lived.

"Okay," I said, ending the call and walking back over to Ben. "They are sending an ambulance now. They said it should only take ten minutes at the very most."

"That'd be great," Ben replied. "But hey, quick question…" he paused for a moment, "just in case I don't make it…do you believe me now? Do you think you can finally trust me?"

I let out a strangled sound, half laughing and half sobbing. I smiled in the dark, tears starting to pool in my eyes. "Yeah," I replied softly, "I guess taking a bullet for me is pretty darn convincing." I leaned in and kissed him. I felt him grinning against my lips.

Ben chuckled again, his voice sounding more raspy and weak. "Alright then," he replied, leaning his head back against the tree. He closed his eyes, smiling. "That's alright then."

EPILOGUE

I slid the key into the lock of the brass doorknob and twisted it. Pushing the door open, I entered the foyer and sighed happily. Turning, I set my keys in the bowl on the long wooden table against the wall. I stopped for a moment, taking the time to fix my hair in the mirror above the table.

Ben and I moved in together about three months or so after the events at Haverford House. We lived in a little townhouse together in New York City. I fell in love with it immediately but had balked at the price tag. Ben insisted we take it. We figured New York was about as far away from Martin's influence as we could get. All the Broadway shows, the music, and the people watching weren't so bad either.

About two months ago, Ben asked me to marry him. I said yes. We opted for a small, private ceremony, with only our immediate family present. I studied the ring on my finger for a moment. We had finally gotten around to telling Emily and Josh we were married just a week or so ago.

Things had been... a little strained since their wedding, nearly a year ago now. In the aftermath of that night, I think we had all said some things that were a little hard to forget. I had begged Emily to leave Josh. I loved Emily dearly, and I always would. But I just couldn't understand how she could stay married to him, not knowing what she did now.

Josh and Emily had sworn up and down that they knew nothing before that night. I wanted to believe them—I really did—but I had a hard time swallowing that. Ben, on the other hand, had been more forgiving and willing to believe them. It was a bit of a friction point for us, to be honest. I hadn't seen or spoken to Emily in months.

When I got home from work the other night, Ben had dinner ready for me. He sat me down at the table and gently explained that he had called Josh and told him we were married. He told me how Josh had told Emily. Emily had gotten on the phone and begged Ben to let them come see us and celebrate with us. I had given in, in the end.

Unfortunately, they had planned to come out this weekend, and I had a big work event that I knew would run late Friday night. Ben had told me it was totally fine. The three of them would figure out dinner, and all I had to do was show up. Well, here I was. Showing up. But I had to be honest. A small part of me was excited to see them. I missed Emily.

I turned from the mirror and made my way down the entry hall. It was strangely quiet, but I could hear soft voices murmuring. I guessed they were sitting in the family room, which had a fabulous view of the city.

I stepped into the kitchen and scanned the room before turning to head through the small dining room into the family room beyond. I stopped short right as I passed the dining table. I slowly turned back towards the kitchen.

There, on the breakfast bar counter, I recognized one of our glass vases. It was full of a massive bouquet of bright, blood-red roses. I froze. The hair on the back of my neck stood up, my heart pounding. I felt a single tear trickle down my cheek, dripping onto my chest.

Slowly, I turned back towards the family room. Ben and Josh were standing on either side of Emily. She sat in the armchair in front of the window. She braced herself on the arms of the chair, slowly getting to her feet. She walked over towards me. One arm cradling her massive stomach. Her hand caressing it. I noticed with shock that she was very pregnant. I looked back and forth from her to Ben. His face was calm but wary, watching me. Emily approached me, taking my hand in hers.

"Oh, Cass," she said softly, "it's all going to be okay." She smiled at me sympathetically. "You're safe. You're one of us now."

"One of you?" I whispered in horror. "What do you mean I'm one of you?"

She smiled again, slowly this time. She held up my hand, examining my engagement ring, the large diamond winking in the light. She looked around the townhouse pointedly. "I mean, you're finally one of us... where you belong."

"Rich? You mean?" I spat at her. "I don't care about any of that. How can you possibly be okay with what his family has done, Emily? Is that why? Because they're even more loaded than you were?"

Emily shook her head. "Don't be silly. That's not what this is about. I love Josh. We belong together."

I stared at her for a long moment. "I just came from a book signing," I told her. "*My* book signing."

Emily's eyebrows raised. "That's wonderful news, Cassie." She smiled, turning her head slightly. "Ben, why didn't you tell us?"

"It's a true crime novel," I continued, "I named it "*Dread House*." She turned back to me, eyes widening. "I decided in the end that Martin was right; local police had probably been covering for your family for years." I shifted my gaze towards Josh. He had the decency to blush before dropping his gaze to the ground. "But the police here in New York? In the rest of the U.S.? I figured they might feel a little differently."

It was Emily's turn to stare at me in horror. She slowly dropped my hand. "Wh-what crime?" She stuttered. "No one died that night."

"That's true. Obviously, I escaped that night, largely thanks to Ben," he smiled at me broadly, "...although," my eyes dropped to her stomach. "If Martin is to be believed, it looks like maybe someone else wasn't so lucky. And Kristy... maybe it's time to find out what actually happened to her the night she died."

"You have no proof..." Emily mumbled, hands on her stomach.

"You're right. I didn't manage to escape with the journal or the photos," I agreed. "I did, however, manage to take one thing with me." Emily and Josh just stared at me. "Remember the page from the journal that I found? I did manage to tuck it in my bra that night. The police here have it now. It's not much, but it's something. That, plus two eyewitnesses. It might just be enough to convince people."

"Why would you do this, Cassie?" She began to back away from me.

I shrugged. "Remember what you told me that first night?" Emily shook her head slowly. I smiled. "That's one of the things you love about me... I always tell the truth."

She swallowed, digesting my words for a moment. "Well, I wish you hadn't done that, Cassie." She raised her gaze from the floor to meet my eyes. "But it can't be helped now. And I hope you will come visit us, sometime. We're going to stay at Hideaway House. It's where we want to raise our children."

"What?" I gaped at her. I looked over at Ben; he watched me cautiously, eyes wide. "Are you insane? I will never step foot in that house again."

Emily just smiled at me sadly. Tilting her head to the side, studying my face, she said softly. "Oh, Cass... but you never really left."

"Wha-what?" My pulse picked up. "What do you mean I never left?" My heart began to pound hard against my ribs, tears of fear gathering.

I looked at Ben in horror for a moment, but I couldn't tear my eyes away from Emily's face. It was... changing. Subtle at first, as freckles popped up, scattered over her cheeks, her eyes darkening, going from hazel to green. Her blonde hair turned copper first, then a deep, rich red. Curling, cascading over her shoulders. A wreath of roses grew as vines wrapped around her forehead. Antlers were sprouting, branching high into the air. I felt a chill wind begin to blow.

"You'll never really leave us..." she whispered to me, in a voice of a dozen different ancient voices combined. A thrill of terror ran down my spine, my gut twisting. I knew that. Somehow, I had always known.

I heard them starting then. The wind chimes. I felt a familiar fogginess begin to sweep over me. "No... no... no..." I sobbed, my gaze swinging slowly, lagging almost, as I turned to look for Ben, to reach out to him. I managed to stretch my arm out as I fell, collapsing to the floor. "NO!" I screamed. My own terror echoed in my ears as the darkness took me.

My hands gripped the steering wheel tightly, knuckles white. My stomach twisted in apprehension. I squinted ahead, trying to see any break in the trees. My only companions were the hum of my car and a faint ding whenever a rock hit the undercarriage. Otherwise, the forest surrounding Hideaway House seemed dead silent and perfectly still. I wondered if there was anything living in here. I rolled my window up. Having it open was making me feel oddly vulnerable. I sighed loudly.

The first mistake I made was the dress.

ALSO BY

Dread House, 2024
Possession, 2024
Mount Snow, 2025
Carl: An Easter Horror Thriller Novella, 2025
Jumpers, 2025
MANIMAL, 2025
Going to the Six, 2026 (Cemetery Dance Publications)

DREAD HOUSE PUBLISHING

Check out our website for news on upcoming releases, and to sign up for a monthly newsletter with ARC opportunities at
www.dreadhousepublishing.com
or scan the QR code below.